MEMORIES OF ANOTHER DAY

SELECTED STORIES

By

Mark Hayden

TO

LIZ

GREAT TO CATCH UP AT

LAST .

Melvin

XX .

2013.

First published in Great Britain

All paper used in the printing of this book has been made from wood grown in managed, sustainable forests.

ISBN13: 978-1-78003-435-5

Printed and bound in the UK
Pen Press is an imprint of
Indepenpress Publishing Limited
25 Eastern Place
Brighton
BN2 1GJ

A catalogue record of this book is available from
the British Library

Cover design by Jacqueline Abromeit

To

Maria and Graham.
With love

ACKNOWLEDGEMENTS

Country Cottage Books and Midnight Magazine: for *Sketches In Horror, Waiting For William* and *Memories Of Another Day.*
Country Cottage Books and Passport Magazine: for *Grave Humour.*
Country Cottage Books and Iceberg 'Two' Anthology: for *Blood Ties.*
Country Cottage Books and The Scribble Anthology Of Ghost Stories: for *Coming Home.*
Country Cottage Books and New Fiction/Forward Press Ltd: for *Where There's A Will*, published in their anthology An Open Mind. *Press-Ganged*, published in their anthology Midnight Crossing. *The Ripper Takes A Holiday*, published in their anthology Pathway To The Unknown and *Mark Of The Devourer*, published in their anthology The Thirteenth Hour.
Country Cottage Books and Infinity Junction/Horseshoe Publications for *Reunion In The Dark* published in their anthology Not For Bedtime.
Country Cottage Books and Acorn Magazine: for *Her Love Will Set Me Free.*
Country Cottage Books for: *Ghost Walk, The House In The Park, Trick Or Treat, One Last Time, The Soul Eater* and *The Shadowean.*

CONTENTS

COMING HOME

"Where are you, you daft bugger?" Taffy muttered under his breath.

Taffy Jones was getting tired of waiting.

Daft Michael had promised he'd be there at nine sharp for the grand opening. Now it was nearly ten and the last of the queue had just disappeared inside.

Taffy knew he was probably being unreasonable. Being beyond employment meant time was something Michael and he had plenty of. Yet, he never could stand wasting a minute of any God-given day. He'd been raised that way since his childhood in the East End, when every spare moment was employed in learning to "better 'isself and get outa 'ere", as his father used to say. Well, he guessed he'd done that all right... and Michael along with him.

Automatically checking for traffic, Taffy crossed to the other side of the road and looked back at the freshly painted house. From here, he had to squint to read the plaque over the door.

MUSEUM OF LIFE IN WARTIME BRITAIN
1939-1945

An entire house, restored to all its former glory.

Taffy was itching to get inside, but knew Michael wouldn't follow in without him. He sighed, his breath as cold as the March day as he paced impatiently up and down. Michael and he had been friends for nigh on sixty years, since joining up in '45 and in their very different ways, they'd always looked out for each other. For that reason alone, there was no way he'd consider going ahead without the daft bugger.

Taffy closed his ears against the noise as a party of school children turned the far corner and headed for the newly opened museum. Their loud, erratic approach was barely held in check by a young, harassed looking teacher, doing his best to herd them towards the front gate in an orderly fashion.

Taffy greatly disliked the modern generation, with their thumping music and computer-controlled lifestyles. In his own younger days, before the Second World War, he understood there'd been hardships of a different kind to face, but life had seemed less complicated and the pace much slower. Now he reckoned youngsters believed the world owed them a living... simply by right of birth. And everyone was in a darned hurry to get nowhere in particular, as fast as they could, polluting the air along the way with their fast automobiles. Often, when he was tired of the turmoil around him, he longed to clamber up once more onto the horse and cart his uncle had used to deliver coal to the hoity-toity in the West End. Just to close his eyes, listen to the steady clip-clop, and allow himself to be taken over by the gentle swaying motion...

Taffy forced his thoughts back to the present. It was past ten now and the London street was waking up to its business of the day. He checked each end of the road for signs of Michael and then crossed back and resumed his pacing.

Finally, Taffy leaned over the front wall of the show house and studied the square of soil to the right of the garden path. Admittedly there wasn't much to see. Several green markers indicated the resting place of early vegetables and a row of pea sticks acted as a divider from the neighbour's garden.

Just when the temptation to cross the black and red tiled path was becoming almost unbearable, Taffy recognised Michael's green beret bobbing towards him, its movements controlled by the man's peculiar, lopping gait. As usual, his friend seemed impervious of others around him as his long, heavily booted steps ate up the distance between them, his unbelted army greatcoat flapping loosely about his thin figure.

"Morning," Taffy said simply, his earlier impatience evaporating as his friend drew near. He always felt a sense of relief knowing just where Michael was at any given time... it gave him an odd comfort factor.

Daft Michael merely nodded and broke stride, staring up at the white painted frontage with large vacant looking brown eyes, waiting for Taffy to make the next move... as usual.

Taffy studied his friend with affection and a smattering of well-concealed sympathy. He would have been surprised if Michael had answered him. A speech impediment had earned him the tag 'Daft Michael' since his earliest days and Taffy doubted if more than two dozen words had ever passed between them; but then he considered this made their friendship deeper and more trusting. The present world was full of spoken promises, from the highest place to the lowest hovel, and most of them were broken in time.

Michael caught Taffy looking at him and frowned his disapproval. Taffy merely forced a smile and tapped his friend on the shoulder, indicating for him to follow in his footsteps.

The front door stood open and the hall was empty, the initial crowd having now moved into the body of the building. Taffy felt a surge of anticipation well up inside of him. This was even better than he could have expected.

The hall was suitably dingy, with cream and brown painted walls, the colours separated at waist height by a wooden dado rail. Orange coloured lino covered the floor. Two cream painted doors led off to the right and bare wooden stairs were straight ahead. Taffy gave a grunt of satisfaction. Wonderful. Not a piece of plastic, Formica or chipboard in sight.

Slowly, they both drifted through the lower rooms; the piano in the front parlour reminding Taffy of Bessie, his nimble fingered grandmother and family gatherings, when each member was called upon to make a solo contribution; Father believing no one got anywhere in life hiding behind their mothers' skirts. Taffy guessed he'd been right at that.

And there was the big family table and chairs in the living room where everyone ate. None of this 'trays in front of the telly' malarkey: in fact NO telly. In his childhood, you were considered lucky if you had a radio.

Taffy inspected the tin bath in front of the hearth with a wry grin, recalling the last time he'd permitted his mother to towel him down, red with embarrassment, rather than from the roughness of the towel. Through the open scullery door, Taffy could make out the top of the copper boiler and the arm of the mangle beside the black kitchen range.

It was all so real, all so *now*. Taffy felt as though he'd never been away and he turned, determined just this once to explain to Michael exactly how he felt.

Except the words never came.

Michael was staring at him. *Really* looking at him in a way he'd never done before. His brown eyes liquid pools, his pale cheeks soaked in tears. It was then Taffy realised what was happening.

As far as Taffy was aware, Michael was raised in an East End orphanage and signed on for the army as soon as he was old enough. Taffy realised he'd probably never known a conventional pre-war home. For his friend, this was probably a totally different kind of trip down memory lane.

Taffy wanted to reach out... to put an arm around Michael's shoulders and comfort him; but he knew his friend wouldn't like that, unaccustomed as he'd always been to any form of affection.

Instead he asked, "Would you like us to go?"

Michael shook his head, dramatically causing more tears to spill over. He raised a thin, trembling hand and pointed a long index finger towards the ceiling.

Taffy nodded that he understood.

The hall was filling up again with a fresh rush of visitors. Alongside two twittering old ladies and an indifferent looking chaperon, Taffy and Michael waited as the school party thundered downstairs and out into the street. The teacher followed at a lesser pace and gave the ladies a despairing shrug of apology as he passed.

Upstairs was much as Taffy expected, with dark oak furniture dotted around each room and iron frame beds - double in the front and singles in the middle and back rooms.

Michael followed Taffy in silent contemplation of their surroundings, giving no signal he was ready to leave, even when they'd clearly seen all there was to see.

Unexpectedly, Michael slipped away and Taffy found him standing at the window of the box room, looking at the makings of another vegetable plot and the mesh roof of a chicken coup.

"Wa... want to... to stay," Michael managed haltingly.

To Taffy, the words sounded oddly disjointed, as though they came from the child Michael had once been.

"Stay where?"

"Here." Michael didn't look at him. "Want a h... home."

The house fell silent around them.

Taffy was surprised how easy it was to take the idea on board. Why not? After all, London was full of squatters. They were both so tired of the City's ceaseless noise and bustle, constantly being forced on by so-called modernisation and progress. Here Taffy realised he could find something of the peace he'd known in his younger days, before the war. Between them, he reckoned they could make a damn good go of it.

"We could give it a try," he concurred.

After all, no one would see them.

In fact, no living soul had seen either of them since their weekend leave when the last V2 bomb had dropped on London.

Daft Michael turned to face him. His eyes glistened now with something other than tears. An emotion Taffy had almost forgotten existed. Hope!

He went to stand beside his friend at the window.

Michael raised a hand that was now quite steady and rested it almost reverently on Taffy's shoulder. Then, for the first time in nearly sixty years... Daft Michael smiled.

BLOOD TIES

The Dungeons - Newgate Prison, 1779

Merciful heaven! What is to become of me?

My dear friends have urged me to go with them - out of this place of darkness that gathers itself around me like a protective shroud.

My initial surprise turned to poorly masked terror as Lewis stood before me, a feverish grin making a gargoyle of his prison pallor. Blind old Culver hovered with one hand at the young man's shoulder, urging us both to hurry. Gaolers were fickle beings, he reminded us, men of little honour and a short-lived memory when it came to recalling who'd crossed their greasy palms with silver.

Filthy straw rustled as I struggled upright, seeking comfort from the cold stone at my back.

"We... I cannot go." I didn't look at Lewis as I spoke - I didn't need to. Even in the rancid, guttering candlelight I knew every plane of his face; the taut lines of his cheekbones, the shadowed hollows where his blue eyes flickered, tortured in their captivity and the smooth line of his throat, broken by the bobbing Adam's apple and the leaping pulse of his jugular - his young vibrant lifeline. Yes, in my mind's eye I could see it all. God, how I hungered to possess him, with my tired body, and tortured soul. I shook my head; for once thankful my shoulder length hair masked my own dark features. "T'is not possible."

"T'is so." Culver insisted, desperation in his voice. "Lewis 'as come into 'is in'eritance an 'as seen fit to use 'is silver to set us free."

Lewis said nothing.

He merely stretched out a steady, eager hand. Another time I would have gladly accepted his grasp, if only to become one with the life force beating strongly beneath his pale skin. I saw that he sensed my hesitation and was confused and troubled by it.

"Radcliffe... understand me. You are a free man!"

I could have laughed at that, but refrained from doing so for fear of hurting my well-meaning but unwelcome benefactor. If only I could make him realize the very freedom he offered could prove the end of me - but I knew with understanding would also come the end of our friendship.

During our months together in this place, he had spoken often of his mother's early death from consumption and the bullying father who had driven his son to the gaming tables and a life of crime to maintain his expensive addiction. Now, it seemed he was free of that tainted blood and had a chance to make good his past deeds. I for one would do nothing to stand in his way. There was much I wanted to say - how confirmation of his long-awaited inheritance gave me joy; yet knowing nothing could ever be the same between us saddened me greatly. I would miss his company, the long hours of merely gazing upon the beauty of his features while he slept and sharing the even greater brilliance of his waking mind; now such opportunities were long past.

"What is the hour?" I asked. The question rasped painfully in my throat.

"The gaoler say's t'is close to dusk," Culver put in, "an' he wants us gone before night patrol or our freedom won't be worth no amount o' silver."

Outside, merciful darkness was falling!

At least therein lay my succour for the hours ahead and the chance to reach Highgate, where a secure place awaited me. Suddenly Lewis's hands were upon my shoulders, raising me up until we were eye to eye.

"Radcliffe... I could not have survived thus far without your good heart and watchful eye. Ye Gods... look at you man," he shook me roughly, as though he would rouse me from a deep and troubled sleep, "always you have seen Culver and myself eat and drink the largest portion... while you have grown old and wasted before our eyes." His jaw became a line of determination. "I for one will not leave Newgate without you!"

I shuddered, for such words as these I did not wish to hear. Great as my loss would be, I could not allow this man to remain imprisoned on my behalf; least time reveal the abhorrent nature of my existence. Indeed I had no doubt the hand of friendship would not have been offered had they truly known the fiend that walked within their midst. Therefore, I must appear equally eager to be gone from this place.

"Forgive me, I waste precious minutes with my cowardly dallying. Too long have I been shut away from the light of day," Oh, such truth my words did carry. "Let us be gone."

Suddenly, all became urgent bustle around me, with Culver unerringly gathering his meagre belongings and Lewis shouting for the gaoler. I took up my spare shirt and breeches and tucked them into my belt. Around my shoulders I draped the tattered cloak that had served as a blanket these past two years and then I remained motionless, silent and as downcast as a man condemned to death, if that sentence were indeed possible twice in one lifetime.

I became aware our hurried movements, combined with the sound of approaching footsteps and the rattle of keys, had caused a stir among others incarcerated with us. Weak murmuring sounds gave life to shadows that solidified and became a dozen or so tattered figures, crawling through pools of their own excrement, drawn by the flicker of hope ignited out of their fear and desolation.

Even in my own wretched state, my heart went out to them. I knew that for some, their crimes were extensive, but for many their only fault was being born to poverty and the simple need to survive. By the fact that I still walked this earth, I knew my own wickedness far outweighed all others and yet I felt a strange affinity with these fellows, because like many of them, the original sin was not of my own making.

The number of lives I had taken to sustain my own miserable existence was beyond reckoning, yet ironically, the solitary death of one man had brought me to this place.

Lucas Trevelin had been a vigorously forceful man. A bachelor by intent, who's entire life had been spent accumulating power and prestige at the detriment of others, both friend and foe - a man hated by the very society that spawned him. One foggy night our paths had crossed in the alleyways behind Whitechapel and I had considered his removal a favour to humanity. I hadn't, however, reckoned on the appearance of his brother and entourage and had finally found myself cornered when I was at my weakest hour.

My deed had abruptly elevated young Marcus Trevelin's position in the family hierarchy and he decided there and then, with typical family aptitude, my reward was not to be a quick dance on the hanging tree at Tyburn, but a lingering, painful death in Newgate.

Now the iron door stands open. The way is clear and Lewis is beckoning me forward. He already has poor Culver by the arm and I feel him take my own cold hand. I meet his gaze and he smiles, his blue eyes full of awakening joy and anticipation at our freedom. Behind us, the gaoler hawks noisily and I hear the slap of spittle against the wall before the gate slams shut behind us. We three then began to climb the first of many stairs that would lead us to the terrifying reality of the outside world.

*

The carriage sped on at a fair pace through the badly lighted streets, away from Newgate and through Holborn towards the Tottenham Court Road.

By the time we had reached street level, darkness had indeed fallen. A fine covering mist was creeping in from the river. Lewis's new title came with a carriage that awaited us a discreet distance from the prison gates, and as we clattered along the cobbled streets our benefactor was eagerly explaining how he expected Culver and myself to remain with him for as long as we cared to do so.

Normally I would have listened to Lewis's every word, mesmerised by the sound of his voice and the beautiful animation of his movements. This time I was content to let him chatter on unheeded as he gripped the leather strap with one hand, while his right cut descriptive movements in the air between us. Culver sat opposite, the swaying lantern casting both their features in alternate light and shadow.

Now we were by all intentions safely away from Newgate, my own mind was becoming plagued with other matters - such as why the house and grounds Lewis was describing seemed so familiar to me, as had been the coat of arms emblazoned on the carriage door? I could have dismissed the latter as mere conjecture, had I not known my night sight was beyond question.

Sooner than expected, I realized Hampstead Heath lay before us and with that I was at least content, as this was also the road to Highgate. The streetlights fell away and the carriage gathered speed as it passed beneath the first canopy of trees onto open ground. A fine mist had descended upon the heath, giving the soft moonlight an eerie character of its own.

Quite suddenly the words 'Hold fast!' burst upon our ears. A shot rang out and the horses reared in their traces as the carriage came to an abrupt halt. The small door immediately swung wide and the steps fell with a clatter. A masked figure appeared in the doorway, well concealed beneath a voluminous cloak and a tricorn hat. A pair of flintlocks glinted dully.

"What in tarnation?"

I stayed Lewis with a hand to his arm, but could not reach Culver before he exclaimed "What's 'appening?' and made to rise. A pistol barrel to the head sent him sprawling senseless at our feet.

I flung myself forward as a second shot echoed across the heath and I felt a searing pain in my chest. My momentum carried me forward, knocking down our attacker, with myself landing in a heap beside him on the frosted grass.

In a trice the fellow was up and running, but you could say by now my blood was also up as I leapt in pursuit towards the first of the trees, where no doubt the man's horse was concealed.

Out of sight of the carriage, I allowed all pretence to fall away, relishing in my newfound freedom; the feel of the night air upon my face, the minute detail of every leaf and bough. Darkness was a veil for mere mortals alone. The hunt was on, poor as the sport might be.

"Come to me, sir," I whispered, "for I thirst and would be quenched."

*

Lewis was awaiting my return several paces from Culver, who was seated upon the carriage step, a bloodstained cloth pressed to the side of his face.

"He got away then," Lewis speculated, seeing me alone. "I'm afraid the driver's dead... took a stray shot to the head. I tried to follow... but you seemed to just melt into the shadows..." He broke off and reached out to touch the front of my shirt. "You are hurt."

I backed away.

"Radcliffe?"

"You had better go."

Lewis stared hard at me.

"The fellow didn't escape... did he." It was not a question, merely a statement of fact.

Having fully fed for the first time in months, I realized Lewis now saw me as never before. My colour was good and I knew my amber eyes flashed with an unholy light. I stood taller, with a full chest and my cloak swayed about me as though touched by a preternatural breeze. All this could be for Lewis's eyes only - I would have permitted no other to live.

"Who are you, Radcliffe?" Although he stood his ground, there was a tremor of real fear in his voice, which tugged at my heart. "*What* are you?"

"Your uncle's murderer," I replied simply, recalling with my newfound clarity why the coat of arms had been familiar. Ironically, I had grown fond of Marcus Trevelin's little whelp.

"You killed Uncle Lucas?" Lewis Trevelin frowned. I merely nodded and he began to laugh then, a musical sound that had once brought me great pleasure, but now seemed full of derision. "Of course you could not take our food and drink. So what did you do," his fine features took on a look of utter revulsion, "feed on your unfortunate companions?"

"Only those I sensed near to death." Even now I needed to justify myself in his eyes. "I gave them a welcome release..."

"Christ!" Lewis advanced, as though protectively coming between dazed Culver and myself. This gesture alone hurt deeper than any words could have done. "God forgive me... what creature have I released. What am I to do?"

"You could let me go." My words silenced him for a moment and in his stillness I saw the glint of tears upon his pale cheeks.

Helplessly, he raised both arms to the surrounding Heath.

"I do not have the means to stop you and t'is clear a round of shot will not."

I drew a long, weary breath.

"A vampire cannot enter where he is not welcome. You have allowed me into your heart. There is now an unspoken link that binds us. Lewis... you must release me now, or ask me to meet death at sunrise... when the last thing I may look upon is the face of a friend."

Silence again settled between us. I could hear the rustle of other night creatures hunting upon the heath. Loudest to my ears was the wild beating of Lewis's heart.

"T'is been over two hundred years since I was made." I felt tears now on my own cheeks and I knew if I brushed them away they would be tainted with blood. "Do you not think that I tire of this existence? That I might seek peace..."

"One such as you does not deserve rest. Go... damn you!"

There... it was said. The bond was broken.

I quickly moved away, my mind already turning to Highgate Cemetery and the family mausoleum that awaited me.

"Did my father know what you were when he had you incarcerated?" His words reached me a mere whisper on the night air.

I shook my head, the distance between us now too great for human ears to hear my answer. I sensed a familiar rushing sensation and Lewis became nothing but a shadow against the backdrop of the Heath.

One day, I promised myself, when Lewis Trevelin had grown tired of his immortal life - I would return for him.

SKETCHES IN HORROR

Most of us, at some time in our lives, have found ourselves drawn to something of an artistic nature.

My moment came when I noticed an ornate Victorian artist's board and easel in the window of 'Recollections' antique shop. The asking price seemed ridiculously low. In fact, I fully expected the proprietor to confess there'd been a mistake. However, there was to be no such disappointment. The man was inordinately eager to sell, and his apparent pleasure reached new heights when I offered to take the easel with me, instead of using his customary delivery service.

In retrospect, as I sit writing this account, which is by way of a confession, considering the short time I probably have left, I realise how differently things might have worked out had I noted the proprietor's relief at my departure; the eager way he ushered me out of the door. But I was too excited to regret my rash decision.

I, by the way, am Gerald Flanders; tall, dark and reasonably handsome in a sophisticated sort of way, being the only seed of an otherwise fruitless marriage, in the realms of what may loosely be termed the idle rich. I might add that I, being jobless, am what my father terms idle, while he, being the tight-fisted schemer he's always been, may be termed the richer half. At the tender age of twenty-one, I was thrust upon an unsuspecting world with Father's words still ringing in my ears.

'By the time I was thirty I'd made my first million. If you can't do the same then you're not a Flanders and have no place under this roof!'

, but this was the landlord I'd seen on the stairs... tight
d and hollow cheeked, with eyes downcast as though
ng for some untold terror to creep over the edge of the
towards him.

ound myself shivering, despite the warmth of the sunlit
. My first thought was someone from the art class was
ng a trick on me and substituted another sketch for my

his was the same conclusion Natalie came to later that
ing, after I managed to convince her I was in no way
onsible. Or was I?

hat night, after Natalie left, I lay awake and restless,
ging the pillow still scented by the warmth of her body. I
dn't get the damn easel out of my mind. Even while we
e love it was there, casting its shadow over us and
ning our enjoyment of each other. Natalie hadn't said so,
was sure she was glad to get away. Her parting kiss had
playfully platonic and she hadn't looked back at the turn
e stairs as she always did.

as it something to do with the easel? Or its previous
er? Again I remembered the feeling of being guided as I
ed, and I saw this now in a different light. Was some
working through me and if so, to what purpose?

ay studying the easel, silhouetted now by soft moonlight,
c from a bygone age of elegance, and a much-hackneyed
e came to mind. 'A thing of beauty is a joy forever'. And
d it be tainted with evil?

*

ing came, and with it a new rush of horror. Eddie's
es had faded to an almost skull-like appearance. Only
es still held a flicker of life... and terror. The reason was
lain to see. An ugly, cat-like creature had appeared at
ttom of the paper. Only the front portion of its body was
 as it hung on by webbed claws at the end of long,
ng legs. The head had normal feline contours, although

I am now thirty-two. Consequentially, while Father lords it
over a spacious mansion near Ashdown Forest, I'm housed in
a dingy bed-sit in Brixton, the sump of the Metropolis. Thus
you will understand the pleasure my find initially gave me,
especially as it was within the bounds of what Her Majesty's
Government allows me to afford.

I stopped off at the local art shop, only long enough to
purchase charcoal and paper before hurrying home, eager to
try out my new acquisition.

*

The first problem was subject matter for my untested abilities.
For me, the natural choice was a self-portrait, although I
eventually rejected the idea, feeling I couldn't be truly
objective about the results. I finally settled on a sketch of my
landlord. Since his skin was the same colour as my charcoal, I
felt I'd have fewer problems when it came to shading and
highlights.

I must confess the easel looked quite impressive set up by
the living room/kitchen/dining room window. The dark
wood gleamed at the touch of a soft cloth and had obviously
been carefully tended by its previous owner.

I worked slowly at first, with hesitance born of a fear my
dreams would fade with reality and I would end up with a
poor man's Lowrie of Matchstick Men and Matchstick Cats
and Dogs. However, as my confidence grew, the charcoal
seemed to glide over the paper as though it had a life of its
own and I was astonished at the clarity and fine sense of detail
I was able to inject into my first attempt... especially as the
subject was drawn only from memory.

Fading light forced a halt to my efforts and with it the
realisation I'd worked ceaselessly for five hours and now felt
both physically and mentally exhausted. Munching a bacon
sandwich, I sat back and surveyed my handiwork with
considerable surprise and a great deal of growing pride. The
sketch was damn good, even if I did say so myself.

I had clearly captured the sunny, fun loving nature of the middle-aged Haitian. His rounded cheeks seemed to glow with vitality and his eyes were bright with the soft laughter of his broad, toothy grin.

'Not bad, Gerry,' I told myself. 'Not bad at all.'

At last I'd proved I could do something other than stand in dole queues. The question was how to harness this ability to bring in some ready cash?

I pondered this problem through the long hours of darkness, only to find the solution came with daylight in the guise of a crude, hand-painted circular. The local activity group were holding free classes for the unemployed. One topic happened to be art, and they asked only that you brought along your own drawing equipment. The idea appealed to me. To join would guarantee my work being seen by others and with the right tuition I might even reach saleable standards. I had to smile at this second stroke of good luck. Perhaps old Flanders's son was good for something after all. That would be one up the old bugger's spout.

*

Within the week, fourteen of us were firmly entrenched in the intricacies of artistic studies, enthusiastically guided by Philip Alton, a young tutor fresh from the London College of Art.

Phil was highly complimentary towards my sketch of Eddie, my landlord, which I'd used as a lever to enter the classes. I must admit I basked unashamedly in a glow of envy cast by the others... especially a beautiful blonde by the name of Natalie, with whom friendship soon extended beyond the boundaries of the classroom.

It may not have been love at first sight, but by week three the relationship was doing very nicely... which was more than could be said for my foray into the field of art.

But, first thing's first.

Phil volunteered to be our live study and as before, I was amazed how easily his features took shape, as though an invisible force was guiding my hand. Sometimes, I felt

convinced the charcoal was several strokes ahead o thought; obviously just my imagination. As explained, I was a 'natural' and coming away fro lesson I only wished I'd spread my artistic wings ye

*

Two days later, I passed Eddie on the basement sta not spoken, he would have slipped by without a wo had I seen such a change in someone usually so cheerful. His normally rounded cheeks were sunken uncommon pallor and as I casually passed the time o answers came as grunts, with a downcast face forever searching the floor. He was obviously agitate presence and only too glad to be away, weaving up eyes still lowered, searching...

Seeing Eddie thus disturbed troubled me all m collected my thirty pieces of silver and studied the board with only half a mind on its contents. Lo returning to the flat, I'd decided to present Eddie wi portrait, although it was quickly becoming one of treasured possessions. Still, if I was a true arti always produce another. The poor chap looked as needed something to cheer him up. The sketch, al pint at the local, just might do the trick.

*

The Victorian easel stood in its usual place before t bright sunlight casting a myriad of colours acro finished drawing of Phil Alton.

I was truly proud of my latest efforts. But wit came a sharp pang of regret over my failed relati Father. There was still enough boy in me to want and say, 'Hey, Dad, look what I've done! Do you unable to do that simple thing hurt more than I possible.

Uncovering Eddie's sketch, I barely stifled a As expected, his familiar features stared back at here the similarity ended. The eyes were larger and the tongue protruded thickly from the gaping mouth, so only the canine teeth were visible between thick salivating jaws.

Even as I watched, I became convinced the creature moved fractionally, the thick shaggy fur shimmering with the reluctant breath of the hunter. Eddie's eyes seemed to catch my own, conveying their message of fear and a mute plea for help. Instinctively, I *knew* I would hear of his death that day, and once again in my mind's eye, I saw him on the basement stairs, eyes downcast, and ever alert for the hell-spawn I'd unwittingly set upon him.

I don't know how long I stood there, engulfed with guilt. By the time I'd pulled myself together to phone Natalie, the gap between the hunter and hunted had definitely decreased. Shakily, and with a sinking heart, I listened to the engaged tone and but finally gave up; remembering Natalie always left the phone off when she slept in.

The thought crossed my mind to destroy the sketch. But would that have helped? After all, Eddie was very real, but so too, presumably, was the creature now pursuing him. With a shudder of morbid fascination, I turned to my sketch of Philip Alton.

*

Eddie's funeral took place three days later. Haunted by guilt, I couldn't bring myself to attend. Instead, Natalie and I spent the afternoon steadily getting stoned. The next day, Carla, Eddie's wife went to stay with relatives, and in her absence word soon spread through the flats of how her husband was supposed to have died.

The story went that, screaming and raving, he had dashed from the basement to the top of the house. Naturally, people came out to see what all the fuss was about. Begging for someone to keep IT away from him, in final desperation Eddie had flung himself from the upper landing.

When Natalie and I summed up courage to look at Eddie's sketch, a blank sheet of paper confronted us.

*

The next art class seemed a long time in coming and you have no idea the relief Natalie and I felt when Phil walked in with his customary cheerful welcome.

As the evening wore on, however, our relief turned to dread as we noticed our young tutor's growing urge to stare at his feet, an action accompanied by long moments of baffled silence. Luckily, the topic for the evening was 'still life', so I wasn't faced with the embarrassment of excusing myself from the class. Earlier, I'd made up my mind to draw no more live subjects and if anything happened to Phil I was determined to burn the easel.

It seemed a terrible thing to walk from that room, knowing what we were leaving Phil to face. Yet, how could we warn him? Who would believe our story and where was the evidence? Signs the horror had started were unmistakable, and on the long trek back to my flat we talked only of how to overcome the encroaching evil. Finally, Natalie and I arrived at one unshakable conclusion. If we did nothing, Phil would be driven to suicide or face something even worse. So we had to take a chance and destroy the sketch. At least then we could say we'd tried.

Back at the flat, I could see no obvious change in the drawing. Perhaps that was a good sign. Maybe things hadn't really started yet. Tearing the paper into small pieces, we watched it burn, the tiny flames giving our first glimmer of hope since Eddie's death.

Then we went to bed and made love, losing ourselves in the rising ecstasy and climatic release. Falling asleep in each other's arms, our last waking thoughts were of Phil and what the next day might bring.

*

By late morning, the news was all round the flats. Driving home after art classes, Phil had a head on collision with an articulated lorry. Trapped in the wreckage, his Renault had

I am now thirty-two. Consequentially, while Father lords it over a spacious mansion near Ashdown Forest, I'm housed in a dingy bed-sit in Brixton, the sump of the Metropolis. Thus you will understand the pleasure my find initially gave me, especially as it was within the bounds of what Her Majesty's Government allows me to afford.

I stopped off at the local art shop, only long enough to purchase charcoal and paper before hurrying home, eager to try out my new acquisition.

*

The first problem was subject matter for my untested abilities. For me, the natural choice was a self-portrait, although I eventually rejected the idea, feeling I couldn't be truly objective about the results. I finally settled on a sketch of my landlord. Since his skin was the same colour as my charcoal, I felt I'd have fewer problems when it came to shading and highlights.

I must confess the easel looked quite impressive set up by the living room/kitchen/dining room window. The dark wood gleamed at the touch of a soft cloth and had obviously been carefully tended by its previous owner.

I worked slowly at first, with hesitance born of a fear my dreams would fade with reality and I would end up with a poor man's Lowrie of Matchstick Men and Matchstick Cats and Dogs. However, as my confidence grew, the charcoal seemed to glide over the paper as though it had a life of its own and I was astonished at the clarity and fine sense of detail I was able to inject into my first attempt... especially as the subject was drawn only from memory.

Fading light forced a halt to my efforts and with it the realisation I'd worked ceaselessly for five hours and now felt both physically and mentally exhausted. Munching a bacon sandwich, I sat back and surveyed my handiwork with considerable surprise and a great deal of growing pride. The sketch was damn good, even if I did say so myself.

I had clearly captured the sunny, fun loving nature of the middle-aged Haitian. His rounded cheeks seemed to glow with vitality and his eyes were bright with the soft laughter of his broad, toothy grin.

'Not bad, Gerry,' I told myself. 'Not bad at all.'

At last I'd proved I could do something other than stand in dole queues. The question was how to harness this ability to bring in some ready cash?

I pondered this problem through the long hours of darkness, only to find the solution came with daylight in the guise of a crude, hand-painted circular. The local activity group were holding free classes for the unemployed. One topic happened to be art, and they asked only that you brought along your own drawing equipment. The idea appealed to me. To join would guarantee my work being seen by others and with the right tuition I might even reach saleable standards. I had to smile at this second stroke of good luck. Perhaps old Flanders's son was good for something after all. That would be one up the old bugger's spout.

*

Within the week, fourteen of us were firmly entrenched in the intricacies of artistic studies, enthusiastically guided by Philip Alton, a young tutor fresh from the London College of Art.

Phil was highly complimentary towards my sketch of Eddie, my landlord, which I'd used as a lever to enter the classes. I must admit I basked unashamedly in a glow of envy cast by the others... especially a beautiful blonde by the name of Natalie, with whom friendship soon extended beyond the boundaries of the classroom.

It may not have been love at first sight, but by week three the relationship was doing very nicely... which was more than could be said for my foray into the field of art.

But, first thing's first.

Phil volunteered to be our live study and as before, I was amazed how easily his features took shape, as though an invisible force was guiding my hand. Sometimes, I felt convinced the charcoal was several strokes ahead of my line of thought; obviously just my imagination. As Phil later explained, I was a 'natural' and coming away from that first lesson I only wished I'd spread my artistic wings years before.

*

Two days later, I passed Eddie on the basement stairs. Had I not spoken, he would have slipped by without a word. Never had I seen such a change in someone usually so bright and cheerful. His normally rounded cheeks were sunken and of an uncommon pallor and as I casually passed the time of day, his answers came as grunts, with a downcast face and eyes forever searching the floor. He was obviously agitated by my presence and only too glad to be away, weaving up the stairs, eyes still lowered, searching...

Seeing Eddie thus disturbed troubled me all morning. I collected my thirty pieces of silver and studied the vacancies board with only half a mind on its contents. Long before returning to the flat, I'd decided to present Eddie with his own portrait, although it was quickly becoming one of my most treasured possessions. Still, if I was a true artist, I could always produce another. The poor chap looked as though he needed something to cheer him up. The sketch, along with a pint at the local, just might do the trick.

*

The Victorian easel stood in its usual place before the window, bright sunlight casting a myriad of colours across the now finished drawing of Phil Alton.

I was truly proud of my latest efforts. But with that pride came a sharp pang of regret over my failed relationship with Father. There was still enough boy in me to want to rush home and say, 'Hey, Dad, look what I've done! Do you like it?' Being unable to do that simple thing hurt more than I ever believed possible.

Uncovering Eddie's sketch, I barely stifled a cry of alarm. As expected, his familiar features stared back at me from the board, but this was the landlord I'd seen on the stairs... tight lipped and hollow cheeked, with eyes downcast as though waiting for some untold terror to creep over the edge of the page towards him.

I found myself shivering, despite the warmth of the sunlit room. My first thought was someone from the art class was playing a trick on me and substituted another sketch for my own.

This was the same conclusion Natalie came to later that evening, after I managed to convince her I was in no way responsible. Or was I?

That night, after Natalie left, I lay awake and restless, hugging the pillow still scented by the warmth of her body. I couldn't get the damn easel out of my mind. Even while we made love it was there, casting its shadow over us and lessening our enjoyment of each other. Natalie hadn't said so, but I was sure she was glad to get away. Her parting kiss had been playfully platonic and she hadn't looked back at the turn of the stairs as she always did.

Was it something to do with the easel? Or its previous owner? Again I remembered the feeling of being guided as I worked, and I saw this now in a different light. Was some force working through me and if so, to what purpose?

I lay studying the easel, silhouetted now by soft moonlight, a relic from a bygone age of elegance, and a much-hackneyed phase came to mind. 'A thing of beauty is a joy forever'. And should it be tainted with evil?

*

Morning came, and with it a new rush of horror. Eddie's features had faded to an almost skull-like appearance. Only the eyes still held a flicker of life... and terror. The reason was now plain to see. An ugly, cat-like creature had appeared at the bottom of the paper. Only the front portion of its body was visible as it hung on by webbed claws at the end of long, tapering legs. The head had normal feline contours, although burst into flames before would-be rescuers could reach him. The time of the fire, as near as we could judge, corresponded with the burning of the sketch!

The effect of this news upon us was immediate and dramatic. I threw up, violently, while Natalie, being a somewhat better class of person, merely fainted.

*

The following morning, I awoke determined to destroy the easel. Natalie, who by now had moved in with me on the principle two people could live as cheaply as one, suggested I take it back to 'Recollections' and try for a refund. Naturally, I baulked at this idea. The damn thing was a killer, and it seemed totally irresponsible to place it back on the open market. Nevertheless, I was becoming besotted with Natalie, and somehow she always managed to get her own way. Also, the cash would come in handy, especially as she was making frequent marital overtures.

'Recollections', however, no longer existed. The shop stood shuttered and empty. Had I not known of the business for a good many years, I'd have believed the proprietor sole purpose had been to sell the easel and move on. The local art shop declined; with the polite explanation there was no call for such outdated models. Today's students preferred the modern lightweight versions. Reluctantly, I returned to the flat and locked the board away in a rarely used storage cupboard, content to let it rot.

*

During the next three weeks, two unexpected events occurred. I landed a labouring job with a local building contractor's, and Natalie and I became an old fashioned married couple. Following a honeymoon in a caravan at Bognor Regis, we returned to spend our first evening in the flat as man and wife.

Thumbing through a magazine she'd picked up on the train, Natalie came across an article describing Father's recent business ventures. Waving a picture of the great man under my nose, she casually commented what a 'nice sketch' it would make, before disappearing into the kitchen to prepare the evening meal. Natalie, bless her, had planted an idea that was to haunt me for days to come.

The more I thought about it, the more I reasoned how unfair it was for me to be slumming it in sunny Brixton, isolated from all that lovely money down in the green belt. Mother had died years ago, weary of life, and I suspected more than glad to escape Father's soul-destroying dominance. So, unless he married again, or his will favoured the local moggy farm, I stood a good chance of inheriting the lot. Why, I asked myself, wait another twenty years or more when I could have it all now? The thought certainly had its appeal.

*

The following Sunday, I packed Natalie off to her mother's and spent the day lovingly immortalising dear old Dad. Then it was just a matter of sitting back and waiting.

At one point I did consider burning the sketch, just to hurry things along. But remembering what happened to Phil, I had visions of the ancestral home going up in flames and decided to have faith in the motto 'everything comes to he who waits'.

*

Within the week, a telegram announced Father's unfortunate demise while night riding alone in Ashdown Forest. Why he should risk such dangers after dark and how he came to be unaccompanied was not explained, and I shuddered to think what it was he'd actually been trying to escape from. Smothering rising guilt, I read on to learn my presence was required for the reading of the will.

*

Unfortunately, I didn't inherit everything, although a house in Cheam, twenty-per cent shares and a cash settlement of eight hundred thousand pounds can't be bad payment for one simple little sketch. Naturally, Natalie was more than satisfied. She had fallen for the good old Flanders' charm and presumably married for love. Now, she was mistress of a beautiful home and part millionairess into the bargain.

The easel, instead of being reviled as a thing of evil, we placed in the spacious drawing room at Cheam... a fitting reminder as to the source of our newfound wealth, as well as proving an attractive addition to the furnishings.

Natalie's first gesture was an elaborate house-warming party, timed to coincide with my thirty-third birthday. As ill luck would have it, I was called away to an emergency board meeting the evening before and knew there was no chance of getting back until late the next day. Holding twenty-per cent share of the business meant I was compelled to attend.

To my repeated promises to return as soon as I could, Natalie saw me off on the London train and hurried home to continue her preparations.

*

The evening was well advanced when I wearily turned my Porsche in at the gates. The house was brilliantly lit from every window and loud music came across the lawns. Obviously the party was in full swing and I felt rather guilty at having left Natalie to cope on her own.

Smiling faces met me at the door, many of which were unknown to me. A drink being thrust into my hand, I was ushered towards the drawing room where Natalie was holding court. This room was as crowded as the rest of the house, but the throng miraculously parted with shouts of 'Surprise, surprise' and 'Happy Birthday' coming at me from all sides.

Natalie had her back to me, and my grip tightened on my glass as I stared over her shoulder at the Victorian easel, stunned to see her busy with a black felt tipped pen. Already a rough character was taking shape, the features comically exaggerated, although there was no doubt to the identity of her study... even before she scribbled 'Gerry' across the top of the sheet.

Unashamedly, she turned and met my gaze. She looked beautiful, radiant... and utterly ruthless. Her blue eyes spoke to me of nothing but greed and betrayal.

The feeling of weariness returned, as swiftly as it had departed. With it came a strange chill, like the coldness of a winter graveyard. With a fixed smile I moved towards the door, eyes downcast so as not to tread on anyone's feet.

My eyes were still directed downwards as I climbed the stairs towards the bathroom, eager to relive my churning stomach. I thought of my old man, and smiled. He must be falling about over this one.

Then I heard it... the faint call of a cat... just beyond the fringes of my mind...

WHERE THERE'S A WILL

My name is Linus and from today my existence will never be the same again.

I've just crawled out of the sack on this dreary November morning, to find myself looking back at my own body... lying on the mattress where I'd drunkenly left it last night. Gave me quite a turn it did, especially with the twelve inch carving knife sticking out of my chest; one from the kitchen set I'd bought Audrey last Christmas.

Naturally my first reaction was to panic and I had to sit down beside myself until my legs stopped trembling. Who'd want to murder me? I was just your regular couch potato, a lager swilling football addict, with no natural enemies... unless you include the mother-in-law. This had to be a nightmare.

I pinched myself, and then my twin on the bed for good measure. Neither responded much and nothing changed. Taking a deep breath and steeling myself against the inevitable, I took a closer look at my other half. I'd heard it said how we never see ourselves as others do and I had to admit, lying there in all my gory splendour I wasn't exactly the handsome devil I'd always envisaged. There was something too turned up about my nose and too pulled down about my mouth. My mousy coloured hair was far thinner than I recalled and that double chin wasn't there last time I'd shaved. Becoming ghoulishly fascinated, I allowed my gaze to wander to the hard won beer gut and cringed at my shrivelled, inadequate manhood. A sense of complete ineptitude swept over me; of broken promises, of lies I'd told... and of dreams unfulfilled. I realized I was seeing myself through my wife's eyes and I suddenly felt ashamed, unable to recall when we'd recently discussed anything of mutual importance or even when I'd last told her I loved her.

I glanced at the right side of the bed, which was still smooth and undisturbed. At least we still sleep together, I thought ruefully, although Audrey had spent last night at her mother's, otherwise we might have both been lying there now. Selfishly, part of me wished that had been the case... then I wouldn't have felt so cheated and alone. Sickened, I stood up and turned away.

Facing me was one hell of a mess. Cupboards were thrown open, their contents scattered around the floor. Drawers had been upturned and pictures pulled from the walls. Shards of glass glinted dangerously amongst our clothing.

Murder - and robbery!

Damn! What a waste, I thought, after winning all that dosh on the lottery. I'd hardly had a chance to spend any of it. At least Audrey wouldn't want for anything; the poor bitch was probably better off without me. I kind of aimlessly drifted across the room. What now? Where do I go from here, I wondered, while the entire range of human emotions hammered through me, finally settling on bullshit... this can't really be happening?

Downstairs, a door slammed. Audrey! I didn't want her to find me like this. I spent ages trying to open the bedroom door, before realizing it was far simpler for me just to walk through it. The landing and stairs were devoid of life, except for old One-Eye, Audrey's ancient cat. As usual, what was left of her was sitting on the top step; the rest was residing in various jars at the local vet. I'd lost count of the times she'd nearly broken my neck and I now took considerable pleasure in seeing her turn tail and clear the stairs without touching a single one. Surely, I thought, that had to be worth another of her nine lives.

Again I heard movement below. On the way down, I checked the spare bedroom and nursery, becoming more and more intrigued how quickly I was able to move from one spot to the other. Everywhere I looked was chaos and wanton destruction and I lingered longest in the 'nursery', saddened to think how Audrey and I still called it that after nine childless years of marriage. Another heavy crash shook me out of my reverie and brought me quickly to the kitchen door. I can't say I liked what I saw.

Stunned, I watched as my brother Junior, upended a drawer of cutlery across the table and followed it with several ripped cereal packets and a bag of flour. I strode into MY kitchen.

"What the hell do you think you're doing?" In death, as in life, Junior ignored me. I recognized the familiar look of smug satisfaction on his handsome face as he righted a kitchen stool and hunkered down, carefully surveying his handiwork. In the presence of this much younger man, I felt the usual anger and frustration begin to rise in me; as much as I loved him, Junior had been the bane of my life. He'd inherited our father's good looks but none of his brainpower. Somehow, his charm had always got him into trouble... while I'd bailed him out of it. From borstal to petty crime! From juvenile prison... and now this. I thought of my bloodstained corpse upstairs and shuddered.

"Why Junior? For God's sake why have you done this to me?"

As if in answer to my question, Junior removed the gloves he'd been wearing and pulled a buff envelope from the pocket of his jeans. Leaning close, I instantly recognized my updated will, with the codicil covering the lottery win. What was going on here? Robbery and murder for a document that favoured my wife before all others. If the little fool wanted a copy this badly, I could have given him one. I watched over his shoulder as Junior began to read, slowly moving his lips over each word and I sensed the content was somehow making him agitated.

"Bloody bitch!" he cursed suddenly, growing red in the face.

I followed as he stood up and went to the wall phone, hooked the receiver back in place and then checked for a tone. Methodically, he punched in a number that seemed vaguely familiar to me.

"Hi, it's me. Yea... I need you here." He paused, listening, impatiently coiling the cable between powerful fingers. "I know that's what we agreed... but I can't go through with it alone. Look... just get over here or we forget everything." Junior slammed the receiver down and I automatically ducked out of his way as he punched the wall where I'd been leaning.

For the next ten minutes, I matched him step for step as he paced the kitchen like the lean, caged animal he'd always been; while I desperately tried to recall whose number he'd just dialled.

I must admit I panicked at the sound of a familiar car pulling onto the gravelled forecourt. I was at the window in the time it took me to think about it. Audrey was back from her mother's. What the hell could I do to protect her, with my physical body stiffening in the bedroom and Junior waiting behind the kitchen door!

"Change your mind, Audrey," I prayed, really meaning it for the first time in years. "Go back for something... please." I'd never felt so helpless since my death.

I watched, in fear for her as the back door opened and Audrey came in, flushed and slightly out of breath; but still beautiful, I realized, with a pang of regret. She stopped abruptly, one hand on the latch, the other sweeping back her blonde, shoulder length hair. I stood between them, knowing I could do no more.

In one lithe movement, Junior stepped through me and into my wife's arms. Pain that was beyond anything physical lanced into my being as I realized the significance of that embrace... *and* of my mother-in-law's telephone number.

"Where's Linus?" Audrey demanded. She was holding Junior from her and I saw a fanatical light in her cornflower eyes. This cold, calculating creature was not the woman I'd married; greed for that damned lottery money had done this...

twisted her out of all recognition. She could have had anything she asked for, except Junior. Going with my younger brother was something I'd never have sanctioned. Anger swept aside my previous feelings and turned them into an all-consuming bitterness that left me suspended and helpless.

"Where IS he?" Even her voice sounded different to me.

"Upstairs... tied up."

Why was Junior lying to her? I wondered.

"Did he see you?"

"Yeah."

"You fool! That means we have to finish him NOW... we'll never get a second chance."

Something was going on here I still didn't understand.

I held back as Audrey headed for the stairs. Not up there! I didn't want to go through that again. Junior trailed after her and I saw him pick up a carving knife as he passed the kitchen table.

"You said you'd do this much for me," I heard Audrey mutter.

"He *is* my brother," Junior mumbled.

Not any more, I thought bitterly.

"Maybe! But he's worth more to us dead."

At that statement, made so crushingly by relatives eager to lay their hands on my millions, I drifted up the stairs behind them, determined now to see this through.

"I've read Linus's will," Junior was informing her as the bedroom door clicked open. I heard Audrey gasp.

"You said tied up!"

"Why didn't you tell me? I'm his next of kin... after you, that is."

At Junior's words, I sensed a change in mood. "I never thought he cared enough to leave me anything," he said

"Look Junior..." Audrey turned in the doorway. I could see her face, now full of doubt and something else, perhaps the makings of fear.

"My name's Christian. Why don't you ever call me that?"

"Ok. Christian." She reached out to him, but he knocked her hand away.

"Don't paw me! I don't need you... not when I can have it all."

I knew what was coming, even before Junior's right hand jerked from behind and sliced downwards. Audrey screamed, both arms going across her gashed chest. She staggered backwards into the bedroom as Junior continued his advance. This time I didn't bother to follow... to try to come between them. I saw her reach out a hand towards the body on the bed... my body, as though begging *me* for help. Then the blade came down once more and I turned back along the landing as Junior wrenched it free in a spray of blood.

Seconds later I heard the bedroom door slam and Junior rushed through me, disappearing round the head of the stairs, one hand leaving a scarlet trail along the wall. Then I heard a yell and a series of heavy thumps, followed by an ominous silence. I looked down the stairs and I think I actually smiled.

As usual old One-Eye was sitting on the top step, seemingly oblivious to Junior's crumpled body in the hall below. Just for once, I thought, in her long, expensive, pampered life... that damn cat had achieved something useful.

PRESS-GANGED

Cornwall - 1836

Nathan cursed as his crippled leg buckled under him.

As he fell, his left arm shot outwards, open-handedly flinging his precious pouch into the shadows. The storm lantern he carried clattered in the opposite direction and went out, leaving him in darkness. His knee-length breeches were no protection against jagged flints that scraped his shins, and he lay still for a moment as the pain of impact washed over him; biting his lower lip against tears of frustration.

Why him?

Why could he not have been made whole, like the other lads in the village; instead he was a creature of ridicule, cuffed by a father who reviled him for his clumsiness and cuffed again because his mother died giving him life; inheriting her dark complexion and vivid blue eyes was a further cruel reminder that led him to walk in his fathers shadow.

Gingerly, he freed his deformed leg and raised himself into a sitting position. His eyes soon became accustomed to the darkness, which was not as intense as he had first believed. Weak moonlight filtered from a cloudy sky and he was instantly able to retrieve his lantern. His pouch, which carried his tinder and flint, and as many plover eggs as fingers on both hands, took a deal longer to find.

All but one of the eggs was broken... and this he dashed to the stony ground in anger and despair. To break their fast with such fine fare might at least have brought a nod of recognition from his father, understanding his son had scaled dangerous cliffs to gather them. Now he would return empty handed and once more be beaten as a wastrel.

Lantern re-lighted, he held it aloft and realized his fall had brought him only paces from the cliff edge. Below lay a place locally known as Wreckers' Bay... a dangerous cove of hidden rocks and treacherous tides. He should have fallen! A sob rose in his throat. He took a lop-sided step nearer. The choice was still his. Come morning, let them find his broken body... or perhaps he should swim out and let the sea claim him when he could go no further.

Ironically, he was the strongest swimmer amongst the village boys. Water buoyed him up and freed him from the restrictions of his twisted leg. Yet he was ridiculed when he tried to help with the fishing nets and was strictly forbidden to set foot on the boats.

"A man's life depends on a strong arm at his side," his father had informed him. "Half a man's as much use as a staved hull."

Recalling his father's words never failed to bite deep and with little caution, he began his descent into the cove, the lantern erratically picking out the treacherous path before him. He would never return to the village, he decided.

In the lea of the cliff, the darkness became deeper and the crash of waves an incessant voice, urging him on towards his doom. When sea spray cooled his burning cheeks he raised the lantern higher and was startled by what appeared to be an answering blink of light, just beyond the headland. Three times he carved a wide arc with the storm lantern and each time received a mirrored answer.

Someone was out there!

Intrigued, he settled on a boulder and watched as a second light appeared; and then a third. The clouds parted, spilling moonlight across the water. In full sail, a three masted schooner was heading directly for the rocks, presumably lured on by his light and the promise of safe harbour.

His reaction was to shut off the lantern. But it was too late. Caught on the tide, he could only watch as the vessels majestic progress was halted by the first juddering impact.

He pressed himself into the cliff face.

He'd seen 'wreckers' at work, but had never been this close. The ship screamed as jagged rocks pierced her heart and the ragging waters boomed their triumph as they breached her. Debris spread a luminous circle of white water as it was thrown from the deck and the canvas sails flapped like the wings of a giant bird, trying in vain to rise above the churning waves.

After an eternity that could only have been minutes, the shattered hulk slowly toppled sideways, her main mast breaking free and wedging itself in the rocks. The hull lifted clear of the water, spewing sea foam in all directions before crashing back with a noise like thunder that echoed from the cliffs around him.

Open mouthed, he waited, shivering now in his worn shirt and breeches. Such a furore would no doubt bring the village out in full force. He measured time against his rapid heartbeat, which eventually calmed as he remembered to breath again. There were no signs of survivors floundering at the water's edge and still no sound of movement on the cliff above him.

The truth gradually dawned.

Single-handedly he'd lured a ship onto the rocks. 'Wreckers' Law' meant the booty was his. A man's bounty. His shallow chest swelled with pride as he continued his descent. Let his father deny him now.

*

Several times, he almost despaired of reaching the wreck, let alone unloading any cargo she carried.

The beach had become a death trap of splintered wood and submerged rigging. He gave the area as wide a birth as possible, deciding to approach the ship from the seaward side and allow the tide to carry him inshore with his bounty.

He swam cautiously at first, fearing to encounter debris and worse still... bodies of drowned seaman. But whatever remained was either trapped in the wreck or now lay ahead of him on the rocks. Soon, he began to revel in his buoyant freedom, rolling and kicking like a young seal gambolling in the moonlight.

At last the wreck loomed darkly before him. He dived to avoid a tangle of ropes and came up to grasp the splintered bulwark. Treading water, he checked the beach and cliff for signs of movement. No lights winked and no figures moved against the skyline. Incredibly, he was still alone.

He pressed an ear to the hull and listened to the vessel's dying heartbeat; the hollow booming of casks, beating time to the lift and swell of the water. He dived again, surfacing where the hull had been breached.

"Nathan."

Startled and more afraid than he'd ever been in his life, he back kicked, treading water - listening.

"Nathan."

This time there was no mistake. The ship seemed to lift and settle again with a watery sigh.

Soft tendrils caressed his legs and then tightened as he recoiled. He tried to dive, but only floundered, gasping for breath as he felt himself being pulled beneath the surface. He expected darkness and skeins of rope or canvas. Instead he found a fluorescent glow and movement all around him.

Dozens of hands reached out, not so much in restraint, but touching and caressing, patting him in a horrendous greeting. He tried to scream. His mouth filled with water and he felt his senses begin to slip. Faces flickered past his vision, white and bloated, with starring eyes and crooked smiles that somehow framed a welcome, even in death.

He knew his struggles were becoming weaker.

The hands were now supportive, preventing him from drifting away with the tide. Their icy touch filled his entire being.

"Nathan – come with us."

And why not!

Who would mourn his passing? What did he have to fight for? A wrecker's bounty he was too weak to defend? The pain in his chest became a dull ache... a mere shadow of the torment that always filled his heart. Unresisting, he felt himself drawn towards the breach in the hull. Darkness descended in his mind as he was gently lifted inside.

*

By dawn, all signs of the shipwreck had disappeared from the cove. All that remained to show Nathan's passing was a leather pouch and a battered storm lantern...

WAITING FOR WILLIAM

Sarah Blande strained against the straps binding her to the hard bed.

'How much longer?' she asked herself. 'Why doesn't he come for me?'

With difficulty she turned her head to the left so she could see the old oak tree through the heavy steel bars of her window, the thinning foliage tossed by a soundless October breeze.

'Be patient, my precious,' William had said, 'wait until autumn... and we shall never be parted again.'

Autumn was nearly over, so he *must* come soon. At the thought of him, she sensed a familiar thrill of excitement, giving her renewed strength and the feeling she could burst free from her bonds if she really wanted to... although now was not the time. Without William there was nowhere to go.

Sarah thought of the other women incarcerated within the asylum. Blind, tormented souls trapped in bodies long outgrown their usefulness, prisoners of their own minds. She was different, and she'd told them so many times. *They* would never leave this place. *She* would. She was merely waiting for William.

It was *because* of him she was here. *Because* she'd done everything he asked off her. *Because* he'd vowed they would be together again. The others knew she was telling the truth. They understood. That's why they treated her differently... why they bound her. They *knew* she could walk away any time she wanted... and the fools hated her for it.

All along, she'd kept her part of the bargain and now it was just a matter of waiting...

Sarah turned over-bright eyes once more towards the window, seeing the tree now black and splintery against the darkening sky.

The nurses would come soon to make her 'comfortable' for the night, to slacken the harness and change the soiled bedding. Then came the injection to make her sleep.

And in sweet oblivion followed the dreams... the memories... and William, with his handsome smiling face and incorrigible laugh, urging her to be strong and patient.

For Sarah, it had been like that almost every day since the funeral. William's funeral!

*

That had been eight months ago. But Sarah could see herself at the grave-side as though it was only yesterday, supported by William's best friend and business partner, Bernard Forster.

Through her tears she'd said, "You know... he hasn't really gone. I only have to whisper his name and he'll be with me again."

Bernard had held her tight; too tight.

"Don't torture yourself, Sarah."

"But it *must* be true," she'd twisted from his grasp, "because he said so... and William *never* lied to me... *ever*." Like a petulant child, she'd knelt and caressed the freshly turned earth. "That's right isn't it William? William my love." Her gently spoken words had seemed to coincide with a gust of wind that swept through the churchyard, stirring floral tributes and scattering mourners' hats and umbrellas in all directions.

Sarah had felt a definite sense of triumph at the expression on Bernard's face as he almost dragged her back to the waiting limousine.

She had never liked Bernard Forster.

*

That night, William had returned to Sarah in all his youthful glory. The years had fallen away and he was young again; renewed... and she'd felt a terrible longing to join him, to be free from the shackles of her ageing body, to escape the new fear in her life... loneliness.

William had laughed at her. Was he not proof she would never be alone? All she had to learn was patience. Their love would achieve the rest.

*

The next morning, in her excitement, she'd made the mistake of confiding in her sister, who of course hadn't believed her. Kind, comfortable, down to earth Annette, who wouldn't have recognized a spiritual visitation if it came to share one of her boring cucumber sandwiches. She'd dismissed the entire episode as the consequences of bereavement, which only time would heal and Sarah had to admit, after a few hours of Annette's company she'd become inclined to believe her sister's sensible explanation... that is until the voice in her head told her she should listen carefully, and only to him, because there were things he would ask of her.

*

After that, strange and unexpected incidents had started to happen. The smell of William's after-shave washed over her in a warm and draught free room. Small, shiny objects moved inexplicably from their usual places in the home. A glass bowl held by Annette shattered as she'd once more decried the possibility of William's continued existence; resulting in a badly lacerated hand. A favourite picture had fallen unharmed to the floor; yet Sarah found nothing wrong with either hook or cord and perhaps, most mysterious and moving of all was the single red rose that appeared beside her picture on William's bedside table.

For Sarah, these events had spoken of a love as strong and undying as ever, but, after experiencing ridicule from friends and relatives she'd fled in tears to her room, resolved to keep such moments close to her heart and never speak of them again.

Then came the lights, floating incandescent colours, tantalizingly beyond the edge of her vision and always when she had least expected them, when her mind was on everyday mundane matters, never when she'd been thinking of William.

She'd also sensed a change in attitude towards her, from strong concern over her early hysteria to scorn at the apparent tranquillity that began to pervade her whole being. To others, it seemed as though her period of mourning had become indecently short lived.

But Sarah was only doing what William had asked of her... learning patience, a patience soon to be rewarded.

*

One evening, she'd been sitting at her dressing table, reading old letters, when she'd glanced up to see William standing behind her, his reflection as clear and positive as her own. She'd made to turn, but the lightest touch on her shoulder somehow held her rigid. As in life, she'd felt herself drawn into the depths of his blue eyes, and as he told her what she must do, and the reasons why, the words had penetrated deep within her mind.

She'd learnt that he had been re-united with his twin brother Michael, who had died at birth and grown to perfect manhood in the spirit world. He'd also met her father, who urged William to help him clear up a misunderstanding he'd had with Sarah before his death. He'd admitted he was wrong to have condemned her early marriage, realising now it had been for purely selfish reasons because, like many doting fathers, he could think of no man as being good enough for his daughter. He understood now how she had desperately needed his approval and begged her forgiveness for the unnecessary pain he'd brought to their marriage. Now, like William, he eagerly awaited their re-union and promised to be there when she took that final step. All she had to do was place her complete trust in the guidance she was being given.

"Now it begins... my love," William had whispered, finally.
At which she'd promptly fainted.

*

Trance-like, Sarah remained unconscious for several days. A
steady stream of doctors, friends and relatives paced her room
while she slept on, oblivious of all but William's presence.

*

Five days later.

Sarah opened her eyes to find Bernard leaning over her, one
hand holding her own where it rested against the coverlet.
Normally, she would have pulled away, but this time she
didn't, much to Bernard's obvious surprise. Instead she
actually squeezed his hand in return and made sure he caught
the welcoming light in her grey eyes.

"At last, Sarah... how are you feeling?" he asked in his
usual unctuous tone, this time tempered with what sounded
like genuine concern.

"Better... thank you," she smiled, in her most encouraging
manner and felt the responsive pressure of his hand, "at least...
I think all that silly business is over now."

"Good." Bernard sounded genuinely relieved. His small
black eyes seared her with their intensity. Then the shutters
came down again as he added cautiously. "You had us all
worried. What with this talk of communicating with William
and wanting to join him?"

"I was being a foolish old woman," she put in a little
breathlessly. "I panicked, instead of turning to others for help.
I've *never* been alone before and I suppose I couldn't come to
terms with loosing him."

"You don't *have* to be alone," Bernard whispered with
emphasis and then unexpectedly released her hand and
stepped back, as though he had encroached on forbidden
territory. "I mean, Annette and the others... they've been here
all the while... should you need them..."

"What about you, Bernard?" Sarah raised herself stiffly on the pillows. "After all, you were not *only* William's business partner. He *was* your best friend and I'm sure he would want you to look after me."

Bernard's colour heightened.

"Yes... yes of course, my dear." His self-pretentious manner had clearly suffered under her direct approach. "William knows... knew how fond I was... am of you." He seemed to draw a calming breath, "I shan't let either of you down."

"That's that then." Sarah gave the flowered duvet a satisfied pat, intentionally leaving Bernard with the feeling they'd just sealed some sort of bargain. "Now, if you don't mind I'm still a little tired and disorientated."

"Yes... right. I'll tell the others not to disturb you for a while longer, although I expect the doctor will want to look in later." He paused at the door and studied her peaceful profile; his own sweaty features a mixture of emotions. Then he was gone, his metal tipped shoes clicking down the hallway.

Sarah opened her eyes again... and smiled.

*

Much to everyone's surprise, Sarah and Bernard spent a great deal of time together over the weeks following her collapse from what became medically diagnosed as 'nervous exhaustion brought about by bereavement.'

Whatever Sarah really believed, she talked of William only in the 'acceptable' past tense and only then concerning the good times they'd had together, noticeably including Bernard in the conversation whenever possible.

One evening, Annette confided how Bernard had spoken of her sister's change in attitude towards him. How, first of all he'd assumed it was another facet of her illness, and was only now beginning to hope they might actually have some sort of future together. Sarah said very little in response to this disclosure. But she did invite Bernard to dinner the very next evening.

*

"Thank you for a wonderful meal." Bernard sat hunched over the remnants of his dessert. "William often boasted of your culinary genius and I used to quite envy him.... until now," he reached across the dinning table and laid his moist palm in hers, "although I wouldn't presume to try and replace him."

Sarah smiled and her grey eyes surveyed the little man in what he obviously took to be an encouraging manner.

"However, given the chance I could very well prove myself an equal." His tone was even more ingratiating than usual, having been well oiled with white wine and brandy.

Sarah laughed and shook her head, although not unkindly.

"As you say, Bernard, no one could replace him." She paused and for a moment appeared to be listening to something. It seemed as though a shadow crossed her face, although it was quickly gone as she added, "William was always... *WILLIAM*." She raised her glass in an obvious toast and ever eager to please her, Bernard followed suit.

"May he rest in peace," he murmured as their glasses clinked together.

"Oh... he will," Sarah promised, sipping the warm amber liquid. Her grey eyes held a strange glow, which may have only been, reflected candlelight. "Eventually."

"That's an odd way to put it, Sarah," Bernard stirred in his chair, but covered the fact by retrieving his fallen napkin from the floor. He found Sarah's next words even more surprising.

"I want you to teach me about *our* loan business. Now I have William's shares I intend to become an active partner." She drew herself to her full, determined height. "It's time I started looking to the future."

*

Blande, Forster and Sons was a reputable loan company of some thirty years standing and although they had never turned big time in the traditional sense of the word, they had built up a wide range of clientele through reliability of service and discretion, many of whom returned again and again. William had once said it was because sensible people preferred to be bitten by a small fish than eaten alive by a shark.

Years ago, health problems had brought the sad news Sarah would never be able to carry William's child. Once, Sarah had feared for their future together, feeling the building blocks of their marriage had been taken from under them. As fate would have it, their lack of offspring had actually cemented their relationship, instead of pulling it apart. Unless Bernard found himself a young wife, the title 'Sons' would remain an empty promise.

Sarah's decision to become an active partner had not gone well with Bernard, who seemed reluctant to share his years of experience with her and obviously preferred to keep their partnership on a purely social level. Undaunted, Sarah arrived every day at nine sharp, visited less important clients and held the fort when Bernard was away, thus saving the added expense of a secretary. Bernard was amazed how quickly she grasped the work, especially computer data. She refrained from telling him that while she slept, William was mechanically repeating everything Bernard taught her until she had it word perfect. After three months Sarah could justifiably call herself a worthwhile partner and despite his earlier misgivings, Bernard couldn't help but agree with her.

Their 'relationship' had remained pretty stable throughout this time, the highlight being their weekly dinner date, always prepared by Sarah herself.

On one such occasion, she suddenly said over her steak, "Do you realise we never talk of how William died?" Although Bernard had obviously heard her, he attacked his meal with added relish, his eyes averted from her own. "I've never been really *sure* of the details," she added, with a note of persistence.

Bernard sighed and at last met her gaze, or at least his dark eyes fenced with hers across the empty salad bowls.

"Knowing the gruesome details won't bring William back, so what can we achieve by pursuing the matter now he's gone?"

Sarah gave no indication she'd noticed his icy tone. She seemed to be absorbed in thought, her head on one side in what had now become a familiar stance to those who knew her well.

"There seems to be a blank in my life," she continued, the old sadness returning to her voice, "as though I fell asleep one night and woke up a week later to find him gone."

Bernard drained his glass of brandy in one go.

"You *know* the brakes failed," he stated simply.

Sarah seemed to flinch.

"Yes... but why?"

Bernard shrugged.

"Unfortunately things like that happen sometimes."

"I used the car that morning... it seemed ok, then."

Bernard positioned his empty wineglass with measured patience.

"What can I say?" he asked gently. "Had the brakes failed a few hours earlier it may have been you who died," he smiled his sickly sweet smile. "That would have been bad news for me."

"Meaning William's death was not?"

Bernard coloured, realising his attempted compliment had somehow misfired.

"Of course it was a shock." He wiped his shiny brow with his napkin. "But they say out of all bad things comes some good. If events hadn't worked out the way they did, I wouldn't be sitting here with you now... would I?"

"No. But you might have been squatting in a prison cell," Sarah said with measured calmness, "especially as I know the car was serviced *after* I used it... and that *you* collected it from the garage."

"How'd you know that?" Bernard blurted, all diplomacy forgotten in his surprise.

"From the accounts data on the computer," she admitted. "A simple phone call to the garage told me the rest. What I *can't* prove is that you tampered with the brakes before handing the car over to William."

Bernard stood up from the table, his piggy eyes inflamed with drink and the suggestion of violence as he swayed before her calmly seated figure.

"You're mad, woman." Spittle bubbled from the corner of his thin mouth. "What possible reason could I have?"

"...Embezzlement of funds?" Sarah suggested. "As far as I can tell fifty percent of William's fees have found their way into your account."

"Well... you have been a busy little bee," Bernard seemed to gather some composure, although his colour wasn't too good and he kept tugging at his shirt collar as though he was finding it difficult to breathe. "By prying into things you don't understand, you've twisted the whole situation out of context." He ran one hand through his thinning hair and gave a long, shuddering sigh. "Sarah... you've had your say... now, please, be reasonable and listen to me. That money was legally transferred because of what William owed me. I know William wanted his gambling kept from you..."

"That's a lie," Sarah snapped, showing real emotion for the first time that evening. "He would have told me."

Bernard shrugged.

"Had he lived he might well have done... the situation *was* beginning to get out of hand."

Sarah gave a funny, knowing little smile,

"Why don't we ask him... he's standing right behind you?"

Bernard didn't appear moved by this statement.

"Let's face it Sarah... which one of our stories do you think will stand up in court? I don't believe William would make a very good *material* witness." He seemed highly amused at his play on words. "I think I'd best be leaving before this conversation goes any further." He gave her what she considered to be a very condescending smile. "You are *still* a very sick woman, Sarah, but because of past friendships and the fact I am so very fond of you I shall ignore your outburst this evening, but I do suggest you stay away from the office..."

"It's gone," Sarah announced in a firm voice. "Blande, Forster & Sons no longer exists. Last night I despatched a standard letter to our clients thanking them for their custom over the years and stating that, in accordance with the wishes of Mr William Blande, deceased, the company was being liquidated and all outstanding debts cancelled in full."

Bernard stared blankly at her for a moment and then laughed, long and loud.

"You can't do that without joint signatures... or unless you happen to be the only remaining partner..."

"At last you have it, Bernard," Sarah clapped her thin hands like a gleeful child. "Tell me... are you feeling tired yet... or perhaps your breathing's becoming a little shallow?"

"I've had enough of this." Bernard turned from the table in search of his jacket. "You're mad. Mad!" He swayed slightly, catching the back of his dining chair and toppling it to the floor. For the first time real fear registered across his sweaty features. "Damn you, woman, what have you given me?" he gasped.

Sarah laughed.

"Your favourite, 'Caesar salad' laced with enough barbiturates to kill a horse, let alone a worthless weasel like yourself." She pulled herself upright and faced him across the table. "You've no idea how I suffered... holding back on those drugs... the endless days and sleepless nights when all I wanted to do was die. William promised it would be worth it and seeing your face now... I can only say he was right... right about everything." Her red lips split in a wicked grin of triumph. "As for the letters... being a bank holiday weekend, they'll not arrive until *after* your death... *this evening*."

Bernard stood wild eyed before her, his jacket crushed in sweaty, trembling hands. Beads of perspiration trickled unheeded to his shirtfront and his breath came in short, laboured gasps,

"You've ruined yourself and destroyed everything William and I ever worked for... *Why?*"

"Because it was what *he* wanted. What *we* planned together to avenge his murder. I'll have no need for money once William comes for me," she smiled sweetly. "Why don't you go upstairs and lie down, Bernard, you don't look at all well. Regrettably, the phone line seems to be down so you cannot call for a doctor."

Bernard said nothing, he just swayed backwards towards the door, his dark little eyes glazed and starring as he fumbled behind him for the latch. The door clicked open and he sort of slid out of sight into the hallway. Sarah heard the hall table fall with a crash and then felt the rush of cool evening air against her burning cheeks as the front door banged open...

*

That had been three months ago.

Sarah never saw Bernard Forster again. No one did, after his car hit the viaduct at ninety-three mph. The resulting inferno fused him permanently with the molten metalwork. Sarah found it ironic that after all her efforts he should have died at the wheel just as William had done. Under the circumstances, she wasn't sure if the authorities could have found traces of barbiturates in what had been left of Bernard's system, but she came forward anyway, to give the remains an identity and proudly state her part in the demise of an embezzler and murderer... because that was also part of the bargain. She knew there was nothing they could do to hurt her... that no walls could ever keep them apart.

Of course certain phrases had been used, such as 'emotional breakdown due to bereavement' and 'while of an unsound mind.' So-called friends had said cruel and hurtful things to her and she had not set eyes on Annette since the news first hit the headlines. But she didn't care. William had warned her it would be like this. Now she understood what the old martyrs must have gone through when they were cast out from society.

*

The ward was in total darkness now.

Sarah stirred from a drug-induced sleep and turned her head awkwardly towards the window, trying to shake the matted grey hair from her red-rimmed eyes, finding herself unable to do so, without the freedom of her hands. She couldn't decide whether the faint light she saw was the afterglow or sunrise. Surely the wings of night had not already passed her by? She always felt so secure in their enveloping shadow.

As sleep fell from her eyes, she realised the light did not emanate from the window as she supposed, but from the floor beneath it. A thrill ran through her aching bones as she recognized the glittering specks for what they really were, swirling and wavering, struggling against the natural darkness that threatened to engulf them.

"William," she breathed. His name seemed to give substance and colour to the form materialising beside her bed. "At last... my love." In her mind, she was already reaching out her frail, wasted arms, feeling the strength of his will draw her upwards, towards the light and warmth of his smile. Momentarily, she closed her eyes, adding her own feeble energy to the miracle... until the drag of her bonds shattered the illusion, bringing back the reality of soiled sheets and her own sweat soaked limbs.

He was leaning over her now, close enough for Sarah to read their future together in the blue depths of his eyes. 'Dying seems to have done him the world of good,' she thought illogically. 'God... he's so beautiful.'

He gave a charming smile, as though he knew the effect he was having on her, and it somehow amused him.

"William." As always, words passed between them in a sequence of loving thoughts.

Unaccountably, she sensed a shake of the head.

"I'm Michael."

The name entered her brain and lodged there like a stone.

"Michael?"

He laughed, the sound reaching deep into her soul and filling her with an unaccountable dread.

"Sarah... you're an old, ignorant fool." His words pierced her like a knife, yet the smile remained. "How easily I have blinded you with your earthly love for another... *Love,* I was never permitted to know or understand. *Why,* was I the one denied my birthright... instead of William?" A shadow seemed to darken the aura around him. "How I hated my brother for that and how eagerly I have sought and planned my moment for revenge."

Her heart gave a sickening lurch as she realised William would not be coming for her... that probably, he had never done so.

"You deceived me. It was all lies?"

"I prefer to think of it as an elaborate game."

"You've left me with nothing…"

"Perhaps that should have been my line, forty years ago. That's a long time, Sarah, to brood upon what might have been... as I'm sure you'll realise as the loneliness and futility of your confinement closes around you."

Sarah felt hot tears well beneath her lashes, spilling over onto the hard pillow; tears, held back for months that should have now been shed in happiness.

"Then Bernard told the truth." It was not a question... just a resigned statement of fact.

This time she sensed a nod of the head.

"Everything was just as he said. William's time had come and there was no way anyone could have prevented it. Yours, however, is far from over and when Bernard is rested... I am sure he will know where to find you…"

"NO! Sarah's mouth opened in a long, drawn-out scream of shock and denial. *What* had she done? *What* was to become of her? *"William... where are you?"* Wild eyed, she writhed and kicked at her bindings, spittle flying as her head twisted from side to side.

*

In the annexe, the Night Sister heard the commotion and carefully prepared another injection for her most difficult patient, thankful that this would probably be the last. At midday, Sarah Blande was to be transferred to permanent accommodation in a high security ward for the criminally insane.

GHOST WALK

Bannerman awoke with a cry and a lurch that brought him instantly upright.

"Oh... God!" Thin pale arms crushed the duvet to his chest and a deep sigh shuddered through him. In time his pulse stopped galloping and his breathing returned to normal. When he was able to take in familiar surroundings, his wide-eyed expression suggested surprise at waking to reality.

He allowed the duvet to fall away and slumped back on the pillows, willing his body to relax. Only when his eyes threatened to close, did he stir and roll to the edge of the bed, fumbling for the light switch and his cigarettes.

God he was so tired!

He ran one hand shakily through his short cropped, grey hair. He daren't risk sleeping again... not before daylight edged the curtains of his hotel room; for with darkness came the dreams and each nightmare left him feeling death was one step closer.

The bedside lamp did little to dispel the shadows in his mind and he pulled deeply on his cigarette. The smoke bit into his lungs and he coughed and took a second drag before checking his Rolex, surprised to find it was still only 7.43 pm.

He had turned in well before dusk, praying shear exhaustion would carry him through to morning light, but nightfall had claimed him once more... forcing his dreams along a now familiar, relentless path.

It was always the same.

He would find himself alone in a dark and dreary place, where the only sound was the muffled drag of approaching footsteps. Automatically he would flee from this confrontation... only to find a solid wall forced him to turn and face his pursuer. Each dream brought this presence nearer and this time he could have sworn he'd caught the sound of harsh, laboured breathing mingled with his own waking gasp of despair.

He might have no conception of the being that tracked him, but he believed he understood the origin of his nightmares. Taking a last, lung-filling drag on his cigarette, he crushed it violently in the ashtray before opening the top drawer of his bedside cabinet. Carefully, he lifted out a black velvet box. Barely an inch square, the container weighed heavily in the palm of his hand. With caution born of respect, he sprung the lid.

The gold nugget seemed to pulse in the soft lamplight, giving life to the intricate swirls and circles engraved on its surface. He had never seen anything that fascinated or attracted him as much as this trinket... this bauble; the possession of which had brought him so much pleasure and pain.

"Look here... the price is irrelevant," he'd firmly informed the jeweller in Chinatown, a wizened little creature who did his best to divert his interest by offering other, lower quality gems. "*I have* to have it!" As an influential man, used to getting his way, even he'd been surprised by the need that filled him.

"This unlucky for you," the fellow had insisted in pigeon English. "Bad omen... no sell!"

Bannerman had never taken '*no*' for an answer in his life and was not prepared to do so now. Finally, they'd reached a favourable deal. He had simply cut the man's throat and taken that which he coveted. The temptation to acquire other valuables had been overwhelming, although he'd finally settled on riffling the till, hoping to make the crime appear as petty theft, gone drastically wrong. There was also the possibility a single gem wouldn't be missed for some time... if at all.

His upbringing in the East End had taught him the strongest survive. Take what you want and eliminate those who stand in your way. With this outlook, by age twenty-three, he was moving in top circles and was proud to know he was feared and despised by all who knew him, including the looser he called Father, now mouldering in a flea-bitten rest home for the mentally deranged. Through sheer guts and determination he'd had some of the most powerful racketeers eating out of his hand... so he was darned if he would let a chunk of metal and an old man's words get the better of him.

He returned the box and closed the drawer, deciding in that instant to book an overnight flight back to Switzerland for the next evening. Perhaps then he could catch up on some sleep and the presence of other passengers just might keep the nightmares at bay.

He was bored with the City and the new blood coming in. For him, there were simply no further avenues to explore and the ones still left held too many tired memories. There was too much *deja vu*. Admittedly, he was pushing sixty, but he already felt as though he'd spent several lifetimes in one place.

With a rally of determination, he raised himself from the bed and headed for the shower. There was life in the old dog yet... damn it. All he had to do was keep one step ahead of the morons that inhabited *his* planet.

*

The autumn evening was cool and dry.

Bannerman shivered as he paused on the steps of the Westbury Hotel. Raising his collar, he thrust both hands into his overcoat pockets and began to head along New Bond Street, intent on avoiding Piccadilly with its restaurant and theatre goers.

Walking with his head down, he turned sharply into Conduit Street and collided with a young oriental woman who promptly apologized, smiled shyly and hurried towards a group of students, loudly being informed of local points of interest. Just once, the woman glanced back at him before disappearing into the crowd. Nice face and legs, he thought appreciatively. He decided to collect a newspaper and something for his headache before returning to the hotel. Then he would phone in his reservation for Switzerland.

Annoyingly, his usual newsagents was closed and several turnings later he found a grotty little corner shop, packed with tourists, all clambering to be served at once. When he finally stepped outside again, a canopy of dark cloud hung over the city and a fine drizzle had begun to fall. Tucking the newspaper inside his overcoat, he popped a couple of Paracetamol and washed them down with a full can of coke. Casting around for a waste bin, he hesitated, suddenly unsure of his surroundings. The road was unfamiliar and there seemed to be no visible landmarks to go by. He turned a corner and soon found himself in complete darkness. So he doubled back, looking for the beacon of light offered by the newsagent, but was astonished to find the shop already in darkness, looking almost derelict behind its dirty, half shuttered windows. Loudly, he rattled the front door.

"Hello... anyone there?" The surrounding buildings instantly absorbed the sound of his own voice; and he stepped back, hoping to see a light come on in the upper storey. But the rain-misted windows remained blind to his presence. Another step and he was surprised to feel an uneven, cobbled surface beneath the souls of his feet. God, he really had wandered into some godforsaken back street. He glanced from left to right, but made no move until logic told him to gauge direction from the sounds of passing traffic.

That's when the silence really hit him.

There was nothing but the patter of rain, which was steadily turning into a downpour. For the first time he seriously took note of his surroundings. Tall, soot blackened buildings, looking more like warehouses than private dwellings. Not a sign of life anywhere. No parked cars... just three cobbled streets, no more than simple alleyways, stretching away beneath flickering gas lamps. Gas lamps for Christ sake! It looked as though he'd stepped into some sort of time warp. A film set! That's what it had to be. Someone was making a period piece in the back streets of Soho. Somewhat reassured, he tweaked the collar of his overcoat and headed determinedly down the nearest turning.

He would never have believed such stillness was possible in the centre of London. The cobblestones seemed to muffle his footsteps and the rain whispered into the gutters. Overhead, low cloud masked any chance of moonlight or seeing the flickering lights of passing planes; the thought reminded him of his un-booked flight and his pace quickened.

The film lot must have been enormous and he was considering trying a different direction when he was startled by the distinct clatter of hooves. Up ahead, shadows shifted and began to take on a solid shape.

He froze, wasting precious seconds as the carriage and four thundered towards him. Suddenly the road seemed impossibly narrow. Moving quicker than he'd done in many a year, he tried to backtrack, but found himself physically thrown against the wall as the vehicle sped past with a clatter and a hiss of spinning wheels. All he caught was a blur of sweating horseflesh and the swaying coachman up top, muffled in his greatcoat.

"Bloody idiot!" Bannerman yelled, severely shaken and undoubtedly bruised.

The carriage rocked to a halt amidst the snort and pant of horses as they settled in their traces. The side door swung open, effectively blocking the passage. Something was very wrong and he decided not to wait around for introductions.

As his pace quickened into a run, hindered somewhat by a breathless pounding in his chest, the horror of his nightmares became reality, and he was almost expecting the brick wall when his evasive action led him slap bang into one. His expensive leather shoes slithered on the wet ground as he turned, *knowing* he was about to find himself trapped.

Out on the road, the gas lamps cast irregular shadows where there had been none at his passing, and above his own harsh breathing he could hear the uneven drag of approaching footsteps, mingled with the sharp tap... tapping of a cane.

With the wall at his back, he waited, the empty coke can crushed between the fingers of his right hand.

Two figures turned into the yard. Although their faces were hidden in shadow, one man was clearly the coach driver, although neither appeared familiar to him, wrapped as they were in heavy, old-fashioned greatcoats. Their determined approach, however, radiated aggression.

Hit men!

Bannerman straightened, feeling sweat gather between his shoulder blades. He knew returning to London had been a mistake... but if this was all his nightmares foretold, he'd wipe the floor with these bastards and leave the owners of the film set to pick up the pieces. Almost casually, he discarded the can and flexed his right arm, reassured to feel a length of warm steel slide down into the palm of his hand.

Both men paused. Cane Man had obviously caught the movement.

"Well lookie here, if it ain't old Jem." His voice had a course, nasal accent, unfamiliar to Bannerman. His companion merely gave an animal grunt. "How far did ya expect ta get this time?"

The question made no sense to Bannerman, but then he didn't know who'd sent these thugs or what they'd been told about him.

"I suggest you guys have made a mistake," Bannerman reasoned, trying to keep his voice level. He even managed to raise a smile, although he was damn near frothing at the mouth. No one in his or her right mind dared call J.D. Bannerman 'Old Jem'... anyone left alive, that is.

"We ain't paid ta make mistakes, Jem," Cane Man replied. "You an' me have been down this 'er road so many times we could walk it blindfold, so cough up ta goods and we'll see Markham says no more about it." The cane flicked up, minus its sheath and Bannerman found himself facing a metre of steel.

His initial doubts returned in a hot wave of fear that set his heart pounding again. Who the hell used swordsticks in the twenty-first century and when had hit men ever arrived in a coach-and-four?

"I suggest you drop tha' little tickler," Cane Man continued. "Markham, he don't like his runners using no weapons."

Bannerman had no idea who Markham was and doubted if he would understand the answer. Clearly the time for words was long past. His gaze flicked to the right, although he moved to the left, intending to take out the coachman, while keeping the man's large body between himself and the sword blade.

Not surprisingly, this ploy failed miserably.

His right hand was seized in a crushing grip and twisted viciously up his back. The knife slipped from his senseless fingers and he heard it clatter on the cobblestones as the tip of the sword raked across his chest. Then someone's fist hammered into his jaw, rocking his head back, bringing instant oblivion.

*

Bannerman awoke to excruciating pain that wracked his body.

He could taste blood in his mouth and his chest felt as though a red-hot brand had been laid across it. It was too dark to see, but he could tell he was only in his shirtsleeves. He was bitterly cold... but at least he was still alive.

He had a vague recollection of leering faces and hands that mercilessly pummelled his body as he slipped in and out of oblivion. Rough voices had demanded the same thing from him over and over, yet he could no longer recall the question and was unaware if he had ever given an answer.

Cautiously, he flexed each limb in turn. Despite the pain, nothing appeared to be broken. The next step was getting out of here while he still had the cover of darkness. Switzerland would have to wait. All he wanted now was the comfort of his hotel bed.

He reached out and touched brick on either side. From somewhere overhead he heard the faint murmur of voices, steadily growing nearer. Cautiously, he stretched out his right hand...

*

"... And just along here, ladies and gentleman, we come to another gruesome reminder of the cruelties of nineteenth century London."

The sightseers were coming to the end of their guided tour.

"This plaque and tiny grill marks the spot where one hundred and twenty years ago, the notorious jewel thief 'Jem' Bannerman was buried alive for stealing from the local mob. His death was intended to be a long and painful one. His tongue was cut out to prevent him calling for help and by design he would have spent days watching people pass overhead while he slowly starved to death..."

*

...Bannerman tried to scream, but only a sob escaped his bloodstained lips. This couldn't be happening to him. He wanted to tell them there'd been some sort of mistake. He was still alive, for Christ's sake. This was the twenty... first century... and he wasn't 'that' Jem Bannerman.

Wide eyed with terror, he watched the nice legs of the oriental woman move away. Very soon the combined voices of the group faded into the night... leaving him with nothing but the sound of his own tortured breathing.

THE RIPPER TAKES A HOLIDAY

I must confess; I have fallen deeply in love.

Elisabeth is the most beautiful, delicate and mesmerizing creature I have ever set eyes upon. She has filled my heart and mind for nearly a month now and although no words can pass between us, already I feel as though my poor existence would never be the same without her presence.

Compared to my years, she is but a child. Yet she displays a grace and serenity that is almost out of this world and is at the same time a living, breathing creature of the most warm and vibrant kind.

Sometimes I draw close enough to feel her heartbeat. I have certainly heard the small, sharp intake of breath she makes whenever anything stimulates her interest; or perhaps when she is startled... then the tip of her tongue explores her finely sculptured lips with quick, darting movements of uncertainty. At such times I feel she is aware of my presence... the intrusion of my gaze upon her and I swiftly, reluctantly withdraw, fearful I should offend that which I come only to worship.

Perhaps here, I should speak a little of myself. My name is Guy and this place is Bonchurch on the Isle of Wight. As an orphaned child, I lived here alone with my Great Aunt Sophy, although there was no blood tie between us, she treated me like a son. Difficult times came when I was killed in the landslide of 1818. They never found my mortal remains and with no man in the family, Aunt Sophy was forced to take lodgers into the Dower House. Others have done so ever since.

Some call this the Garden Isle. If indeed this is so, then Elisabeth must be choicest bloom and I dread the day her convalescence ends and she must return to the mainland.

You may consider my words harsh and even selfish in their content, but to understand you must appreciate the depth of my feelings and realize her illness is all that keeps her near me... they say the sea air can drive away the virus said to have brought her low.

Her affliction, however, does not keep her tied to her room. Every day, around the hour of one, she takes the air between Bonchurch and Ventnor. Unfortunately, in this promenade the odorous Mr Samualson, with his bulbous eyes and wet, slobbering mouth, barely concealed by his great moustache, accompanies her. He arrived here shortly after my fair Elisabeth and being at present the only other lodger, offered himself as her chaperon.

If she were able to allow me the smallest of such considerations, I would believe myself the luckiest of fellows, yet Samualson seems to show no great emotion. Indeed, he clearly takes it as his right to stand beside her, their heads bobbing gently together as comments pass between them. Were I in his position, I could not refrain from casting sideways glances at my Elisabeth, fearful lest I miss the slightest turn of her head or the sheer beauty of sunlight playing on her dark fall of hair.

Despite Samualson's gentlemanly reserve, there is something in his manner that disturbs me greatly. Today, for the first time, I did not follow my beloved but left them to their perambulations, eager to enter Samualson's rooms and make what I can of the man.

Although the window is open, there is a musty smell of soiled linen combined with the fellow's cologne, which I find as equally cloying and unpleasant as the former. From long experience, I know full well the variety of possessions that clutter people's lives, yet what I see does not strike me as the trappings of a fine gentleman; rather those of a man of limited means who perhaps aspires to stations above his calling.

I was drawn to the writing table under the window, where some form of diary or notebook had been left open. Aunt Sophy never taught me my letters, so the content is beyond me. Several newspaper cuttings lay scattered around... markers... perhaps dislodged by a book too hastily thrown down? Some were faded with age, but the pictures were clear enough. Women. All of them women!

What had I stumbled upon? Was this fellow a journalist... or some voyeur? I cursed my inability to delve further into these writings, overcome by dread thoughts my dear, sweet, innocent might be in danger.

I must go to her!

My fears were temporarily allayed by the sound of familiar voices floating in through the open window and for once I was relieved to see them *both* at the gate.

*

It is dark now.

I cannot... dare not rest. My beloved sleeps as I sit beside her. As usual, she is heart wrenchingly unaware of my presence. In sleep her beauty is almost ethereal and there is a great temptation to lie down beside her, so that for a short time I may imagine we have become one, touched by the same moonlight and shadows.

The notebook has now gone from Samualson's desk and without moving from this place I know that he sleeps, although I cannot sense what thoughts fill his dreams.

The house is silent, yet it is not still, for this land is old and there are others like myself who were here before my time. We cannot communicate, for they are now mere shadows, without substance. No minds. No emotions. Just ragged tags of darkness that no longer know why they are here or what first tied them to this place. If it were in their power, they would probably envy the great love I have for this woman...

He moves!

Samualson stands behind me in the doorway, a dark shadow where the moonlight cannot touch him. I turn and see the glitter of his eyes and sense the evil thoughts in his heart and I rise up, a powerless barrier between them.

I watch helplessly as he leans over the bed, looking down at my beloved, very much as I have done this long night, although there is no affection in his gaze. For some reason he inspects the glass on the night table and draws back his full lips in a smile of satisfaction.

Elisabeth's cordial! What evil have I missed here?

He lays a hand upon her shoulder and shakes her, at first gently and then with an urgency that would wake her. I sense the life force within Elisabeth flutter... but she does not stir.

He raises her into a sitting position and then drags her to the edge of the bed as though she were no weight at all. Stooping, he lies my beloved swiftly over one shoulder, the whiteness of her nightgown concealed by a carelessly thrown blanket as he carries her from the room.

Once clear of the Dower House, I was startled to see Samualson turn left and make for the cliff path. As we climbed higher towards the old church, what I had believed to be a still night unleashed upon us a raging torrent of wind that plucked at Samualson's greatcoat and weaved the blanket around my beloved like a tattered shroud.

I prayed Samualson would seek rest from his burden... anything to delay the awful certainty of his step; but he continued on, surefooted, higher and higher into the darkness, with me pawing at his heels like a fawning spaniel.

At last the path levelled off and I knew we were near the graveyard wall. Samualson faltered at last and I heard his breath as a rasping growl. He shifted Elisabeth against his shoulder and I reached out, wanting desperately to touch her dark hair where it cascaded down his back; but the gesture was as a fist clenched in a cloud of hearth smoke and my hand came away with nothing. Then they were both gone from me, through the gate as Samualson laid my beloved upon a flat-topped tombstone.

There are tears now, as real as any I have ever shed, yet all I could do was pace up and down with the wall between us, calling upon a God I no longer believed in and with equal force, cursing the elements that condemned me to be a mere spectator.

Samualson stepped back, and I saw a glint of steel against the darkness of his clothing. As he stooped again over my beloved, I knew that I cried out, swearing I would forsake my futile love for her... that I would remain forever tied to the landslide that claimed my life... if only she might live...

For the first time Samualson appeared to hesitate. More than once, I saw him glance into the shadows, as though disturbed by something seen from the corner of his eye. Finally, he sat back on his haunches and listened, his head turned slightly to one side.

Then I saw them, the souls whose domain Samualson had dared to disturb. At first they were mere shadows, rising out of the ground, gathering and dispersing and coming together again, as though unsure of their purpose, yet each time becoming more substantial.

Samualson must also have sensed them, so great was their combined energy compared with my poor self, for he suddenly stood up, my beloved clearly forgotten with this new preoccupation.

As one, they began to advance upon him. I knew not if he actually saw them, but their presence was enough to drive him backwards towards the gate, stabbing and slashing at the air about him. Several times I saw him stumble, as though jostled by a force beyond his control. Then with a mighty drawn out cry, he dashed past me. Such a look of terror I have never before seen on any man's face.

His retreating footsteps ended abruptly with the sound of crashing bushes. I heard another cry then, fainter, but somehow more desperate. Then nothing! Just a smattering of boulders falling into the sea!

Then came voices as people were roused from their beds. Close by, I heard the sound of heavy bolts being drawn. Wood grated on stone and candlelight flickered across the path, illuminating the place where my beloved lay.

All is at peace now... those other goodly souls have returned to their resting places.

I would like to stay, to see my Elisabeth safely down... but I must honour my oath so desperately given. There are others gathered who will minister her needs and see her to the shore. Farewell, my beloved. Fare thee well!

GRAVE HUMOUR

So, this was death, the hand that strikes all mortals, high or low. The great and final mystery, inspiration to scholars and seekers after the truth, and a pain in the ass to everyday human beings who just want to get on with their lives.

It all seemed pretty boring really, Ron thought, as his coffin abruptly ceased its descent, jolting him out of the stupor he'd assumed precluded total oblivion. In inky darkness, he lay wondering what came next... and then began *wondering* how it was possible for him to *still wonder* what came next, and then, being the unadventurous type, decided he didn't really want to know anyway.

He *had* sensed momentary panic when they'd first screwed the lid down. The old claustrophobic tendencies came rushing back, accompanied by the urge to scream for help. Foolish really, considering he'd been dead for eight days now.

At first he'd enjoyed the attention; the nice young lady who'd washed and laid him out and then there'd been the emotionally confused male assistant, who'd shown considerable interest in his private parts, not that he was complaining, mind you.

Being single, and now very much alone in the world, there'd been few mourners at his funeral. Mark, his brother had come to smirk, but Ron knew *that* would change at the reading of the will. Never brothers, but always rivals, Ron had happily and productively invested the best years of his life coveting Nancy, Mark's wife, until her untimely death two years previously. An aunt and uncle had travelled down from Scotland, the uncle red nosed and combustible and his aunt, diminutive and sincere, shedding tears into an impractical lace handkerchief. He sincerely hoped the old dear would be allowed to enjoy the proceeds of *his* meagre estate before her husband drank it all away.

Now, humming the last few bars of 'Rock of Ages', he listened to the receding thud of soil on the coffin lid. Very soon, silence reigned, except for the small sounds of settling earth. He closed his eyes and waited, thinking back over his life and wondering if he was about to hear the call of Gabriel's trumpet or the scrape of the Devil's pitchfork. Instead, a nagging itch developed along his right calf, reminding him he should have complained about low grade embalming fluid. The cramp it gave him was a killer, and on one occasion he'd been forced to sit upright and take a turn around the table while the undertaker was out of the room answering a phone call.

The stillness deepened. If this was Eternity, it was going to be one hell of a drag. Restlessly, he drummed his fingers against the imitation satin, wriggling his long form until his best patent leather shoes touched the end panel, surprised how loud the movement sounded in the confined space. Oddly enough, the sound continued after he lay still, and he found himself holding a non-existent breath as a general tapping and scraping developed around him. His first thought was of the fabled rats, come to feed off his corpse... but that wasn't feasible unless they were equipped with miners' helmets and shovels. Unexpectedly, he felt the wood vibrate beneath his leather soles. There followed a hollow splintering sound, made all the more awesome by the complete and utter darkness.

"Come on, lad, on your feet. I'll have no shirkers in my section." A strange phosphorous glow illuminated his shoes as the sagging lining parted and bone white hands reached in and gripped him round the ankles.

Silence of the grave, be damned. Ron's vocal response would have made a speech therapist proud. His frightened yell was swiftly followed by a firm declaration,

"Er, get yer bleeding 'ands off me!"

The hands receded.

"It's always the same with you first timers," the disembodied voice commented, adding with a hint of childlike petulance. "Well, you can't stay in there forever... it's not allowed."

"*Who* says it not?"

An irritated sigh, not unlike the rustle of dry leaves.

"Don't try to confuse me."

"How'd you think I feel?"

Silence. Then,

"Look, do come out, there's a good chap." The voice now held an almost apologetic tone. "You *have* to be booked in before the next arrival."

"Booked in *where*?"

"Here, of course."

"Where's *here*?"

Another sound, like sucking on greasy dentures!

"Where'd you think?"

It was Ron's turn to hesitate. He wriggled slightly in his coffin.

"Not Hell," he finished on a hesitant whisper.

"Of course not... you've just come from *there*."

Ron thought about that for a moment.

"Ok," he said. "So, what do I do?"

"Just relax... take a deep breath."

"You trying to be funny?" Ron felt a firm tug on his legs and he shot forward with a soft crackle of static electricity. A grey glow enveloped him. His new body fluids threatened to evacuate themselves as he swayed dizzily against a hard earthen wall and a bony hand hauled him upright on feet that felt like plates of jelly.

"That's a mistake you all make. Don't use your muscles," the dark shape beside him advised, in a voice like leaking bellows. "*Feel* the bones. *They* support you now."

"Yea... right." Ron gasped, instantly missing the womb like security of his coffin.

"I'm under-brother Arnold."

Ron cautiously stretched... and farted.

"Sorry!"

"Low grade embalming fluid. Does it every time."

"When do I get to meet him?" Ron asked conversationally, attempting to hide his embarrassment as another crescendo rumbled from his nether regions.

"Who?"

"Brother Arnold."

"I'm brother Arnold."

Ron frowned.

"You *said* you were under him."

"We are all *under*-brothers and sisters here."

"I... see" Ron squinted sideways, trying to sneak an indirect look at Arnold, who seemed to comprise nothing more than a blazer and peaked cap. He couldn't decide if the fellow's face was in shadow, or if he simply didn't have one.

"It's my job to welcome you down and show you round your patch," Arnold explained.

"Hmm. Have you been doing this long?" Ron was amazed how naturally the question came to him, yet at the same time he felt totally stupid.

"Nigh on sixty under-years," Arnold said with obvious pride in his reedy voice. "I expect they'll pension me off soon. I'd like some time to myself, there's one or two hobbies I'd like to catch up on... but I shall certainly miss the teeth."

"Teeth?" Ron asked, despite a strong urge not to.

"Sure. They come with the job. Regulations stipulate we welcome new customers with a smile... sets them at ease, so to speak." A pair of ivories flashed under the cap and Ron thought he caught a glimpse of watery, expressionless eyes.

"You mean... they're not yours?"

"Of course not. We share everything down here... which reminds me. First things first." Wavering slightly, like a man walking on stilts, Arnold shuffled a few steps along the passage and reached into a niche in the hard packed earth. "You *have* to sign this before we can go any further." He held out a grey card and a piece of charcoal. "Best do it now mate, before the fingers go," he encouraged, kindly.

Ron froze.

"What is it?"

"A donor card." Arnold's teeth flashed again. "Just a formality, of course, but you *must* carry it with you at all times."

Ron swallowed, uneasily.

"Must I?"

"Well, down here one never knows what the next under-day may bring, and remember, there are *always* others needier than ourselves," Arnold finished on a somewhat pious note.

Gawd blimey, Ron thought, can't get away from blooming do-gooders and charities even down here. Reluctantly, he signed the card and watched it disappear into Arnold's empty looking sleeve.

"Now, *this* is the main under-passage," Arnold explained, suddenly warming to his subject. "You're in a much sought after position here, with access to all amenities... right outside your front door, so to speak."

Ron squinted along the gently glowing corridor to where it curved away into total darkness, and shivered. The walls and floor consisted of hard-packed clay, buttressed by the occasional tree root and strategically placed headstones. A cool breeze flowed around him, bringing with it a damp, earthy smell, mingled with a less definable odour, which he preferred not to think about. In other words he was standing in the middle of his worst nightmare.

"Ah... I see you've noticed our little rogues' gallery," Arnold exclaimed, with discernible remnants of human excitement. "Here, we have epitaphs of the famous and infamous going back over four under-centuries, and when you've settled in and studied them at your leisure, I'm sure they'll give you as many hours of contentment and pleasure as they've given me." He stooped towards the nearest piece of stone. "Mind you, some have grown a little faint, so you *do* need a good pair of eyes." A muffled grating sound signalled a change in posture. "Remind me to put you down for some when we pass the dispensary." So saying, he strutted on, wheezing softly to himself, straw-like hair jutting out from beneath his cap, his threadbare blazer and trousers occasionally flashing a hint of grey bone. He was at the turn in the passage before Ron caught up, suddenly more afraid of being left alone than off what could possibly lay ahead.

A few paces farther on, the tunnel narrowed slightly.

SHROUDS ONLY BEYOND THIS POINT

exclaimed a large notice.

"Ignore that," Arnold advised, shuffling on. "There's a strong contingency here that insist the old ways are best. I maintain a good suit of clothes adds a little character to a body." He flicked an imaginary speck of dust from the front of his blazer and something rebounded off the wall and scuttled away into the shadows. Ron didn't look to find out what. "Mind you," Arnold continued, "under-brothers and sisters only retain one layer of clothes. Anything else goes over the other side to the under-paupers. Those poor devils never have much to start out with."

'Over my dead body', Ron murmured, thinking of the expensive shirt he wore beneath his suit. "How commendable," he said aloud to Arnold, guiltily wondering if telepathy was one of the old fellow's attributes. "What does one actually do down here?" he asked, clumsily attempting to smother his selfish thoughts.

Arnold appeared encouraged by his interest.

"We do not ask a lot of our under-brethren. Most of us have our little hobbies to keep us occupied. Our main request is that you remain honest, upright and together for as long as possible. You *must* see our chapel," he suddenly took an unsteady left turn. "Of course, there are no religious or racial discriminations here. After all, colour is only skin deep and as you'll soon learn, that's the first thing to go." A low archway appeared, and Arnold motioned for a cautious approach, at least that's what Ron assumed he meant, with only one finger on Arnold's left hand, he could have misinterpreted.

Another sign announced,

SHOES MUST BE REMOVED BEFORE
ENTERING THE CHAPEL

"We're getting that changed," Arnold whispered. "The under-cleaner's forever complaining about returning toes to lost property."

Despite himself, Ron stifled a giggle.

"That could give the 'first footing' tradition a whole new meaning."

Arnold rattled to an abrupt halt.

"*I do hope* you're not going to be cynical about our little community." He sucked indignantly on his dentures. "Count yourself lucky you were not cremated."

Ron was beginning to wish he had been.

"Those poor devils need endless counselling. It takes them months to find themselves again."

"Counselling?" Ron managed.

"Shhh!" Arnold peered cautiously round the archway. Ron thought he caught a murmur of voices like the rustle of reeds on a riverbank. "I thought so. We can't go in now. There's an under-wedding taking place."

This was too much for Ron.

"Oh, come now, surely..."

Arnold urged him back up the passage.

"Why shouldn't under-couples marry if they desire?"

"But... what for?" Ron thought of Nancy, his brother's lately departed wife, and decided that was *another* foolish question.

"Company, of course. Someone to give your coffin the homely touch." Ron felt the shadowed, watery eyes bore into him. At least the one facing outwards did. "I can see you were never a married over-man."

"No. But even so..."

"You might change your mind down here. In time, unless a relationship falls apart, they can make their union complete by adopting an under-child from the orphanage."

Ron stopped so abruptly, Arnold walked straight into him and Ron backed up, hastily, brushing the sleeve of his jacket. Arnold didn't appear to notice.

"Enough." He raised heavy feeling arms. "The joke's over. Take me back to my coffin." The line sounded ludicrous, but somehow appropriate under the circumstances.

Arnold shrugged, disturbing something which immediately sought sanctuary beneath the lapel of his blazer.

"I'm sorry, Ron, I've obviously burdened you with too much too soon..."

"And I don't believe a word of it. What are you, some sort of escapee from Hammer House of Horror?"

Instead of being offended, Arnold rewarded him with another of his famous grins.

"I always wanted to be an actor. Mother said I had remarkable stage presence for my age..."

"*Arnold!*"

"Er... yes, proof?" Arnold removed his peaked cap and proceeded to scratch the flaky, straw-like substance beneath it. "Perhaps you should meet Errol, our under-gardener?"

Ron gave an irritated sigh.

"Well, let's face it," Arnold continued reasonably, "what other pressing engagement do you have at the moment?"

*

Several well sign-posted passages later, Arnold led him into a large underground cavern, the roof and walls of which were a maze of fibrous roots and suckers.

"Please, mind your head. Under-brother Errol is very proud of his work."

Despite his earlier outburst, Ron found himself nodding in admiration. Here, the atmosphere felt different. There was a rich loamy warmth that had nothing to do with death or decay, and a deep sense of peace one would expect from a garden that was loved and well tended. A movement against the far wall caught his attention and he saw a tall figure reach up and tuck in a stray tendril, causing soil to powder down onto the upturned skull.

"Under-brother Errol is very dedicated, but he does find the work difficult since his accident."

"What accident?" Ron asked; intrigued to know what further calamity could possibly befall a corpse.

"Well, you *know* what these over-gardeners are like. They plant a commemorative rose and then ten over-years later, no renewal of fee... no rose, and up she comes. Unfortunately, under-brother Errol's right hand was still holding the roots. It obviously gave the over-gardener quite a shock because he decided to join us a week later."

"Poor fellow. Will he be alright?" Ron was becoming practised at asking dead end questions.

"Your compassion is commendable, but don't concern yourself. Under-brother Errol has just found a suitable donor."

"Actually I meant..." Ron broke off, remembering his donor card and self-consciously clasped both hands behind his back.

"Would you care to meet him?"

"It seems a shame to disturb his work," Ron put in quickly.

"I'm sure he won't mind."

Some unspoken signal passed between the two figures, for the under-gardener suddenly set down his trowel and came shuffling towards them with an odd, lop-sided gait, his shroud flapping in the under-breeze. The tall skeleton shed soil at every step and as he wavered to a halt, Ron was startled to see the jaw drop into the semblance of a smile.

"Hello, Errol." Ron said lightly, keeping both hands out of sight.

The under-gardener bowed slightly, scattering soil over Ron's patent leather shoes. There was a suggestion of a second smile and he turned away, intently studying the ceiling as he went.

"I'm afraid he's very shy," Arnold explained.

"So I see." Ron eyed his shoes distastefully.

"He's one of our first successfully re-habilitated cremations and has great affinity with the earth and all growing things. As he was originally sprinkled over the Garden of Remembrance, I suppose you could say it's in his blood." They left the cavern down a narrow passage opposite the one they'd entered by. "Do you have an interest in gardening?" Arnold asked. "Perhaps you'd like to work with under-brother Errol, he could certainly use another hand." An odd, whistling sound erupted beside Ron and he realised it was Arnold, laughing. "I do believe I've just made a funny." His dentures flashed briefly. "Now, one more stop and I simply *must* leave you."

Ron experienced a sudden sense of panic. What was he to do alone in this underground maze?

"Don't worry. I'll see you back to your quarters," Arnold said, as though he *could* read his thoughts after all. "You'll find certain preparations have been made for your future comfort. How are you with animals?"

"Er, depends. I used to breed rabbits... that is they did the breeding while I..."

"We're quite proud of our under-animal husbandry here, as you'll soon see." The passage began to slope downwards and Ron sensed an increase in temperature as the under-breeze died away. Suddenly he found himself in a low roofed cavern, full of rough-hewn coffins on wooden trestles, set in a semi-circle around the walls. "That's a shame," Arnold sucked on his teeth, "under-brother Farmer doesn't appear to be here. Still, I don't suppose he'll mind us looking in on his pets." Arnold hobbled over to the nearest coffin and Ron followed out of sheer curiosity.

Maggots!

Millions of them filled the coffins. Some had spilled over onto the earthen floor and seemed to be struggling to return to base.

"Poor lost little mites," Arnold cooed, leaning forward. Ron thought he was going to gather them up, but a sharp grinding sound put paid to that theory. "Damn arthritis," Arnold cursed. "Never mind... under-brother Farmer will see they're safely returned." Sidestepping the 'little mites', he turned to the next container. "Wonderful! It takes a very special under-person to be this dedicated to their work."

Ron shuddered.

"You mean there are... people in there." As if in answer, a hand lifted clear of the seething mass and gave a thumb's up signal. The thumb promptly dropped off and the hand disappeared, groping frantically for the lost digit.

Arnold sighed.

"I have such respect for someone who can give themselves so totally to the care of animals."

"I... I think I'd like to go back now." The non-existent contents of Ron's stomach threatened rebellion.

"Yes... yes, of course. Time presses." Arnold reached inside his blazer and threw something that wriggled into the nearest coffin. "Goodbye my little children," he whispered. "No personal pets allowed," he added, by way of explanation. Now I'd better get you back." Arnold wobbled on, muttering various other rules about *no* co-habiting between unattached under-couples and how it was advisable never to go above ground before dark. Apparently, the last under-person to do so had been badly savaged by a dog, which ran off with his left foot. Thus incapacitated, the under-brother had been unable to give chase and as a result still suffered prolonged nightmares, despite months of professional under-counselling. Ron followed weakly behind, too tired to comment, wanting only to close his eyes and rest. He hadn't realised death was such hard work.

Arnold finally left him at the end of Rogues Gallery. A neat-hinged door, bearing his full name, burned into the wood, had now covered the damaged panel of his coffin. Inside, a black card lay on the white lining. He picked it up and squinted at it in the half-light.

Heard you were down this way.
Looking forward to seeing you again.

Nancy.

He smiled, and old memories stirred.

His brother's wife *had* been buried somewhere nearby. Until now, the connection and its possibilities hadn't suggested themselves to him. It would be good to see Nancy again, he thought, picturing her delicate elfin features, so in contrast with the heavy fall of hair he'd once loved to run his fingers through. They'd had a perfect understanding. She wouldn't leave her pompous husband because of the children; which suited Ron fine because he'd never wanted to be tied down in a permanent relationship. He'd been a man who needed his own space and Nancy had clearly understood that on occasions she was welcome to share that space with him. They'd been ideal contrasts, his quiet and timid nature against her outgoing, fun-loving approach to life. Somehow, even on bad days, she'd managed to make him laugh, sometimes calling him by his pet name...

"Bob-tail."

Yes... that was it.

"BOB-TAIL"

Startled, he turned, afraid to believe his ears. A figure stood in shadow at the end of the passage.

"Rag-tag?"

"You remembered." She sounded pleased, her voice hollow, without the old lilting quality, but he would have recognized it anywhere.

"How could I ever forget?" He sensed a surge of emotion and felt a trickle of fluid on his cheek. "I've missed you, Nancy."

"I've missed you too," she returned. "It's been... different."

Ron held out one hand, aware that it was visibly trembling, but she made no move to come closer.

"Mark did this to me." A sigh rattled from her. "He said he could forgive a one night fling, but felt a thirty year affair with his naff brother was a bit over the top. So he doctored the electric heater in the bathroom."

"Accidents *do* happen..."

"*He told me...* at the funeral parlour. Of course he didn't realise I could *still* hear until I called him a 'murdering bastard'. That's why he didn't attend the funeral."

"And I thought it was because of grief."

"More likely in a blue funk."

"Nancy... come, let me see you."

"I've changed, Ron. The last two years haven't been kind to me."

"We can make up for that now we're together again."

"Down here, unexpected things... happen. I'm *afraid* that you won't like me any more."

"Perhaps I should be the judge of that," he suggested boldly, his weaker nature wondering what he was letting himself in for. Nancy moved then, out of the shadow into the glow of the passageway. Ron remained with his hand outstretched, waiting for her to come to him.

Her walk was the same, elegant and upright and as she drew closer he could see she still had her long hair, cascading over her shoulders in a dark halo that masked her once fine features. Now her skin, broken in places, stretched tightly over white bone and as she raised her face to his he could see the fear of rejection in her one good eye.

"You... you've lost weight," Ron said conversationally. He wasn't sure if she smiled or if her lips were making an all out attempt to avoid her blackened teeth. She raised a skeletal hand and self-consciously touched her hair.

"I don't smell too good, either," she declared with her old, forthright honesty, shaking loose the black hairs that now clung to her finger bones.

To *hell* with it, Ron decided suddenly. You're a long time dead and after all, what's a little decay between corpses in love? He raised the flap and took her cold, hard hand in his own.

"They have some law down here banning co-habitation, so it looks as though we're going to get hitched after all." He suddenly remembered his brother's smirking face at his own the funeral... and grinning broadly, he crawled in beside Nancy and closed the flap behind him.

THE HOUSE IN THE PARK

Darren coughed and felt a fresh trickle of blood run from the corner of his mouth.

For the hundredth time in as many days, he wondered if this was about to be his last on earth.

'An Aids Related Illness,' the doctors had called it; but then death had several names and many guises and the end result was always the same... you were a goner.

Today, the sheer effort to wipe the blood away was more than he could cope with. There was bound to be more before his carer arrived for his evening round and he knew Paul would clean him up; Paul always did... without a word of reproach or condemnation, his large grey eyes filled only with concern as he changed his soiled linen, washed and patted him dry and spoon fed him liquidized food they both knew would no longer stay down.

Paul was too sensitive for care work and he'd told him so on his second visit.

"I'm doing what I didn't have the guts to do when my own partner needed me," he'd admitted. "Trouble is, Darren, it doesn't make me feel any less guilty."

Having never had a full time partner, Darren wasn't sure if he totally understood. Too many one-night stands had got him where he was now... and nothing had been the same since Stephen, his beautiful hero, the elusive shadow that haunted his days and nights and palled all others in comparison.

He coughed again and wished Stephen was here now to soothe his pain-racked body. There were no other sensations left to him; even when Paul carried him to the bathroom and tenderly bathed the foulness from his body... there was nothing but agony.

But he still had a clear mind and his memories...

*

...Darren knew he was in for the worst beating of his life.

The old park had seemed as good a cruising area as any, but this time he'd stretched his luck too far and returned once too often to the same place.

"Queer bastard!" There were five of them gathered round him. Big lads from the town, one of whom he recognized in the fading light... one whose voice, on this particular night, was no longer breathlessly coaxing as he urged his mates to violence. "Dirty sod tried to touch me up."

He went down under a hail of fists and rolled into a foetal position as boots and trainers began to thud home. Someone grabbed the belt of his jeans and fumbled for his manhood, squeezing viciously.

"How d'ya like that then? Ha!" The hand tightened and twisted sadistically. "Anyone got a knife? Let's castrate the bastard."

Through half closed eyes he saw the glint of steel.

"No! Please don't." He despised the sound of his own voice, begging these thugs for mercy and he tried again to roll clear of their clutching hands. Someone kicked the side of the head and his mind reeled in an explosion of pain.

Then came the pounding in his ears... louder and louder... abruptly changing timbre as the ground vibrated to the unmistakable sound of hoof beats. Shouts of aggression turned to exclamations of surprise and a stream of abuse.

"Fucking 'ell... run for it lads!"

He flinched as heavy boots rose and fell around him, but none of the boys singled him out in their flight of panic. A great mass thundered past, seeming to sweep all noise and movement before it... finally leaving him trembling and alone.

Through waves of pain he became aware of night sounds and how damp the leaves felt beneath him. Every muscle screamed in protest as he rolled onto his back... and abruptly back again, choking on the vomit that erupted from his throat.

When the worst of the nausea had passed, he dragged himself to the side of the path, resting his back against a stunted tree. He shivered, suddenly aware how cold the night had become... or perhaps he was going into shock; not surprising really after nearly having his head kicked in and his pecker sliced off.

He wrapped both arms protectively around his chest, wishing he'd worn a tee shirt under his shirt and perhaps a jacket... but when you're cruising, too many layers could prove inhibiting and how was he to know he would end up a beaten wreck. He shivered again. One of his mum's chunky-knits would have been handy. In fact what he really needed right now was the old girl herself. She would have seen him right... but she'd been gone eight years now. A shuddering sob escaped him and tears of self-pity brought on a new sense of panic. He couldn't sit here blubbering. He had to get clear of the park in case those louts came back; perhaps even get a rare cab home. He never carried a wallet when he was on the make, but there was twenty quid in his sock; some tricks liked to be paid for their services.

He scrubbed his hands over his face and saw fresh blood on his palms. He *had* to be the one who's bleeding. He doubted if he'd landed a single punch... he'd been too busy grovelling in the dirt. Perhaps it was a good job his mother wasn't here... she'd have been ashamed of him. He forced himself upright, finding it easier than he expected. Two steps later and he was on his knees again, waiting for the world to right itself.

"God help me!"

"I expect he's busy saving souls somewhere else." The soft cultured voice came from behind him, back the way the lads had gone.

Darren felt cold sweat break out all over. Resignedly, he slumped on his haunches and painfully turned head and shoulders.

A young man stood several paces away. Like Darren, he wore a white shirt, but this was tailored to the waist, with loose baggy sleeves gathered at the wrist. A broad leather belt emphasized his long legs, encased in dark breeches, tucked neatly into immaculately polished riding boots. The reason for his attire nuzzled gently at his shoulder.

"Patience, Rufus." Long fingers curled lovingly into the white mane. "We must remember the rules of hospitality." He smiled warmly at Darren, and ran a hand through his dark wavy hair, which he swept back over his ears in what seemed a self-conscious gesture. He moved nearer, the horse matching his step. "Are you able to ride?"

"I doubt it... I wasn't able to before they kicked the shit out of me."

"Ah, good." His dark eyes held a hint of amusement. "A man with a sense of humour in adversity. I like that. Can you at least stand?"

Darren accepted the offered hand, surprised by its coolness.

"I was out walking and they... they came from nowhere..."

"I know exactly what they did... and why they did it."

Darren found himself blushing.

"I promise they will not go unpunished."

"I don't want to make trouble."

Again; that enigmatic smile!

"I am responsible for this land and must ensure travellers have safe passage."

Jesus, Darren thought. Who was this bloke? Some kind of Park Ranger! And why didn't he speak like a regular guy?

"I have seen you often and would have introduced myself... but the time was never right. My name is Stephen. Stephen Monck."

"Darren... just Darren," he confirmed cautiously.

"You shall ride with me."

"I... I'd prefer to walk."

"Do not worry. Rufus is very gentle."

After several abortive attempts, Darren found himself sitting upright in the saddle. Stephen had shortened the stirrups and was now behind him, his strong arms reaching round to gather in the reins.

"My home is just beyond those trees."

This guy must be a Ranger, Darren thought. No one else would live in the middle of a Municipal Park. He leaned back, enjoying the soothing movement of man and horse. If he closed his eyes and concentrated, he was sure he could feel this strangers heartbeat against the curve of his back. He'd been told to keep both hands on the saddle horn, but he let his right hand drop to the knee tucked in behind his own.

The firm, answering pressure of Stephen's encircling arms told him all he needed to know.

*

Darren stared up at the ceiling and wondered when this dream would turn into the usual nightmare... and the beautiful man lying beside him would become some grizzled old park ranger who'd arrest him for loitering.

There had to be a catch somewhere.

Stephen's home had indeed been just beyond the trees... a semi-derelict mansion, lit only by candlelight. He had stabled Rufus and almost carried Darren through an adjoining door into the main building.

In a small, ground floor bedroom, which he explained once belonged to servants, he had stripped him and washed the mud and blood from his pale-skinned body; all the time quietly apologizing for any pain his touch might have caused, pointing out the cut in his hairline and places where bruises would probably come in time.

No-one had ever touched Darren in such a way, with such consideration and tenderness and when he himself could no longer hold back, when he to longed to touch and caress in return, Stephen merely smiled and allowed Darren to ease the beautifully tailored clothes from his strong, eager body.

Fire and ice, Darren had thought as they finally came together, Stephen's cool limbs captured in his burning embrace.

He had never met anyone like Stephen... a reassuring, consummate lover who nevertheless showed moments of childlike vulnerability that plumbed his own, long hidden depths. The night seemed endless as they loved, laughed and cried themselves into an exhausted sleep.

Now morning had come. The candle on the bedside table had burned down and daylight edged the curtains. Darren wondered what the day would bring as he rolled over and studied Stephen's profile, still in shadow against the pillow.

Carefully, he reached out and traced the smooth brow with his forefinger... down over the bridge of the nose, round the full, slightly parted lips to the square chin, now freshly stubbled. The thought that he was taking a mental picture to take away with him suddenly alarmed him. He mustn't think like that. They'd been good together; this time there would be more than one night. There had to be!

Breakfast!

That was the least he could do, he decided, slipping reluctantly from the warm bed. He ignored his own muddied clothes, now folded over the back of a chair and opted for Stephen's long shirt, which smelt slightly of horse sweat and felt good against his skin.

With a swift backwards glance, he padded from the room.

In daylight, the house appeared less romantic and more derelict. Everywhere, nothing but cobwebs! Gutted candles scarred the ancient looking furniture and as he walked, dust lifted cloyingly from the threadbare carpet.

"Jesus! I thought my flat was bad enough. This guy needs a housekeeper pronto."

He turned his back on the hall and main staircase with its faded portraits and dull chandeliers; Stephen could give him a guided tour later. Logically the kitchen would be on the ground floor. By the time he found the correct door, he was becoming concerned. The 'scullery' was nothing but a burnt out, rat infested hovel, without a scrap of food in sight.

"Perhaps he eats out a lot," he told himself, hurriedly urinating in the great cracked sink before turning back.

Stephen was no longer there.

The bed had grown cold and the impression on the pillow could have been made by anyone or anything. If it hadn't been for the presence of his own clothes, Darren would have sworn he'd returned to the wrong room.

He never saw Stephen Monck... or Rufus again.

*

...Darren hauled himself up on the pillows as fresh blood erupted from his mouth.

Of course he'd searched and waited... long into the hours of the night and the next day, until sheer exhaustion and hunger drove him from the house. After that, he never found the place again and in time he stopped looking. It could have all been a dream... except he still had Stephen's shirt, neatly folded beneath his sweat soaked pillow.

He tried desperately to reach it now, but the effort was too much for him and he fell back, exhausted.

He wished Paul would come.

His urge to use the bathroom had just stopped becoming a problem, but he badly needed a mouthwash and a change of bedding. The room was growing dark, but he couldn't reach the table lamp. He was beginning to feel cold; one of his mum's chunky-knits would have been nice now. He fought back the tears. He shouldn't have gone over all that again in his mind. Stay calm... the doctors had warned. Don't get emotional.

God he was so cold.

He crushed the damp duvet to him and closed his eyes against a fresh rush of nausea. Out in the lounge, a clock struck nine and downstairs a door opened and closed. Heavy footsteps on the stairs brought a sigh of relief that left him in one long, drawn out plea,

"God... help me."

"I expect he's busy saving souls somewhere else," said a hauntingly familiar voice.

Surely... he was still dreaming? Darren opened his eyes.

The room was much brighter now and his vision seemed to have cleared for the first time in days. Stephen was standing by his bed, hand held out in a familiar gesture of assistance.

"Come on, Darren." He smiled, his other hand self-consciously sweeping dark curly hair behind his ears. "Rufus is waiting to take us home."

MEMORIES OF ANOTHER DAY

England 1729

A light breeze whispered through the forest, stirring faded bracken and rustling autumn leaves, warning of the stranger's approach. All became still as the dark cloaked figure flitted between the trees, following the neglected path towards the old house. The dying sun dipped beneath the treeline, touching the highest boughs with burnished gold and casting fingers of shadow amongst the lower branches.

Calantha hurried through the dusk, trying to reach the house before darkness claimed her. Despite apparent haste, her step was gracefully light and in order to manoeuvre the overgrown path, she raised the hem of her heavy woollen cloak with a slim hand, disclosing silver buckled shoes and a white stocking ankle.

At the great gates she paused and looked back for the first time, her head to one side, listening for any sound that was not part of her flight through the woods. Her full lips curved in satisfaction and she turned her attention to the gravel drive ahead, gleaming grey in the fading light. The rusty framework swung wide with a screech that sent several ravens winging their way towards the rooftop of deserted Scar Manor.

Calantha hurried on, her dragging cloak forgotten, a different urgency to her step as she neared the burnt out hulk that had once been her home. As the sweeping drive opened before her she stopped abruptly and stared at the dark expanse of stone, still somehow majestic in its towering presence. Two marble columns gave entrance to a gaping maw where double doors once opened onto a balconied hallway. A few remaining windows at ground level caught the last glimmer of sunlight, while those higher up reflected nothing but darkness, their edges blackened where flames had once burst from them, hungrily seeking the ancient rafters above.

Scar Manor had been the home of her family for over three generations, since Scarface Seaton acquired property after Naseby, in 1645. He immediately retired from army life and set about establishing a dynasty that would shortly witness the execution of a King and be forced to barricade them selves against a countryside, ravaged with plague. For nearly a century, the Seatons weathered religious wars, the rise and fall of the Old Pretender, the end of the Stuarts and the appearance of a hated fat German Prince on the English throne. However, while they were successfully riding outside influences, the family was being torn apart from within by tyranny, petty squabbles and forbidden love...

At Calantha's approach, all was silent save the distant caw of crows. Weeds sprouted from cracks in the marble steps and windswept leaves whispered secretively together in the doorway. Without hesitation she passed through into the Great Hall.

Immediately she sensed the overpowering charisma of the house, still evident, despite years of desertion and in her mind she saw it all as it had once been. Instead of the blackened walls and the lighter patches where sky showed through, the hall was filled with bright candlelight and off to her left, the tinkling notes of a harpsichord competed with a pleasant murmur of voices from the withdrawing room.

Amidst the darkness and dust, Calantha flung wide her arms and welcomed the memories. Her cloak fell unheeded from her shoulders, allowing a mane of golden ringlets to tumble freely down her back. Head thrown back, she laughed aloud, her blue eyes closed against the reality of her surroundings. She began to pivot gently, bowing graciously to an imaginary partner as she turned faster and faster around the hall, oblivious of the charred remnants that dangerously scattered the floor. At the foot of the main staircase she paused, breathlessly, apparently rebuking a companion for following too closely upon her heel. With a childish giggle of delight she ascended to the upper level and leaned precariously over the blackened balustrade, searching the hall way below with wide, eager eyes...

*

...From her vantage point at the head of the stairs, Calantha could easily watch the country gentleman arrive in their fine city-bought clothes, accompanied by their buxom wives, squeezed into impossible silks and satins of the most outrageous colours.

She had no interest in these people, although one or two were handsome Corinthians, clearly down from London, demonstrating to these country bumpkins how a waistcoat and breeches should be worn. She *knew* why they were here. Most of them were either in debt to her father or wished a favour from him. There was only one man for her, but her Tom could never be part of this social gathering... Father would never allow it. Daniel Seaton was a proud and arrogant man who would consider a common drover unfit to look upon his daughter. Calantha didn't care about that for she loved Tom and intended to marry him... with or without her father's consent.

As though conjured by his daughter's thoughts, a giant of a man in a silvered mulberry waistcoat divested himself of the gathering and headed towards the library with a young red-faced buck in tow. The door closed heavily behind them, causing an interested lull in the conversation, followed by a burst of speculative talk.

This was the opportunity Calantha had been waiting for. Casually she descended the broad staircase, aware appreciative eyes were turning her way. Her step remained unhurried, her printed sack-backed gown rustling softly, flickering candlelight enhancing her pale features and highlighting the halo of blonde hair she refused to hide beneath a fashionable mobcap. She wanted nothing more than to run, to be free of this house and its hypocrisy... to spend a few precious moments with Tom. She controlled her haste until past the library. Then she hurried down the secondary staircase to the kitchens, from where a side door led to a small courtyard beside the stables.

Once beyond the shadow of the house, Calantha ran, a light breeze tugging at her gown, dust from the courtyard swirling in eddies about her dainty feet. She skirted the stables, wary of being noticed by the grooms as they scuttled back and forth with each new arrival. Moonlight showed the way across the Tudor garden as she headed for the folly, their meeting place.

Flushed and breathless, she flung herself beneath the overhanging fronds of ivy, turning instantly lest her flight be discovered. She could see no movement and hear nothing above the beat of her heart. Thankfully she found the marble seat and as the night air-cooled her burning limbs, Calantha wished she'd had the foresight to bring her short riding cloak, but guessed that would have drawn more attention to herself.

Minutes passed.

Alarmed, she rounded as a twig snapped, somewhere off to her left. A shadow fell across her hiding place... and he was there, gathering her to him.

"Tom!" she gasped, both relieved and elated.

"Clary!" He held her at arms' length, drinking in her fragile beauty while she herself took pleasure in his strong hands against her shoulders and the taunting laughter in his dark eyes.

"Take me away," she begged. "Tonight!"

"I cannot," he returned instantly.

"Then you do not love me," she stated simply, her blue eyes at once wide and reproachful.

"You know I can offer you nothing until old man Johnson's cattle are sold. Then we can catch a ship to France..."

"I can raise something..."

"No!" He spun away from her, suddenly all anger and pride. "Not Seaton money. We shall not start our lives together with tainted gold."

Despite his anger, Calantha had to smile at this tousle headed young man in woollen shirt and gaiters, talking so strongly of their future.

"I love you so much," she whispered.

Tom paused mid-stride and caught her to him again. She felt his breath, warm and urgent against her cheek and she raised her lips to his, hungry to feel his rough stubble against her soft mouth.

Gently, he eased her further into shadow, his hands caressing her hair, her throat, cupping her small eager breasts and kissing them through the thin material of her gown. She gasped, thrusting both hands beneath his shirt, relishing the warm flush of his body.

"Yes... Tom," she breathed, her face pressed against dark hair that smelt of cornfields and freedom. "Yes..."

Suddenly the all-protective darkness receded as a flaming brand was thrust into the folly and Calantha felt Tom dragged roughly from her. The towering figure of her father came between them, bringing with him a wave of anger that instantly extinguished her feelings of happiness and release. Daniel Seaton grasped Tom by the scruff of the neck and with a bellow of rage flung the boy aside like a piece of unwanted sacking.

"Whip him to within an inch of his miserable life," he commanded and as strong hands hauled Tom to his feet Calantha realised her father was not alone. She recognized several local squires leering at her in the torchlight and also the red-faced youth who'd followed Seaton into the library.

"Please... Father, you cannot do this." She reached out a trembling hand. "I love him dearly..."

He shrugged off her touch.

"Go to the house," he stated with quiet authority. "If your poor mother had lived to see this day it would have broken her heart."

Calantha drew herself to her full height.

"If Mother had been alive, Tom would have found himself a welcome guest at our table..."

"Enough!" For an instant she thought he was going to strike her, but he merely thrust her aside with his raised hand. "I shall deal with you later." He stepped heavily down to where Tom stood with pinioned arms. "As for you my young cockerel, it seems you do not crow so loudly now the master of the roost has arrived?"

"Perhaps t'is because I do not strut and boast like some animals." At this, a murmur ran through the gathering, leading to open laughter as he added, "I'm as good a man as any of you... if not better," he finished, meeting Daniel Seaton's gaze with a boldness that sent a chill through Calantha.

Her father eyed the youth with obvious contempt.

"Are you even remotely aware how *gentlemen* settle their differences?"

"Tom, do not listen to him..."

Seaton rounded sharply.

"You see, Mistress Calantha, where your foolishness has led you. You are about to watch this common yokel die like a *man*." He squinted against the blurred circle of faces. "One of you escort my daughter to her bed-chamber and then bring steel to the stable courtyard. The rest may do as you damn well please."

*

Despite efforts to the contrary, Calantha was firmly led above stairs to her chamber, much to the amusement of the remaining guests whom by now realised something of greater interest was about to occur outside.

Hearing the key turn in the lock, she crossed to the window and dragged aside the heavy velvet drapes, allowing herself an unhindered view of the stables and adjoining courtyard.

Seaton had discarded his mulberry waistcoat and buckled shoes and now stood in his shirt and breeches, casually folding back the lace at his cuffs. Tom stood immobile in the circle of onlookers, a rapier hanging loosely from his right hand. Briefly, his gaze swept upwards to where he knew her window to be, but Calantha doubted he could see her beyond the arc of light. She knew he had little experience with the small sword, save for friendly sparring between his village fellows and her heart leapt as she watched the brief salute and the first thrusts of blue steel.

For some minutes both men paced back and forth across the cobbled forecourt. The faint yellow light seemed to enhance their determined features as they judged one another's reach and strength. Calantha pressed close to the latticed pane, flinching at each scrape of steel. Seaton suddenly lunged forward and she felt sure the flashing blade must find its mark. There followed a quick and forceful parry. Forte touched forte! Tom appeared to stagger. There was another erratic scuffle of blades and the two men parted, each warily circling the other.

Calantha stifled an involuntary cry as they came forcibly together again, so close they appeared as one distorted outline. Tom broke away much more slowly than his opponent, shaking his head as though dazed. Seaton, seeing his advantage pressed forward, driving the boy towards the stable wall, the crowd scattering before the onslaught.

In apparent desperation, Tom lunged into quarte. Seaton parried and thrust, his flickering blade drawing a red line across the boy's sweat-stained shirt. Tom grimaced and as his back came up against the stone wall he stepped swiftly sideways, receiving Seaton's foil in a clumsy, half-hearted parry that left his guard open for his opponent's downward thrust. Tom closed his eyes and ducked as the returning steel raked his shoulder. Almost in reflex, he sprang up again, taking Seaton by surprise. The tip of Tom's blade, point upwards, entered Seatons throat and brought the uneven match abruptly to an end.

Calantha gasped as her father staggered a pace or two towards the house. His rapier clattered to the cobblestones as both hands clutched the blade still embedded in his neck. With an effort he wrenched the steel free, bringing with it great gout of blood that soaked the front of his shirt, glistening darkly in the candlelight. Then, like a felled oak, he toppled backwards with out flung arms and lay still, his lifeblood flooding the stones beneath him.

For an instant silence touched the stunned gathering. Tom spared time for one swift glance towards the manor, before he backed off and turned, sprinting towards the trees.

With a strange calmness, Calantha watched pandemonium break loose. Earlier that evening, her life had promised an uncertain but exciting future. Now her father lay dead and Tom was a hunted man.

Seaton's guests poured out of the house in eager pursuit, although Calantha wondered how many were just eager to place Scar Manor as far behind as possible. Last to leave was the red-faced Corinthian, trailing after a pack of her father's hunting dogs. She watched until his white mare was just a blur between the trees and the only sound left was the baying of the lead hound as it scented its prey. From her solitary vantage point she stared down at the lonely figure sprawled in the courtyard and found she could feel only pity. Where now were the hangers on... men who could once have been made or broken at the whim of this lifeless form? Not one had remained to straighten her father's limbs or close his eyes against the cold moonlight.

Her hands began to tremble where they rested against the window seat and as she scanned the trees, imagining she might catch one last glimpse of Tom, signalling as he had often done... tears spilled onto her pale cheeks and fell unheeded amidst the velvet folds at her feet.

Listlessly she turned to face the refuge that had become a prison. She made no effort to test the door again, knowing from past experience the servants would let her out at morning light. All she wanted was to lose herself in sleep... to let this nightmare end. For the first time she noticed the chill of the room and the unprepared hearth. Fully clothed, she slipped off her shoes and crawled between the cool covers, surrendering her self to the tears that threatened to choke her.

*

Raised voices dragged her from welcome oblivion. Heavy-eyed, Calantha turned, disappointed to find no glimmer of light in the night sky. Slipping back against the bolster, she listened again for the sound that had awakened her, expecting to hear servants' chatter from the gallery outside. Then came the sharp clatter of hooves on cobblestones and the softer tread of human feet.

"Tom!" Calantha flung aside her covers and hurried to the window, only to have her hopes dashed by the scene below.

A ring of torchbearers circled the manor in either direction. None appeared to be the gaily-clad guests from earlier, but local villagers, who stood staring at the house as though waiting for someone or something. The flickering brands gave colour to their hostile expressions and reflected off the farm implements they carried with quiet menace.

Calantha felt a strong urge to pull the drapes against this new nightmare, to slip back beneath the covers and leave men forever to their own devices, but familiar faces drew her to the cold glass. She recognized several of her father's servants and realised his body no longer lay in the courtyard. Perhaps their apparent hostility was a figment of her distressed mind? She was wondering if they'd come to show their respect when thick smoke drifted past her window and with numbing horror she understood the true purpose of their vigil. Scar Manor had been put to the torch.

Frantically Calantha rushed to the door, only to find it still locked against her. With clenched fists and renewed strength founded on fear, she hammered upon the heavy panelling, her screams for help becoming gasps as smoke poured beneath the door, driving her back towards the window.

Surely, they *couldn't* have known she was still inside! The leaded panes offered no escape, but *were* a means of drawing attention to the tower room. She snatched steel tongs from the cold hearth and flung them at the aperture, shards of glass following their descent to the courtyard below. Momentarily, smoke shifted on the breeze and she was relieved to see at least a dozen faces glance upwards.

"Help me!" she screamed, her parched throat rasping painfully. In response, the smoke returned, leaving her with a fleeting impression of their un-moving, passive reaction. Calantha staggered back, afraid to face their cold gaze a second time. They intended to let her burn.

Nearly at the point of collapse, she cast about for a place of refuge. Barely able to breath and almost blinded, Calantha crawled into the hearth recess and drew her knees under her chin. Making herself as small as possible, she watched death fill her bedchamber.

"Oh... Tom," she whispered, raising smoke reddened eyes to the small circle of sky above. Dawn light brushed its fingers gently across the opening. "Wait for me my love..."

*

...Calantha shuddered. Death had come so close. She had no recollection of her escape... just drifting into a deep healing sleep and waking, cramped and alone. After that, no one returned to Scar Manor. No passers-by came to sift through the debris or stare at the blackened shell, pondering over the great house that once stood there.

Without Tom, Calantha often believed she could never go on. The memories were too strong and too painful. On such days, she would crawl inside the overgrown folly, which had somehow escaped the villagers' wrath and sit on the marble seat, pretending he would come to take her to France. Some evenings she would climb to her old chamber with its charred doorframe and panelling and look down on the courtyard... remembering.

She sighed. Shadows were receding across the hall as cold moonlight invaded the ruptured brickwork. The night was well advanced and Calantha felt there was something she should be doing... but couldn't quite recall what it was.

Halfway down the staircase, she froze, hearing her name softly spoken, in a voice that sent her mind reeling.

"Tom?"

Movement! There, in the partial darkness at the foot of the stairs.

"Yes... Clary."

Her special name came like a blow to the heart.

"Tom... you're *alive*," she stammered, doubting her own words as she added, "you've come back for me?"

"I always promised I would." His voice sounded tense and weary. "I could never leave you here alone."

A surge of emotion swept over her as she took another uncertain step towards him.

"France, Tom... take me to France!"

A moment's silence fell between them.

"If that is still your wish."

"We must hurry." A note of urgency crept into her voice. "If you're seen they'll take you from me again." Eagerly she closed the distance between them.

"Clary... there's something you have to understand."

In that instant the moon uncurled her fingers, bathing the staircase in silver light. Calantha stopped so abruptly she almost fell against her lover's motionless figure. This was not the Tom she remembered.

His broad frame appeared bowed, as though a great weight rested upon it and as he raised his eyes to hers, there was no suggestion of light in their once smouldering depths.

"What in God's name have they done to you?"

He gave a small sob before answering, like the whimper of a terrified child.

"Your father's friends cornered me in the church." He began to unwind a heavy muffler, his hands strangely pale in the moonlight. "At first no one would enter, so... so they set the dogs on me... knowing the poor creatures have no understanding of sanctuary." The scarf dropped unheeded to the dusty floor, revealing torn and bloody ligaments that no man could possibly live with... and Calantha finally understood the meaning behind her utter loneliness and desolation.

He held out a hand to her, and after the merest hesitation, she accepted it, the cold, hard touch matching her own.

"Then I *didn't* escape the fire," Calantha stated simply.

Tom made no reply. There was no need for further words. Grasping her hand tightly, he drew her down the last steps, guiding her across the littered hall and out between the marble columns. Hand in hand they returned to the folly for the last time, lingering over past memories.

Just once, Calantha looked back at Scar Manor. They were both free now. Their love could be boundless, with no need to skulk in hidden places. Tom had come for her as he always promised he would and now they could be together until the end of time.

REUNION IN THE DARK

The decision to dispose of my wife was not a difficult one to make.

Having been separated now for almost eight years, I feel the time to end her worthless existence is long overdue. Concern for my son's future, combined with Vanessa's drug-ridden, ever more unstable behaviour has led me to monitor her movements on a daily basis. I guess 'stalk' is the operative word, although mostly I watch her comings and goings from the small copse at the front of the house, rarely venturing inside. Since my spell in prison, four walls and a roof fill me with a sense of dread.

I enjoy the shelter of the trees, especially as darkness wraps its velvet cloak about me, endowing me with a sense of security daylight no longer brings. Then I am content to remain for hours, watching the house that would still have been mine... had I not been so careless! At such times I become one with the dappled shadows, listening to the sounds around me, trying to distinguish the rustling of dry autumn leaves from the foraging of night hunters; thrilling at the agonized cry as they seize their prey... or become victims themselves.

You see I know what it's like to become a victim... of circumstance. Once, I loved Vanessa with all my heart and soul; nothing had been too good for her. I scrimped and saved, worked and slaved and each time I thought we finally had it all, there was Edward Remmington-Smythe, urging his daughter towards bigger and bolder schemes; all the time reminding her the good life would come quicker if she'd married in her own league... or better still, returned home to good old Dad before it was too late. When the latter option became a serious point for consideration, I decided it was time to step in and take control of our marriage. So I killed the interfering old bastard!

This deed was not as premeditated as it sounds. Vanessa was at one of her coffee mornings and Edward had driven over to 'inspect' my progress on the extension of the conservatory extension... if you get my drift. I was negotiating a tricky piece of carpentry when he rolled in and with his pompous, deprecating air started suggesting alterations to plans I happened to be particularly proud off... plan's Vanessa and I had worked on together. Words such as 're-shape' and 'knock-out' were used.

On that particular day, it was Edward's misfortune I happened to be holding my favourite claw hammer... with which I 're-shaped' his head and 'knocked-out' his brains. I shall never forget his startled expression at that first blow; his insipid blue eyes went wide and his jaw dropped as a trickle of blood seeped from his nose onto his mousy moustache. Edward was probably dead by the second impact; reducing his head to a bloody pulp was merely a satisfactory conclusion to years of verbal and emotional abuse.

I couldn't have been in a more perfect situation for disposing of Edward's lifeless blubber. Dustsheets were down and in the corner stood my trusty work-mate and circular saw. Beneath my feet was an un-filled floor cavity, which I could easily skim over during Vanessa's next coffee morning... these were becoming more frequent.

Just over an hour later, I was about to rest on my laurel's, via freshly laid work sheets, when I recalled Edward's car, parked rather obviously out front. Solving the problem seemed so simple and I remember thinking how clever I was at this murder game. All I had to do was drive a hundred yards or so down the lane, catching the bank and hedgerows along the way, suggesting the driver had been out of control. Then I would turn into a ditch and leave her with doors open and engine running.

As I slipped cautiously back towards the house, I realized here was the perfect opportunity to prove what a model husband I could be. I had pleasant visions of the various ways I would comfort Vanessa, while the police searched for Edward Remmington-Smythe, presumably concussed and bewildered, roaming the Dorset countryside. Daddy's message on the answer phone that 'I'm on the way over', would add a further poignant note.

However, my self-congratulatory bubble had soon burst. The police became suspicious when they noted the car was facing the wrong way down a one-way lane. Also, having thoroughly wiped my fingerprints from the steering wheel, Edward's prints were questionably absent. In came the sniffer dogs... and I soon found myself behind bars for first-degree murder.

Within months of being inside, I'd learned Vanessa was pregnant with my child, conceived no doubt on the day of her father's death, when emotions between us had run high. Later I also discovered Michael's birth had left my wife with a convenient heart condition... convenient for me, that is; this time there would be no mistakes.

With its messy connections to her father's death, I'd been surprised to learn Vanessa kept the house. Any self-respecting person would have at least demolished the conservatory. She, however, had turned the extension into a shrine and was holding weekly séances in an attempt to communicate with the 'great man'.

My close watch revealed everything which should one day pass to my son, was in danger of being lost to a charlatan Medium, aptly named Conner, who was currently charming the knickers off of my wife. Personally I'd lost everything the day my hammer parted Remmington-Smythe's hairline, but I still had Michael's future to consider and had to act while Vanessa still favoured the lad in her will.

So here I was... nightfall once more found me watching from the trees at the end of the garden. I knew Michael was at the cinema with friends. Vanessa was alone in the house and

Conner had just pulled up in an expensive Mondeo, presumably purchased with money fleeced from previous clients.

God knows what Vanessa saw in him. He was tall and thin, almost to the point of emaciation and walked from the car with an odd, lopping gait. The attraction had to be his supposed ability to communicate with 'dear old Dad'. As he began transferring holdalls and boxes to the house it rankled me simply because the fellow had his own key.

Not wishing to reveal myself too soon, I waited until his third trip before slipping diagonally across the lawn and into the spacious hall. Conner's luggage was piled neatly at the foot of the stairs, looking for the entire world like the guy was moving in.

Even amidst familiar surroundings, I sensed a claustrophobic urge to flee back into the night and perhaps would have done so had not a familiar laugh drawn me through the dinning room towards the place of my ruination... the conservatory. And *there* was the reason for it all.

Vanessa looked as beautiful as ever. Unlike me, the years had not outwardly scarred her. I wondered if Conner was aware of the unstable, drug-ravaged mind that functioned behind those lovely features; inheriting Daddy's money had done Vanessa no favours at all.

The windows of the conservatory were heavily curtained against the deeper shadows of the night. The dividing doorway was similarly masked and I slipped gratefully into this pocket of darkness and waited.

I listened patiently as small talk drifted on to weightier matters... re-decorating the master bedroom, expensive holidays abroad. Several times Conner looked towards my place of concealment and once, there was the strangest sensation that our eyes locked... but the moment passed. Then, in the faintest whisper, I heard Michael mentioned. Conner was saying something about being back in Vanessa's life for good... and how his son would at last carry his rightful name after they were married.

His son!

Then Conner had known my wife before I killed her father! Before I went to prison! Never had I felt such anger well up inside me and I'm sure Conner perceived something, for he glanced again in my direction and this time Vanessa followed his gaze and smiled, perhaps believing Conner sensed her father's presence in the room.

All I understood was that *two* people would die this night!

Conner switched on a tape recorder while Vanessa dimmed the lights. Both re-settled round the table. I shifted my position slightly, so I could concentrate fully on Conner. From him would come the cue I needed?

Silence settled over the house, except for the muffled ticking of the grandfather clock in the hall. That sound to somehow faded as I felt the air in the conservatory become heavy and oppressive. Conner seemed to be doing a fair impression of a trance medium. Minutes passed, during which his breathing became at first loudly laboured and then almost silent. His posture changed several times and I tensed in readiness when his head finally came up from his chest. His eyes opened and lips that were no longer slack began to shape soundless words.

Shielded by impenetrable darkness, I slipped from cover and stood directly behind him. He sensed my presence immediately and I felt his aura contract as he tried to push me away. But I was far stronger than any make believe entity he could conjure up.

Vanessa obviously saw the change in Conner and as realisation dawned I saw her throat working as she tried to scream. Finally, she shook her head in disbelief as I leered back, overshadowing Conner with the agonized features of the man who'd once been her husband... recently hanged for the murder of her father. Showing her the rope burn round my neck seemed a particularly effective touch and I watched dispassionately as her face turned ashen and her lips blue. When one hand fluttered weakly to her chest I knew my moment of triumph was near...

"Follow the light!" Someone whispered in my ear. I sensed a massive shift in energy. "You *must* follow the light!" The voice urged again.

Darts of colour flickered around me as I tried to earth myself to Conner, but something more powerful was pulling me in the opposite direction; and that damn voice... was rapidly becoming the most soothing and compelling sound I'd ever heard. Something seemed to snap within me and I found myself looking down at the table... at Conner, comforting Vanessa. *My* Vanessa. Then another movement caught my eye and I kind of spun slowly round to see Edward Remmington-Smythe standing in a shaft of brilliant white light.

Without really understanding why - I drifted towards him.

TRICK OR TREAT

"Shit!" the boy cursed aloud as the branch whipped across his face, not hard enough to draw blood, but with a vicious backlash that brought stinging tears to his eyes. Standing perfectly still, he fumbled for his grubby red bandanna, and realised it was at home in the pocket of his school uniform. "Shit!" he said again, wiping his face on the sleeve of his father's old padded work shirt.

Of all his stupid ideas, this one had to take the biscuit. He could easily have won back his classmates' respect by lipping the maths teacher... or doing a spot of graffiti on the new school gates. But no! *He* had to pledge to steal that old bag's cat. He surged forward with renewed determination to have his task over and done with, one hand pushing aside the thick undergrowth while the other grasped the sack in which he hoped to carry his prize... unharmed of course.

The 'old bag' was their much-feared ex-school mistress, Miss Williams, who'd officially 'retired' from Edbury Manor two years ago. However, it was well known amongst the pupils she'd been asked to leave after her famous temper left a pupil unable to sit for a week. Thus, Miss Williams' twenty-three years of service had come to an abrupt end. At that thought, he squared his narrow shoulders and gave a wry grin. You definitely weren't allowed to hit school kids nowadays. They were the future up and coming generation and as such deserved a little respect... his baseball cap snagged on an overhanging branch and disappeared into the gathering darkness.

"Son of a bitch!" he declared, nearly wetting himself as the hat came back at him from a different direction and cuffed him round the ear. He stopped again, struck for the first time by fear he may have lost direction. A wind was rising and the green canopy that had kept off the rain now shuddered and deposited large drops over him.

It was common knowledge Miss Williams watched all comings and goings along the top road, so his approach had to be by the back path, which scarred the cliff edge between the woods and the void beyond. For very personal reasons, he chose to keep as close to the trees as possible, which was why he now found himself being snagged and whipped by the thin, thorny branches.

His stomach lurched as he heard the crash of waves above the sighing wind. He looked down at the rough ground and then sideways, where the cliff edge and darkening sky became one, and cursed himself for not bringing a torch. With luck the storm might move on and God willing his return journey could be made by moonlight... not that he was much into prayers these days.

Eighteen months ago, Scott, his best friend... his only friend if he was honest with himself… had been killed on these cliffs. All the police found was his scarf, and it was a fair assumption his body had been swept out to sea by the strong currents that plied the coastline. Because Scott had come from the local children's home, there had been no relatives to ask *why* he'd been out on the cliffs that night. Had he been alone? Had he fallen... or had he jumped and if so, why? Day and night he'd been tormented by questions about his friend's death, but no one had been prepared to listen and what could one schoolboy do alone? It seemed kids like Scott just didn't count. Other than Mr Phips, the headmaster, he'd been the only classmate at Scott's funeral. The home had done their duty by sending a representative, but the service had been a cold, emotionless affair and soon over.

He *had* felt the loss. For the first time in his young life he'd experienced the empty panic that comes with the loss of someone close. Then came the guilt that accompanies death. Instead of fading with time he felt it more keenly than ever.

Now that it had time to play on his mind. Guilt that he'd noticed the troubled look in Scott's eyes several days before he died. Guilt that he'd accepted Scott's curt "Nufin" when he finally asked what was wrong. He'd been Scott's best friend. He should have asked again and again. He should have made him spit it out. That's what friends were for. Instead, he'd let it go and now Scott was dead. Suicide was common amongst *his sort*, they'd said. Right now he badly needed to know what 'Scott's sort' really meant.

Now, stumbling alone on the edge of the woods, tears welled in his eyes... tears that had nothing to do with battling against the elements. He missed his friend. It was as simple as that. This escapade could have been fun with Scott there to share it with him. Then again, if Scott hadn't died, he probably wouldn't be doing this now.

He forged on, getting colder, wetter and more pissed off by the minute. I had better make this a good one, he told himself with brittle determination. Halloween. The timing couldn't have been more perfect. It would take something as spectacular as this to get back his 'street cred' after being caught in the showers with 'Pinky' Davis. Despite the cold, he felt his blood run hot at the memory, bringing back the fumbling confusion and emotion of the moment.

He'd sprained his ankle during football practice and Pinky, the head prefect, had suggested alternate hot and cold spray to reduce the swelling. Minutes later, naked and leaning on Davis' broad shoulder for support as the water did its soothing work; he'd been horrified to find he was getting an erection. No matter which way he turned it had been impossible to conceal his condition. Completely unfazed, Pinky had stepped fully clothed beneath the shower and began touching him in places he'd barely discovered in his own early explorations. In a very short time, he'd found himself simultaneously crying, wanting to come, and pouring out his guilt and pain over Scott's death as they clung wetly together, his head buried against the older boys' chest.

It was then two of his 'gang' had crept into the shower block for a quiet smoke and his private hell had suddenly doubled.

He staggered as unseen brambles snaked round his legs and kicked back in anger and frustration as thorns pierced his damp jeans, hungrily seeking flesh. Using the thick sacking to protect his hands, he tugged himself free with a violent backwards movement that brought him closer to the cliff edge. He felt the updraft snatch his shirt as he inched carefully round. Far below, white-capped waves glimmered faintly, their thunderous voice erasing all other sounds from his mind. He remained perfectly still, the sack clamped to his chest, blue eyes closed against the finely driven rain, his other hand keeping the baseball cap firmly in place.

Was this how Scott had felt, he wondered, this strange shadow land between fear and power, where an entire lifetime hung in the balance? What mixture of strength or cowardice did it take to turn away, or plunge into darkness... and what had made his friend choose the latter?

"Why, Scott?" he cried, his eyes still closed, his face raised defiantly against the elements. "We were friends, damn it. You had no right... we should have faced this thing together." He staggered back and began to run, stumbling and swaying along the footpath, oblivious of all danger in his haste to be far from this place and free of the guilt that followed him like a shadow.

The trees ended abruptly and he'd blundered halfway across a clearing before coming to a wheezing halt. The rain had stopped and he now welcomed the cool breeze as it fanned his flushed cheeks. Removing his cap, he wiped his forehead with its soft crown, squinting at a white walled cottage across the way, made grey and ghost like beneath its covering of night. From twenty yards, the building looked lifeless to the point of dereliction. Mismatched curtains shuttered the windows and the only sign of life was a wisp of smoke spiralling from the central chimney. Darkness came from within, competing with the lesser darkness as his longed-for moon finally broke through the clouds, playing shadow games on the rough walls and moss covered roof tiles.

He shivered, resetting his cap in a boyish gesture of bravado. He was a lot closer than he'd realised, although he couldn't remember crossing the short track of ground. Yet here he was, ready to crouch low against the balding privet hedge, immensely relieved to find no further signs of life. Being Halloween, the old witch was probably out on her broomstick whooping it up with the rest of her cronies. He giggled nervously at this picture of Miss Williams and hoped she hadn't taken her familiar with her.

"Where was that bloody cat?" He risked a quick glance over the bush and was rewarded with an immediate answer to his question. A black and white shape lay huddled on the back door mat. Simple. All he had to do was creep up on the animal, shove it in the sack and run like hell. He meant the creature no harm and would release it in the woods... once the gang knew of his success.

Taking a deep breath, he edged round the privet bush, trying to silence the gravel that lanced his palms and no doubt caused even worse damage to his jeans. Luckily, the distressed clothing look was still in. He was so close now he could see the rhythmic rise and fall of the cat's fur. "Just reach forward, grab, into the sack... and run," he told himself; wishing Scott was still here. His friend had been incredible with animals. Keeping as far back from the side porch as possible, he stretched out, his arm muscles instantly starting to protest. "Just another inch." Unfortunately for him, it was an inch too many and with a soft groan of despair he toppled forward, landing squarely on the unsuspecting feline.

"Aw... shit!" he breathed. The cat said nothing, and for several seconds neither moved. Eventually he managed to get an elbow underneath and raise his weight, but the startled creature remained firmly attached to his shirtfront. That's when real panic set in and he started to ask himself questions like "What the hell was he doing here?" and "Did he really care what the gang thought of him?"

"Piss off," he suggested fiercely, tugging desperately at the cat's scruffy neck. So engrossed was he with this Velcro moggy he didn't notice the door opening until a cultured voice said,

"I see you have made friends with Demelza."

Electric light flooded the scene. Miss Williams' diminutive figure faced him squarely across the step.

"Oh hell... Miss." His knotted fingers subconsciously began to caress the mangy fur. "I was just passing, Miss and, and er... stopped to admire your beautiful cat," he explained. His heart dropped like a stone into the pit of his stomach as Miss Williams' sharp little eyes flickered from his face to the sack and back again.

"How disappointing, Master Duncan. Aren't you supposed to say Trick or Treat?" She gave an open-mouthed, high-pitched laugh displaying yellowed dentures that clicked as she added, "Don't look so startled, boy. I taught your father and the family likeness is unmistakable. I never forget a face... especially if it belongs to a trouble-maker."

Duncan decided there was little point in denying the charge with the evidence hanging round his neck.

"Come, Demelza." The cat disengaged itself from his shirtfront and dropped at her mistress's feet, where she commenced a deep-throated rattle. "Isn't she a dear?" Miss Williams's coo-ed. "I can understand why you were so attached to her."

Her sarcasm was not lost on Duncan, who backed up a pace... too late to avoid the gnarled hand that seized his sleeve and held on with surprising strength. "Why, you are all wet." A thousand wrinkles played tag across her face. "You had best come in and get yourself dry."

"I... thanks all the same, Miss. I really ought to be getting home..."

"Nonsense," she snapped firmly. "If we don't get you out of those damp clothes it'll be the death of you. And while they're drying we can look out some of your father's old class photographs."

Without really understanding why, Duncan allowed himself to be drawn over the step with Demelza rubbing affectionately round his ankles.

*

The living room was surprisingly warm and cosy in an old fashioned way, with overstuffed armchairs and a log fire burning brightly in the grate. Drapes that had looked dreary from outside were in fact colourful chintzes that perfectly complemented the chair coverings. In the only alcove, an oval cased radio whispered classical music and Duncan couldn't help noticing the small table before the hearth was already laid for two.

"Oh God," he thought, "the old witch was expecting me."

He hovered awkwardly in the middle of the room. "I didn't realise you had a visitor, Miss. Perhaps I should go..." he offered, hopefully.

Miss Williams frowned and then following his gaze, she gave a sad little smile.

"You must excuse my eccentricities. Habits can be hard to break." A sigh wheezed from her. "I'm afraid I still set a place for my poor Arthur."

It was Duncan's turn to look confused.

"How long's he been gone?" he felt compelled to ask, wondering who in fact "he" was. It was common knowledge the old bag had never married, after all, who would have been willing to saddle them selves with such a harridan? Whatever sadness Miss Williams may have felt at leaving Edbury Manor, her pupils certainly hadn't mirrored it. Her departure lifted a cloud from the school and even her fellow teachers had breathed a sigh of relief.

"The poor little mite was no bigger than yourself when he passed." Her dark eyes judged him in one sweeping movement. "In fact you could have been two peas from the same pod."

"Was he your son, Miss?" Duncan instantly regretted his question, so full of surprise and curiosity. He'd seen the shadow that passed across Miss Williams' face and considered an apology.

"Son?" She repeated the word slowly, as though savouring it, and then surprised him with a smug little smile that lit up her entire face. "Yes... I suppose in a sense he was, although you are the first person to have called him that in my presence." Unaccountably, Duncan shivered, an action which didn't go unnoticed. "Now then... that's enough of my prattle, young man. Let's get you changed before you catch pneumonia."

Miss Williams' scuttled away and just as Duncan considered making a bolt for the door, she returned with a shirt and trousers, neatly folded on top of a fluffy blue towel. "Now, you slip into these while I go and brew a nice cup of tea."

*

Ten minutes later, Duncan was settled in a comfortable armchair, smelling mildly of mothballs and lavender while his own clothes steamed gently over the hearth. The kidnapped moggy had seemed like pure genius, but taking tea with the old witch of Edbury Manor went beyond question, and would surely guarantee his 'street cred' until the end of time.

Cautiously, he studied Miss Williams over the rim of his teacup, seemingly content as she placed another sandwich on his plate and cut a large slice of fruitcake in readiness. Contrary to expectations, she didn't seem any different to his aunty down in Clacton. Perhaps a little greyer and more wrinkled, but there were no obvious warts and her nose was quite like his own mother's as was her yellow, hand-knitted cardigan. He risked a swift sideways glance into the alcove, from where the radio still gave soft accompaniment. Not a broomstick or cloak in sight.

"Eat up, Master Duncan," she encouraged, giving no sign she was aware of his scrutiny. "I know how it is with you growing lads." She smoothed the front of her skirt, and

Demelza jumped onto her mistress's lap, where she padded for a moment before curling into a tight ball.

"Thank you, Miss." He leaned forward and helped himself to another jam sandwich. "Did your Arthur attend Edbury?" he asked, after a moment's hesitation.

Miss Williams studied him for a moment and then shook her head, he thought, a little sadly.

"No. He lived in Devon with his father and spent one summer here with me... his last summer... as it happened."

An awkward silence touched the room. Duncan fidgeted in his chair. Miss Williams seemed to look through him, perhaps seeing another who'd once sat there. He thought he caught a glint of tears in her dark eyes and in that moment sensed real pity for what she appeared to be... a frail, lonely and embittered old woman who must have spent a lifetime trying to conceal what sounded to him like a broken marriage... or perhaps the existence of an illegitimate child. She'd concealed her unhappiness beneath a cloak of respectability, until one extreme outburst cost her a lifetime's dedication to teaching. Had she realised then what a mess she'd made of her life, he wondered? Had she finally understood how the pupils hated and feared her, and had a single one of them come to visit since her disgrace? He thought she must now live a very lonely existence and realised since Scott's death he understood a little about that himself.

The fire coughed and spat a shower of sparks into the hearth, bringing them both out of their silent reverie. Duncan yawned and discreetly checked his watch.

"I'm sorry, Miss Williams, but I should be going. I only slipped away for a moment and my parents will be wondering where I've got to." Noting her look of disappointment, he surprised himself by adding, "Perhaps we can look at the photographs another time... if you wish?" To his even greater astonishment, Miss Williams laughed openly at his suggestion, with head thrown back and her thin throat exposed above the yellow cardigan. "I'm sorry, Miss," he began, feeling his confidence take a serious nose dive, "I thought you'd like... I mean..." he broke off as her watery gaze pinned him to the chair.

"Forgive me, Master Duncan," she gasped, "*I have* enjoyed your company and *shall* continue to do so. It's just," she wiped her eyes with the back of one hand, "I find your notion to leave so very, very amusing." She lent suddenly towards him across the table, scattering Demelza and sandwiches in different directions. He felt the cup being taken from his grasp and realised with a shock how little choice he'd had over the action. His fingers felt numb. In fact, as he backed from her leering face, his limbs seemed heavy and lethargic. "You shall never leave here," she promised, her breath sickly sweet against his face.

Mesmerised, Duncan watched a line of spittle drip from the corner of her mouth onto his borrowed trousers and found him self-wondering if Arthur had worn them before him. Words crowded his mind, tumbling over themselves in their haste to be out. He wanted to apologise for the attempted kidnap of her cat and promise he'd come visiting any time she liked... he'd do small jobs around the cottage and garden... anything, so long as he could go home right this minute. He wished his friend Scott was here, or even Pinky Davis, but most of all he wanted his mother, because no words would come and he was frightened. His tongue lay like cold, dead flesh in his mouth and his eyes began to burn with unshed tears.

Miss Williams stood over him now, clammy hands covering his own. He shuddered as her bony knees pressed against him.

"Don't fight it, Master Duncan," she advised. "Young Arthur found the sensation not altogether unpleasant... I could almost have wished he really was my son... and not just a hitch-hiker stealing milk from my doorstep."

He could hardly keep his eyes open. Each laboured breath brought a deafening rush of blood to his ears and with horrifying clarity he realised he'd messed himself. He knew if he looked down, a damp patch would be spreading over the front of his trousers. Ridiculously, he wondered if he should have asked teacher's permission to leave the room. Then darkness came, bringing with it a welcome friend... oblivion.

*

A return to awareness was something Duncan hadn't expected.

It started with a pinpoint of light, hovering like a firefly in his darkness. Then came the sensation of being dragged upwards from a great depth, making his first conscious breath a frantic gasp that brought him instantly awake. At first he could see nothing but a grey haze, like the first light of dawn through his curtains at home. But this was not his bedroom, and if it was Heaven, he didn't think much of the seating arrangements. The hardwood chair bruised his buttocks and the backrest sliced painfully below his shoulder blades. He shifted experimentally, finding full use of his limbs again. His wrists, however, were secured to a flat surface in front of him.

"Aw shit!" He tugged experimentally at his bonds. Nothing happened. Time to panic. "Help!" He began to stamp and kick his feet against the legs of his chair. "Will some mother-fucker come and untie me?" He heard a click close by. Light momentarily blinded him to Miss Williams' entrance.

She'd changed into a neat grey suit, her hair scraped back into a tight bun. She now wore make-up, and in the harsh overhead light the heavy lipstick and eye shadow turned her features into a distorted mask. At least... Duncan hoped it was the light. He risked a sideways glance, finding himself in a classroom similar to those at Edbury Manor. The desks on either side were empty.

"Miss?" The single word was a child's heart-rending plea for freedom.

"Silence, Master Duncan. Speak only when you are spoken to." She moved towards him, her thin fingers wrapped around a wooden ruler. "Be so good as to stand while I introduce you to the rest of the class."

A burst of hope lanced through him. If he was not alone, there was still a chance to escape this nightmare. Leg muscles screamed in protest as he pulled himself eagerly upright.

"Master Duncan has joined us today as a new and welcome pupil." Miss Williams appeared to be addressing someone behind him. Confused, Duncan twisted as far round as his bonds would allow... and froze.

Two figures occupied the rear desks, their decayed faces attentive, eyeless sockets winking at him and mouths slack jawed as though enjoying a private joke. Dry hair plastered their skulls and peppered the shoulders of their faded school uniforms. Open books rested on the desks in front of them, hemmed in by fleshless fingers... manacled like his own.

From a great distance, Miss Williams voice droned on.

"I hope Arthur and Scott make you welcome, Master Duncan. They're good boys, now, and hardly give me any trouble. If you're prepared to work hard I'm sure we shall get on famously."

"Scott?" His stomach lurched and bile filled the back of his throat. His best friend! What crime had he committed to end up here? Duncan shook his head in violent disbelief, hoping to wake himself from this nightmare. But the truth persisted. "Noow." The room began to spin, turning the corpses into grinning gargoyles that pranced and leered around him. He felt himself slipping sideways, feeling the ropes burn his flesh as they held him upright.

Miss Williams slapped the ruler on the edge of her desk.

"Master Duncan, be so good as to sit down. We are waiting to start. Today's lesson will concern Modern Society and its lack of respect for elderly people and their property..."

HER LOVE WILL SET ME FREE

1900 - Newport, Isle of Wight

The dormitory is silent now... although the house is not empty.

The youngsters are down in the chapel; at least those who were able to make the stairs. The others, currently three in all, are sitting out on the landing, where they can look through the balustrade and join in the service below.

My name is Arwin and I have not been to the chapel in many a long year. It may seem strange to some that I still consider myself a child amidst the others; but then I have not left this chamber since my death in the small anti-room, nearly one hundred years ago. By all intents and purposes, I am still the twelve-year-old boy I have always been.

Since long before my time, the good Sisters of St Benedict's have cared for the children here at St Radigan's. Few of us have ever left this place... for we are the flotsam of life; the maimed and sick; both in body and mind... for whom nothing more can be done.

I too was once amongst their number, a ragged little church orphan. A runaway cart had caved in my chest. Despite this misfortune, I count those days as the happiest in my short existence... for in my earthly time here I had come to know love. Not the physical kind the older lads sniggered over beneath their bedclothes at night; but pure and platonic... for at St Radigan's I had discovered a soul mate.

Esther had been all things; gentle and caring, shy and softly spoken, yet strong in her belief that God had brought her into this world for a purpose other than to merely die of consumption.

From the moment of her arrival we were drawn together. Esther was the first true friend I had ever known and she claimed the same of me... although I believe her words were spoken only out of kindness; for none so pure could have walked this earth for eleven years without winning more than the heart of a mere crippled boy.

We were to become inseparable.

I came to delight in Chapel, when I could sit on the pew facing my beloved and listen enraptured as her angelic voice soared to the rafters, her radiant face uplifted, her golden hair framed by a myriad of dancing colours from the stained glass window behind her.

As you can see, I was very much in love.

We laughed and played as only children can. We pored over the meagre books in the library; neither of us could read, but we were mesmerised by the illuminated illustrations. Weather and health permitting, we would walk hand in hand down by the lake and sometimes go skinny-dipping when dear old Sister Angelica was taking one off her unofficial naps. We even dared to plan what would come 'after' St Radigan's... refusing to accept a bond that felt so right could ever be broken.

But in those far off days, the shadow of death frequently stalked the corridors of this house and as God would have it, I was the next to be taken. Pneumonia! Following a cold swim in the lake. But I would not... could not bear to leave my love and when the moment came, I turned away from the light and chose to remain earth bound... a spirit of darkness.

'I shall wait,' I had told myself, assuredly. 'I shall remain with my Esther until we can pass over together.'

I became her constant shadow, her echo in every thought and deed and I truly believe she sensed my presence when it mattered most and understood that I was always at her side. Waiting. Her distress at my passing only strengthened my resolve that I had made the right choice.

Our time was not long in coming and my dear Esther bore the pain of death as bravely as she had faced the rigours of life. I suffered at her suffering, yet at the same time felt elated, confident we would soon be together. The boys had carried her into this very dormitory and I had held her hand, while the nuns fluttered, like grey moths around a dying flame, as helpless against the inevitable as I was.

Upon her last breath I was sure Esther looked straight at me. Her blue eyes grew wide and she had smiled, our special, secret smile. Then I sensed a change in her frail body; a kind of reduction, of folding in on itself... an altered state I have experienced with many others since that day.

A golden radiance had spread upwards from the foot of the bed, bringing with it a sense of absolute peace and tranquillity. I sensed its welcoming touch where our hands were entwined upon the coverlet and just once, I was convinced I heard my name whispered in her very own voice. Then my dear Esther was rising up... free at last from her earthly torment.

To this day I do not understand what went wrong.

I tried to follow. Believe me. I tried with every ounce of by spiritual being and with a litany of Saints tumbling from my lips. Tears flowed freely as I begged for God's intervention, of his mercy and understanding of my predicament. But all was to no avail. That wonderful light receded, taking my beloved Esther with it and I was left alone. So very alone!

Now, time has no meaning for me.

I do not leave the dormitory; because there is no earthly reason for me to do so... her voice no longer calls me from my bed. Her laughter no longer touches my ears, neither her smile my heart. I can only sit patiently and wait upon God's good grace for her return; for I am convinced she would never have willingly left me here.

Sometimes the solitude weighs heavily upon me. Off the hundreds of souls I have watched gain their freedom, none have elected to remain. I know not whether other spirits walk the corridors of this place. Perhaps one day loneliness may force me to venture forth... but in truth I am as frightened of meeting a 'ghost' as the next man... or boy.

I watch my young flock now as they file back from Chapel, some assisting those less able than themselves and sometimes I pretend there is one who has not yet returned. I watch the door, waiting for her delicate hand to curl around the jamb and for her round, pale face to light up the dormitory. When you have all the time in the world, one can indulge in such imaginings and when the pain of reality returns, I always have my memories to fall back on.

Tomorrow, there is to be a new intake. As always, I will be the first to meet them at the door, to gaze into their eyes... to see if my Esther has returned; because even if I have to wait a thousand years... I know my love will one day come to set me free.

MARK OF THE DEVOURER

2003 - Guy's Hospital, London

My name is Panhar, son of Wendle, secret messenger of Anubis; Jackal headed Guardian of the Underworld.

I have carried this name for nearly four thousand years, since the keystone to mighty Amenhotep's tomb was first carved in the Valley of the Kings.

Of course, none of the fools inhabiting this so called twenty-first century understand who or what I am. To the addle-brained girl at reception, I am merely Edom Scott, expectant father and Assistant of Egyptian Antiquities at the British Museum; a fitting occupation, for I actually work amongst old friends and handle artefacts that are known to me.

Pending fatherhood is a condition I have long grown accustomed to! Over the centuries, I have procured many fine women to bear me strong, handsome sons and beautiful daughters. Although I love my present wife, I am not concerned for the health of either; Miquel will be born at thirteen hundred precisely and shall bear his mother's blonde hair and blue eyes. I know these facts, just as I am given to understand many things as a servant of Aman the Devourer.

I find it entertaining to sit quietly in this waiting room and watch other men pace up and down, attempting to make trite, humorous comments to hide their nervous agitation... and to my mind, failing miserably. I do not feel predisposed to make small talk and I know the others sense this, for they discreetly skirt the corner where I am sitting. Even in my silence, they *know* I am different.

I do not live as other mortals... merely to be born, procreate and die, although this is a path I am forced to follow, to maintain my anonymity. My sole purpose in every incarnation has been to search out those who carry the *Mark*, placed upon their foreheads by the ancient ones, whose Temple's they'd once dared to desecrate. Physical death does not bring a release from this sacrilege. We live and die and are born again... this has always been the way and shall continue to be so, while the one true God Ra rides his solar barge across the daytime skies. There is no Heaven and no Hell. But there is always cause... and the effect is the retribution I bring, for I am a portal into the past and through me, the wrath of the Gods can be terrible to behold.

The souls I have taken back for punishment are now beyond number. Throughout every century and from every walk of life I have hunted them down. Power, wealth and position have no meaning in my quest and I care not what purifying deeds have been committed through other incarnations... their first unpardonable sin was in the Eden that was once my beloved Egypt.

One such act of retribution took place only hours ago, causing a delay in my arrival here at the hospital. There could be no question, which task took priority; the criminal had become sufficiently well known to me and I could feel the nagging pull of time and space that indicated the channel was open to receive us both.

I do not question what I am or ask if there are others who serve in the same way as myself. I know only that I have full recollection of all that has passed before me... I have seen nations rise and fall and have witnessed great progress and terrible atrocities. Yet man still does not accept his simple position of servitude, clinging to the blasphemy that he alone rules this Universe.

I can read it now in the body language of those who agitatedly strut back and forth before me, like cocks of the roost, proud in their act of successful procreation, totally unaware no soul arrives without the blessing and consent of the Great Ones.

Feeling the rise of anger and frustration, I closed my eyes and ears against the incessant prattle around me and allowed my thoughts to drift back to this morning's satisfactory conclusion...

*

It is midday.

I am in the Valley of the Kings and Ra beats down unmercifully upon the limestone tombs of the faithful. A breeze teases the woven awning beneath which I stand, but brings no relief; its touch is like fire on my naked skin.

My stifling suit has gone. I now wear only sandals and a loincloth. My head is covered with a white skullcap, symbol of a servant of the Necropolis. My right hand rests lightly on a bamboo staff, carved with the head of a Jackal. Other men stand behind me. I do not need to look at them to sense the tension... their air of expectancy.

High above the cliffs, a dark speck appeared upon the horizon, dipping and weaving through the heat haze, growing ever nearer. This is the signal I have been waiting for; mighty Horus himself had taken flight to witness the prisoner's punishment. The falcon swoops low over the gathering and then with a solitary cry of benediction, heads away into the west.

The scuff of sandals and an agonized gasp of pain broke the sacred silence as a semi-conscious figure was hauled across my path, incongruous in twentieth century jeans and t-shirt, torn and bloodstained where the inquisitors had been at work. I too tensed in anticipation of what was to come.

Before me stood Joe Parker, bearer of the *Mark,* whom I had met and befriended in a London bar... whose trust I had encouraged and allowed to blossom almost to the point of intimacy. I had done my job well, for in Joe's own words 'I had filled a space where only crushing loneliness had existed'. But that had been in another time and another place. Here he was known simply as Ayat, a desecrater of Horemheb's sacred resting place.

Joe had seen the stake embedded in the sand and his struggles had become more frantic. With a slight movement of my staff I signalled more guards to come forward and lay their hands upon him.

Twisting round, Joe saw me for the first time.

"Edom... thank God." Dark eyes met those of a lighter hue, full of fear and confusion. "Tell them there's been a mistake."

I smiled and raised my left hand, but this was not intended as an acknowledgement of past friendships, although Joe had clearly taken it as such for I saw the makings of relief in his expression, still tampered with a lack of comprehension. The fool still didn't understand the enormity of the crime he had once committed... or the agony of its consequences.

"Edom?"

Still smiling, I allowed my hand to fall.

Silently, the guards raised Joe's body as though it were as light as the feather of Thoth. In that exquisite moment, I believe realisation dawned on him, for stark terror swiftly erased all other emotions.

"Nooo..," was all the sound he managed before the guards let him drop, his own weight driving the sharpened stake deep into his bowels.

A murmur rippled through the gathering as Joe's screams echoed and re-echoed off the surrounding cliffs, loud enough to wake the sacred dead and hopefully appease the owners of the tombs he had plundered.

I waited until his cries had subsided to broken sobs before approaching him, careful to avoid the pool of blood and faeces splattering the sand.

"You didn't he...lp me." He coughed and blood gushed from the corners of his mouth.

"I shall, Ayat. I promise." I handed my staff to an attendant and I rested both hands on Joe's twitching shoulders, feeling the skin, moist and clammy beneath his t-shirt. I leant forward slightly. "Thoth awaits you in the Halls of Justice," I whispered. Then gently, like a fond embrace between two lovers, I began to exert a downward pressure...

*

"Mr Scott. *Mr Scott?*"

Centuries flashed past in a matter of seconds and for an instant I struggled to remember where I was and who I was supposed to be.

I looked around. The waiting room was empty and I guessed I was the last to be called. The clock on the far wall read thirteen forty-seven. Miquel should have been born by now. I stood up and automatically headed towards the door marked 'Maternity Ward.'

"Mr Scott!" The receptionist came scurrying across my path. "The doctor would like to see you... first."

"Everything *is* alright?" I was surprised I needed to ask the question; that wasn't like me.

"I'm sure he will explain," the girl responded lamely, ushering me into a side office.

The nameplate read Dr Fiord, but to my mind, the person sitting behind the desk was little more than a schoolboy, complete with owlish glasses and a floppy fringe.

"Ah, Mr Scott. Please, sit down."

I remained standing.

"Can I get you tea or coffee?"

"What's happened?"

He studied me for a moment. Obviously realizing I preferred the direct approach, he said, "I'm afraid your wife... never made it."

"And my son. What of Miquel?"

Dark brows arched briefly above gold frames.

I knew what he was thinking. Why didn't I show some emotion? Right now I was too busy wondering why I hadn't *known* this would happen.

"You have a perfect boy," Fiord said.

"I want to see him." I knew that to Fiord's ears, my words sounded callous, more like an order than a request. I guess most men would have rushed to their departed one's side... perhaps even sensed resentment towards the living child. But then as I have said before, I am not like other men.

Without another word, Fiord pressed a button on his desk phone.

A little black nurse led me to a side ward.

As I leant across the cot, Miquel opened brilliant blue eyes and returned my gaze with the unerring confidence of an old soul. I moved the blanket to expose a mass of fine blond hair and sensed the first gut-wrenching tug of reality; he was so like his mother.

I stretched out one hand and small fingers curled against my palm. Instantly, the bond was made and there and then I swore this beautiful child of mine would never want for anything; that he would grow big and strong. Side by side, we would make our way in the world. As a servant of the Devourer there was so much more I could teach him.

Just then, as I stooped to kiss my son, the *Mark* flared briefly on Miquel's wrinkled forehead...

HOME FARM

Baines hated driving at night, especially in the rain.

He dimmed his car lights and cautiously took the bend in the country lane, just as a ragged figure lurched out from behind a hedge and froze in his path like a startled rabbit.

"Shit!" Too late, he slammed on his brakes and felt a definite impact as the Metro slewed across the wet surface.

Turning on full beam, he released the driver's door, only to find it wedged against the bank. Rather than risk backing up, he slid across the passenger seat and out into the freezing November rain. Heart racing, he checked around the car. Finding nothing, he fetched a powerful torch from the glove compartment and paced the lane on either side for at least fifty yards, checking the mud filled ditches and peering through gapes in the hedges where an injured person might have crawled or been thrown.

Relieved, yet puzzled, he trudged back towards the car, shoulders hunched against the rain. He allowed himself the luxury of a rare smile. If he hadn't known better, he'd have sworn he'd just mowed down a scarecrow... not bad for a man renowned for having absolutely no imagination at all.

The smile froze on his face as the beam of his torch picked out a dirty clump of straw, plastered to the Metro's front bumper.

*

On his forty-ninth birthday, Baines decided he had to escape the rat race before he hit the big five-o and declined into old age. He would retire and write his masterpiece on the Cinque Ports of England.

Being single and a man of simple requirements, he'd worked hard and invested well. The payoff was Home Cottage and five acres of prime grazing land overlooking Pevensey Levels, in Sussex, remnants of a large farming community dating back to Saxon England.

Home Farm was a ramshackle building that successive generations had modified and extended; resulting in a two storied cottage with odd shaped rooms, sloping ceilings and passageways that seemed to go no-where or end in quaint latched doors that concealed nothing but musty storage cupboards. The garden was extensive, although somewhat neglected by the previous owners. The grazing land extended on three sides and a large, ramshackle barn marked his northern boundary.

Baines fell for the cottage before the estate agent had the key in the door. Considered a bit large for a single man with few material possessions, Home Farm was billed as an ideal family residence. However, Baines maintained his money was as good as the next man's. He could pay cash and wasn't locked in a chain; his current flat went with the job he'd left.

So, three weeks before his fiftieth birthday he hired a long based transit van and moved in. That same day, he'd found a note tucked under the latch stating a local lady named Doris Gooding would 'do' for him if required... at least until he settled in. There was a phone number, but no address. Unaccustomed to such bonhomie, Baines set up an informal interview across the scrubbed kitchen table, left by the previous owners... a horsy crowd who considered the cottage too small for their expanding family and aspirations.

Three days later, following the incident, which would henceforth be remembered as 'The Night of the Scarecrow,' a large lady arrived at the cottage and navigated her way into the kitchen with a determined sideways shuffle.

Never a people person, Baines however took an instant liking to Miss Gooding... no wedding band! Over coffee and biscuits he discovered she was a gentle, outgoing person who already knew the layout of Home Farm... having 'done' here on more than one occasion. It was agreed she would clean for him, but only cook if specifically requested and most important of all, she would respect his privacy as a single person; being one herself.

Baines said he didn't require a reference. Miss Gooding emphasized her wish to always be home before dusk. Both admitted three afternoons would suit. Remunerations were settled and Miss Gooding promised to return tomorrow.

*

A week later, Baines awoke to the feeling he'd finally 'come home' as the saying goes.

He loved the cottage and had discovered an unexpected urge to potter around the garden. Local farmers had already shown interest in grazing rights on his land. Despite her size, Miss Gooding was an invisible dream come true and he'd successfully roughed out the first chapter on Cinque Ports. Everything was perfect... except the view from his study window. So today, he was determined to have a closer look at the barn and see if there was anything could be done with it.

*

Baines closed the side door and took a heady breath of fresh air. The morning was bright and dry, although the winter sun was not yet strong enough to drive the frost from the lawns and flowerbeds.

The barn stood on a slight incline, some six hundred yards beyond a thicket that marked the end of his vegetable garden... to be. Halfway up the slope, he looked fondly back at the cottage, with its erratic rooftop, the small orchard and pond with its stepping-stones to the rose garden.

Before continuing up, he waved to Miss Gooding, out by the old chicken coop, distance making her look quite slim and twig-like. In the shadow of the barn he stopped and looked back, squinting against the morning sun, realizing he must have been mistaken about Miss Gooding; Sunday was not one of her days. He shivered, suddenly feeling cold in the lee of the old building.

Whether by design or decay, the front of the barn was totally open to the elements. The back wall was of old planking but the sides were of solid stone, similar in style to Home Farm. High up to the right, there was an aperture and a pulley and what looked like the remains of a hayloft. Several bales had fallen through and lay scattered in one corner, flattened in places where some wild creature had sought a resting place.

He sat and studied what was left of the roof, none of which looked very safe; perhaps he should have the place pulled down. Testing the floor with his heel, he was surprised to find a stone slab beneath the hard packed earth. He widened the area and found where this finished another started. Although he knew absolutely nothing about barns... somehow he still sensed this was an unusual feature.

He sighed and stood up, dusting the back of his jeans.

"Please help us!"

He spun round.

"Who's there?"

A shadow passed over the sun and as from nowhere, a wind howled and moaned through the rotting timbers, rustling the straw and sending three great black grows screeching from the roof. Then there was nothing. Nothing but total silence and when the sun broke through again, Baines felt its rays lacked some of their previous warmth.

*

"Doris, did you pop round for anything yesterday?"

 Miss Gooding was mopping the kitchen floor.

"Yesterday?"

"Around tenish."

"Why no, sir. I was at my sister's place all day."

Baines disappeared into his study.

"Do you know anything about the old barn?" he asked, returning immediately.

"Hasn't been used in years."

"Yes, but is there anything else... history and whatnot."

"Doesn't it say anything in them there deeds you brought home?"

He shook his head, running a hand through iron-grey hair.

"Just shows a rectangle with dimensions and the word BARN stamped across it."

"Well, there you are," Doris concluded, raising a flushed face. "A barn is all it is then."

Somewhat disgruntled, Baines returned to his study.

For some minutes he stared blankly at his computer screen, trying to convince him self what he'd heard yesterday had been a trick of nature... or even local kids trying to frighten the village newcomer. But that didn't explain the figure in the garden.

"Something bothering you, sir?" Miss Gooding came edging through with a cup of coffee.

"Please... everyone calls me Baines." He smiled a thank you as she placed the steaming mug before him. "And yes Doris, I'm beginning to wonder if I've bought more with Home Farm than I imagined."

Doris stood quietly by him for a moment.

"Perhaps you should have a word with the vicar of St Nicholas," she suggested, with noticeably less than her usual exuberance. "He's also the local historian."

Baines checked his watch.

"I'll ring him in the morning," he said.

*

That night the nightmares started.

Baines had retired around eleven, having spent a frustrating evening writing up the notes he'd made earlier on the original five Kentish and Sussex Ports. Nothing however sounded right and he'd decided to come to it fresh in the morning.

He had no recollection of falling asleep, only a vague awareness of the bedroom becoming hot and claustrophobic.

Sometime after, came an odd sense of confinement, from which he tried again and again to break free, hampered by a raging thirst and crushing darkness.

He was relieved to awake to a lesser darkness, his duvet on the floor and his sheets tangled around his sweating body. It seemed ages before the gut wrenching tension left him; however, the thirst remained. Even then, he lay and listened to the night sounds of the old building, finally rising, cold and exhausted to answer the call of nature.

Moonlight flooded the bathroom, giving the faded porcelain a false, clinical brightness. He padded to the sink and filled a plastic beaker, draining it twice before his need began to slacken. Then he leaned forward, resting his forehead against the cool glass of the window, wondering what the hell all that had been about.

Outside, a movement on the lawn caught his eye and he froze.

A figure was looking at the cottage... possibly at the very window where Baines stood. He was certain this time. There could be no mistaking the tattered trousers and the twig-like limbs jutting out at odd angles. The long coat hung open and ragged tufts of straw flapped in the breeze. A floppy, old-fashioned hat kept the features in darkness, but Baines somehow knew bright button eyes would be staring back at him. He flung the beaker aside.

"What do you want with me?" he cried, hammering his palms against the pane of glass. "I wish I *had* run the bugger over," he muttered under his breath. Baines tried his old childhood trick of closing his eyes for a few seconds; when you did that, nasty things usually disappeared.

The figure remained motionless. Or had it?

This time the scarecrow was standing side on, one skeletal arm pointing up the incline towards the old barn.

*

"I need to see you as soon as possible. Yes." Hollow eyed, Baines nodded down the receiver. "It's urgent. Thank you Vicar... I'm leaving now."

The previous evening, Miss Gooding had informed him the Parish Church of St Nicholas could be found in Church Lane, barely one hundred yards from the ruins of Pevensey Castle. She had kindly offered to accompany him in order to make the necessary introductions, but after the events of last night Baines was glad he'd decided to go alone.

Vicar Rubicond could have stepped straight from the annuals of history. Naturally tonsured through premature balding, his rotund little body and bright rosy cheeks exuded a most charitable welcome. He gestured for Baines to join him on the front pew where he was sorting old sheets of organ music.

"Bought Home Farm? Excellent. Don't find it too rambling? Good. Good. Hope you stay longer than the last owner. But of course you will, a dependable looking chap like yourself. Planning to lease the grazing land? Fine idea. Nice little income there."

Baines quickly realized Rubicond had a penchant for answering his own questions.

"Interested in the old barn. Unusual that. Still I suppose you know what you want. Now I could tell you a thing or two about the parish..."

"The barn! Please," Baines cut in a little more sharply than he intended.

Large, doe-like eyes widened in gentle alarm.

"Of course. Of course." Plump little hands massaged each other, generating thought as well as warmth. "I guess you want me to start with the archives? Good idea really. That's what I'll do then. Take some time though." Raised eyebrows indicated Rubicond actually required an answer.

"Can you ring me?" Baines stood up, fighting the urge to say, "Of course you will. Excellent idea."

Rubicond nodded and jotted the new number of Home Farm on a discarded sheet of music.

*

The rest of the morning and afternoon seemed endless.

Before returning home, he'd walked to the end of Church Lane, through the arched gateway and into the grounds of Pevensey Castle. For some time he'd stood on the site of the old drawbridge, looking down into the moat and wondering if he should go back and tell Rubicond everything.

But what evidence did he have? A voice, a nightmare, and a scarecrow... all of which only he'd experienced.

Tension increased towards evening and he wished Miss Gooding were there to keep him company. He considered calling her in on some pretext, but today was Tuesday and they had rigidly settled on Monday, Wednesday and Fridays. Besides, he recalled her insistence on never remaining after dusk and in the light of recent events, began to wonder if Miss Gooding knew more than she was telling him? He would have a word with her in the morning, he decided.

He worked half-heartedly at his book for an hour... mainly hoping to receive a last minute call from the vicar. When this didn't come, he considered phoning the vicarage, but decided Rubicond would have been in touch if he'd found anything important. Checking all was secure; he climbed wearily to his bedroom, convinced he would never sleep.

*

The nightmare came again.

It was the same pattern as before, cloying heat, claustrophobia, confinement and darkness... and this time an overpowering odour of decay, which had brought him retching to the edge of the bed. His flesh crawled as he determinedly stood with his back to the bathroom window, downing three glasses of water.

Knowing sleep would now be impossible he returned to his study and switched on his computer. The file opened and Baines stared open mouthed at the screen, reading the last words he had apparently typed.

"Please help us... in God's good name!"

*

Baines descended before Miss Gooding was out of her coat.

"Doris... does Home Farm frighten you?" he demanded, getting straight to the point. "Is there something I ought to know?"

He had just taken a call from Rubicond. There had been nothing in the Parish records except a dispute over land boundaries back in 1801 and because he was feeling somewhat deflated, he finally told the vicar about his nightmares and seeing the scarecrow, holding back only on the voice he'd heard at the barn. Surprisingly, Rubicond had listened without question.

Now Miss Gooding noticeably blanched.

"Well, sir," she blustered. "You know what small villages are like."

"I don't actually." Perhaps unfairly for Miss Gooding, Baines didn't feel inclined to make this easy.

"People talk..."

"About what... precisely?"

Miss Gooding couldn't meet his questioning gaze.

"Strange figures. On the top field..."

"Near the old barn?"

She nodded, her generous cheeks trembling.

"And sometimes near the cottage," she added.

"But never inside?"

"No sir, not unless you've..." Her hazel eyes grew wide and questioning and Baines finally relented, explaining the strange and frightening occurrences since his arrival.

Miss Gooding had gone as white as a sheet.

"That's what the Spicer lad must have seen when he asked me who built the wicked looking scarecrow?"

Baines had bought Home Farm from the Spicers. It was gratifying to know others had witnessed the same phenomena. But what did it all mean?

"Doris... why do you think an open barn would have stone slabs on its floor?"

"Could be an old threshing floor," Miss Gooding considered this while slipping out of her coat and making them both a much needed cup of coffee. "Although that would normally be outside, so the breeze could carry the chaff away."

The phone rang and deep in thought, Baines wandered off to answer it. He was gone for some time and when he returned Miss Gooding noticed his blue eyes were alight with excitement.

"This may sound weird, but Rubicond thinks he knows who Scarecrow is. Around the time of this boundary dispute, a simpleton by the name of Jethro lost his rights to sleep in the barn."

Miss Gooding looked doubtful.

"That's a bit vague."

"I know. But listen to this." Baines took a hasty sip of coffee. "Jethro was a well known figure of fun in the area; one of his tricks was to stuff layers of straw inside his clothing to keep warm."

"Bloody hell." Miss Gooding's hand flew to her mouth.

Baines nodded.

"My sentiments exactly. Something's keeping Jethro tied here..."

"But that doesn't explain the nightmares... and the voices."

"I bet I'll find the answer in that damn barn."

Miss Gooding looked worried.

"What are you going to do?"

Baines glanced out of the window at the darkening sky.

"It looks like a storms coming." He finished his coffee in one gulp. "Before it breaks I'm going to take another look at those stone slabs."

*

The storm broke long before Baines reached the incline.

He'd stopped to don his parka and had then doubled back to fetch a shovel from the garden shed. He didn't know what he expected to find... part of him didn't want to find anything at all, yet at the same time he knew none of this would go away simply by ignoring it. He wanted a peaceful retirement.

By the time he reached the top field, sleet was driving in sheets across the coarse, frosted grass and an icy wind was buffeting him from all directions. The mouth of the barn loomed, full of unwelcome shadows and creaking timbers and he stepped inside, holding the shovel defensively across his chest. All seemed as he had last left it. Even the scuff-marks made by his heel were still there.

As good a place as any to start...

*

Chores forgotten, Miss Gooding stood at the study window and watched Baines struggle against the elements.

Beside her on the desk, the phone rang and she absently reached for the receiver, more concerned about Baines, who was now in the lee of the barn. She could no longer see him against the lowering clouds.

"Home Farm. Hello Vicar... no, I'm afraid Mr Baines isn't here at the moment. Yes, that's right." As she listened, her expression became fuelled at first with disbelief and then horror. "I'm afraid I can't... he's up there now."

*

Baines had cleared the outline of six slabs.

Oddly enough, the rest of the area seemed to be beaten earth. Maybe Doris was right about the threshing floor. He removed his restricting parka and had just prized up the first slab when he caught a movement at the base of the incline.

Miss Gooding was scrambling up the slope towards him, her coat and arms flapping, her face a glowing beacon of exertion. Baines looked on in dismay as behind her, a misshapen figure lumbered out of the orchard and also started to climb, seemingly oblivious of winter's onslaught. Fired with a new desperation born out of fear, Baines started to dig.

*

Miss Gooding felt as though her heart would burst.

Why didn't Baines stop digging? He must have seen her by now. Soaked to the skin, she forged on, Rubicond's words ringing in her ears. By the time she staggered into the barn, Baines was leaning on his shovel, staring down at something at his feet.

"Oh gawd," she gasped, following his gaze.

Just below the surface Baines had uncovered human bones and a few shreds of clothing. This was only one corner, so there could be more. Hollow eyed, he looked at Miss Gooding.

"Rubicond phoned again, didn't he?"

She nodded, swaying slightly.

"Jethro was hanged. Some sort of serial killer," she gasped. "They found his victims... when they moved the barn."

"Not all of them apparently."

"His specia...lity was burying them alive." Miss Gooding shuddered. "Poor devils."

Baines whistled softly through clenched teeth. That explained his nightmares, the heat and claustrophobia... and the voices calling for help. He was beginning to understand. They *were* standing on the old threshing floor, which had once been outside the barn. The nineteenth century boundary dispute changed all that. He looked past Miss Gooding and stiffened, the spade coming up between them.

"Don't look round."

Naturally, Miss Gooding did just that... and fainted.

The creature once known as Jethro the Simpleton shuffled towards them with a primal, lop-sided gait that was terrifying to behold. Baines held his ground, unable to move away from Miss Gooding's inert body. He brought the point of the shovel down with a resounding crack on the slab beneath his feet and Jethro rustled to a halt. The breeze shifted, bringing with it the stench of decay.

"You wanted me to find them, didn't you? To put an end to their torment... and your guilt."

The figure seemed to bristle.

"To give them a marker in consecrated ground." Baines swallowed. "Where do you go from here, Jethro? I hear there's good summer work for scarecrows." He realized his fear was making him dangerously flippant. "But not on my fields." He brought the spade up again, edge on, prepared to use it as an axe.

Jethro seemed to sway, as though genuinely uncertain which way to turn. Then he lurched sideways, not towards Baines as he'd expected, but towards the open grave. The round head tilted forwards and for a fleeting moment, Baines thought he made out features beneath the floppy hat, shifting and twisting like someone uncertain of their identity. Straw crackled as the arms came up, almost in a gesture of prayer or benediction and for few seconds time seemed to stand still as a pitiful keening sound rent the air.

Mesmerized, Baines watched as the scarecrow started to fold in on itself. Pieces of straw and hay fluttered to the ground. With nothing to support them, the ragged coat and trousers tumbled into the pit Jethro had prepared two hundred years before. His rounded, yokels hat rolled past Baines' feet and a gust of wind caught it and sent it skittering down the slope... to be chased by a beaming Vicar Rubicond as he climbed hurriedly to meet them.

Behind Baines, Miss Gooding gave a small gasp as awareness returned...

ONE LAST TIME

1962 - Steephill, Isle of Wight

I shivered and raised the collar of my threadbare jacket against the driving rain. God I was cold.

"Jamie, you have to stop doing this," I told myself loudly, above the rising wind. "This has to be the last time."

Despite my words, I felt a familiar thrill of anticipation as I climbed the slippery, wooded path. Up ahead of me, a brick built folly was just visible through the gathering darkness.

'Why stop now?' As usual, the voice of my alter ego stepped in, soft and wheedling. 'They can't hang you just for looking.'

I shivered again, this time at the mere thought of such an end, twisting and turning, kicking out my young life at the end of a hempen rope.

"Maybe not," I retorted breathlessly. "But they'd hang me for what I did over in Portsmouth... for what *you* made me do. I should never have let that happen."

'The kid might have talked.'

"I doubt it."

'But *we* weren't prepared to take that risk... were *we* Jamie?' I sighed, struggling to equate fact with my conscience.

"I guess not," I relented.

That's why I was here now, back on the Island, safe and secure in my old village, with nobody the wiser that I'd crossed the Solent since spring. The locals were so accustomed to 'daft' Jamie's presence, they hardly noticed me anymore; and that was just the way I liked it.

I forced myself to concentrate on the twisting path, skirting brambles and branches brought down by a storm that had been raging since first light that morning; desperately trying to shut out the young face that still haunted me, day and night.

I hadn't intended to kill the boy; the situation had somehow got out of control. One minute there were two naked lads horsing about, unaware I was even watching them. Then a dog started barking and the taller of the two had run off. Urged on by the voice in my head, I had stepped from the bushes, finding myself reaching out, wanting to touch and be touched. For the briefest of moments, the feeling seemed to have proved mutual. Then everything became confused. The lad was trying to explain something, his voice at first soft and coaxing... then suddenly strident and aggressive. The other voice kept interrupting and in the end I panicked. To this day I still couldn't remember picking up the rock... but suddenly there was blood everywhere and like the other boy, I was running away.

At least I'd had the foresight to hide the rock inside my jacket until I could dispose of it in the harbour. That had been three months ago... three long months, sweating over every caller at the Home, constantly expecting to have my collar felt by the law. My lettering not being up to much, I couldn't check the local papers and daren't have asked for help, for fear of drawing attention to myself; after all, what interest would 'daft' Jamie have had in mainland matters.

I was glad I hadn't got to know the lad's name... that would have given him an identity, with grieving parents and a life brutally snubbed out. In hindsight, I knew I'd had no choice. My alter ego was *never* wrong... he *would* have talked. In all of my seventeen summers I'd never yet met man or boy who could keep his word... and no other woman had held my trust since they carted my mother off to die in that newfangled hospital on the undercliff. Tuberculosis, the doctors had said; but I knew different. She'd died of a broken heart. After her passing I'd felt the need to start 'looking'. That's why I was here now...

I hawked and spat vehemently into the shadows, thinking bitterly of the aggressive father who'd constantly molested me as a child... until thankfully, the sea had taken him; of my mother lying cold in her grave and the string of petty offences that had once brought me in daily contact with the law; until I'd hit on the 'daft' approach. Only recently, in more lucid moments back at the Home, I'd begun to wonder where 'daft' Jamie ended and the real James Monroe stepped in. If I could no longer tell the difference, what chance did anyone else have?

Dejectedly, I kicked out at the brambles, their moist scent rising in the air as I forged ahead. The last part of the path took an even sharper incline and I paused breathlessly, pushing my cap to the back of my head as I checked out my surroundings.

"Who the hell would come here on a night like this?" I asked myself.

'You for one.'

I hesitated, suddenly uncertain.

"Perhaps tomorrow."

'Defeatist'.

As always, I gave in to my other half. It made life easier.

I could just see the familiar turret now, rising above the trees and one end gable, long since stripped of tiles. Automatically, my step changed into a slightly stooping gait, although I had no real fear of discovery. Nobody came here anymore, except those like myself, with a purpose.

I recalled how the folly was said to be haunted, which struck me as totally out of order, with the ruins of Steephill Castle only a stone's throw away. I guessed there was no accounting for taste where ghosts were concerned; not that I believed in them, although down in the village they spoke at great length of an on-going scenario of unrequited love, treachery and foul murder, still being played out, several decades after the event.

I didn't enter by the wrought iron gate, with its rusted spikes and presumptuous, headless lions, but lurched abruptly to the left, stooped under dripping sycamore boughs and followed my usual path towards the conservatory.

I sensed the rain was easing off now, but the moon was up and the wind was rising again, stirring the branches overhead and causing unfamiliar shapes to writhe across the clearing ahead of me. Eagerly, I headed for the only place where cover reached the walls. Windowless, this part of the building was nothing more than a gaunt framework resting against weathered brickwork; but it gave me entrance to another world...

"Great night for a lovers' tryst."

For once my inner voice made no answer. But I thought I heard a soft laugh, that seemed to come unbidden from the back of my throat and despite the heat of my exertions, I shuddered, feeling the clammy night air close around me. This really had to be the last time.

Quickly, I ducked out of sight into the warm, earthy tunnel and crawled forward on my stomach. Raindrops trickled down the back of my neck and I felt the tug of cobwebs against my face. I was about to slide below the first wooden lintel when I caught a flash of movement over to my right, something light against the darkness.

Someone else was out there.

My first reaction was annoyance at finding trespassers on my patch. But when the man came into sight, I decided I had to admire the balls of this guy; walking upright, soundlessly heading towards the gate, confident in his stride and destination. Totally assured. I sensed a pang of envy and found myself wishing I could go through life like that, instead of crawling around on my belly in the dead of night.

A surge of icy wind sought me out, rustling bushes and whispering through the conservatory. The structure creaked loudly and as I watched it seemed as though the figure hesitated for the first time, turning a handsome, leonine face directly in my direction.

Instinctively I ducked, breathing heavily.

"Phew! That was close."

'Don't be stupid... he couldn't see you.'

When I dared to look again, the clearing was deserted.

Touched with a sense of urgency, I moved forward until I felt familiar stone slabs beneath my hands and knees. Then the peak of my cap butted the inner wall. Heart thumping, I turned, resting my shoulders against the brickwork, all the while listening for sounds of movement inside. I almost cried out when a pool of candlelight bathed my outstretched legs with an eerie glow.

"Christ!"

'Be quiet... you fool.'

"Shut up!"

I froze, realizing I'd shouted out loud.

The light became suddenly disjointed, as though someone had moved the candle or passed between its source and the window; which meant whoever it was could be standing directly behind me.

I swallowed. Had they heard me?

"I can't look."

'Coward! Always were... always will be.'

I resented that.

Easing off my cap, it was anger rather than bravado that brought my eyes level with the ledge. I'd never seen the interior of the folly. Until now I'd been guided by sound and my own vivid imagination. The room was larger than I'd expected. Sparsely furnished, but with good quality in an old fashioned kind of way. What I'd always assumed to be a mattress, thrown across several tea chests, was in fact a magnificent four-poster bed.

This guy obviously had class.

The tall stranger was there, languidly removing his jacket and kicking off his shoes, his dark, hungry eyes never once leaving those of a women stretched provocatively across white linen sheets. High breasted, with a slim waist and powerful looking thighs, she was nothing like I'd ever seen before; or particularly wanted to see again. In my state of excited anticipation, it never occurred to me to question how she came to be there in the first place.

Hungrily, my gaze flicked back to check the man's progress and I stifled an involuntary gasp as the last of the guys clothing fell away. Candlelight turned his muscular shoulders, tapering waist and rounded buttocks to alabaster. It was then I sensed the first stirring in my loins.

"Oh God!"

'Pervert... dirty, bloody pervert!'

"Don't say that," I begged, overwhelmed by conflicting emotions.

'If Mother could see you now.'

That was the last straw.

There and then I decided my alter ego had to go. As much as I wanted... needed to watch, I would stand up and walk away; or at least crawl to begin with.

"Bastard!"

I knew hot tears were scalding my cheeks.

'Cry baby.'

Never would I return here to be tormented like this.

Even so, as I replaced my cap, I was unable to leave without risking one more sideways glance. Instantly I knew a change had taken place within the folly. The candles were beginning to gutter as though time had passed and it suddenly dawned on me the room was bathed in total silence, as though I was watching an old, silent movie. The couple, now entwined on the four-poster was making interesting progress, yet instinctively my gaze was drawn to the deeper shadows on the far side of the room.

I almost levitated on the spot when my eyes locked onto those of a short, swarthy man, enveloped in an old fashioned greatcoat that smothered all but his face. The man's skin was heavily pockmarked and almost translucent, reminding me of how my mother had looked just before she died.

"We have to go," I whispered urgently.

'*No*! Wait.'

With a terrible sense of impending doom, I watched as the intruder shuffled towards the bed, his shadow rising and falling in grotesque relief against the walls. The startled couple rolled over just as the man reached them. His overcoat fell open and I caught a glint of steel as a curved blade arced once... twice, turning the sheets crimson as man and women writhed together in a macabre dance of death.

Stunned, I fell back on my haunches, bile rising in my throat. A sob escaped me and I looked up again to find the man was at the window, within touching distance through the broken frame. I could see the sheen of perspiration on his skin and shuddered, as the glazed, soulless eyes seemed to seek me out.

Suddenly I was consumed with a terrible self-awareness, realizing this man's face was a reflection of my own... the face of a murderer. Was this how I would one day look upon the world? Even now, could others read the guilt in *my* eyes and know the terrible crime I had committed?

"Sod crawling," I announced, desperate to get away.

Instantly, I was over the lintel and heading for the gate.

'Don't look now... the bogey man's right behind you.'

Spurred on by an urge to escape from what I now saw as myself, I reached effortlessly for the rusty framework and leaped up and over, twisting as I did so. Whether I misjudged my hold or my hand simply slipped on the wet metalwork, I would probably never know. I came crashing down on top of the gate, the central spike driving upwards into my chest with the full force of my momentum to assist it.

At first there was no pain; just a strange jolt that reached down into my very soul. Then gravity began to take over and I felt my body start to swivel. Desperately my feet scrabbled for a purchase as the spike scribed an agonizing arc inside of me.

"Je... sus!" I screamed.

It no longer mattered who heard.

'Clumsy.'

"Fuck yeeew!"

'You wish.'

Through red tinted vision, I saw a black garbed figure detach itself from the folly, greatcoat flapping open, moonlight glinting on the blade still held before him. I tried not to look, but my skewered position made it impossible; I didn't want to take that pale face and those staring eyes to my grave... because that's where I was damn well heading; I knew it would take more than 'daft' Jamie to get me out of this one.

"Oh... God!" I gasped as the murderer leaned into me, as though he would confide some long dead secret; but in effect passed through both the gateway and myself, on a path preordained by past deeds.

'Do something... you fool.'

I recognized panic in the other voice.

"Dying ain't nothing... and I'm bloody taking *you* with me."

Silence at that!

Christ it hurt! My legs were turning numb and I could feel myself sliding sideways. My fingers were loosing their hold as my life force began to pour from every orifice.

"Please God... make this quick."

It was then I sensed, rather than saw another presence near me, one that brought with it aura of waiting for the inevitable.

"Mum?" I hoped.

But then why should life be kind to me, even in death.

"Simon." The name was spoken softly, almost shyly and instinctively I knew it was the lad from Portsmouth.

"C... ome to gloat?" Typically, my alter ego said nothing... just when I could have done with a little moral support.

"Neither of us would gain from that, Jamie."

The boy's voice was already fading as he moved away.

"Wa... it! What should I do?"

An agonizing silence followed. Then,

"Just let go, Jamie. We all have to eventually."

What choice did I have?

Cautiously, I released my hold on the gate and stepped down, determined not to look back at the ruins of my physical self... afraid I'd look into the sweaty, pockmarked face of a murderer.

There was no more pain. Nothing. Just an incredible sense of freedom!

Simon was at my side again, looking remarkably healthier than when I'd last seen him. However, the floppy fringe and hazel eyes were just the same... and so was the way he looked at me as he held out his hand.

"I don't quite understand why," he began, "but they thought I should be the one to bring you home."

"Home?" I echoed, desperately wanting to ask who 'they' were and to beg Simon's forgiveness for what I'd done to him. But my tongue felt as though it was stuck to the roof of my mouth and the words just wouldn't come.

"Hurry up," he urged, glancing past me towards the folly. "Unless you want to be trapped here like the others. Your Mother would never forgive me if that happened."

Eagerly I accepted Simon's outstretched hand; finding it cool, yet unexpectedly firm for the hand of a ghost.

As I left the folly behind me for the last time, I found myself walking like that other guy had done; head up, confident...and just for once, prepared to face whatever was out there waiting for me.

BOARDING OUT

1873 - London

In his own unique way, Oliver was frightened.

He had just watched Mr Flowers showing his new pupil and her sombre looking guardian into the downstairs study.

Flowers ran Heberdeans, a summer school for wealthy, but 'difficult' children, who were not permitted to return home during recess at their boarding or convent school or were merely too unruly to fit in with their fellow pupils and required tuition of the more 'singular kind' in which Flowers specialised.

*

Early that morning, as soon as Oliver heard talk of the new arrival; he had stationed himself at the attic window. His high vantage point overlooked the narrow drive, so nothing approaching *his* house went unnoticed. Oliver was still living there, so it *had* to be his house and the attic was his favourite room, where he felt safe and secure. The room where he had died over fifty years ago!

Habitually, he glanced reassuringly behind him. The trunk was still there in the corner; the one with the heavy curved lid and the simple hook and eye catch that had been his undoing.

He could still recall shouting for his twin sister, Clara, his cries no doubt insulated by the thickly quilted interior. They had been playing their usual game of hide and seek; she should have come... she should have known. Then came the claustrophobia and panic; the heat generated by his small body in the confined space and an awareness of his own laboured breathing. Then sweet oblivion!

Upon reawakening on that fateful day, he had felt strangely light and unencumbered as he stepped from his prison into a house divided. Parents blamed themselves, each other and finally Nanny Bina, who had been elsewhere in the rambling Georgian house. Shortly afterwards his family moved away; but he had been unable to leave with them. The house seemed to hold him in thrall, as though there was something unfinished he had to do and even now, a terrible sense of emptiness and desolation overcame him whenever he tried to cross the garden perimeter.

Oliver shivered; not that he felt cold. He felt nothing much anymore, except lonely... and now frightened of course, for this young girl. Other than his dear Mother, in all his short life and long death, Oliver had only ever known Clara, so he was naturally intrigued and eager to see 'this girl'.

The wait seemed endless, which was strange in itself for someone to whom time no longer had meaning. Outside, the day had been gloriously sunny and bright, full of colour and sound, yet it was dusk before the carriage rocked to a halt at the gates. The side door opened and the steps unfolded with a clatter to the gravel path. Oliver found himself leaning forward with a mixture of dread and anticipation as a diminutive cloaked and hooded figure stepped down, followed closely by a pasty-faced adult who seemed intent on herding the child unceremoniously before him.

Despite the fellow's haste, or perhaps merely because of it, the petite figure seemed to hold back, head raised, all the time looking up at the house. It had to have been Oliver's imagination, but for a fleeting second it seemed as though their eyes locked, as though the young girl had actually seen him. Oliver's raised hopes were dashed again immediately as she stumbled and would have fallen, had it not been for the cane concealed in the folds of her cloak. Oliver then understood her caution had been purely functional, because the new pupil was blind.

Despite his disappointment, his heart went out to her, for he alone knew the terrors awaiting her within Heberdeans; the bullying and depravation that went on in the name of 'correction'. To Oliver's knowledge, no child had ever died in Mr Flowers' care, but all had left the boarding house broken in spirit and mind... becoming the docile, obedient offspring the exorbitant fee guaranteed.

Oliver wanted to rush down and bar her entrance into *his* home, to warn her of the dangers to come. But he knew that would do no good. He had tried that tactic many times before; people just did not see or hear him. And why should they? He had spent the last half-century being his mother's blond, blue-eyed boy. If he had only managed to mature, to become a little more forceful he could have been of some use to these poor misused wretches.

With such thoughts as these, the anger and frustration would finally come through and that was when things really did start to happen... nasty things beyond his control, that mostly frightened pupils and made their term at Heberdeans even more unbearable. So instead, Oliver quietly mooned about the place, keeping to the attic where no one ever came, insulated against the living, but far from immune to the waves of pain and sorrow that percolated from below.

But today, in the darkening attic, Oliver found himself pacing back and forth between the chest and the window. Right now, Mr Flowers was downstairs in his study, planning how to break a young girl's spirit. Oliver saw again the pale face lifted towards him... the dark fathomless eyes and the suggestion of auburn hair beneath her hood. He knew nothing about this girl; he didn't even know her name. But this time he *would* find a way to make a difference...

*

Oliver descended rapidly through the ceiling... and landed expertly in the leather bound armchair behind Mr Flowers' great oak desk. He had, after all, done this many times before.

As expected, Mr Flowers was in full flood as he rocked on his heels before the cold hearth, driving home the advantages of Heberdeans to his male guest.

Oliver studied Mr Flowers closely.

By no stretch of the imagination could he have been considered handsome. He was not very tall; standing barely five-two in his highly polished riding boots. His lack of stature was greatly emphasized by the unusual length of his arms, which enabled him to scratch behind his knees without stooping to do so. Due to the good living afforded by Heberdeans, his figure was slightly rotund; but by the same token he was able to afford perfectly tailored clothes to conceal this imperfection from all but the most discerning eye. He wore his hair long, swept back in a thick greasy mane that brushed the shoulders of his velvet smoking jacket and from his ruddy, moon-shaped face, blue eyes of the most piercing and demonic quality challenged all newcomers.

She was also there, sitting still and silent in the corner, while her future was neatly dissected and disposed off by two men who cared nothing for her. She still wore her cloak, despite the warmth of the evening. The hood had fallen back, either by intention or neglect, to disclose heavy tresses that fell almost to her waist, shimmering like burnished gold in the candlelight. Her features were small, the mouth firmly rounded and set against the injustice of her situation. But it was her eyes that mesmerised Oliver, drawing him into their dark, liquid depths like nothing and no one had ever done before.

"Your niece informs me Rebecca is unyielding," Flowers was saying, "and that she breeds malcontent amongst her brethren at the convent school." His fierce gaze settled on the motionless form. "If I find this to be so... I assure you such self-contained practices will cease forthwith," he took a threatening step towards the girl and then spun swiftly back on his heel "or I shall know the reason why," he concluded, with a genial nod at her guardian.

Mr Phips' pockmarked face crumpled into the semblance of a smile. He leaned forward.

"Some say Rebecca claims her affliction to be a gift from God," he confided in a soft, nasal tone, casting a surreptitious glance over his shoulder. He sniffed and noisily cleared his throat "Wouldn't surprise me if 'er peepers were as good as yours and mine."

Flowers nodded benignly.

"Such deceptions have been known, particularly in association with religious houses. Rest assured Mr Phips," he tapped the side of his broad, veined nose, "if such trickery is found in my establishment... the perpetrator shall rue the day."

Phips pursed thin, cruel lips.

"I shall sleep better knowing that, Mr Flowers." He massaged greasy palms down the front of his jacket. "As you know... a great deal rests on your findings."

"Yes, yes... enough said!" He offered Phip's his hand, which when accepted, was used as a lever to prize the gentleman unceremoniously from his chair. "Soonest begun, soonest done as my dear wife always says."

Oliver snorted derisively.

He knew there had never been a Mrs Flowers in residence, only a succession of dubious housekeepers, duped into actions that made it criminally impossible for them to back out or talk afterwards. The book-lined study and adjoining classroom was a front for 'soft' visitors and the dormitory no more than a filthy cellar at the back of the house. And there *were* no other pupils; Flowers found it safer and more satisfying to deal with one 'correction' case at a time.

*

Indeed... now would begin the part Oliver dreaded.

It did not help him at all knowing *her* name was Rebecca or that he now thought of her as a beautiful angel beneath that quiet, determined exterior. None of that mattered... because before long she would be like all the others; hollow eyed and subdued. A wealthy child, who could be easily manipulated by her mentors!

The sound of carriage wheels on gravel marked Mr Phips' departure, having been handed his cloak and virtually frog-marched out of the door, albeit with a smile and another firm handshake. Oliver cringed at the return of Flowers heavy, measured tread and thought the man looked surprised to find Rebecca still seated where he had left her. Other pupils had tried to make a break for freedom, or even hide somewhere within Heberdeans.

"Come child." Flowers held out one hand, as though testing her.

Rebecca stood, calmly shaking out the folds of her cloak.

"I am not a child, Mr Flowers and I should not be here." Her voice was young, but firm.

Flowers brought the same hand hard against her face. Oliver flinched, but Rebecca remained still, although her cane trembled slightly, as though she considered striking Flowers with it.

"Do it, girl," he hissed. "Give me an excuse to break you."

"Don't make it worse!" Oliver cried, ineffectually stepping between them.

Candlelight flickered and the clock above the mantle shelf measured precious seconds while nobody moved.

"Mrs Twain!" The veins stood out on Flowers neck.

Somewhere in the bowels of the house a door slammed, followed by heavy footsteps along the passage outside. The housekeeper huffed into the study, mobcap askew, bringing with her the odour of sweat and gin.

"Sir?" She bobbed unsteadily.

"Take this creature away," Flowers ordered, disdainfully. "You know what to do with her."

*

Oliver felt utterly useless.

He could only turn away as Rebecca was stripped of her clothing, doused in cold water and given a coarse, homespun shift to wear.

"You won't be needing tha', my lovely." Mrs Twain snatched her cane and prodded the shivering girl. She laughed, brashly. "Not 'less the Master decides you need a good birching."

Rebecca remained staunchly silent until the door was bolted and the housekeeper's heavy footsteps climbed the stairs. Then she slumped onto the pallet bed and began to sob quietly.

"Please don't do that," Oliver begged, rushing forward, wanting so badly to put his arms around her. "Rebecca... don't cry."

Naturally his plea went unheeded.

Oliver backed away, feeling the damp wall behind him and sensing the urge to drift backwards into it, to let the house absorb him once more. What good was he doing either of them? He clenched his small fists and felt the anger and frustration begin to rise. While others were being starved and beaten into submission... what had he ever done? What he was about to do now... hide!

He took one long look at Rebecca, memorizing the pale features framed by her long fall of hair, the delicate hands clasped beneath her chin... almost in an attitude of prayer, and the angry red welt left by Flowers' hand, moist now with salty tears.

And something in Oliver snapped.

He moved clear of the wall; aware the air around him was beginning to change. He knew what was happening... knew he could stop it if he wanted to. But this time he was determined to make his presence felt... whatever the consequences.

He tried to let the energy build slowly, but failed, realizing it would have to come at once... riding on an upsurge of his anger. So he closed his eyes and allowed Heberdeans to envelope him in its current evil and all the terrible things he had seen there. The atmosphere in the cellar began to feel heavy and charged; Oliver always likened this stage to the coming of a summer storm.

Suddenly, the floor seemed to lurch sideways, knocking him backwards. He heard a scream as the walls leaned inwards and the ceiling sagged like a water filled balloon. Rebecca was on her feet, arms outstretched in panic.

"It's all right," he shouted, struggling to reach her. "It's only an illusion."

Yet, for the briefest moment, before they were thrown apart again... he could have sworn he felt the touch of her hand against his arm.

*

Oliver was totally stunned. So much so, that all activity ceased abruptly.

Footsteps thundered on the stairs. Bolts were drawn and the door flew open, crashing back against the wall. Oliver glanced round and breathed a sigh of relief. The cellar had stopped shifting and Rebecca had returned to her bed.

"What's going on down here?" Flowers bristling figure filled the doorway, a three branched candelabra throwing a pool of light across the floor.

"N... Nothing... sir." Rebecca's voice sounded suitably startled by his arrival.

"Hmm! Nothing begets nothing," he snorted angrily. "So there'll be no supper for you, my girl."

The door slammed. Eventually silence descended once more.

Oliver whistled. Whatever he had done, Flowers had felt it too. Nothing on this scale had happened before. He stared hard at the shaken girl... wondering. She seemed calm enough now, almost resigned in her posture.

"Rebecca?" he whispered. Was that the faintest flicker of response? He repeated her name again... louder.

"I heard you the first time."

Oliver almost dropped through the floor.

"Are you real?" Rebecca questioned, "or are you some sort of familiar, sent by this man to torment me?"

Oliver sniggered. He had never thought of himself like that.

"I'm just a seven-year-old ghost who's trying to help you," he explained.

Rebecca lapsed into a long silence. This clearly hadn't been the answer she expected. Carefully, she brought her legs round and lay back on the bed, hugging the cotton shift to her knees.

"Then you are not a test... to trap me?"

He didn't know how to answer that.

"You see... I've always heard voices that others cannot hear... and because of that some consider my blindness to be the mark of the devil."

Again Oliver didn't know what to say.

"Are you still there, boy?"

"Yes."

"Mother Superior has faith in me, but Sister Verona, my guardian's niece, believes I consult with demons. What do you think?"

He hesitated.

"I don't know."

"Don't know a lot... do you?"

Oliver bristled.

"I wasn't around long enough to get much schooling."

"I guess not," Rebecca sighed. "I'm sorry! What did you do to this room?" she asked, changing the subject.

"I was trying to attract your attention." Suddenly he felt stupid.

Rebecca actually laughed. He decided he liked the sound.

"I think you succeeded, don't you? What's your name?"

"Ollie... Oliver."

"That's a good, strong name." She licked dry lips. "I don't suppose you could conjure up some water?"

"Sorry, can't do that." He hated to disappoint her. "No need... you see."

"Never mind, Oliver."

He liked the way she said his name.

"Come and sit by me." Rebecca patted the pallet beside her. "There are things we should talk about."

*

And talk they did, through the long dark hours.

For the first time in fifty years, Oliver had a reason not to return to his attic; and for him the experience was like being born again. He was captivated by Rebecca... fascinated by the sound of her voice, the colour of her hair, the way her nose turned up slightly and most particularly he loved her eyes, so unbelievably brimming with life for someone who had never looked upon the world of men.

Rebecca laughingly admitted that although she couldn't see him, the sound of his voice did conjure a picture in her minds eye... a remarkably accurate one as it turned out. Her description reminded Oliver what it had felt like to blush and he had wriggled self consciously down alongside her, kicking ineffectually at the filthy blanket. Constantly, as they talked, his colourless shade brushed against her on the narrow bed... but for Oliver that first feeling of contact was never repeated; and if Rebecca sensed anything, she remained silent about it.

Oliver told her of his own short life, quickly skipping over his manner of passing, to relate amusing and unusual incidents about families who had since come to share his home with him. Rebecca considered him justified in still looking on Heberdeans as his own; after all, where else would he go?

Where indeed, Oliver thought, a little sadly.

Rebecca explained how her parents, both now deceased, had been landed gentry in a place called Yorkshire. When she came of age, she would inherit considerable wealth, all of which would go to the convent once she had finished her schooling. However, if Phips succeeded in proving she was of an unsound mind or consorted with demons, the funds would fall into his hands. Sister Verona, her guardian's niece, would be proved right... Mother Superior would turn against her and she would never be allowed to take her vows. Everything rested on what happened at Heberdeans; which brought them back to the unavoidable present.

Oliver just knew he was *meant* to help in some way... and said as much.

"Tell me about Flowers and that Twain woman," Rebecca urged, her voice harsh with thirst. "Don't leave anything out."

Gradually, as daylight filtered through the high grill, a plan began to fall in place. Two things were required of Oliver; to chaperon Rebecca when Flowers or Mrs Twain were present and, perhaps more difficult, somehow learn to control the unpredictable energy that flowed from him. This, he decided, could only be practised in the attic, to prevent drawing undue attention to the girl.

As Rebecca finally slept, Oliver was already wondering what would become of him when his new friend walked free from Heberdeans.

*

Rebecca's term of 'correction' started at six p.m. that morning.

Oliver was still in the cellar when Mrs Twain arrived to administer another ice-cold sponge bath, which Rebecca bore with the same quiet fortitude as before. To save mutual embarrassment, Oliver had turned his back until she donned her rough smock. Rebecca was then presented with a lukewarm bowl of gruel, for which she smiled and thanked Mrs Twain with considerable enthusiasm, remarking that, "A slice of Mr Flowers' game pie would go down well with this." Mrs Twain was about to leave.

"What's tha' you say, girl?"

"Why, the game pie, Mrs Twain." Rebecca focused directly where Oliver told her too. "Like the one you pass out to your brother every Thursday evening."

The Housekeeper's countenance became ever redder than usual.

"How'd you know?" She broke off and studied the girl suspiciously. "Where'd ya get such a wicked idea?" she bristled, crossing her massive arms and gathering in her ample breasts. "Mr Flowers shall hear of this, my girl." She snatched the bowl from Rebecca's grasp and headed for the door.

Oliver giggled. They both knew Flowers would hear of no such thing.

"You've forgotten your candle," Rebecca reminded her, once again following Oliver's guidance.

Mrs Twain stopped in her tracks and turned as though stung. Clearly troubled, she came back to the bedside and picked up the candleholder, which Oliver noticed trembled in her grasp. She leant forward and studied Rebecca closely, her bloodshot eyes never leaving the girl's face as she passed the candle back and forth, her ravaged face consumed with spite. Long seconds passed.

"Huh!" was all she could find to say; where words failed her however, actions obviously didn't and she brought her hand hard across Rebecca's face, knocking her sideways across the pallet. "Don't mess with me, girl." Mrs Twain backed out, slamming the door behind her.

Distraught, Oliver sat beside Rebecca as she righted herself, fighting back tears as she rubbed the red weald on her cheek, the second in as many days. They had both known this would happen; that Rebecca alone would have to bear the brunt of their malevolence. They also knew it could get worse before she won through and Oliver suddenly became frightened, fearful at the cost of his friend's freedom.

Rebecca had only managed two mouthfuls of gruel and as the morning advanced, began to suffer seriously from thirst. In this situation, Oliver felt totally inadequate, wishing he could somehow bring her something and once again the anger and frustration began to build in him. When the pallet bed suddenly bucked beneath them, Rebecca laughingly suggested he take the opportunity to go and practice in the attic.

Reluctantly Oliver agreed, simply because he knew she was right. The attic no longer held any draw for him. It was just an empty place, with a trunk full of memories. Heberdeans didn't feel like *his* home anymore. Once again he wondered what he would do when Rebecca left; broken in spirit or not, the day would have to come. It all seemed so unfair.

Suddenly he felt as though he wanted to bring the house crashing down around his ears. Fifty years of restraint and loneliness left him in a wild rush that hammered into the walls of his prison and sent them tumbling away from him in a creaking, groaning mass of wood and brick. He knew it was all illusion, but it felt good as sunlight poured in and the stale air was swept away on a cleansing, summer breeze. Bird song and the scent of flowers enveloped him in a halo of childhood memories and for the briefest moment he heard his mother's voice and the sound of childish laughter... of Clara calling to him.

Then another sound reached him; a high-pitched scream he recognized as Rebecca's voice.

*

Flowers had raised his cane for the third time when Oliver came bursting through the cellar wall, carrying with him a residue of energy that knocked the bully off his feet and sent him sliding across the grimy floorboards. He gave a startled grunt as his head met the skirting board with a resounding crack, rolled partly onto his side and then lay still, groaning softly.

Oliver clambered to his feet.

"Oops!" He grinned sheepishly at Rebecca, who was shakily gathering her torn shift about her shoulders, not quickly enough though, to prevent him seeing the raised welts against the whiteness of her skin.

He glared at Flowers, feeling both angry and elated. Talk about attracting unwanted attention; the incredible thing was, once again he had sensed the contact, albeit fleeting. So much for illusion!

Flowers was beginning to gather his wits and was pulling himself upright, one eye masked by his thick mane of hair, the other staring murderously at Rebecca, as though he believed the girl had actually dared to strike him.

"The door's still open," Oliver informed her urgently. "Go!" Rebecca took a faltering step in the wrong direction.

"I can't."

"I'll talk you through it," he promised.

Flower's was reaching for his cane.

"I'm afraid."

"So ya should be, my girl." Mrs Twain's large figure now blocked the way to freedom. "Honest folk don't take kindly ta witches."

Oliver saw Rebecca's shoulders straighten indignantly.

"I am *NOT* a Witch," she stated firmly.

"Try telling Mr Flowers 'tha," Mrs Twain sneered, taking in his dishevelled figure. She hurried to his side and bending awkwardly, attempted to raise him up, but his boots slipped on the floorboards and he dragged her heavily down on top of him. There followed an embarrassing disentangling of limbs, during which Flowers twice lost his cane and on the second occasion elbowed Mrs Twain in the ear while retrieving it.

Had the situation not been deadly serious, Oliver would have considered this the most amusing scene he had ever witnessed. Yet at the same time, his heart went out to Rebecca, who remained motionless at his side, awaiting the inevitable return of their attention.

Eventually Flowers steadied himself sufficiently to relinquish his grasp of his housekeeper's ample bosom.

"I told ya she were evil," Mrs Twain gasped, straightening her mobcap. "Send fer Phips. We knows enough."

"May I remind you, Mrs Twain, who runs this establishment?" Flowers flicked back his hair and tugged at the points of his waistcoat with his free hand. "Evidence we may have... but I have not yet broken this girl." He sliced the air before him with the thin birching cane. "And break her I shall." Despite the return of his dictatorial manner, the end of this statement brought him considerably nearer the door than the beginning had seen him. Without so much as a backward glance, he was gone, his footsteps pounding up the stairs.

Finding herself alone, Mrs Twain seemed uncertain what to do with herself. Cautiously, she took a step towards the girl; Oliver advised Rebecca to take a corresponding pace backwards, which seemed to visibly unsettle the woman.

"Mrs Twain?" Oliver heard Rebecca take a deep, steadying breath. "Does Mr Flowers know of the silverware you conceal at the back of your bureau?"

The housekeeper pursed thin lips.

"I warned ya not to play games 'wi me, girl." Her powerful hands clenched in readiness to strike out.

"We both know this is not a game. Speak up for me against Mr Phips and you shall benefit by more than a few pieces of silver."

The women's heavy lidded gaze narrowed.

"An… if I don't?"

Her stale breath hung in the air between them.

"Then Mr Flowers shall know of your dishonesty," Rebecca assured her. "No doubt a simple search of your rooms would prove me right."

"Hmm!" Twain surprised Oliver by merely turning her broad back on the girl.

"I'm sure your brother wouldn't want you to go to prison again…" The door slammed against her words, leaving Rebecca trembling, but with a certain sense of satisfaction.

*

"You have to get away," Oliver insisted, full of admiration for his blind friend's strength of character. He wondered if all girls were as brave as this in the outside world.

"It's not that easy."

"I'll help you."

"I know you will. But if I run from Heberdeans Phips and his niece will have been proved right and I could never go back to the convent. I'd not only be loosing my vocation… but my home. I *have* to face my accusers and prove them wrong."

Oliver tried a different approach.

"Why was Flowers beating you?"

"Apparently three strokes of his cane starts his morning class of correction." Rebecca visibly shuddered. "God knows what would have come next if you hadn't intervened."

Oliver felt himself blushing, if that was at all possible.

"You know, Rebecca, our plan isn't working. I hate to say this, but either Flowers will break your spirit... or Twain will murder you in your sleep." Oliver saw Rebecca blanch and regretted his bluntness, although he knew he was right.

"We'll just have to hope I can hold out... and that Twain's greed is greater than her fear of Flowers or the law."

*

It was well past midday before they heard approaching footsteps and the bolts being drawn back. The door opened only wide enough for a wooden tray to be pushed through and immediately closed again. Oliver thought he recognized Twain's thick, stubby fingers.

Water, a chunk of stale bread and some cold cuts of beef... for Rebecca a veritable feast and as she set to, they both wondered if the meal was on Flower's instructions, or the housekeeper's first step towards capitulation.

Neither of them stopped to wonder if the food might have been poisoned.

*

The answer was to come within the hour.

They had been discussing how Oliver's energy release was becoming more actual and less illusory, when Rebecca suddenly groaned and doubled up. The bed began to shake with her convulsions and within seconds a white froth appeared at the corners of her mouth.

Even as he watched, dumfounded, Oliver saw her eyes roll up into her head and he reacted in the only way he knew how, by letting the energy flow from him in one long scream of anguish that vibrated through the walls and rocked the very foundations of Heberdeans.

It wasn't long before Flowers rushed into the cellar with Mrs Twain huffing behind him. He took one look at the girl and the discarded tray and rounded on the housekeeper.

"You stupid woman... what have you done?"

Mrs Twain looked genuinely frightened.

"It were only cold cuts..."

"For your sake it had better 'ave been." His eyes burned into her. "Anything more and we'll both swing for it. Go and get that fool Phips and fetch Dr Belcher; he knows how to keep his mouth shut."

Red faced, Mrs Twain fled from his presence.

"And don't bother to come back if you're alone," he announced in a great voice that echoed after her.

Oliver could only look on as Flowers paced the cellar, pausing only to mutter over the girl and once to kick the food tray out of sight under the bed. He never once touched his charge, which continued to writhe and thrash about with such force Oliver feared she would suffer further harm, if that were at all possible.

The wait seemed endless and just when Oliver began to fear help would never come, he heard hurried footsteps overhead and then on the stairs outside.

"Mother Superior!" Flowers gasped as two nuns swept into the cellar, the first Oliver had ever seen at close quarters. "I don't understand... I sent for Mr Phips and Dr Belcher..."

The tallest of the pair gave him a cursory glance.

"Mr Phips' gardener sent your messenger on to the convent, where Mr Phips was visiting Sister Verona..." Her eyebrows lifted. "A far too common occurrence of late, which I shall be looking into. Under the circumstances, I decided to visit your 'House of Correction' myself. As for Dr Belcher," she gave what sounded to Oliver like a snort of derision, "Sister Theresa is far more practised in dealing with Rebecca's fits."

"Fits?" Flowers repeated, his mouth hanging open.

Mother Superior fixed him with steely blue eyes.

"The child is prone to seizures when emotionally distressed, particularly after a long period of fasting." She appeared to take in her surroundings for the first time. "Is this your sick room?" Her tone echoed the disgust she felt. "Where is the dormitory? And the other pupils?"

Flowers coloured critically.

"My term has just started," he explained. "Rebecca is the first to arrive..."

"And shall be the first to leave."

"But... but fees have been paid... in advance," he blustered, "and cannot be returned."

"That is between yourself and Mr Phips. Understand, Mr Flowers... I find your methods and motives highly irregular."

"With due respect, madam," Flowers drew himself up to his full diminutive height. His veined nose twitched arrogantly. "I don't see what it has to do..."

"Now is *not* the time for discussion." She gave a firm nod of dismissal, one she was clearly used to having obeyed. "You will permit us to continue." It was not meant to be a question.

"Yes." Flowers backed towards the door. "Yes... of course." He disappeared, bellowing for Mrs Twain, the sound of his voice preceding him through the house.

As far as Oliver could tell, Flowers received no response from his housekeeper, although he wasn't really listening. He was totally mesmerized by the Mother Superior... by the sound of her voice and the gentle, dignified way she moved; seeming to dispense authority, yet understanding with the simplest glance.

"How is the child?" Mother Superior knelt beside Sister Theresa and Oliver cautiously sandwiched himself between them. All three considered the still figure on the pallet.

"It seems she has already slipped into her restorative sleep. Other than these..." Sister Theresa pulled aside the torn shift to display the marks on Rebecca's shoulder, "probably sustained during her convulsions... I doubt there's any harm done."

Mother Superior gave a sigh of relief, which Oliver echoed.

"Then we must remain while she rests and escort her back to the convent when she awakens."

"No!" Oliver gasped, unable to prevent himself. "I don't want her to go." Of course his words fell on deaf ears; he knew he was speaking against the inevitable.

"Not yet..." he added forlornly. He was being selfish, but he couldn't bear the thought of returning to his attic, trapped in Heberdeans with Flowers and his wicked accomplices. Ironically, he couldn't even wish himself dead.

With a supreme effort he managed to suppress the emotions building within him. He didn't want to frighten these good people away... to leave Heberdeans a second before they had to.

Sadly, he knelt and watched Rebecca's face for the first sign's of wakefulness that would take her from him.

*

"Mother Superior... if I may be permitted to ask you something?" Sister Theresa broke off, tutting over the filthy blanket she was forced to tuck round her patient. "Your compassion is renowned and I understand your concern for Rebecca's well-being, yet... I sensed you had another purpose for coming here today. Is that so?"

Mother Superior actually laughed. It was an unexpectedly soft, tinkling sound that sent a shiver of pleasure down Oliver's spine and carried with it an odd sense of familiarity.

"Astute as ever, Sister Theresa," Mother Superior accused, although not unkindly.

The younger nun flushed beneath her wimple.

"But you are correct," she admitted. "I used to live here."

Oliver's ears pricked up. Surely, he would have remembered a woman of such presence.

"I was only a child at the time... around fifty years ago."

He sat transfixed as Mother Superior told Oliver's own sad story and then the tale of a young girl named Clara, driven to a life of penance by the death of her twin brother.

CLARA!

Could it be true? Oliver was beside himself. He didn't know what to do first... to suppress the energy rising in him or to hug his long lost sister. Wait until Rebecca knew; she would be so pleased for him. Suddenly, he wanted her to wake up as soon as possible.

By the time Clara finished, Oliver was sitting on his sister's knee and Rebecca was awakening to the presence of her rescuers. Explanations were exchanged while Oliver fidgeted around, eager to tell his own news. But before he knew it, they were all on their feet and Rebecca was being helped up the stairs.

"Rebecca! Clara! Please... wait!" Oliver called after them, his young voice breaking with emotion.

Rebecca heard him and pulled back a step.

"What ever am I thinking off," she said. "We can't go without Oliver."

Clara swayed and put a hand to the wall, deathly pale.

"Oliver! What do you know of Oliver?"

"He's the little boy in the attic..."

"Wicked girl," Sister Theresa snapped. "Mother Superior, can you not see... Rebecca must have been listening when we thought she was asleep."

Oliver noticed Clara didn't look convinced, either way.

"Is Ollie... Oliver with us now?" she asked, her voice all a tremor.

"Yes," Rebecca said, without hesitation.

"Tell her the trunk's still in the attic," Oliver instructed. He was on the stairs ahead of them now, as though in some way he might prevent their leaving.

Rebecca relayed the message.

"Both of you... wait for me outside. Call the authorities if Flowers tries to follow you." Clara's right hand sought the rosary at her breast. "There's something I have to do that's long overdue."

*

The climb to the attic was more strenuous than Clara recalled, making her realize how the years had taken their toll.

She couldn't know it, but Oliver matched her step all the way, chattering excitedly about past times and adventures they had shared together. He knew she couldn't hear him, but it felt good all the same. The old anger and frustration seemed to be falling away from him.

They reached the sloping door and Oliver let Clara go first, watching as she stooped hesitantly on the threshold before striding boldly into the middle of the room, as though finally prepared to confront the demons that had haunted her for half a century.

She stepped into a patch of sunlight and slowly pivoted on the spot until her gaze fell on the trunk. Oliver heard a sob escape from her as she softly crossed the bare boards and laid a hand on the curved lid.

"Ollie... I'm so very, very sorry," she whispered. "Can you ever forgive me?"

He couldn't see her face, but she still sounded like the sister he remembered, apologizing for some childish disagreement. Gently, she released the hook and eye and lifted the lid. He knew then that she was crying as she ran her hand round the quilted interior. Quickly he went to her side as she sank to her knees.

Clara's once serene face was now a mask of tears. She rocked back and forth, repeating his name over and over, her left hand clutching the side of the trunk, while the other still fretted with her rosary.

Amidst a sea of emotion, Oliver felt incredibly calm as he let the energy build, this time out of love and compassion instead of anger. The change in the atmosphere seemed subtler and it was obvious Clara was too distraught to notice, so he concentrated harder, placing his small hands on the rim of the trunk.

Sooner than he expected, Oliver felt the wood begin to vibrate gently. He stepped up his efforts until Clara broke off mid-sob and pulled her hand away as though stung. Then she eagerly reached out again... and smiled as contact was renewed.

"Is that really you?"

Carefully, he removed one hand and placed it on her shoulder, stunned to feel material and certain warmth. Clara must have sensed it too, for she quickly laid her own hand over his, increasing the sense of union for the merest second before it was gone completely. Wiping tears from her cheeks, she sat back and stared at the trunk and even as she watched, Oliver managed to slowly bring the lid down.

"Thank you, Ollie." Her words were almost a sigh, torn as she was between sadness and elation. Automatically, she reached out and closed the hook and eye, just as they had done for each other many times before.

She stood up then, brushing the dust of ages from her habit, making her intentions clear as she took one last look round. Panic stricken, Oliver hurried after her, realizing he could no longer delay their moment of parting.

The house was silent. Flowers and Mrs Twain were conspicuous by their absence and Clara's departure went unchallenged; as she also hoped her colleagues had been. But she was determined that would not be the end of the matter. As Mother Superior, Clara was determined to use her influence to see Heberdeans closed as a 'House of Correction'.

Outside in the sunshine, Oliver skipped noiselessly beside his sister as she crunched down the gravel path, looking out for the others. He stopped abruptly at the great wrought iron gate, disappointed to see Sister Theresa had already guided Rebecca across the road, well beyond the garden perimeter.

By the time Clara joined them, Oliver noticed she had regained her poised manner and was once more their Mother Superior. She said something to them both and all three faced Heberdeans, making a slight obeisance.

"Goodbye, Rebecca! Clara!" he shouted. "Come and see me some time," he added. He knew it would never happen, but it helped him to say it, anyway.

Rebecca was the last to turn away and as she did so, Oliver recalled that first moment, when she appeared to look up at his attic window and he had lost himself in those wonderful eyes. He swallowed hard, knowing in the endless, empty years ahead, he would never forget her.

He continued to wave until all three were almost out of sight, leaning forward in order to catch the last glimpse of them as they turned the corner of the road. Then, before he knew it... he found himself lying face down on the pavement outside.

"Ouch!" he said, although he hadn't felt anything... except surprise.

Cautiously, he rolled onto his back and formally tested each limb, like someone who had fallen from a great height and feared the worst. Then he sat up, feeling none of the expected nausea and distress he associated with straying too far from the house.

He stood and backed into the road. The further he went, the more Heberdeans looked just like one building in a row of many others and he began to wonder if, like his sister, the house no longer had a hold over him... as if between them they had sprung his prison door.

Without a moment's hesitation, he turned and began to run... faster and faster, excitement lending him speed over unfamiliar ground.

Rebecca and Clara were out there somewhere... and so was a whole new world, the like of which he had never seen before.

THE SOUL EATER

1285 - Sherwood Forest, Nottingham

Father Thomas was lost. He should have reached Nottingham before nightfall. Now the city gates would be closed against him and the watch unlikely to open up for a mere hedge priest. Hopefully he might find a postern gate, but first he had to find the city.

The path was beginning to peter out and was now nothing more than a dirt track, with scrub closing in on either side. The last travellers had passed him a long way back, both in distance and time; a young knight with his squire in attendance and a flaxen haired maid on a gentle, soft mouthed Palfrey.

He must have missed the turn off. He leaned firmly on his staff and studied the way ahead. The setting sun cast his shadow before him, distorted by the broken ground. He could see and hear nothing; too late in the day for all but the most foolhardy of travellers and too early for creatures of the night. He raked the ground with the tip of his staff. The earth was soft, still moist from the morning's rainfall, but there were no hoof prints or cart ruts to show others had passed this way.

He sighed and sent up a prayer for guidance, wondering why the god who granted him a vocation and stamina to wander the length and breadth of this land hadn't also endowed him with a good nose for direction. He unhooked the wine skin from the rope round his waist and took a thoughtful sip. Come morning, he'd probably be forced to drink the phial of holy water he'd carried in his pouch all the way from the shrine of Saint Thomas a Becket in Canterbury.

The way he saw it, he had no choice but to turn back. If the path still eluded him, he would climb a tree and sleep until dawn.

He had retraced but a few steps, when the sensation of being watched caused him to turn abruptly. Nothing, yet from years of experience travelling these roads, his tingling spine told him he was not alone. Cautiously, his right hand dropped to the Welsh stabbing-dagger at his belt; a legacy from a wild, misspent youth. He knew the forest hereabouts to be full of outlaws, but wolfsheads usually allowed poor priests to pass by, unless called upon to shrive one of their numbers.

"Father."

Spoken softly, the single word reached him easily on the still, moist air. Urgently, his blue eyes scanned the path on either side. The sun was down and heavy clouds obscured the full moon. Darkness hung over the forest like a shroud.

"Father!"

This time there was a note of urgency.

"Who speaks my name?" he demanded in a strident voice, designed to mask his own fear. Beneath his cassock his heart beat wildly as he recalled tales of night-hags and demons who ensnared the unwary. Dagger half drawn, his hand went to the plain wooden cross on a thong about his neck. "God protect this simple sinner," he prayed.

Ahead of him, shadows moved where none should have been. The darkness seemed to fold in on itself, as though consumed by some great advancing maw.

"Jesu," he muttered, swiftly blessing himself and taking an abrupt step backwards. He sensed, rather than felt a touch on his sleeve and spun round, dagger drawn.

"Devil's teeth!"

The young boy stared hollow eyes at the long blade.

Of a sudden, moonlight cut a swath through the woods. Like a welcome beacon sent from God, Thomas used it to check the path in both directions... and shivered.

"Where did you come from?" he demanded.

The boy said nothing.

Thomas sheathed his dagger and the green, almost feline eyes shifted to meet his own. He judged the lad to be barely seven summers and in need of a good meal and a bath. Skinny arms and legs jutted from a rough sacking smock, tied at the waist with a frayed piece of rope.

He steeled his nerves long enough to sketch a blessing.

"I asked you where you came from, lad?"

The boy pointed west, back the way the priest had come.

"I am Father Thomas. And what is your name?"

"Fox."

"Do you wish me to accompany you?"

Fox nodded.

Thomas smiled, showing white, even teeth. Other than remaining on this path like some moonstruck fool, he had little option but to follow the lad. By the look of him, his parents might welcome a coin in return for a night's lodging.

"Lead the way."

Fox slipped a warm, calloused hand into his own and led him gently back a hundred yards or so before branching off into the forest proper. The track, if indeed there was one, was single file and Fox bounded on ahead, yet never once out of sight of the good father who stumbled uncomplaining after him, despite the bracken that snagged his cassock and lacerated his unprotected calves and ankles.

Fox abruptly stopped and waited as Thomas stepped cautiously into the small clearing. Moonlight filtered through the overhanging branches, silvering the sparse grass and hard, impacted earth surrounding what appeared to be a charcoal burners' hut.

Thomas starred around at the conical, turf-covered mounds of logs. No scent of wood smoke hung on the air... just the smell of decay and the damp odour of the forest floor. Fox pointed at the hut, which looked equally abandoned. A corner of the roof had caved in and the hide door stood open to the elements.

He hesitated.

There was something wrong here... a feeling that went deeper than mere desolation. Had he been alone, he would rather have slipped back into the woods and taken his chances with the outlaws. But Fox was still jabbing a grubby finger towards the cabin. He began hoping frantically from one foot to the other.

"Ok, lad." Thomas placed a hand on the boy's head, almost in a gesture of absolution. Then he ruffled the matted blond hair. "Come on then."

Halfway across the clearing he realized Fox was no longer at his side. The boy stood his ground, shaking his head, his eyes now looked dark and cavernous, as though he was terrified by someone or something within the hut. Automatically, Thomas reached into his pouch and tossed a coin to Fox. The lad caught it and was gone in a blink of an eye.

Thomas swiftly scanned the glade, checking for any sign of habitation he might have missed earlier. With Fox's departure his own sense of unease increased, yet there seemed no visible threat.

Cautiously he approached the cabin's single, unshuttered window, unable to see anything but a dark, empty shell. He wondered if he should return at daybreak; or bother to come back at all? Then he recalled the fear in Fox's eyes and wondered if this had once been his home... his refuge and if so, what had driven him to run wild in the forest. He backed off and skirted a pile of overgrown logs, attempting to still the trembling in his limbs as he approached the open door.

"Blessed Father," he breathed. "You *must* know I also am full of fear. I do not question but merely..."

A rasping moan sent his hand reaching for his dagger... only to grasp an empty sheath. With a sinking heart he realized the knife must have been lost as he stumbled after the boy. The sound came again, this time more like a man in agony than any imagined soul in torment. With renewed determination, born of his sworn vocation, Thomas stepped into the musty interior.

A shaft of moonlight pierced the ruined roof and picked out the beaten earth floor and a broken, upturned stool. The cabin was larger than he expected, clearly extending back under the shelter of the trees and in the far wall was another door, beneath which he caught the faintest flicker of candlelight.

This time he heard an unmistakable gasp, followed by a faint rustle. A bench or floorboard creaked and then all became still. Outside a night owl screeched. He reached out, brushing long fingers over the rough boards. His hand settled on a wooden latch.

"Come in, *Priest!*"

Thomas froze.

"What are you... waiting f...or?" Although laced with pain, the harsh, guttural voice managed to convey a note of mockery. "Frightened of a... dying man," the taunt faded in a bubbling cough.

Unaccountably, Thomas recalled the words of his own father confessor. 'No matter what sins he has committed in life... no man should die outside God's Covenant.' He raised the latch and gagged at the smell of corruption that engulfed him. Covering his mouth, he squinted into the dim, smoky interior.

A figure lay on the pallet bed, covered with a filthy blanket. Only head and shoulders were visible and one wasted arm, folded across the sunken chest. This fellow once stood tall, Thomas reflected, noticing the long boned feet hanging over the edge of the straw mattress. Cautiously, he stepped closer and almost recoiled at the baleful brilliance of the sunken eyes. He gave the sign.

"Bless you, my son," he intoned, determined to see this through.

The man's expression never changed. His nostrils remained distended, thin lips drawn back, rotting teeth clamped against the pain. Only the eyes shifted, watching him guardedly, appearing to change colour in the flickering candlelight.

"I knew... you would come," he gasped, his fingers fretting with the blanket.

Thomas smiled in acknowledgment.

"You sent your son to find a priest."

The man's lips curled, but he said nothing.

"I am Father Thomas. What is your name?"

Again silence, although the eyes watched as he trimmed the spluttering candle with his fingernail and pulled a rickety stool to the bedside. He sat... allowing his cross to swing forward and settle comfortably between his palms.

"My name is Legion... for we are many!" The man hissed the words, as though intending to shock. His corrupted breath hung in the stale air between them.

Thomas' expression remained impassive.

"You know your script, my son. Were you once a priest... or perhaps a lay brother?"

Something akin to laughter rattled in the man's throat. A line of pink spittle dribbled to the mattress.

"I've been many things."

Thomas bowed his head before the fanatical gaze.

"Then perhaps I should hear your confession, my son."

"Indeed!" The concealed arm shot out from beneath the blanket, gnarled fingers grasping the hem of his cassock. "What would you hear first... Priest? Of the boys I've sodomised?" The clammy hand brushed Thomas' knee. "Of worthless lives snuffed out... of blood that has sustained me...?" Head and shoulders lifted with the effort to spit out the words. "Of a soul no longer... mine..." He fell back again in a paroxysm of coughing. His eyes momentarily closed. His left hand held fast to the brown woollen robe.

Despite his revulsion, Thomas leaned forward to place emphasize on his words,

"You must return to the path of righteousness. Understand, my son. God's forgiveness is infinite."

The disturbing eyes locked with his again, seemingly at first red and then becoming flecked with gold.

"Will... your God fight for... for my soul?"

"Yes. If you open your heart and let him in."

Thomas sensed his answer gave some satisfaction.

"Would *you*... fight for me?"

He nodded, the thought filling him with apprehension.

"Will you die for me, Father?" Against all odds, the man struggled into a sitting position. The blanket fell from his ravaged body. "Will you die for me?" he asked again, his voice seemingly growing stronger, "so that I may live?"

Thomas swallowed, fighting for physical and mental control.

"The scriptures tell us..."

"A piss on your scriptures, Priest. Can you not see what is happening her?

Thomas gaped, open-mouthed.

"Why do you believe I sent the wretched child?"

"To shrive a dying man."

The man laughed, the sound heavy with phlegm and blood.

"Then prepare to shrive thyself!"

Thomas tried to stand, but his legs refused to respond.

"Why don't you run, little worm?" the man taunted, knowing it was already too late. He swung his own legs round and planted his large feet squarely before the priest. "What will you do when the candle gutters and dies? Sit here in the dark and pray that *your* God will save you?"

Thomas struggled to raise his cross, but his arms felt like lead and the polished wood slipped through his fingers. His temples began to throb and he could feel a terrible pressure at the back of his head, as though an invisible force was crushing his skull.

"Behold *Priest*!" Effortlessly, the man rose from his pallet, towering over him. "Know *you* that I am an Eater of Souls." He placed calloused hands on the priest's shoulders and Thomas cried out as ice-cold fire lanced through his body. "My kind were ancient before your weak, snivelling God ever walked this earth."

Their combined weight caused the stool to rock backwards and both men tumbled to the earthen floor. Drooling with anticipation, the man squatted over him and placed one hand on the front of his cassock. Thomas felt his wildly beating heart flutter like a trapped bird.

"No! Damn you!" he cried, his sandals thudding against the bed frame, fingers digging vainly in the dust for leverage. His surroundings began to blur.

Fox suddenly materialized beside them and Thomas felt something heavy pressed into his hand... even as the boy was sent crashing back against the wall. Summoning every ounce of his fading strength, Thomas thrust the Welsh dagger upwards. The man screamed and jerked back on his heels, clawing at the knife embedded in his scrawny side.

The priest scrabbled backwards towards Fox. The abomination leered across at them and began to withdraw the blade. Frantically, Thomas fumbled in his pouch for the phial of holy water, biting through the wax seal. The candle at the bedside guttered and died, plunging the chamber into darkness.

"Can you move, lad?" The ragged form stirred beside him.

"Yes."

"Then go... do not look back."

Fox required no further bidding. The latch rattled and he was gone.

Thomas listened. He could hear nothing but the blood pounding in his ears. Had his blow been more decisive than he thought... was the creature dead?

"No *Priest!*" The answer came out of the darkness, like his worst nightmare. "I can see you... little worm. And I can smell your fear."

Thomas heard a dry scuffling and pulled his knees up as something brushed his left foot. Two yellow orbs blinked in front of him as the man hawked and spat. Thomas flinched as thick globules of phlegm struck his face. Seconds later, cold steel scored a line across his throat, stunning him into action.

"Blessed Saint Thomas, protect this poor sinner from evil." His right hand came up, propelling an arc of water through the air.

His next breath took a lifetime to come. Those pitiless eyes, now blood red, returned his gaze and Thomas realized he was looking into the pits of hell... then suddenly they flickered out like a snuffed candle and the screaming started.

The darkness became filled with noise and movement, as of a mortally wounded creature, throwing itself about the chamber. The acrid smell of burning flesh brought him retching to his feet, the empty phial crushed underfoot as he fumbled for the door. The blade sliced his shoulder as the creature rushed past him, out of control in its blind haste to escape the agony that consumed it.

For once, Thomas was grateful for the darkness. He did not wish to witness how God punished the unrighteous.

Fox was waiting at the edge of the clearing as Thomas staggered from the cabin. Behind him the howling reached a gibbering crescendo and then abruptly ceased.

Man and boy faced each other.

"Brave thing you did, lad," Thomas gasped, extending his hand, which the lad ignored.

"He destroyed my mother," Fox said coldly, without a flicker of emotion.

Silently, he led Thomas through the trees to a small brook and left the priest to strip and wash the blood and filth from his body. The slight cut on his neck had already stopped bleeding, but the wound in his shoulder was deep enough to leave a permanent reminder of this day.

By the time he reached, shivering, for his robe, Fox had returned. Thomas was stunned to see the lad had actually gone back and retrieved the dagger, which he now held before him like a miniature sword.

"You can keep it if you wish." He smiled and unhooked the empty sheath from the belt of his cassock. "I think you've more than earned it."

Fox slid the blade into the outstretched scabbard and pressed the weapon back into Thomas's hand, as though the gesture meant nothing to him. Wordlessly he headed back towards he charcoal burner's cottage. Thomas shrugged and wearily followed, suddenly intrigued by the faint glow between the trees.

The cabin was an inferno. Fox stood watching with morbid interest. Thomas came and stood beside him, one hand on the boy's shoulder.

"Thought that was your home?"

"Still is." Fox looked up at him, the reflection of his handiwork turning his green eyes a fiery red.

Automatically Thomas walked forward to extinguish a hot cinder near one of the woodpiles... and froze. There was something damned familiar about that lad's eyes. He recalled what Fox had said about his mother. Could a father not destroy his wife and turn his own child against him?

Like father like son?

His hand hovered near the hilt of his dagger, praying he wouldn't have to use it again... and wondering if this time he really could.

"You know, lad," he began casually, extinguishing the small flame. "Whoever or whatever that creature was... he claimed he sent you out to find me." He recalled how the boy had silently materialized behind him on the forest path. "Is there anything you wish to tell me? In God's good grace... there is always time for confession." He turned.

Fox was gone.

Thomas shivered. After a cursory glance around, he raised his cowl and cautiously picked his way across the clearing.

Before slipping away, he placed a small pouch of coins at the base of a tree – knowing Fox would be watching.

THE WATCHER AT THE GATES

St Bride's Churchyard, 1771

Hugh Pragnall was bored.

Having been a man accustomed to living a full and varied life, to find his self both bored *and* tied to the earth plane seemed an unpardonable waste of time; although time seemed the only commodity left to him now.

"Someone should have warned me," he muttered sourly, as he continued to stomp back and forth between the headstones.

In death, as in life, he cut a bold, upright figure. His grave shift was of the finest linen and those who prepared him for his final rest had taken time to secure his jet hair at the nape of his neck and slip the softest moccasins upon his feet. His newly gained pallor served to enhance the dark, fiery depths of his eyes... his finest feature, or so his beloved Nell, Lady Pragnall, had maintained. A cravat of the finest French lace was gathered at his throat, a concession, not to fashion but an attempt to hide the mark where the lead pistol shot had torn flesh and shattered bone. He thought then of Nell and the child she carried; his child... the last in an illustrious line, established by Sir Hugo De Pragnall in the footsteps of the Conqueror.

Despondently, Hugh settled on what had become his favourite spot... the steps of an ancient mausoleum, the highest point in the graveyard, from where he could survey his domain as he had come to call it. Domain indeed! That had to be the biggest joke his side of hell. It was a month since he had passed over. The trouble was he *had not* actually 'passed'

anywhere! He was still in St Bride's Churchyard, where those faithful to the house of Pragnall had buried him.

He sighed, stretched and resumed his restless pacing, knowing his steps could take him no further than the boundary stones. He had tried countless times to break free; to leap the wall, run at the rusted, sagging gate... even tagging on to a departing group of mourners while one of their own number loitered at the graveside. Nothing worked. Every attempt felt as though he had walked into a brick wall... and was just as painful; so much for the idiots who preached death brought an end to physical pain. He wondered idly how they would feel in his position and finally allowed himself a wry grin... one day, high or low, they would all come to it.

The other chap had warned him what to expect. His predecessor, he guessed you had to call him; all skin and bone with a leering, toothless grin and a laugh like the rustle of dry leaves. The fellow had materialized out of nowhere, frightening the death out of him.

"You're late, guv'nor!"

Hugh was not particularly aware of hanging around after Benjamin Trew's pistol did its damage. He recalled the numbing impact; the sudden rush of pain...

The fellow had thrust a greasy parchment in to his hands. "All pres'nt 'n correct... your job now is ta keep it tha' way." A few basic do's and don'ts and the man had literally faded on the spot. "An don't s'pect me ta come back, niver," he had rasped in Hugh's left ear. "'Cause I ain't." Rustle, as Hugh had instantly dubbed him, had remained true to his word.

The manuscript was a record of internments. Rustle was listed as Nick Farrow. Most disquieting of all was the line drawn beneath the name of Pragnall, followed by a boldly printed 'LAST INTERNMENT'. It appeared no one was scheduled to relieve Hugh of his graveyard watch. Clearly, Rustle had been privy to this information, assuming the fellow could read; no wonder the creepy bastard had been so eager to disappear.

Still muttering under his breath, Hugh changed direction and set out counter clockwise, eyes downcast, his long stride carrying him effortlessly between the headstones.

The unanswerable, unendurable questions that haunted him day and night surged into his mind once more. What had become of Nell? Why had she not been amongst the mourners at his graveside? Unlike him, had she managed to escape their pursuer and make it back to Osterly their home; or had Trew forced her to return to the streets... and if so, what would become of the child? Their child!

Two years ago, Nell, Lady Pragnall had been nothing but a street urchin, until he had taken her under his cloak... literally, as it turned out, for that was where he found her, picking his pocket in the jostling crowd along Newgate Street; an unwashed cutpurse, sweet-faced and as innocent looking as her days were undoubtedly long.

For one of them, it had been love at first sight.

New to the Pragnall inheritance, his blessed mother had died giving him life and his father had been buried these past ten months... instead of dragging the girl off to the authorities at Newgate, Hugh had taken Nell into his home and offered her everything within his means; including the family name, sealed in wedlock before three months had passed. On their betrothal, he proudly presented her with the Pragnall amethyst; a precious stone set in a ring of beaten gold, worn by the female line since the time of the Norman Conquest.

Never, in an age of marital convenience, had he hoped to meet such a match. With every passing day, what could have proved a one sided bond of gratitude, swiftly become one of mutual passion and understanding. Nell had an enticing vulnerability about her, which from the first he found totally enchanting. Life could not have felt more fulfilled when she eventually informed him she was with child.

God! How he had loved her. He still did. He kicked a stray stone and sadly watched its trajectory over the wall, wishing he could so easily gain his freedom.

Blinkered by all that was so good in life, Hugh hardly gave thought to Nell's 'street family'. If only he had not been so blind! It never occurred to him how terrified she was of those indelibly linked to her past, separated as they were from 'Southwark Stews' merely by the thin ribbon of the Thames.

As the weeks passed, and they began to build a life together, Nell became quiet and reclusive, like a beautiful, frightened butterfly, trapped behind the walls of Osterly, rarely venturing forth unless accompanied by Hugh or at least two maidservants. When gently questioned, she begged him to be patient with her; her 'condition' made her wary of mishap. She wanted nothing more than to give him a healthy heir.

If only he had not left it at that! If he had been more vigilant, things could have turned out so different. And it had come upon them so swiftly...

*

...Lady Pragnall stood at the window of the drawing room at Osterly, one small hand resting on a handkerchief of delicate pink chiffon, pined in such a fashion as to conceal her spreading waistline.

Behind her, on the mantelshelf, Westminster chimes marked the fourth hour in the afternoon and the long case clock in the hallway answered back in a deeper voice. Hugh would be home soon, she thought with the usual rush of excitement, marred this day with an uncommon touch of apprehension. The hand that held aside the curtain trembled slightly as she allowed the heavy drapes to fall back into place. She stepped back a pace and faced the beautifully appointed room, her mulberry coloured sack-backed gown rustling about her as she moved towards the hearth.

Frowning at her reflection in the gilt overmantel, she recalled Hugh's voice, as he had gently chastised her the previous evening.

'My dear, a young *Lady* should fill her mind with books and minor household matters, and occupy her hands with such things as needlework and the playing of music. *Never* should she be *seen* to pace the room in agitation or loiter behind curtains in anticipation of events to come.' He had kissed her then, a long, lingering embrace that left her breathless yet longing for more. 'Even if that fortuitous occasion should herald my return.'

The trouble was, she did not feel like a *Lady* and doubted she ever would.

She sighed and turned her back on the powdered and painted doll reflected back at her; seeing a stranger, with pale, elfin features and wide, fawnlike eyes... frightened eyes! She knew she should be grateful for her lot in life. Yet nothing would change the fact beneath the expensive dress and fine undergarments, she was still the ragged street urchin she had been these past fifteen years. The wedding band on her finger and other fine jewellery Hugh had given were not the sole reasons for her love, or even the child she carried. Just recently, she found herself wishing they'd met under different circumstances, that he had not been of the gentry; class would be their downfall... she sensed that deeply.

Already the past was coming back to haunt her in the name of Benjamin Trew, her street father - although whether there was any blood tie she knew not and cared even less. Only once, in a drunken stupor, had he tried to take her by force, having cornered her in a blind alleyway behind the gin shops of Tooley Street, in Bermondsey. She would never forget the crushing weight of his powerful body, his stale, gin sodden breath, and the peculiar odour of sweat and death he carried proudly, like a badge of office. Terrifyingly aware of his brutal reputation, she had fought like a wildcat, scratching and biting. Loud indeed must have been her cries, to attract the attention of passers-by in an area where rape and murder was commonplace. No man present who valued his own life had dared intervene; yet Trew had backed off, bloodied, but not bowed; his notoriety and control depended largely on his street credit. Time would tell. No one held the upper hand with Benjamin Trew for long.

Since that time she had slept with a knife at her side, aware he was always watching, waiting... giving him no reason for confrontation by ensuring she never brought *less* than her quota to Aggie's gin shop by nightfall. Best cutpurse in the Southwark stews, or so she had thought, until she had tried it on with Lord Hugh Pragnall. She smiled at the memory. He could have taken her to the thief-taker; instead, he had taken her as his wife.

Now, here she was; Lady Pragnall, in possession of a beautiful home, with child by a loving husband and in danger of losing everything if she did not do what Trew demanded; and could still end up as gallows' bait if she did. What a choice! To steal from the man she loved or forfeit his life and probably her own. She had considered warning Hugh, but he was not the kind to skulk behind doors. He would insist on facing up to whatever came. She knew the way of it. It would not take much... a moment's jostling in London's narrow byways and a blade would find its mark; she had witnessed it many times already in her short life.

She wondered if Hugh already had his suspicions, being convinced he had overheard her recent conversation with one very frightened kitchen maid; it seemed Trew was prepared to use any means to get to her... even her household was under threat.

She pressed both hands to her temples. Sensing the makings of a headache, she shook out the treble ruffles at her wrist; seeking the square of scented muslin her maid had tucked there that morning. Casting around, she spied it on the boards beneath the window; and there was Hugh, crossing the square... and here she was, still with no decision made!

Finally, unable to face her husband, she hurriedly left the drawing room.

*

Hugh Pragnall paused at the corner of Bloomsbury Square and gave a long, drawn out, unashamed sigh of satisfaction.

Since taking his first faltering steps, he liked to stand here and watch the comings and goings of the rich and famous, the poor and infamous; listening to street vendors crying their wares, the creak of carriages and the clatter of hooves across the cobbles.

Osterly was the third house from the left. In appearance, no more imposing than those either side, with its smooth cut Portland stone and Georgian windows just now catching the sun's dying rays. What made it special was the fact it was all his, and that a beautiful young lady awaited him... what more could a man want?

How he hated being away and vowed each day would be the last. There was no need for it; he had money enough to pay another to control his business matters in Lombard Street.

Filled with pleasant thoughts of the future, he crossed the square at a leisurely pace, cutting a fine figure in a dark blue cut-away coat with matching waistcoat, beige knee-length breeches with white stockings and highly polished, red heeled shoes. In one hand he carried a beaver hat and in the other his silver topped swordstick. His one concession against fashion was always to wear his dark hair un-powdered, and secured at the nape of his neck with a black velvet ribbon. Hugh Pragnall was not one for the shaved head and the discomfort and frippery of wigs.

Keating, an austere looking butler of long standing, opened the door to him. Man and boy, Keating had been at Osterly since Hugh's Grandfather's time and Pragnall knew the pinched-cheeks and shrewdly pursed mouth concealed a cutting humour of rare quality.

"Good evening, Keats. Lady Pragnall at home?"

"Madam *was* in the front drawing room, Sir, but I believe she has since descended to the kitchens." He gave a slight sniff, which Hugh understood to mean the lady of the house should *never* be seen below stairs. Servants were there to be summoned!

Hugh laid aside his hat and cane. Collecting the *London Chronicle* from the hallstand, he crossed towards the drawing room, his stride unhurried, by all appearances a man at peace with his surroundings. The panelled door stood slightly open and he unconsciously paused, recalling two evenings previously when he had hesitated just so at the sound of Nell's raised voice.

"You can't go, Essa. I need you here with me." There came a rustle of skirts as Lady Pragnall paced, just the other side of the door. "More than ever with a child on the way."

"It's me 'usband, Milady. Wilf's a good man but I fear fur 'is life." The older woman sniffed thickly. "There 'ave been threats... an demands made of me as well."

"This cannot be happening," Nell had muttered, her words barely audible and had Hugh not know differently, he would have sworn his wife was talking only to herself. The long case clock in the hall behind Hugh chimed the fourth hour. "It's *him*, isn't it?" she whispered her voice sounding subdued. Defeated!

"Yes, Milady," Essa confirmed with another throaty sniff and Hugh heard her out with a sinking heart. "Tha's why I av ta go. Benjamin Trew'll neva let up."

Like many other Londoners, Hugh was aware few villains were as widely known, or feared, than this man, born and bred to the Southwark underworld. Rumour had it Trew remained at large due to his remarkable hold over the local roughnecks. Towards anyone foolish enough to cross him, his justice was harsh and usually fatal and fear alone held sway, more so than any local Charlie or runner could have done; even with the horrors of Fleet Prison within spitting distance of his stomping ground.

Until that night, Hugh never considered Trew's web of terror extended this far beyond Southwark, let alone into his own household. Clearly, at least *one* of the servants was terrified of the man; as it seemed, was Lady Pragnall herself.

He regretted not bringing everything into the open. Instead he had slipped quietly into the library, not wishing to be thought an eavesdropper in his own home. After all, he had reasoned, if the situation were serious, surely Nell would come to him?

Now, as he entered the drawing room, he was beginning to suspect his wife was actually avoiding him. Keating had been right, as always. Nell's delicate perfume still lingered, warming the chill solitude of the room.

Hugh poured himself a glass of Madeira and tried to settle with his Chronicle. But the words soon became a meaningless jumble and he was all too aware of the minutes ticking by. When the fifth hour chimed and there was still no sign of Lady Pragnall, he decided it was time to bring matters to a head.

Fortifying himself with a second glass of port, he headed for the kitchens... ensuring of course, that Keating was not witness such a dire discretion of etiquette. There he found Essa, mobcap awry, tear stained and distraught.

"Where's Lady Pragnall?" he demanded, as the maid tried to rise from her stool.

"Gone, sir." She blew her nose into her apron and gave another heart-rending sob.

"Gone! Where?"

"Was'na my fault, sir," Essa hiccupped. "All I said wer me 'usband wer beaten up last night... set about 'e was. I neva meant fer er ta take off." She tried to turn from him, but Hugh grabbed her none too gently by the shoulders and forced her round to face him again.

"I'm not here to cast blame, woman. I simply want to know where Lady Pragnall's gone?"

"Back to 'im, sir."

Hugh saw nothing to gain from feigning ignorance.

"Benjamin Trew?"

Essa nodded. Her mobcap slipped unheeded to the floor.

"Mistress sayed there wer somefink she could take ta set us all free of 'im."

To Hugh, that could mean only one thing.

"And she went alone?" He tried to keep the crushing dread from his voice, and then turned away as he read the answer in Essa's stricken gaze.

Oblivious as to who might see him, Hugh dashed up the back stairs, his red-heeled shoes clattering on the bare boards, and along the servant's corridor to the main landing leading to the master bedroom.

Going directly to Nell's dressing chest, he pressed an inlaid panel on the left hand side and a corresponding panel, on the right side slid open, revealing a square, silver gilt box. Foregoing the luxury of hesitation he quickly flipped back the lid and stared dumbstruck at the contents. As he had guessed, the Pragnall amethyst was gone. What he had not been prepared for was to see Nell's wedding ring pressed into the velvet enclosure.

He picked up the gold band and held it for a moment... almost believing he could still feel the warmth of Nell's body. Then he slipped it onto the finger of his left hand and flinging aside the box, he hurried into the adjoining closet.

*

Just as she had walked barefoot into Hugh Pragnall's life, so it was Nell left it, her old darned and patched shift concealed by a heavy woollen cloak, the hood raised to hide her dark fall of hair, brushed out now to shoulder length, and free of silver combs and pins.

With practised ease, she lifted a ripe peach from a vendor's stall on the corner of Drury Lane and slipped unnoticed into the stream of London's low life.

*

When Hugh again descended to the main hall a rapier hung at his side, its tip beating a feint tattoo against the balustrade.

He threw a hooded day cloak round his shoulders and shook out the lace at his cuffs, to ensure their length would not hinder the use of the pistol tucked into the front of his breeches. With the door into the street open, he hesitated, wondering if it would be wise to say anything to Keating. He decided against it, shutting the door firmly, but quietly behind him. Time for explanations later; if Lady Pragnall ever returned to Osterly it would be with him... or not at all. It was not until he had reached the street he realized his silver tipped swordstick had gone from the hall table.

To anyone following the movements of Hugh Pragnall that day, they would have thought a different man exited Osterly than the one who had entered nearly two hours earlier. Gone was the casual air. His stride was full of purpose and there was determination in his upright carriage. A grim line marred his generous mouth and anger flashed in the dark eyes, swiftly concealed as he pulled the hood of his cloak well forward over his face.

His moccasins silent on the cobblestones, he headed south east, through Holborn towards Drury Lane, intending to cross London Bridge via Fleet Street and from there into Southwark, where he expected to encounter Benjamin Trew. Shadows were lengthening across the square as darkness descended on the city; very soon a different breed of person would be abroad, he thought. His hand dropped to the hilt of his sword. Let them come... because if they held back, he had every intention of seeking them out. He would find Lady Pragnall, even if he had to spend the rest of his days scouring every rookery in London.

As Hugh turned out of Bloomsbury Square, a rat faced little figure in a torn jerkin and cut off breeches dodged round a passing sedan chair and padded silently after him.

*

Nell had no fear of the streets at night.

Darkness meant she could pass unobtrusively through the ill-lit runnels and alleyways of Holborn and Fleet. Not for her the congested thoroughfares of Drury Lane and Cannon Street, with there painted doxies, street vendors and city dandies... she dare not draw attention to herself, not with the Pragnall amethyst knotted in the hem of her cloak.

At last London Bridge loomed mightily before her. It was high tide, and down in the swirling darkness, water slapped against the stonework and sucked greedily around the great wooden pillars. She shuddered. Being unable to swim, the close proximity of water brought out the greatest of fears in her.

Despite the advanced hour, lights still flickered along the bridge's length and trading was still in full flow. The noise seemed deafening after the peace of Osterly and Nell found herself pushed and jostled from all sides. She managed to keep her hood up and her eyes downcast, watching where she was stepping, ever mindful of the greasy water slipping beneath her. She hugged herself inside her cloak, one hand on Hugh's sword-stick; all too aware if she gave a Charlie or Thief-taker reason to stop her, no-one would believe she was Lady Pragnall. The valuables she carried would be considered ill-gotten gains and she would be carted off to Newgate without a chance.

Back on what she considered firm ground, her pace quickened. Not far now. Just Duke Hill Street and round into Red Cross...

A strong hand grasped her arm at the elbow and something like a dagger pricked her ribs as she was deftly eased out of the flow of people.

"Well, hif hit hain't the little princess," rasped a familiar voice.

"Hello, Snape."

"How'd yer know?" the man demanded petulantly.

"I recognized the smell."

Snape's grip tightened.

"Boss wants yer hunmarked, huverwise I'd..."

"He'd slit your throat for even thinking about it."

"We'd see habout that." Snape spat and a gobbet of spittle slapped against the wall in front of her. Keeping the pressure of the knife constant, he took his hand from her arm and slipped it adroitly inside her cloak. "Nice little tickler," he said, tucking Hugh's swordstick into his own belt. "Hi just might keep hit..."

"Trew wouldn't like that."

"Hand who's gona tell him?" Snape laughed and spat again. "Reckon he'll hexpect more'n that, Princess." His free arm snaked round her slender waist as he pulled her hard against him. "Know what hi mean?"

Nell stopped abruptly, causing Snape to swing round in front of her.

"Where's Trew?" Her unexpected smile seemed to pose more than just a question for Snape.

"Usual place." His breath was foul on her face, but she steeled herself not to turn away. His face was pockmarked and festooned with blackheads.

"Well?" Nell made sure their eyes locked and held. "First we go to Aggie's gin shop, and then..." She pressed one hand against Snape's chest and held it there for as long as she could bear before seeming to reluctantly ease her self from his grasp.

With a new swagger to his step, Snape eagerly followed Nell into the rat-infested runnels of Southwark, unaware the swordstick was no longer tucked into the front of his breeches.

*

Hugh reached the city end of London Bridge as the sharp, clear night succumbed to rain.

A heavy downpour swiftly turned the filth and ordure of the streets into a slippery morass. Lights were blinking off all along the bridge as vendors closed the fronts of their shops. Travelling salesman, some pushing handcarts, covered their wares with pieces of sacking; scant protection against the sudden deluge. En mass, the populace fled for cover. One traveller, leading a donkey piled with bales of cloth, was loudly protesting his right of way over a dozen pigs, happily rooting between the stalls. The result was deepening darkness, chaos and virtual gridlock, which suited Hugh fine as he slipped between a wheelbarrow and a bullyboy arguing ownership of an upturned barrow of stinking fish.

Leaving Osterly, Hugh had known straight away he was being followed, a task at which his pursuer appeared eminently unsuited. He prayed he was right in his assumption this was Trew's man... perhaps he could make this situation work for him. If the rat lost its quarry, it stood to reason it would eventually return to its nest. Find Trew and he was convinced he would find Nell.

He almost ran then, unashamedly using people and obstacles as leverage and cover until he literally slid down the ferryman's steps at the Southwark end of the bridge. Breathlessly, he concealed himself in the noisome darkness; aware he was not only in a place of concealment, but a virtual death trap, with a watery grave at his back and an unknown quantity out front.

To give his pursuer credit, he was not far behind. He came of the bridge in a sudden rush, like a cork out of a bottle and frantically cast left and right, mouthing obscenities, their meaning masked by the general hubbub. The fellow changed direction three times before coming to rest within touching distance of his quarry. The man was shivering violently, his hair and clothing plastered to his scrawny frame. Hugh noticed his hand continuously went to the crude knife at his belt. Finally, he shook himself like an enraged bulldog, and padded off into the darkness.

Hugh had no option but to follow.

*

Aggie's gin shop was nothing more than a front for Trew's business empire.

From here his web of fear and corruption reached throughout the boroughs of Southward and Bermondsey and across the river into Holborn and the City itself. Not that he needed to skulk behind doors. There were some who said he could conduct his affairs under the hanging tree at Tyburn and the authorities would still turn a blind eye. Unfortunately, that was probably true.

Nell's arrival caused quite a stir amongst Aggie's customers, most of who were known to her. The interior brought back a familiar smell of gin, sweat and stale urine as barefooted, she picked her way across the hard packed earth floor. Snape scuttled along behind her, enjoying the attention.

Aggie didn't gawp like the others. She merely removed the ever-resident clay pipe from her mouth and gave a gap toothed smile. Nell returned the smile; Aggie had never shown her anything but kindness, and was probably the only person she had missed out of this hellhole. She would like to have gone to her friend first, but with Snape drooling at her heels, the confrontation with Trew had to be *now*. Time to talk later; she hoped. Dumb since birth, nevertheless Aggie would be dying to learn what it had been like living in a big house, with servants and fine clothes. Even in thought, Nell realized she was using the past tense; she could never go back to Osterly, not with the Pragnall amethyst burning a hole in her cloak. She pointed to the heavy door at the end of the room and Aggie nodded, her expression becoming grim as she replaced the pipe and leant against the makeshift bar of barrels and rough-hewn planks.

She was a large women, with forearms the size of hams and an overabundance of facial hair. A moderately clean mobcap was pulled well down over her forehead, beneath which bright blue eyes kept a discerning watch on the comings and goings of her customers.

Nell smiled grimly to herself as she clocked several people edging into the street, no doubt eager to spread word of her return. Not for long, the fools. Either Trew accepted the amethyst as an end to her persecution or else... her small fist closed round the concealed swordstick.

She raised the latch to Trew's inner sanctum and found herself hesitating, wanting even now to believe she could turn back. Snape, however, shoved her forward with such force the door opened and crashed back against the wall.

"Look ho hi've found," he jeered, "skulking huround..."

"Snape's a liar," Nell cut in with a defiant turn of the head. Benjamin Trew sat behind a great scared table, his hands already on the brace of pistols in front of him. "I've come to deal."

Trew stood up.

He was a giant of a man, of indeterminate age. Some said he was nigh on fifty, yet his powerful physic and the way he moved round the table towards her made liars of them all. His ruddy complexion marked him as an outdoor man; just as his rheumy eyes suggested he drank too much... believing that, many had paid the ultimate penalty. He was no fool.

He wore a battered, old-fashioned tricorn hat, from under which a great mop of mouse coloured hair fought to escape. His shirt had once been of the finest cambric, yet quality had given way to age and colour to the status of the great unwashed. A heavy leather belt circled his powerful loins, carrying a bunch of keys and a leather money pouch. His breeches were cut offs, below which powerful calves bristled thickly with matted hair, darker than his head. His feet were thrust into shoes from which the buckles had long been pawned.

Benjamin Trew was a man of contrary nature. It was known by some and guessed by many that he possessed wealth enough to wear fine apparel and conduct his affairs from one of the great houses across the river and yet...

"Get out, Snape," Trew spoke softly, yet his henchman jumped as though he had been pistol-whipped.

Nell sensed, rather than heard the door close behind her.

Trew studied her slowly, from head to toe, square jawed and unsmiling, as though reminding his self what she once looked like. When he finally spoke, his first words to her were not what she expected.

"So, girl... you've finally come home?"

*

Hugh found himself hard pressed to keep up.

The conditions enabling him to reverse the situation were now telling against him. Darkness, rain that turned into an icy river mist, the maze of unlit alleyways and the speed the fellow moved over familiar ground compelled him to follow at a less than prudent distance. More than once he believed they had doubled back; the shadowy buildings seemed familiar and the sounds from the river close by... then another twisting turn would set him wondering again. He had no choice but to keep going; if he lost the fellow... then *all* was lost.

Over a low wall, then another alleyway. Ducking under a broken archway, stepping through the rubble. The blow came from an unexpected quarter while he was looking ahead at the short figure, weaving through the shadows. The back of his head exploded in a riot of pain, sending signals to his brain that this was not good... this was not part of his plan. His knees buckled and rough hands dragged him upright by the back of his cloak. Automatically he clutched for his sword, but his fingers felt rubbery and disconnected and he could do nothing to prevent the weapon being taken from him.

A piercing whistle, swiftly answered by another; and footsteps came running.

"Blindfold?" rasped an unfamiliar voice.

"Na. No point, mate." They pulled his hood well down over his face. "He ain't ever coming back."

*

"Home?" Nell echoed, trying to keep the surprise out of her voice. "I have no home... either here, or Osterly." This was clearly not the answer Trew wanted. His dark eyes registered anger, yet they also held a question. Nell answered by holding out the ringless fingers of her left hand. "It's over. I want you to leave him... them alone."

Trew laughed. It was not an unpleasant sound; he was a man given to self-appreciating humour, usually at the expense of others. Nevertheless, it sent a chill down her spine.

"Why?" He threw the word in her face; a simple question, yet one she found too complicated to answer.

Instead, she said,

"I've brought..."

"...The Pragnall amethyst."

"How..." She was thrown by the casual, almost disinterested way he said it.

"Because I *know* your mind." He sounded disappointed in her. "You forget I taught you everything."

She resented that.

"I guess you did. If you mean how to lie," she flung back her hood, her dark hair tumbling about her shoulders, "cheat and steal."

"It kept you alive, didn't it!"

"In your company, death would have been preferable."

Trew raised his hand and would have struck her, but was stalled by her unflinching manner. They faced each other for a few silent heartbeats and finally he laughed again. This time the sound was scornful.

"I suppose *he* taught you niceties beyond my under-standing?" Nell kept her silence. "So, you think you can survive out there without him... or me to watch your back?"

"I did before."

"Not as often as you believed, girl." He leant forward, close enough for her to smell the sweat on him. "Snape or one of the others was rarely far behind. Sometimes it was me," he added, as though he were proud of the fact.

"I don't believe you. I... I would have known."

Trew merely smirked at that.

She flinched unavoidably as he reached out and touched her hair where it fell to her shoulder.

"I've never seen you look so beautiful," he whispered, an odd, wistful note in his voice that frightened her more than any threat could have ever done. His fingers trailed round the curve of her throat and she raised her chin in order to escape his touch. Their eyes locked and he licked dry, cracked lips as though discomfited by the hostility he saw in her; then why should that bother him, she asked herself, this beast had once tried to rape her, but never again. Heart racing, her small fist slipped inside her cloak and closed over the swordstick.

"How could a dung heap like me have created something so fragile... and filled it with such loathing?"

Unexpectedly, he let his hand fall away with a gesture of hopelessness totally alien to the man she knew as Benjamin

Trew. Nell gasped, there was something in his expression she had never seen before. Something she didn't want to see; not now... it was too late to face such truths.

"You're right, girl... you don't belong here." He raised his hand again, palm upwards. "Give!"

Nell stared, mesmerized by the sweaty, dirt-engrained lifeline that seemed to travel well up into the corded wrist; that hand had brought nothing but death and destruction to all it touched. Had he been trying to tell her this was the hand of her father; was his tainted blood beating in the pulse that even now threatened to choke her. Suddenly her mind was in turmoil.

Behind them, something hit the door with a thud that rattled its hinges and jolted Nell out of her painful cogitations. Then came another blow, louder and more violent. She spun round as Trew, cursing wildly, reached past her and lifted the latch. Snape and another henchman she knew as Maggs, filled the narrow doorway, a figure slumped between them. Lord Pragnall's hood was back. Blood covered his face and shirt front from a large welt above his right ear.

"Hugh!" Nell cried as Trew pushed her roughly aside.

"We ad'ta clobber him," Maggs muttered. "Follering er'e were."

"More's like leading him here," Snape contradicted, his face full of malicious cunning.

"I'd no idea." Again she tried to reach Hugh and again Trew dragged her back. The swordstick slipped from inside her cloak and dropped at his feet.

"What trickery's this?" Trew sideswiped her hard across the face. She staggered and would have fallen if not for the table at her back. "Bind him and throw him in the river."

"No!" Nell cried, unsteadily righting herself, one hand going to the red weald flaring on her cheek. "You promised."

"We didn't get that far, girl," Trew reminded her with a sneer. In the presence of Hugh and the others, Trew had reverted to the man she had always known; a towering figure of anger and violence... a man not to be crossed.

"But... my offer can still count." It took every ounce of determination to prevent her voice from trembling. Her head was swimming as she blinked away tears of pain. "Doubly so... if you let him go."

"Don't talk in riddles, girl."

She touched his arm and bile rose in her throat.

"The amethyst," she swallowed hard, "and anything else you want." She forced herself to unflinchingly meet his gaze. "Anything."

Trew glanced at Hugh and back again. Nell read the hesitation in his eyes, the doubt... and the hunger. Beneath her cloak, she shivered; the way he was suddenly studying her... this man could not possibly be her father?

"Throw this *gentleman* in the cellar," he ordered Snape and Maggs, without looking at them. Suddenly, he had only eyes for her. "I'll let you know come morning whether to set him loose... or send his carcass out on the morning tide." Snape made to pick up the swordstick. Trew stamped viciously on his hand and then his rich laugh followed as he kicked it out the door. "Keep it," he muttered with sudden generosity. "I think I have the better prize."

*

Hugh felt an utter fool.

When he finally gained consciousness, the prison in which he found himself was pitch black and reeked of sewage and river water, so he guessed he was situated well below ground. He no longer knew what time of day it was or how long he had been there. His head ached abominably and he was suffering from thirst as well as the call of nature.

Mercifully, they had not bound him, so the later problem was easily dealt with. Purely through touch, he covered every inch of the chamber, including the ceiling, which was low enough to cause some hindrance in movement. One door, no window and no furniture, save for a couple of empty barrels and the pile of foul smelling straw on which he had awoken. Naturally, his pistol was gone, but they had had the forbearance to leave him his cloak, which he pulled about him against the damp air.

Where was Nell now? he wondered, almost too afraid to consider the possibilities. And where was he and why were they keeping him locked up? After a second blow had left him senseless he could recall nothing, just an odd sense of movement and just once, the murmur of voices, no more than a painful droning in his head. He punched his fists together in self-admonishment; what a fool he had been not to tell Keating he was following Nell to Southwark.

A frustrated bout of shouting and kicking having elicited no response, he lowered himself on to the upturned barrel. Like a man condemned, Hugh, Lord Pragnall, began to contemplate a bleak future.

*

Trew locked the door and leant against it, leering at Nell as he tucked the key down the front of his breeches.

He had led her upstairs to a chamber above the bar, one she had never seen before. From behind the counter, Aggie had watched Nell go past, pale faced and placid... a lamb to the slaughter, and she had not liked it one bit, especially when Trew pointedly told her they were not to be disturbed. No, she had not liked that at all.

Nell's gaze darted swiftly about the room with an odd mixture of fear and resignation. There was nothing there to help her... just a single cot bed and an earthenware jug sitting on a battered chest.

"Not much of a room," she offered, trying to keep her voice light and casual. "Now you have the amethyst you can leave all this behind."

Trew grunted as he sauntered towards her.

"But I haven't got it yet, have I?" he said, waging a thick finger at her.

"Let's get it now." Nell made to push past him, but he caught her cloak and swung her back round towards the bed.

"First I have a mind to taste a little of what's coming to me."

"Give me a knife," Nell thought, "and I'll soon show you." She flinched as Trew reached for her throat. With a flick of his powerful wrist her cloak fell away, leaving her shivering in her tattered shift.

Trew laughed.

"Cold, my girl? My lips will soon warm you." Despite his confident words she caught a momentary flicker of doubt before his mouth crushed down on hers, his tongue instantly probing, his bear like arms crushing her against his sweaty chest.

Trew gave her no option. He used his weight to force her back on to the cot. His breath was rancid and his hands were everywhere... hurting her with their urgent fumbling. The fabric of her gown was torn away and all too soon he was pulling at the front of his breeches. Her hands scrabbled along the edge of the cot and beyond, seeking leverage to push her further up the bed, anywhere, away from this nightmare. Trew merely crawled after her, enjoying the sport, breathing heavily as his knees locked between her own.

Naturally, when the water jug smashed against the side of his head, he was not expecting it. Surprise turned to a glazed look and his body went crushingly limp. She wasted precious seconds fighting hysteria and trying to get out from under him. Panic again, when she could not find the key, which had slipped down the side of the straw mattress.

Flinging on her cloak to hide her near nakedness, she unlocked the door and as an afterthought locked it again behind her.

"Hi'll take that, Princess."

"Snape!"

"Smell me, could you?" His sarcasm could not have been more frightening.

"Key!" He held out his bony hand, palm upwards. A dark form loomed behind him, blocking out what little light there was at the head of the stairs. Snape followed Nell's gaze with an exclamation,

"What hew doing hup here?"

The answer came in a pair of powerful hands that easily lifted him off his feet and smashed his head against the wall. Pieces of plaster reined down on his inert form.

"Aggie!" Nell gasped, relieved, but afraid for her friend.

The woman's response was to take her hand and drag her down the rickety wooden stairs, past her own quarters, the rear entrance to the bar and on down into musty darkness.

*

Hugh readied himself when he heard hurried footsteps.

A key scratched in the lock and the door opened, bringing with it more darkness and an exchange of air that told him nothing.

"Hugh?"

"Nell!"

She came out of nowhere in a rush that brought her into his arms and virtually bowled him over. They clung together, making small sounds of happiness as they rediscovered each other.

"I've been such a fool," she admitted at last, breaking away. "Take me home."

"You'll have to lead the way."

"Aggie, can you get us out of here?"

Hugh tensed at the other's approach, but Nell went willingly, drawing him with her, up the side stairs again, this time taking a left out onto the street. It was still dark, although it had stopped raining. The moon was up, admiring its reflection in the scum-covered puddles of the alleyway. Hugh had never been so glad to see the sky and breathe cool air again.

"Come with us," Nell begged of her friend, even now stepping back into the shadowed doorway. The woman gave her familiar gape toothed smile, head cocked to one side, clearly listening for movement within. Nell embraced her one last time, kissed her cheek and turned quickly away before she made a fool of herself. Before they were out of the alley, they heard the door shut firmly behind them and the rattle of bolts being drawn.

Aggie hurried back to where she had left Snape. Breathlessly she stared down at his inert figure, nothing more than a bag of bones, huddled against the wall. There was no pity in her bright blue eyes. Eventually he would wake and go running to Trew. She could not allow that. Effortlessly, she hoisted him across one shoulder and carried him down to the cellar. Dropping him face down on the earth, she calmly placed a knee in the middle of his back and pulled back his head with one swift jerk of her powerful arms. There was a satisfying crack and Aggie smiled her gap toothed smile.

From somewhere above came the sound of splintering wood.

*

In no time at all, or so it seemed to Hugh, they had passed through the maze of alleyways and were approaching the Southwark end of the bridge.

As they hurried along, Nell told him how she had left Trew unconscious and of Aggie's timely intervention with Snape. Hugh guessed by her halting speech there were other things she could have said; perhaps in time, he hoped.

Had he been alone, he was all for going back and settling with Trew; but he had Nell's safety to consider. Here they were, travelling in the dead of night, without even a blade between them. Getting her back to Osterly was paramount. So far, no one had tried to stop them, although their flight had earned enquiring glances over their bloodstained and dishevelled appearance, particularly from a water seller, with whom Hugh slacked his thirst; then again, it could have been because he was collecting his 'pure water' from the Thames in the middle of the night.

The bridge was virtually deserted and in full darkness, save for a solitary candle. No doubt a tradesman working late. Halfway across, Nell faced him.

"Take this!" She lifted the hem of her cloak and fished out the Pragnall amethyst, but saw Hugh had eyes only for the torn state of her shift. It was the first time he had *really* looked at her since leaving Aggie's. "It doesn't matter." She pressed the precious stone into his hand. "Really... it doesn't." He dropped the bauble into the breast pocket of his shirt and in the same move produced her wedding ring.

"Lady Pragnall, I believe you mislaid this."

A smile transformed Nell's face.

"My Lord."

Hugh placed the ring back on her finger. Their eyes locked and they both knew a new bond had been forged between them, stronger now and full of promise for the future. He kissed her bruised cheek and then her upturned mouth, finding her lips warm and compliant.

"How touching," Trew's voice cut between them like a knife. They fell apart and Nell gave a cry of despair as Hugh stepped in front of her.

"Just you and me, Trew," Hugh hissed. "You'll not threaten my wife or household again." He leapt forward, but before he had covered half the distance, Trew pulled a pistol from his breeches and fired in one fluid movement. Momentum kept Hugh going, but the lead ball had caught him full in the throat and he was dead on his feet before Trew casually sidestepped his careering figure.

Without a word, Trew started dragging the stunned girl back the way they had come. Near the end of the bridge she managed to scratch his face and break away, but he hauled her back, suddenly finding he had a wildcat in his grasp as biting and kicking, she threw him off balance and together they rolled down the steps where Hugh had concealed himself the night before.

Trew was far stronger, but Nell had anger and hatred on her side and a determination never to be taken back. The tide was ebbing now and the steps were slick and dangerous underfoot. They started to slide, one atop the other until Trew came up against one of the great support pillars, the jolt shunting the girl from his grasp. Nell slithered over the edge and would have gone under had Trew not grasped the folds of her cloak. She hung there, her pale, elfin face framed by the dark, surging water.

Trew rolled on his side.

"Take my hand."

Nell stared dispassionately into the face of the man who just might have been her father. Then, with terrible purpose, she released the clasp at her throat and let the current take her, bobbing and ducking under the bridge.

Trew cursed and stood up, bunching the cloak in angry fists. Something hard in the lining drew his attention and he hurried up the steps and out into the moonlight, ripping the cloak apart as he went.

A plumb stone was all he had to show for his efforts...

*

...Hugh shivered, drawing the nightshirt they buried him in close to his wasted body, although he felt neither heat or cold, he still found he aped human characteristics and actions.

He paused suddenly, mid stride, squinting through the early morning mist, curling around the gravestones near the western perimeter of his domain. There it was again... a speck of light, blinking on and off, hovering above the headstones. He had seen such lights before, erratic and quickly gone. This one, however, moved with a purpose.

Keeping low, he cut across ground. Perhaps here was something to break the monotony of his vigil. His preternatural hearing missed nothing and he thought he heard the faintest scuff of a shoe against stone. He was ahead of the light now and he crouched as the mist shifted to reveal a hooded figure coming directly towards him. He could not help thinking that something in the way the person walked struck a not of familiarity with him.

*

Holding the lantern high, Nell stepped cautiously between the headstones, her cloak and gown dragging heavily through the damp grass.

It had been barely a month since the ferryman fished her out from the far side of the bridge and had taken her across with him. Wrapped in nothing but a coarse, dry blanket, she had continued on to Osterly, carrying with her the dire news of Lord Pragnall's death; knowing in her heart nothing would be done to apprehend his murderer. After that, the indomitable Keating had taken over.

Fear had kept her shut in Osterly. Fear had prevented her going to her husband's funeral and fear wracked her now as she hesitated, alone in this terrible place. Keating had told her where to find the grave; indeed had begged to come with her. But this was something she had to do alone.

She was surprised how easily she found his marker. With a little gasp, she fell to her knees and thrust back her hood, her dark fall of hair masking her features as she brushed a pile of leaves from the stone. Then she sank back on her heels and raised her tear stained face to the night sky.

*

Hugh stood rooted to the spot.

Nell! At last she had come to him, alive and seemingly well. With needless stealth, he moved nearer, until he was close enough to reach out and touch... oh, how he longed to run his fingers through her fine hair, raven black in the moonlight.

She was speaking softly, her words interrupted by gentle, hiccupping sobs, telling how Trew believed her dead. She had to keep things that way. She would go away until their child was born... perhaps even until he or she were old enough to inherit Osterly. That the Pragnall amethyst had been buried with him and how she wished she had never taken it and started out on that fatal journey. How much she loved him...

Hugh suddenly became aware of another figure approaching through the mist. So engrossed had he been on Nell's lament, the man was almost upon them before she turned in terrified recognition.

*

"I knew you'd eventually come here," Trew laughed as Nell leapt to her foot, turning left and right for escape. "It's no good, girl. You can't outrun me. Where's the bauble?"

"Bottom of the Thames."

"Don't lie to me!" He was close enough now for her to see the red wealds she had clawed down the left side of his face; they did little to improve his appearance. "I'm gonna teach you a lesson you'll never forget." He unbuckled the broad leather belt from his waist, slapping it against the palm of his hand. Instinctively Hugh moved between them, but Trew walked through him as though he were nothing but mist.

Out of nowhere, another figure came lumbering towards them, mobcap askew and skirts flying. It seemed Hugh was the only one to see Aggie, before she collided with Trew, knocking the belt from his hand and sending him staggering backwards. A knife materialized in his hand, even before he regained his footing, but Aggie kept coming, allowing the blade to slice across her shoulder as she wrapped powerful arms about him.

For seconds they were locked together, like two great tree trunks refusing to be felled, while Nell and Hugh looked helplessly on. Trew gave a mighty grunt of exertion and Aggie toppled backwards, taking him with her, keeping his knife hand trapped beneath her armpit. Blood spurted as he butted her face, splaying her nose and adding to the gaps between her teeth. Aggie responded by bringing her knee up hard into his groin and using the same leg as leverage to roll them over.

The movement freed the knife and Trew slipped it between them, slicing her breast as he tried to drive the point home. Aggie pulled back to avoid the blade. Grabbing his hand in her bone-crushing grasp, she twisted hard and Trew yelped as his arm snapped at the elbow and then gave a greater cry of agony as the blade sank to the hilt in his chest. His heels drummed a tattoo on the soft earth, as though even now he would run from the face of death. Then he gave a rattling cough and lay still.

Blowing bubbles of blood through a shattered nose, Aggie rolled on her knees and then onto her feet, swaying as she used her mobcap to staunch her wounds.

Nell flung herself at the woman and they clung together for a long moment. Hugh suddenly realized how radiant Nell looked, as though a great weight had been lifted from her, just as she had once looked when he held her in his arms.

"Come back to Osterly with me," she insisted, heart-stoppingly aware such a dream was now possible.

Aggie shook her head, scattering droplets of blood.

"Please," Nell begged. "Let me tend your wounds. Thanks to you, neither of us have anything to fear anymore." She glanced back at the headstone. "Hugh was such a kind and generous man... through Osterly I can show you what he was really like."

Aggie grunted some kind of assent and Hugh watched them go with a mixture of envy and regret, for here they would indeed part company. On impulse, he accompanied them as far as the sagging gate... the perimeter of Lord Pragnall's domain. All too soon darkness claimed them and he was left starring out into the night.

Sensing movement, he turned sharply.

"Pragnall!" Trew was advancing towards him.

The bastard could see him!

Hugh pulled the scroll from his sleeve in time to see the name 'Benjamin Trew' flare brightly in red and then darken as the ink dried.

"Yours I believe," he flung the document in the man's face.

"I don't... come back. You can't leave me here!"

But Lord Pragnall had already found he could jump the low wall. His pace quickened. Lady Pragnall might no longer be aware of his presence, but for now he still considered it a husband's duty to escort his Lady home. After that, who knows? He smiled, and his dark eyes flashed in eager anticipation.

Perhaps, here was the beginning of a new adventure...

THE SHADOWEAN

PROLOGUE
St Oswald's Church School – 1951

It was some time since darkness had fallen.

Brother Martin continued to wait, leaning forward slightly one hand on the polished wood of the window ledge, his breath misting the glass from the icy chill of the room. When he could no longer make out the trees in the circular walk below, he knew the moment had come; there would be no going back.

Whatever apprehension he may have been under was not evident to the others as he turned and faced his three Companions in Christ. The movement caused the hood of his cassock to fall back and beneath his blond tonsured head, his light blue eyes and finely boned features held their usual calm serenity. His gaze passed over Brothers Vernon and Askew and settled on Ezekiel, the youngest novice in the school; in fact the only novice, as by necessity the building had been hurriedly emptied of all life.

He gave a slow, encouraging nod and the boy steeled himself to light the three branch candelabra, determined his hand would not shake. Standing shoulder to shoulder with Brother Martin and a good head above the others, Ezekiel stared round the library, his favourite place in the school, except of course the chapel. The room felt strange to him, as though he was seeing it for the first time; or perhaps the last... if this night went badly! Somehow, the chamber seemed smaller as the candle flames struggled to push back the darkness; no more than a book lined cubicle. Shadows danced over the ancient leather bound volumes and polished oak shelves. The moon shaped faces of Brothers Vernon and Askew struck him as paler than usual and Ezekiel didn't doubt he too looked just as strange, with his spiky ginger hair and freckles you could barely place a pin between; as an old aunt had once relentlessly teased him.

To their left, where the thick walls came together, the door to the treasure vault stood open, although all church valuables had this day been removed to a safer place. As candlelight took hold, it seemed *that* was where darkness retreated; like the gaping mouth of hell, it waited to receive a creature they doubted God intended to walk the earth, let alone the corridors of St Oswald's... and *never* would have, but for old Abbot Gregory's foolish dabbling in the occult. Because of him, the Brothers had had no choice but to transfer the novices to a safe house, supposedly to escape a mysterious epidemic that threatened to decimate their numbers.

Those remaining, with little chance for spiritual pre-paration, had reached this penultimate moment, when faith must pass from trust into reality, where doubt would risk not only lives but also their very souls. The *idea* seemed simple enough; once the creature found the dormitories deserted, its relentless urge to kill would bring it to where they waited; armed only with bell, book and candle and a simple trust in the Almighty... and hopefully, one another. Each should have carried holy water, but Brother Vernon had dropped all but one phial as he crossed the courtyard... becoming distraught at his clumsiness, because there was none left in the font to go back for. In truth, Ezekiel guessed the good brother feared to return to the chapel through the gathering dusk; and who was he to judge whether he himself would have fared any better. Still, there had been enough to fill a shallow paten, from which Brother Martin consecrated the corners of the chamber and the very boards upon which they stood.

It had taken considerable strength of mind for Ezekiel to overcome his fear and urge Brother Martin to let him remain; consent no doubt influenced by common knowledge as the

Seventh Son of the Seventh Son he had 'the sight'. His father claimed such a gift was wasted in solitary service and should be used for the benefit of all. In the darkness of his cell, however, Ezekiel reckoned a successful outcome to this venture would erase any doubts his father might harbour regarding his vocation.

Nevertheless, it had been *firmly* explained his task was *only* to support the ancient missal, while Brother Martin read the invocation to bind and hold the creature in the vault. Brothers Vernon and Askew were to give spiritual support in prayer and assist in any way they could.

So, the four of them waited, with the stoical patience that came with their calling. The biting cold made short work of their thin cassocks and sandaled feet, but they dared not light a brazier, for fear the fire might act against them in the turmoil that must surely come.

Ezekiel seemed the first to feel a change in the atmosphere. Brother Martin appeared calm, as always, his eyes closed in silent meditation. Behind them, Brothers Vernon and Askew chanted softly but evenly, only the slightest quaver evident in their voices. Clearly they had noticed nothing untoward, but to Ezekiel, it seemed as though a heavy veil was being lowered around him and unexpectedly he found himself wishing he could be any place other than here, where to some his gift branded him an outcast. His eyes began to mist over and he felt close to tears as a shuddering sigh escaped him.

Why was he helping these people? Perhaps, if he just set aside this heavy book for a moment. He wanted to rest. He needed time to think... to give himself up to the doubts that assailed him...

Brother Martin nudged Ezekiel sharply in the ribs and the boy's eyes snapped open to face crushing reality. Brother Martin's voice was rising strong and vibrant beside him.

"In nomine Patris et Filii et Spiritus Sancti. Amen."

It had begun!

Almost instantly, the shadows in the room began to change, becoming unnatural and at abeyance to the flickering candle-light. The ominous silence was shattered as a howl of beastly rage filled Ezekiel's stunned mind and he knew a presence full of anger and hatred was beginning to build, bringing with it an icy maelstrom that circled the room, dragging books from the shelves, rattling windows and whispering under the door; *they* remained untouched however, the candles undiminished in their brilliance and Ezekiel instinctively knew the creature was testing them, measuring their strengths... and searching out their weaknesses. He tightened his grip on the precious missal; *afraid* it might be torn from his grasp... *frightened* Brother Martin might lose the place he'd so carefully marked with a strip of white alter cloth.

The unearthly wind died as swiftly as it had come, leaving behind a lingering stench of decay and a stillness Ezekiel found even more unsettling. Then Brother Askew sneezed, making them all jump, spraying the back of Ezekiel's neck with droplets of moisture.

"Bless you, Brother," Vernon muttered, causing a break in their joined litany. In response, Brother Askew sneezed again. This time pink droplets spattered Ezekiel's shoulder. As the novice glanced down in surprise, another blast followed and thick, dark gobbets of blood shot in stringy ringlets across the open book, obliterating some of the precious text.

"My head!" Brother Askew gasped. "Mother of God... it's in my head." He gave an agonized gasp and Ezekiel felt him grab the back of his cassock, presumably to stop himself collapsing. In that same moment Brother Martin lifted his right hand, in a parody of benediction, to ward off something that rushed at them out of a strange, gauzelike haze. Ezekiel flinched, but held his ground. He glimpsed fishlike eyes and a long snout before the creature withdrew; and straight away his own voice rose in unison with Brother Martin's, anticipating the beast had found a chink in their armour.

Brother Martin suddenly staggered and gave a mighty cry. A ragged claw mark appeared on the back of his raised hand and travelled up his arm, ripping through his cassock. The bell he carried in his right hand clattered to the floor as he was lifted from his feet and flung backwards. Ezekiel heard a sickening crunch as his body struck the wall beneath the windows and for the first time he faltered... long enough to know the terror that came to his companion in that last moment. Then the creature was in Ezekiel's own mind, whispering, low and malevolent, filling him with a crushing lack of self worth and unrealised, unspoken doubts.

He could achieve so much more, if only he'd taken a different, darker path. It was not too late, if he would but listen to one who understood how he suffered...

Brother Askew was sobbing like a child and Brother Vernon had dropped to his knees behind the novice's lanky frame, babbling incoherent sentences that were of little help to any of them. Ezekiel swayed and would have gone down; but then something else kicked in, something that always came to him unbidden when needed; the ability to close his mind against outside influences, to channel his thoughts, until nothing existed except his point of concentration.

The great book slipped to the floor, hitting the bell and sending it skittering noisily away into the shadows. But that didn't matter; the necessary words had already ignited a fire in Ezekiel's brain and now they poured forth like bolts of flame he *knew* burned into the creature. Correspondingly, the pressure in Ezekiel's head increased as the beast retaliated; but the boy ignored it, using the words as a shield, turning aside promises of hellfire and damnation that threatened to break his mind; asking Christ and his Angels to destroy this abomination.

The battle of wills seemed endless as the creature railed before them, showering the Brothers with books and papers, buffeting them from side to side, gradually separating them from the novice until he stood alone.

When he least unexpected it, Ezekiel sensed a lessening in resistance. The outline of the creature became more discernable as it gathered itself in. He thought he saw silver, scale covered limbs as it finally turned and bolted for the dark maw of the open vault.

Instantly Ezekiel was there; although how he made his legs respond he never knew. Perhaps it was hearing the demon scream as it sensed a trap. With supreme effort, he slammed the door, even as hooked tentacles snaked towards him. The heavy metal bolt slid in place with a screech of tortured metal; and the wheedling, intrusive voice in his head died instantly.

It seemed an age before Ezekiel turned, afraid of what might confront him; amazed to find the candles still burning, although they were considerably lowered, marking just how long the struggle had raged. Covered in each other's gore, Brothers Askew and Vernon clung together in the corner nearest the door, suggesting they'd done their utmost to escape... and who was Ezekiel to blame them?

"Well," he began, his voice hoarse as his throat closed on him, "that wasn't too bad..." He broke off as his gaze fell sadly on Brother Martin's inert form.

Three paces would have taken him to his tutor and friend, but despite every effort, the walls seemed to recede as he advanced, spinning away from him in a kaleidoscope of colour that belonged only in a summer's garden.

Then his legs *did* finally buckle under him. A different kind of darkness descended; one that felt deservedly right and good, drawing him into gentle oblivion.

DAY ONE

St Oswald's Respite Home – 2003

The sledgehammer fell with a practised, even stroke that sent reverberations through the old walls of St Oswald's, Residential and Respite Home for the elderly.

Barry Paterson, maintenance man and general dogsbody, gave the plaster and brick dust time to settle before stepping over the debris and squinting into the carefully positioned breach.

At first he could see nothing but a dark cavity, barely inches deep. He pushed the shaft of his wooden mallet through the opening; it met no resistance. Then he tried again with a length of broom handle and was rewarded with a dull, metallic thud. He rummaged in his tool bag for a torch. The narrow beam of light reflected off a pitted surface, streaked with rust.

His thick, beetle brows came together.

"What the devil?" He thrust again with the broomstick. A base echo vibrated from floor to ceiling... some kind of metal door or screen? Sims Cordell, the owner, would be none too pleased; the original plans indicated this room should be three foot wider at this point. Removal of the wall would have brought room five up to registration standard for letting out.

*

Behind the steel partition something quickened.

The Shadowean had lain dormant for decades, ancient, full of anger and hatred. The creature stirred from its timeless sleep as its prison vibrated from the external onslaught. It raised itself warily into an upright position, stretching and flexing its transparent membranes as far as the cramped space would allow. A snarl rippled along its snout and its round, cold eyes became fixed and unblinking, awakened now to an insatiable hunger and an even greater appetite for revenge on those who had dared imprison it.

*

As the day wore on, more of the partition joined the pile of rubble in the corner of room five.

Some residents complained to the manager about the hammering, while others, unknown to each other, sensed a reluctance to leave their rooms and go about their daily routine.

Outside, the day was bright and reasonably warm, despite a light autumn breeze. Inside St Oswald's, however, the chill of deepest winter was beginning to permeate the building.

Barry probably noticed it first, being closest to its source. The opening was wide enough now to disclose a metal door and two long bolts. The first slid across easily; however, he hesitated over the second one. Should he get permission before going any further? He scrubbed a calloused hand through short cropped, grey hair. Trouble was, Cordell was on the mainland, as usual, and wanted the job finished by the time he returned. To hell with it!

The bolt screeched in protest, setting his teeth on edge. Flakes of rust fell away as the bar scored a fresh groove; and then it came free, clattering to the floor. The door partly opened of its own accord, faltered and swung back against the wall, its weight taking more of the partition with it.

A foul stench filled the room.

Barry's stomach churned and he'd barely taken a step backwards before he violently threw up, spattering his boiler suit and trainers. Clutching his stomach, he flung open the door of number five and headed for the bathroom opposite. Despite tripping over Mia, the resident tabby, he made it to the toilet. Unfortunately his bowels opened before he could unfasten his overalls.

*

Full darkness had now fallen and the Shadowean was free at last to roam its old domain.

It had chosen a new nest. A bolthole it recalled from the past; a place of warmth and darkness, deep in the cellars. The creature felt disorientated. Its surroundings looked much the same, yet nowhere could it find evidence of those strangely garbed beings responsible for its incarceration, especially that young one; tall and gangling, with spiky ginger hair. *He* had been the harbinger of its downfall. Recollection brought again the sting of *his* words, like red-hot knives being driven into its flesh, forcing it back. Never had it known such pain! Yes, *he* it particularly hungered for, but where to look? Their strange cages were now full of musty smelling creatures of indeterminate age, ripe for the picking, yet not what it remembered; soft flesh and impressionable young minds were what it had come to know and expect.

The Shadowean's cautious pace quickened as its powerful limbs again became accustomed to movement. Lights flickered and dimmed at its passing and in some rooms went out altogether. Soon, it thought, lives would be just as easily extinguished. It would enter their minds and discover what each soul feared; and then mould their terrors to its own bidding. The creature raised its snout and tested the air. Hot, rancid breath rasped in its throat.

Up ahead a door stood slightly ajar...

*

Annie Booker lay staring up at the ceiling.

Thankfully the overhead light had come on again. Nothing had changed, however. The faded plaster looked the same as it had done an hour ago, or last year for that matter.

She turned her head on the pillow, a grey head of tight curls, with grey eyes and a grey tinge to the skin. She knew she was dying, had known for some time now, but what the heck; weren't we all from the moment we were conceived. There was no need to make a song and dance about it.

Her throat felt raw with thirst, but she felt too weak to reach for the glass of juice on her bedside cabinet. Someone might come by soon... perhaps one of the carers. That's why she'd left her door open; always had done from the day she'd arrived, all those long, empty years ago. On principle, she refused to ring unless it was what *she* considered an emergency; otherwise it made her feel like a hospital patient, instead of an independent resident.

Independence. That had been her byword. No friends. No family and definitely no hangers on. St Oswald's would get her meagre savings, other than a donation to the Donkey Sanctuary, down at Lower Winstone Farm, Wroxall. Animals had been her life... and she'd refused to enter the Home until Midge, the last of her seven cats had slipped peacefully away; the memory still brought tears to her eyes. She swallowed and blinked them away. She mustn't upset herself. That only made the pain in her chest worse and really, she didn't have anything to worry about... except where her next breath was coming from. Resignedly she returned her gaze to the ceiling. That was new!

An exceedingly large house spider was working its way towards the centre light fitting. She hated the things; always had done since that damn holiday chalet over in Birchington, Sussex. Her parents had caught forty-eight in three days. Cut the second week short, they had, because she was becoming hysterical.

No problem now though... as long as it stayed where it was.

Pain lanced through her chest again. She squeezed her eyes shut, fighting for breath. Knotted arthritic fingers sought comfort from the duvet. The pounding in her chest peaked and slowly declined to a dull ache and when she opened her eyes it was to a room that had grown considerably darker. The central source of light seemed to be receding from her.

This is it, she thought. This is the big one.

True to character, she widened her gaze, determined to face whatever came. She sensed movement; dark shapes slipped in and out of her vision. Only then did she begin to understand; the ceiling and walls were festooned with hundreds of spiders of every shape and size, clambering over each other to gain a foothold amongst their eager companions.

Feeling an unexpected weight on the coverlet, she looked down, expecting to see Mia, who sometimes kept her company. The pain in her chest flared again. Her bed was the same as the ceiling. Row upon row of dark bodies, except these were all stationary. Watching her.

Waiting...

*

In the corner of the room, the Shadowean held sway over Annie Booker's waking nightmare.

Controlled by the creature's powerful mind, the images deepened and multiplied and at its command the spiders on the coverlet rose up as one and swarmed towards their prey.

The Shadowean stretched to its full height, its tendril like arms touching every part of the room, siphoning of the terror that emanated from the unfortunate woman as she tried in vain to push herself up the bed. It sighed in scornful ecstasy as one hand futilely scrabbled for the call bell, now buried beneath fat, hungry bodies. It moaned in delight as the spiders surged up and over the women's head and shoulders, nipping at the tissue thin skin. When Annie Booker finally opened her mouth to scream, the horde surged in… and as death came to St Oswald's, the creature leaning over her raised its snout and roared in exquisite pleasure.

The hunt had begun.

DAY TWO

Brother Ezekiel clambered into the back seat of the cab, clinging stubbornly to the Satchel containing all his worldly goods.

Being an excessively tall, angular man, he was forced to sit with his knees drawn up, long, thin arms wrapped around the bag cocooned in the bony curve of his chest. The simple action of getting comfortable was accompanied by an excessive number of grunts, followed by a drawn out, weary sigh of exasperation and finalized by a throaty fit of coughing that unintentionally sprayed beads of moisture over the driver in front.

At the end of a life-long vocation, blighted throughout by self-doubt and a wilful, contrary nature, Brother Ezekiel, seventh son of a seventh son, having never admitted to a day's illness in his life, had finally succumbed to bronchial pneumonia. Father Abbot had given him two options; spend a month swopping religious anecdotes with a bunch of decayed old boys back at the Retirement Home or go for respite elsewhere. Fearing the Carmelite House might prove the death of him, Ezekiel had opted for St Oswald's at Ventnor, on the Isle of Wight, where he first received his induction into the church; although the property had long since been developed as a Residential Home.

He stared out at Shanklin Station courtyard. A solitary fluorescent tube mutated the daylight into something unreal and ghostly. The enclosed area channelled the chill wind and turned a discarded carrier bag into a whirling dervish that swept past the cab and up and over the platform.

'That's just how my mind feels,' Ezekiel thought, wondering again at the sense of his decision. Other than Father Abbot, he was probably the only one left alive who understood why St Oswald's was more then just a house where he'd spent his novitiate... much more.

He was beyond tired. His chest felt as though he was breathing through an iron lung and he longed for a hot toddy and something other than what British Rail considered food. The journey down from London had seemed endless and he prayed the end result would justify the discomfort.

"Ready when you are, driver." He stifled a cough and grasped the seat in front, longing now for this day to end. "Drive carefully... and *do* spare the petrol. Holy Mother Church might be disgustingly rich, but its minions are exceedingly poor."

*

Until recently, Reverend Dimpleton had loved living at St Oswald's.

Life had seemed simple and uncluttered; a joyous montage of memories, surrounded by good books and music that had once given wings to his heart. He'd never been a robust man; just one of life's plodders who somehow achieved mammoth tasks, drawing energy from his religious convictions and the ceaseless variety of human nature around him.

Now he was ninety-four, and feared death more than he'd ever done as a younger man. Distressingly, he found his faith was no longer a barrier against the nightmares that plagued him, for they came frequently now... and always in darkness.

That was why he'd had his bed moved in front of the broad bay windows. With the curtains thrown back, daylight bathed him as he slept and at night he would turn on all the lights and perpetuate the ritual of washing, eating and drinking. Always a considerate, self sufficient man and not wishing to inconvenience the kitchen staff, day time meals were left on a table outside his door; to be reheated later in his own microwave. Then he would tend his beloved orchids and read or perhaps write letters to friends who no longer replied, probably because they were all long dead; but he wrote them anyway, to keep the lengthy hours of darkness at bay.

Today, despite having followed his usual routine, he was unable to sleep. And he felt frightened. Numbness had crept into his bones and the word 'confession' kept hammering at the back of his mind.

He turned over restlessly and stared out at the extensive gardens, resplendent in their autumn coat of many colours and then raised his gaze to the sea beyond. His rheumy eyes filled with tears and uncharacteristically, a trail of saliva escaped his slackening jaw and trickled down his chin.

Why... should one minor discretion, blight a lifetime of service to church and charity alike? How could one foolish deed turn his dreams into nightmares and his days into night?

"God in heaven, help me." He closed his eyes against the beauty that confronted him and buried his thin face into his pillow, begging for sleep to come while the sun still rode high in the sky.

Today however, Reverend Dimpleton's God in heaven wasn't listening.

*

"Mr, er... Brother Ezekiel. You *may* have specifically requested room five." The manager of St Oswald's short, rotund body quivered and his bald pat bobbed up and down as he consulted the register in front of him. "But you *must* understand, I *never* permit respites to chose their own rooms. That privilege is normally left to permanent residents."

Ezekiel tapped the book with a long, bony finger.

"You won't find my name listed there, Mr Lyons," he informed him. "In essence, *that* room has remained church property since the good Brothers of Conscience ceased teaching here fourteen years ago." He leaned forward, clutching his satchel in front of him. "Believe me... there *are* good reasons why it *should* remain locked."

"It is... was!" Lyons insisted. "It's just... with this new registration ruling, Mr Cordell felt with the wall down..."

"You've breached the partition?" The words came out as a wheezing gasp, not really a question, more a declaration of total disbelief.

Lyons blinked owlishly.

"Not me personally," he began. "Cordell wishes to enlarge the room," he added assertively.

"I see." Ezekiel felt the tightness in his chest increase. "And *has* the vault been opened?"

Lyons frowned suspiciously.

"You *know* about that?"

"Of course. It *is* as I have said... church property. Has it been opened?"

Lyons hesitated.

"I understand there was nothing in it."

"*Nothing* indeed!" Ezekiel snorted, praying Lyons was right; God willing the Shadowean should have turned to dust long ago. Unknown to Father Abbot, one of his reasons for choosing St Oswald's was to enable him to renew the Binding Spell, just as a precaution. "I *must* speak to whoever did this," he insisted.

"Of course, as soon as Barry... that's our maintenance man, is released from hospital. He went down with a mysterious bug and couldn't stop shitt... er, spent hours in the bathroom he did."

Ezekiel's face remained stony.

"When you next speak to this Barry... I suggest you tell him to get on his knees and thank God he's still alive."

"Er... right, Brother." Lyons offered a key, clearly eager to end this confrontation. "Room seven, just across from five."

"At least that hasn't changed," Ezekiel snapped sarcastically, breaking off in a painful fit of coughing.

"Luggage?" Lyons was watching him closely, squinting through black, piggy eyes.

"All I need is here." He tapped the satchel.

Lyons gave him what he considered an understanding smile.

"I guess you Brothers travel light when you have God's weightier matters to deal with."

Ezekiel couldn't believe the idiot had actually said that.

"When was the vault opened?" he asked abruptly, refusing to be sidetracked.

"Sometime yesterday morning."

"One night." He glanced at his watch. "Time enough..."

"For what?"

Ezekiel hesitated.

He wanted to confide in someone. Looks could be deceiving, but Lyons was not the *one*.

"Sleep, Mr Lyons. The journey down was most unsettling." At that he was gone; to return seconds later, leaning round the door jamb, wisps of ginger-grey hair making him appear more like a refugee from a soup kitchen than a man of God. "This may seem an odd and perhaps morbid question, but have any residents died within the last twenty-four hours?

Lyons looked totally taken back.

"Who told you about Annie Booker?"

Ezekiel felt his blood run cold.

"I hope, Mr Lyons, that you are about to."

"Not much to say, really," Lyons paused and for a moment Ezekiel thought he was going to suggest he mind his own business. "The laundry girl found Mrs Booker when she went in to make up her bed this morning."

"Was there anything unusual about the manner of her passing?" Ezekiel's Adam's apple bobbed erratically around the question.

"There *has* been talk amongst the staff. Wrongly so... and I shall look into the matter. It appears the poor woman suffocated." Lyons looked uncertain whether to continue, but clearly his love of the dramatic outweighed his sense of discretion. "Word has it a large spider was lodged in her windpipe."

Ezekiel blanched. He detested spiders.

"A most unfortunate way to go," he admitted.

Lyons nodded.

"Statistics claim we swallow at least seven of the blighters during out sleeping lives." The Manager seemed proud of this piece of information. "I guess the answer's to sleep with our mouths shut..."

Ezekiel was already closing the door between them.

"I wish to God that was all we needed to do," he murmured, crossing him self as he climbed the stairs.

*

Angelica Miers studied her reflection in the bathroom mirror and smiled her singularly cynical smile.

She felt equally satisfied and amused at the decision she'd just made regarding her latest client. As 'Madam Tourvey' she had achieved considerable success in her younger days as a healer and a wise woman. She had been respected, not only for her abilities but also for her generosity, frequently cutting fees to suit the sitter's means, often giving services for free.

But travelling up and down the country at all hours of the day and night had eventually taken their toll, both financially and on her health. Bedridden with a viral infection, she had continued to work by post and had been inundated with letters from the sick and needy; letters full of pain and sorrow, listing hopes and dreams and what some considered as transgressions, minor and major, against themselves and others.

Armed with such lucrative information, an idea blossomed and was at first shamefully cast aside. However, the struggle with her conscience hadn't lasted long... and so the blackmail had started.

It had been so easy. First, a letter of sympathy requesting further details in order to make the sitting more potent; all in the deepest confidence of course. When she had the who, why and where, a different kind of letter was dispatched; outlining unexpected overheads and hinting at an incurable illness, which could suddenly leave her 'delicate' papers in the hands of her executors.

Incredibly, she faced little resistance and was amazed how eagerly people parted with their money when afraid of disclosure. Replies came to St Oswald's via a P.O. Box number and what better cover than Miss Miers, retired headmistress, school unspecified, who spends her lonely days corresponding with ex-pupils from all over the world. As far as she was aware, no one had ever checked the validity of her claims. As long as her rooms were paid for, she was confident the manager couldn't have cared less whom she was.

Her latest acquisition was a gem, linking a well known politician with an up and coming starlet, who just happened to be married to one of the country's leading police commissioners; with careful handling this one could run and run.

She smiled again and blew a kiss at her faded reflection, not seeing the cruel slash of a mouth and the bloated features, overlaid with thinning, orange dyed hair. In her mind's eye she was still Madam Tourvey; slim, auburn and mysteriously beautiful.

She stifled a yawn. Blackmail could be so exhausting and her afternoon nap was long overdue. Still in her voluminous pink fluffy dressing gown, she padded towards the bedroom and stopped abruptly.

Her front door stood open; again.

Automatically, she reached for the telephone on the side table; then thought better of it. She wasn't in the mood for a slanging match with that slime ball of a manager and if the man came up here, she'd feel obliged to get dressed... a woman of her standing couldn't deal with servants while in her night attire.

She shuddered and pushed the door to, making sure she heard the latch click. The last thing she wanted was that moth-eaten moggy pocking around and leaving its hairs all over the furniture. As far as she was concerned, the damn thing should have been put down ages ago, along with any residents who encouraged its presence.

Tomorrow, she would ask that much more approachable maintenance man to have another look at the catch. She shivered again and wondered if there was a connection between yesterday's hammering and the fact her rooms were now icy cold. Perhaps the central heating had packed up.

Muttering about withholding the exorbitant rent until jobs were completed properly, she climbed beneath the covers of her bed; with luck, her latest victim might prove lucrative enough to get her out of St Oswald's and set her up elsewhere.

Barely had her head touched the pillow when she sat upright again as her psychic intuition came into play. A sense of utmost evil filled her being, stronger than anything she had ever experienced, even in her days as Madam Tourvey.

Being the type of person she was, Angelica Miers was not consumed by fear, but with a burning desire to know the source of this power... and whether she could harness it for her own use.

*

Brother Ezekiel breathlessly climbed the stairs to his room.

He *had* been right to come back, even if it meant facing his old adversary. One death did not make a plague, but if the Shadowean had gained its freedom, it would be more wary of entrapment and unless he acted quickly, would grow strong on a new crop of victims.

Wheezing heavily, he paused on the halfway landing. Room three and four to his left and five, six and seven to his right, just as he remembered it. He hovered outside five and the years rolled back, like an ebb tide, uncovering something he wished had remained buried.

Five decades had passed. He had been a young novice, full of ideals and convictions; determined not to take the psychic path his father had mapped out for him. However, the legacy of generations of Seers was not lightly ignored and like it or not, the calling had remained with him... a taunting voice at the edge of his conscience, eating away at his faith. Now, it was too late; he no longer knew or even cared what he believed in.

His one certainty was the existence of the Shadowean, a mind altering demon, summoned from the dark realms by his mentor and headmaster, Abbot Gregory, the original founder of St Oswald's.

Unknown to the Brothers of Conscience and pupils undergoing their novitiate, Ezekiel included, Abbot Gregory had been a practising warlock; powerful enough to call up the Shadowean. No-one admitted knowing the extent of the Abbot's demonic practices; his personal papers having been consumed by a mysterious fire... but clearly something had gone wrong, for Gregory lost his life and it was assumed his soul in the process, leaving his unfortunate successor to deal with the Shadowean as best he could; as well as keeping events within church bounds, in order to protect the good name of the school.

The creature had claimed the lives of three novices before being brought under control; strings must have been pulled, Ezekiel recalled bitterly, for their untimely deaths were blamed on a flu epidemic currently ravaging the country.

Heart thumping, Ezekiel tried the door; it was not locked. Room five had once been a library and vault, where the Brothers kept their most ancient manuscripts and relics, free from the ravages of time and vermin. Guardedly, he felt himself flinch, although there was nothing to see... just a pile of rubble in the corner and a few discarded tools. The door of the vault stood open and from where he stood, he could see great gouges in the metal, where he alone knew the Shadowean had tried to claw its way to freedom.

It had been in here they had set the human bait... himself and three other Brothers, now long gone; the choice had been theirs. In a school intentionally emptied of all other life, they knew the creature would eventually seek them out; homing in on the fear that emanated from them, despite their trust in God's deliverance from evil.

He had felt, rather than heard the Shadowean's approach, like a creeping malaise; that spoke of every hurt he had ever known... his mother's early death... the painful clash between father and son... and then it was there, in the room with them, like a wisp of smoke, seemingly transparent and wholly terrifying.

As a novice, it had been his instruction to hold the heavy volume while Brother Martin read the invocation; but the good man had faltered and the Shadowean had thrown him aside, bloodied and broken. Brothers Vernon and Askew had thrust Ezekiel forward, crosses and candles held high, prayers trembling on their lips as they did their utmost to conceal themselves behind his gangling frame.

So he had been forced to take control and from the first command he had felt the ancestral power course through him. He still recalled the words of the Binding Spell, as though he had spoken them only yesterday. His voice had rung out with vibrant clarity and each word had hammered into the Shadowean. From a confident advance, the creature had been forced to back off, roaring in anger and pain as it railed damnation upon them.

The Brothers had gone down in a hail of precious books and manuscripts, but Ezekiel had remained unscathed and undaunted. Unholy obscenities had rained on his young ears and constantly he had felt the Shadowean trying to probe his mind, seeking to use his own fears against him. He may not have followed his Father's path, but he had been schooled well... taught how to reach down to his inner self and focus the mind so that it became a powerful tool and an impregnable barrier.

It seemed like the battle of wills had continued for hours, but in reality it could have only been a matter of minutes before the creature had made a mistaken bid for freedom. Metal bolts were swiftly drawn and not until then had he allowed himself to collapse out of sheer terror, the last scraps of paper fluttering around the three of them as Brothers Vernon and Askew clung together, thanking God for their deliverance.

In the days that followed, while he had lain seemingly at Death's door, the vault had been bricked up and the room locked. Brother Martin had been quietly interred and the House of Conscience had eventually returned to a semblance of calm under the gentle, but firm hand of Father Ansalem, Abbot Gregory's more than worthy successor.

Upon awakening, Ezekiel's one instruction from the Council had been *never* to repeat a word of what had occurred. If questioned, the church would deny everything and start proceedings towards his committal.

"Bigoted fools!" Ezekiel said aloud, off a religion that sanctioned exorcism and in the next breath denied its part in the scheme of things.

There was nothing to be achieved here, Ezekiel decided. The least he could do was to persuade them not to dismantle the vault, it might well be needed again. He glanced sadly at the pile of rubble, thrown carelessly in the corner where Brother Martin had died. With a whispered prayer for the departed, he closed the door and crossed to number seven.

*

Ignatius Wirrel had led a good life.

There was 'no gainsaying that' as his old Gran would once have said. And it was true. He'd had a happy and contented marriage with a wonderful woman who had given him six healthy boys; these in turn had fathered eleven grand children, all of whom were now in their teens and beyond.

The fact none of his family came to St Oswald's hurt more than he cared to admit. Nevertheless, his conscience was clear. He had done right by all of them, offering long years of love and support.

The money had changed everything.

His wife's life insurance, added to the sale of their house, reached quite a substantial sum. Each offspring was favoured equally in his Will, but what with mortgages and college fees, he knew the funds were needed now.

So he'd decided they could have it all.

He was comfortable at St Oswald's, but why waste money perpetuating a life that had grown empty. He felt like the dregs of a good bottle of wine... the quality stuff was gone. He stared at the envelope propped against the sugar bowl. It was addressed to his eldest son. Arnie would understand; he would know how and what to tell the others.

He shoved aside his empty dinner plate and stood up. Today, he'd eaten in his room, instead of the lounge. The food had turned to rubber in his mouth, but he'd persisted, assuming the tablets would be more effective on a full stomach. For a seventy-eight year old, his step could still be considered sprightly as he crossed to the dresser; just a slouch in the narrow shoulders and a slight tremble betrayed his nerves as he poured a full glass of whisky.

The pills were already waiting for him, lined up like little death-dealing soldiers on the window seat. He sat for a few minutes looking out over the bay. It promised to be a glorious evening. The sea was like a millpond, lapping gently against the rocky shore, beneath a sky laced with every colour of the rainbow.

"Just one more sunset, Ignatius," he said aloud, popping the first of the pills into his mouth. He would allow himself that much. Making himself comfortable, he stretched out and made sure he could still reach the side lamp from where he was sitting.

Ignatius Wirrel wasn't afraid of death... but he had always been terrified of the dark.

*

The Shadowean was playing mind games.

It had tagged on to a middle aged, rotund carer as she went about her rounds, switching on lights and looking in on residents. The creature found it easy to probe her mind, preoccupied as she was with the task at hand, injecting scenarios and assessing her subconscious reaction. When the woman suddenly miss-stepped, as though avoiding something unpleasant and apprehensively followed its progress down the corridor... the Shadowean knew it had her. This human creature was scared of rats.

With consummate patience, born of centuries, the Shadowean began to weave its spell...

*

"Goodnight, Robert," Mariel said. "I'm sure they'll 'ave the 'eating sorted by morning." She too shivered at the extreme chill that pervaded the resident's rooms. "Sleep well, love." Closing the door to room twenty, Mariel backed into total darkness.

The fire doors at each end of the corridor were shut and the only light entered through a small window, either side of the drugs cupboard. Could she have known the fate awaiting her, Mariel would have gone back to Robert Sadler's room and pressed the call-bell for assistance. Instead she edged her way along the wall, towards the nearest light switch.

A slight sound made her turn and then turn again as a similar noise seemed to come from both sides. At first she thought it might have been Mia. Then she gave a nervous gasp as something scampered across her feet. She looked down and numerous pinpoints of reddish light stared back at her, blinking on and off.

Rats?

A heavy body brushed her ankle and then she felt the first bite, needle sharp, at the base of her heel. She screamed and kicked out, feeling the teeth loose their grip. She heard a squeal and a satisfying thud and frantically fumbled for the light switch, still terrifyingly beyond her reach. Sobbing breathlessly, she took another faltering step, trying not to loose control as more rats took their companion's place, clawing at her legs and clambering over each other to gain purchase on the hem of her overall.

Her mind screamed in protest as she lashed out at the rising tide of dark bodies. This *couldn't* be happening to her, not here... not at St Oswald's.

She felt an additional weight on her back and fell against the wall, intending to use her bulk to crush the life out of the rodent nuzzling at the nape of her neck; but the creature merely hopped onto her shoulder and sank its teeth into her left ear. The pain was excruciating; she felt as though her entire body was on fire as the rodents tore at her clothing and freshly exposed flesh, maddened now by the smell of blood.

The sheer weight of numbers brought Mariel to her knees and finally onto her back. She snatched a rat from her ample breast, oblivious of its teeth gnawing viciously at her fingers as she hammered its squirming body against the wall. As consciousness began to slip away, her fear of the inevitable came out in one, drawn out scream of protest.

*

Brother Ezekiel sat bolt upright.

Disorientated at finding the room in darkness, he slipped from the bed. He was still dressed in his habit, having intended to doze for a few moments before going in search of something to eat. It took several seconds for him to realize what had awakened him.

A scream! He'd heard an awful, bloodcurdling scream.

The passage outside his room was brightly lit and empty. However, it was the bitter chill that drew him on, past room five and up half a dozen stairs to the next landing. It felt as though he was wading uphill through an icy stream... a feeling that for some reason seemed unpleasantly familiar. Wheezing softly, he hesitated before the closed fire door, suddenly afraid of what he might find on the other side.

Despite his frequent lack of faith, one hand automatically clutched his simple wooden cross as he eased the door open a crack. An icy cold blast took his breath away. He could see nothing in the total darkness and it felt as though someone was holding the door shut from the other side. He pushed harder and as the gap widened, a beam of light crept down the wall, highlighting the obstruction.

A large woman lay on her back behind the door. Even as Ezekiel watched, she made a soft mewing sound and flapped one hand weakly over her clothing. Her other fist, tightly clenched, was held aloft.

"Get 'em off me. Pleassss."

Terror-filled eyes begged Ezekiel for help. He reached for the wall switch, bracing himself for the worst. Lights flickered on.

Mariel stared up at him, blinking furiously.

She wriggled into a sitting position, frowning at her empty fist. Then she checked her legs. There was not a mark on her. Not a drop of blood stained her overall.

"I... I don't understand."

Ezekiel squinted along the brightly lit corridor and for a moment thought he saw a smoky shadow, drifting away towards the far end. By the time he'd blinked and focused his tired gaze it was gone.

"I don't understand," Mariel said again, wide-eyed and still very much afraid. "Rats... wuz all over me."

"Here." Ezekiel offered a thin, veined hand. "Let me help you, my dear."

A door banged down below and footsteps sounded on the stairs. Despite her large bulk and state of mind, Mariel managed to pull herself quickly upright.

"Please Brother... don't say anyfing ta the others. I'll loose me job if you do."

Before Ezekiel could respond, Mariel was heading back towards Robert Sadler's room, sobbing quietly to herself as she straightened her clothing and tucked strands of mousy coloured hair behind her ears.

*

The Shadowean had never known such fury since the day of its incarceration. It wanted to rend and tear, to drain the life force from the human who dared intervene in its pleasure.

It watched from the alcove beside the drugs cupboard, struggling to keep itself transparent, to prevent flares of colour coursing through its veins, indicators of its anger and frustration. The large human would not escape. It had tasted her essence; she had its mark upon her. It was just a matter of time.

As for the other one, standing motionless in the doorway. The creature suppressed a snarl as it recognized the strange garb of those who had once persecuted it... yet there was also a deeper familiarity in the way the man studied the corridor, his head slightly to one side, one hand fingering the useless icon around his neck. What was he looking for? What was he expecting to see? The Shadowean felt the grey eyes settle briefly on its place of concealment. Had the human somehow sensed its presence? It would prove simple enough to find out. Silvery tentacles snaked the length off the corridor... but made contact with nothing but the closed fire door.

The man had gone.

Doubly frustrated, the Shadowean countered the urge to follow. The time for games was over. Retracting its sensors, it went in search of easier, more accessible prey.

*

Brother Ezekiel's worst fears had now been confirmed.

With the briefest of glances at the male carer who brushed past him on the stairs, he returned to his room and slipped the catch. He leant against the door, aware his breath was coming in short, tortured gasps as he considered what he had just witnessed; the bone numbing cold, darkness, the personal, all consuming fear... indicators of the Shadowean's presence. He didn't need to ask that unfortunate carer what was her greatest nightmare. Somehow, he would *have* to speak to her again... and soon.

He unzipped his satchel and allowed the meagre contents to slide across the bed. On top of his few personal items, rested a thick, leather bound volume of indeterminate age. His father's Book of Shadows and his father before him, Generations of Spells and Potions. Words of power to harm or heal. Despite their ancient manuscripts, the Brothers of Conscience had clearly not possessed the ultimate knowledge, but herein he hoped to find an answer, a way of sending the Shadowean back into darkness. But he knew he couldn't do it alone. Whatever powers had been his by birthright had waned with physical age and his disregard for their importance.

Wearily, he carried the book to a high-backed chair by the window. He was tired and hungry and very much afraid, because he *knew* no matter the outcome, for Brother Ezekiel of the Holy Brothers of Conscience... there could be escape from the abyss opening before him.

*

Reverend Dimpleton slept on as darkness descended, twisting and turning as he sank deeper into his nightmare.

It always started the same... as though he was suspended from a great height. He would see himself as a much younger man, slipping out of his robes after Sunday morning service. Nolan, his head choir boy would come in and Dimpleton would again think how inappropriate he looked in his smock; he may have had the voice of an angel, but his body was that of a teenage rugby player. He can see that the boy is clearly distressed... almost tearful, undoubtedly having been the pawn in yet another row between his parents.

Dimpleton would go forward and comfort the lad, as he would any member of his flock. His words appear to ease the boy's distress. He gives his blessing and gently kisses the top of the tousled, blond head. Then suddenly his lips are caressing Nolan's smooth brow, the bridge of his nose, moving down... until their eyes meet.

The boy does not flinch, but there is such an expression of surprise and loathing in his blue eyes that it is Dimpleton who steps back, stunned at the enormity of what he has done. Nolan stumbles out, choking back fresh tears at this new, unexpected betrayal.

Even in his dream state, Dimpleton struggled against what he knew was coming next; how Nolan had hanged himself in Priory Wood that very same morning.

He had gone along with the distraught parents blaming themselves, but what he'd never come to terms with was the way he had allowed them to believe the responsibility was theirs alone... knowing his own actions had probably turned Nolan's already troubled mind.

One stupid mistake... so many lives ruined!

For the thousandth time, tears of guilt and self-pity spilled over onto his seamed cheeks, soaking the pillow on either side... but they would never be enough to quench the flames of his torment.

*

Mariel knocked lightly on Reverend Dimpleton's door.

Despite being badly shaken, she'd decided to say nothing to her colleagues and finish her night shift as usual. As an epileptic, she'd just learned an unpleasant lesson and would never again allow her medication to lapse; it was more than her job *or* her sanity was worth. However, before going of duty, she would find out if that kind Brother was still on the premises and offer a discreet explanation.

Receiving no answer from Dimpleton, she looked in to find the Reverend was sleeping uncharacteristically late into the evening. His stentorian breathing reassured her and she backed out again, placing his evening meal on the side table as pre-arranged.

Suddenly, she gasped and swayed against the wall as an icy dart pierced her through and through.

Savouring Mariel's essence for the second time that night, the Shadowean slipped past her into the Reverend's room.

*

Reverend Dimpleton stirred, fighting against the restricting bedclothes, trying to resurrect himself from this nightmare, which had suddenly taken an unfamiliar path.

Organ music had started up again, drawing what had become an older Dimpleton out into the body of the church. The largest congregation he had ever resided over, waited for him; all those souls he had committed to the ground during his long, wasted life. Row upon row of blackened faces, uplifted, their ruptured flesh crawling with corruption, their sightless eye sockets filled with an unholy light. Nolan was there, in front of the choir stalls, with a rope still tight around his neck, his swollen tongue making a parody of the hymn 'Abide With Me.'

Dimpleton followed the boy's gaze. Over the pulpit, an empty noose awaited his convenience. Drawn by a power beyond his control, he mounted the steps, accompanied by a slow handclap that became a deafening crescendo of stamping feet until he had placed the hemp about his own neck. The organ music abruptly ceased and a hush fell upon the congregation. Dimpleton cast around at the gathering as he had done so many times before... yet there was no hint of compassion, just an awful expectancy. Finally he singled out young Nolan.

"Please forgive me," he mouthed, before stepping out into space.

*

The Shadowean spread its membranes like a canopy over the bed as Reverend Dimpleton began to gasp and flail around.

It gave a satisfied, sucking noise as the man's bony fingers clawed at his scrawny throat, the Adam's apple bobbing wildly as the creature watched the haggard features turn from grey to the darkest purple. A deep, expectant sigh trembled through the Shadowean's frame and it leant nearer, almost lying across the struggling figure as the Reverend's tongue began to protrude, forcing gobbets of saliva to fly from the frantically turning head.

There would be no escape... not like the fat one. This time the Shadowean would have its way. It gave a slow, sibilant hiss of disappointment as all too soon, Dimpleton's struggles became weaker and more sporadic... finally ceasing with a wild kick and a shudder that shook the entire bed.

DAY THREE

It was almost dawn when Brother Ezekiel finally closed the Book of Shadows.

With a far from steady hand, he carefully tucked the volume down beside him in the chair. If he had been afraid before, he was absolutely terrified now. Terrified... and filled with despair at what he had read; at the impossible situation in which he and St Oswald's found themselves. He closed his eyes and scrubbed at his face with stiff fingers and for the first time in many years he longed for his father's presence; he would have known what to do.

Just as he'd expected, the incantations and ritual were all there. But a sacrifice was also required... a willing victim the creature would be unable to refuse, one whose faith and willpower was essential to drive the Shadowean back into darkness; a requirement he knew he could no longer fulfil, both as a human being and a man of the church.

He raised re-rimmed eyes and stared out at the breaking dawn. It was going to be a beautiful day. For long minutes he sat and watched crimson fingers of light spread across the sapphire sea and actually shuddered at the scene before him, as always, questioning... questioning. If indeed there was a

God, why did he allow evil to walk the earth in the face of such beauty.

*

Ignatius Wirrel awoke to bright sunshine and a thumping headache.

He was surprised to find himself still propped upright in his chair before the window. The once neat line of tablets, now greatly reduced in number, were scattered over the window seat and on the floor at his feet; after months of careful hoarding, now there wasn't enough left to cure a headache.

Cautiously, he stood up and stretched, patting his sides as though rediscovering his body... feeling the blood course through his veins, warming his cramped limbs and awakening unexpected pangs of hunger. With a markedly renewed spring in his step, he made a circuit of the room before picking up the manila envelope addressed to his son and tearing it open, frowning over the neat, copperplate hand as though he had already forgotten what he'd written and the reasons why. After a moment's hesitation, he crumpled the single sheet and dropped it into the waste bin beneath the table.

He closed his eyes, took a deep, steadying breath and opened them again to view his surroundings with newfound confidence. Always a strong believer in fate; he maintained a lifelong insistence in there being no such thing as coincidence; there was a purpose for everything, no matter how illogical it might seem at the time. Perhaps, after all, this hadn't been his moment to go.

The family would have to wait for their inheritance. Something told Ignatius Wirrel he still had a little more living to do.

*

It was an accepted fact that Millicent Toppler was always the first resident down to breakfast.

Any break in this long standing routine would have caused instant concern amongst the carers. Occasionally, greeted by

Mia... who associated her arrival with the first meal of the day. This morning, however, the grey tabby obviously had business elsewhere.

Millicent had her own special chair by the window, padded out with cushions to ease the painful curvature of her spine, which she always approached in a crabwise manner, assisted by two strong walking sticks and an even stouter heart.

In all of her seventy-three years she had never allowed anything to visibly bring her down, especially her health, which had been poor from day one. Luckily, in an age when the only support for premature birth was hope and plenty of tender loving care, her parents had supplied both in abundance.

Physically deformed she may have been, but until recently her mind had been as sharp as a razor. From an early age she had developed the knack of comparing herself with those she considered less fortunate; those maimed not in body, but in spirit, whose dull, lacklustre eyes masked a trapped and frustrated soul. Consequentially, her life had become dedicated to working alongside the mentally handicapped. From age ten, she had started selling toys on her grandmother's highly polished stoop and six decades later, she was still being asked to sit on the Board of Directors of numerous societies and institutions; although admittedly the invitations came less frequently now.

Upstairs, the mantelpiece in her room groaned under the weight of awards and diplomas gathered along the way. Every one was important to her, not for reasons of self-gratification, but as markers for a failing mind; they were islands in a once busy life that reminded her who she was, where she had been and God willing, gave some indication of where she might yet venture.

Now she approached all things with a positive, no messing frame of mind. Tomorrow could look after itself... today she was determined to be the woman she had always been. Each morning, when she opened her eyes, the first thing she saw was a notice that read:

*'Don't waste precious moments worrying about what might have
happened yesterday... you probably won't remember anyway.'*
Dementia may have been steadily claiming her memory,
but it hadn't curbed her love of studying faces... of locking on
to a troubled gaze with brilliant blue eyes that were both
gentle and compelling. People still opened up and told her
their problems. Total strangers went away feeling uplifted...
that perhaps their dreams could after all become reality; that
life was not so bad. Some claimed she had missed her vocation
as a counsellor, but she doubted that would have brought her
anywhere near as close to the wonderful characters that had so
enriched her life.

With practised caution, she eased herself into her chair,
remembering too late, there were papers in her bag intended
for Reverend Dimpleton, regarding a charity they were both
acquainted with. She would take them along this evening; she
knew he would not come down to breakfast and she had no
wish to disturb the gentlemen's peculiar sleeping arrangements. She pictured his drawn, aesthetic features and felt the
usual rise of concern for her friend; now there was a troubled
mind if ever she saw one.

One face she would miss was Annie Booker's. Her passing
had greatly saddened her, although she also saw it as a
welcome release, however unexpected. Many an enjoyable
afternoon had been spent at Annie's bedside, swapping
anecdotes jointly spanning fifteen decades, although of late,
her own recollections had become sketchier. She had
recognized much of herself in that gentle, unassuming woman
and wished now their paths had crossed earlier in their lives.

She shuddered, wondering, not for the first time, why St
Oswald's had grown uncharacteristically cold over the last
few days. She was just considering asking one of the breakfast
girls to fetch a cardigan for her, when an unfamiliar face
distracted her, bobbing briefly round the doorjamb.

She glimpsed spiky ginger hair and a rumpled, concerned
expression before the head withdrew to fetch a long neck and
a lanky body clothed in a monk's habit; despite the man's

deep set, kindly grey eyes and obvious age, Millicent instantly sensed the robe didn't sit too lightly on the slim frame.

*

Brother Ezekiel hesitated in the doorway, not wishing to intrude on the solitary figure seated by the window, even though the woman beckoned him over.

"Good morning, Brother?" Despite an apparently frail demeanour, her voice was strong and held a firm invitation.

"Good morning," Ezekiel returned, exchanging one foot awkwardly for the other like a shy stork, glancing round at the empty tables.

"Looking for someone in particular?"

"The refectory... actually." Ezekiel failed to keep the desperate note from his voice. Physical hunger was not helping the mental anguish he was going through. "Things have changed since I was last..." he broke off, thinking it best not to go down that road.

The woman appeared not to have noticed.

"I'm always early," she said. "The girls will be along in a minute... they start upstairs with assisted feeders and those who prefer to eat in their rooms. I'm Millicent Toppler."

"Brother Ezekiel."

"Spoilt for choice!" The women's smile was infectious. "But you're welcome to camp here if you wish."

Ezekiel weaved his way between the tables.

"Resident, or just visiting... Oh my!" The pale hands clutching two walking sticks gave an involuntary shudder. "There *hasn't* been another death?"

Her unexpected exclamation startled Ezekiel.

"I've heard of only one, my dear. A Mrs Booker."

"Miss Booker."

"You knew the lady?"

"Not as well... or for as long as I'd have wished," Millicent admitted. "Annie was confined to bed. We often chatted to help pass the time of day."

Ezekiel nodded.

"Haven't seen you around. Just arrived?"

"Midday, yesterday. Here for my health." *And everybody else's,* Ezekiel muttered under his breath. "Respite for bronchial pneumonia..."

"Yet you already know about Annie."

Smart bird this one. Piercing blue eyes met his gaze and it was Ezekiel who broke away, shunting chairs as he played for time.

"You *can* tell me to mind my own business," Millicent allowed. Again giving that disarming smile. "Yet somehow I have a feeling you wouldn't want to do that."

Ezekiel tucked in his habit and settled, facing Millicent across the table. Instantly, he felt enveloped by this women's aura. The sensation was not unpleasant, very convivial for conversation. Yet how could he express the terrible danger they were all in, without having her believe him totally insane?

"I'm a good listener, you know," Millicent persisted.

"That's a rare commodity these days," Ezekiel responded diplomatically.

"Been here before then?" she asked disarmingly.

"Er..." For Ezekiel, the rattle of cutlery heralded a welcome distraction.

*

Angelica Miers just *knew* something odd was going on.

Her mind had been in psychic overdrive since long before dawn and now her head felt as though it was about to burst.

In desperation, she'd resorted to dealing the cards; something she hadn't done for many a year. The pack had belonged to a batty old aunt who gave readings to holidaymakers on the south coast; admittedly, Angelica was a bit rusty, yet no matter what method she tried... twelve card spread, the Horoscope, Bohemian... the result was the same. Nothing but death and destruction! And the coming of a prophet of doom!

The Madam Tourvey streak was still strong enough in her not to leave it there. A massive surge of negative power had encroached on the tranquillity of St Oswald's and she wanted to know its source. Control was what her life was about. The red slash of her mouth curled with vicious determination... she *had* to know!

With dangerous disregard, she swept aside the tarot and hurried through to the lounge. Upending her coffee table, she dragged aside the circular rug. The faded outline of a pentacle showed on the dusty floorboards; a discovery she'd made and disguised again many years before. She was not totally unfamiliar with such devices; undoubtedly a previous occupant had also been a seeker of knowledge.

The day was young. Time enough for her to prepare. With the coming of darkness, she would search out this source of power and demand that it bow before her.

*

Robert Sadler may have been blind, but he was not stupid. There was something seriously wrong with Mariel, his favourite carer.

Yesterday evening, having settled him for the night, Mariel had returned to his room in a high state of agitation. She'd fluffed around, claiming to have mislaid the keys to the drug cupboard, although Robert now believed differently... and then seemed reluctant to leave, occasionally giving a soft, hiccupping kind of sigh, worlds apart from the women who'd wished him a good night's sleep only moments before.

St Oswald's was now his home and Robert cared about the staff and other residents, just as he'd considered people all his life. When they were troubled, he was troubled too.

Blind since birth, his sighted parents had nurtured and protected him until he was of school age. Then their tactics had abruptly changed, teaching him to be strong and confident in the face of adversity.

He soon learned the outside world could be cruel to those considered less than perfect. But he never allowed himself to see it that way. He decided very early on that perfection came from within and was reflected in the way you lived your life.

As far as he was concerned, we were all entrusted with the same task... to make this world a better and safer place for every living thing.

The races he ran were on paper. His thirst for knowledge and understanding outstripped his colleagues in every school and college he attended and carried over into his adult life. Accolade followed accolade. Humanitarian awards came from all sides. Even consultants consulted him, trusting implicitly in his uncanny understanding of human nature.

All things, however, come to an end.

Retirement came and the adviser of princes and paupers alike, realized he'd neglected to consider the emptiness and solitude of his own future. Using his life savings and valuable business contacts, he'd formed the 'The Society for the Single Sight Impaired', a network that spanned the world and gave people like himself the opportunity to communicate, whatever their financial or personal circumstances. Then, three years ago, the funds of the 'SSSI' had vanished, along with a trusted member of staff, and he was forced to declare bankruptcy.

The man who'd given his life to society, found society was prepared to give very little in return. Now, classed merely as a pensioner, with few possessions and of no monitory value to the state, St Oswald's had become his retreat... the only light in his world of darkness.

Now, having spent a relatively sleepless night worrying about Mariel, he'd finally pressed his call-bell; something he rarely did, only to find she had gone off duty and wouldn't be back until the following evening.

This news brought the strangest of sensations to Robert Sadler... a feeling that he was never going to see Mariel again.

*

Brother Ezekiel had to admit, breakfast with Millicent Toppler had been an enjoyable experience.

The woman was an entertaining conversationalist, a perfect foil for his own dry sense of humour. It was enlightening to talk to someone other than his fellow Brothers, whose views were somewhat limited, closeted as they were from the realities of the world. Ezekiel sensed Millicent knew he was tiptoeing around the opportunity for 'more serious' confidences. This fact was brought to a head when his second delicious cup of coffee arrived with a gentle tap on the shoulder. Startled, Ezekiel turned, expecting to find Father Abbot standing there, ready to admonish him for partaking off such luxuries.

A familiar face, no longer fearful, elicited a guarded smile from himself and a welcome from Millicent as she exchanged introductions.

"Brother Ezekiel... I just wanted ta thank you for last night."

Ezekiel was aware Millicent's gaze held them both.

"An fer not saying anyfing to the uvers," Mariel added, sounding slightly uncertain if this was *still* the case.

"It was nothing, Mariel." He wished that were true.

"If you only knew 'ow important..."

"Believe me, my child," Ezekiel faced her squarely and grasped both her hands lightly in his own. "*I do know!* I understood exactly what was happening."

Something in his words or expression registered.

"S'funny. Didn't expect someone in your profession to understand about epileptic fits."

Ezekiel hesitated for a second.

"I assure you," he gave her hands a gentle squeeze before letting them go, "some servants of the church have greater afflictions than many on the outside world." Mariel's expression clearly told him a weight had been lifted from her mind and Ezekiel decided it was best to leave it at that... for now.

"I must be off." She shuffled her large bulk expertly backwards between the tables, still smiling at them both. "My shift ended 'alf 'our ago an me old ma'll be wondering where I've got ta." At that she was gone, hopefully back to a much safer place.

"Hmm?" Millicent raised thick, questioning eyebrows.

The bustle and chatter of other residents settling down to breakfast faded into the background. One glance at Millicent Toppler's expression and Brother Ezekiel knew the game was up.

*

Five urgent strides took Ignatius Wirrel into the hall.

He had just been considering taking a walk, in order to shake off the after effects of the sleeping tablets, when he'd heard a distinct crash from the suit of rooms opposite.

Reverend Dimpleton's door stood open, held that way by Todd, a new carer Ignatius had been introduced to earlier in the week. All credit to the white-faced lad as he tried to block Ignatius' view; but not before he'd seen Dimpleton stretched out on the bed, his contorted features, blue-black against the pillows, one hand clawing his throat in apparent desperation and the other held outwards, not in panic, as would have been expected... but suggesting a gentle gesture of benediction.

"Sorry you had to see that, sir," Todd quietly closed the door, as though the resident inside were only sleeping. "Shook me rather," he admitted, "his evening meal still being here like." He hesitated, glancing down at the mess of food and broken crockery. Mia arrived as from nowhere and began industriously lapping at an upturned jug of milk.

"Best go tell the Manager," Ignatius suggested. "Mr Lyons, isn't it?"

"Yes sir." Todd sounded relieved to receive positive direction.

"I won't mention I've seen anything," Ignatius promised soberly. "Could be upsetting for the other residents."

"Thank you, sir," Todd called back. He was already halfway down the corridor, eager to get away.

Ignatius felt the least he could do was scrape the meal back onto the tray, which he returned to the side table, much to Mia's disgust; head and tail erect, she wandered off in search of a more considerate human being.

Waiting until he heard Todd's footsteps descend the stairs, he eased open the Reverend's door and hovered on the threshold, wondering why. Voyeurism wasn't his thing. He was barely acquainted with Dimpleton. He allowed his gaze to rest briefly on the bed and then pass over the tidy interior, not really sure what had drawn him in; yet disturbed to know something had done so.

He backed out; doubly glad his attempted suicide hadn't worked. Seeing young Todd's face made him realize he hadn't once considered the effect of his actions on the poor devil that actually found his body.

He'd exchanged slippers for outside shoes and donned a lightweight coat before the answer came to him... something totally out of character. One fact he *had* gleaned about Dimpleton was his love of plants, particularly orchids.

He realized every piece of greenery in that room had been nothing but a dry, shrivelled husk.

*

Brother Ezekiel held his breath and waited.

Millicent Toppler had said nothing throughout his lengthy explanation, although he had her full attention, which wasn't surprising, with such a tale as his, believable or not. Residents came and went, including Mia, who was whisked away to be fed by one of the staff. Tables were cleared, their own included, all seemingly unnoticed; trivial details that no longer mattered at this moment in time. Millicent's expression gave nothing away, although tension showed in her constant white knuckled grip on the walking sticks.

"Poor Annie!" she finally exclaimed, no longer able to contain her emotions. "You *really* believe that creature... this Shadowean caused her death?"

"I don't have any proof and I doubt we'd find any at this stage, but," he shrugged narrow shoulders, "after what I witnessed with Mariel..."

"She must have been terrified."

"That's why I didn't say anything just now," Ezekiel admitted. "Better to let her believe she suffered one of her attacks."

"At least she's safe at home."

"But for how long?"

"Speak to Lyons," Millicent suggested in a lowered voice, although they were now quite alone. "Maybe advise closing the place... for the time being."

Ezekiel sighed. He knew she was right, but his hands were tied.

"I can't, not without authorization from church superiors. Trouble is, there's nobody else left alive who knows the Shadowean truly exists; Father Ansalem died several years ago... the creature's nothing but the stuff legends are made off."

"Or nightmares." Millicent leant back on her cushions, walking sticks crossed against her chest. "So! What can I do to help?"

Ezekiel wasn't ready for that one.

Millicent virtually knew as much as he did; which meant he'd probably broken every church ruling in the book and when the facts came out, he could expect to face excommunication at the very least. His own grey eyes met her bright-eyed gaze and his heart sank.

How could he tell this genuine, caring lady what he needed most of all was someone willing to accompany the beast back to hell.

*

The Shadowean was restless.

Cold, hooded eyes watched the grill in the wall that measured the passing of time. The daylight hours were too long. Already it wished to feed again. Very soon, hunger would force it out before the cover of darkness had fully formed. So far, each of its prey had been a mere husk, their life force almost spent. That fat one, however, would have sustained it, had the scrawny creature not intervened.

The Shadowean stirred angrily, flexing its membranes in the confined space of the boiler room; colours pulsed through its transparent veins, flashing like a million fireflies in the darkness.

At first it had believed destroying *that one* would prove compensation enough; convinced the strange, flapping garb shrouded a thousand terrors, all there to mould to its own bidding. Now, the Shadowean was *almost* sure why the figure seemed familiar... and if it were right, it would demand more than mortal suffering; it would flay *his* very soul and suspend it eternally over the pits of hell.

*

Angelica Miers was also impatient for darkness to fall.

The pentacle was ready. Candles were in position, to be lighted at each point. Unfortunately these were not black, as she would have wished... pink jasmine were all she could find at such short notice; although she understood the importance of ritual, she doubted if it mattered in this case. Plastic cups stood on the side table, filled with holy water, filched from nearby Trinity Church; luckily there'd been a christening that very morning. The final touch was the summoning ritual, hand printed on a card pinned to the adjacent wall, a concession to poor eyesight and a memory that failed her when nerves took over.

She checked the wall clock. The day was still young. There were letters she could be writing to 'clients', she thought, pacing the room; that would help pass the time, but it wouldn't bring her down, which was what she needed.

Selecting a meditation tape and portable player from her bookcase, she headed for the bathroom. Soon, all that could be heard was gentle music and the relaxing sound of running water, incongruously in contrast with the dark thoughts inhabiting her mind.

*

As manager of St Oswald's, Lyons was a man who preferred the quiet life.

He liked co-operative, easily manipulated staff and low maintenance residents; no serious nursing requirements or advanced cases of dementia. Everyone jogging along, including an owner who rarely showed his face or asked embarrassing questions... as long as the books and head count tallied.

Lyons inevitably got his way, until this last week.

One death he could deal with; but now it seemed there were two, inconveniently close together. He scowled at his most inexperienced carer and wondered briefly if any blame could be laid in that direction. Annie Booker's death was no problem. She had seen a doctor in the last two weeks and her demise had been virtually expected. The Reverend, however, hadn't accepted medical attention for many months, possibly a year or so.

'My faith in God heals all ailments,' Dimpleton had tirelessly echoed.

Unfortunately, his stubbornness could now mean an autopsy.

"Are you quite sure?"

Todd nodded, wide-eyed and a bit green round the gills.

"Yes, Mr Lyons. He was all twisted..."

"Spare me the details," he snapped. "We'd best go and have a look." Reluctantly, he stood up from his desk. "Just don't tell the other residents. Dimpleton's death isn't officially confirmed until the examiner says so. Then you can get one of the girls to help you wash and lay him out."

"Yes sir..." was all Todd managed before slumping against the wall and sliding gently to the floor.

Lyons found it difficult to refrain from kicking the helpless boy; and probably would have done so had another carer not come hurrying to his assistance.

*

Of course word did get around.

Todd was carted off to the sick room and eventually sent home. The shortage of staff brought Mariel back on the floor and the first thing Lyons told her to deal with was the Reverend Dimpleton.

When Millicent heard the news she was still ensconced in the dining room with Ezekiel. To say she was distraught was an understatement. She had been 'fond of the old fellow', as she put it and concerned by the torment that entered his latter years.

For very different reasons, Ezekiel was equally troubled and considered requesting to view the body. However, Lyons would have asked difficult questions and the Shadowean would have been out of the vault, so to speak. It was Millicent who suggested slipping in to the Reverend's room on the pretext of the charity papers she carried in her bag. Brother Ezekiel's acceptance of this idea as they made their conspiring way upstairs, confirmed he now had an ally at St Oswald's.

*

Mariel had not wanted to return to work so soon. Normally she couldn't wait to get back to her 'old luvvies' as she called them; so much so that her ma jealously claimed her daughter preferred their company to her own.

Walking reluctantly along the top corridor, Mariel shivered as she passed the drugs cupboard and hesitated outside Robert Sadler's door, feeling guilty over the concern she knew she'd raised in him the previous evening. Firstly however, she had to check out the Reverend's room before IDOC arrived.

"You know the score," Lyons had warned. "Just don't touch anything." From past experience, Mariel knew that also meant, "Not unless you notice something that might land us in the shit!"

Sometimes she wondered about her manager.

*

The Shadowean could wait no longer.

The creature slipped from its lair and sped up the back stairway, lured on by the scent of helpless prey waiting on the floors above. Like all hunters, it was becoming accustomed to its surroundings, to the heartbeat of St Oswald's.

As it moved, it allowed its membranes to touch every surface, to infiltrate beneath doors and through windows, seeking out and memorizing every detail that might maintain or threaten its existence; from the place of its incarceration right down to the life force that scurried beneath the floor and behind the skirting boards.

Tonight it was determined to feed long and well... to reinstate its presence once and for all on the world of lesser mortals.

*

The doctor duly arrived and Mariel found her self waved aside by her impatient manager.

After a brief examination, he announced Reverend Dimpleton deceased from this world and departed leaving a disgruntled Lyons with a declaration of 'autopsy required'.

Before the day was over, Mariel guessed most of the residents would know; that always meant a drop in moral, which made her job harder.

Against Lyons' instructions, she worked on alone, needing time to think as she tenderly washed and dressed the Reverend in what was literally his Sunday best, thinking sadly how she would miss the old boy and his funny, nocturnal ways.

She might not have 'inerited' her father's brain box, as her ma was fond of saying; but she knew when something was wrong. She had already removed the plants... shrivelled, dried out stalks; knowing twenty-four hours ago they'd been living, green and vibrant; now she found Dimpleton's skin was unusually dry and there was little evidence of body fluids. It was as though all moisture had drained away, not only from the body, but from the room as well.

No wonder IDOC wanted an autopsy.

She was just trying to recall if Dimpleton had ever mentioned any living relatives, when a faint sound made her turn...

*

Robert Sadler had decided to call it a day. He'd hardly slept the night before and he felt exhausted. He would be warmer in bed... his room remained freezing cold, no matter how he adjusted the central heating. Apparently the maintenance man was laid up with a stomach bug, so true to character, he could see no point making a fuss.

So, time to retire; as always, with the door propped open so he could hear the comings and goings within the house. His 'refuge' his parents had called it, the place where as a child he had retreated to laugh or cry, rant and rave, or when there was nought else for it... just to lie still and contemplate the eternal darkness of his world.

Even now, when he felt the day left nothing more to achieve, he liked to curl up beneath the covers and assess its highs and lows; although admittedly the lows were more frequent of late. Trouble was, so were his moments of lengthy reflection; and for the first time Robert Sadler began to wonder if age, that great leveller, might have finally taken the upper hand.

*

Mariel was the last person Brother Ezekiel expected to encounter in Reverend Dimpleton's room.

He instantly noticed the tension in her manner as she jerked round to face them... and something else. Was it fear?

"Sorry!" Ezekiel whispered. His gaze flicked to the figure on the bed. "We didn't mean to startle you."

"Came to have a word with the Reverend," Millicent began, a little breathless from the stairs. "Oh my," she gasped, taking in the scene before her. "I... that is, we thought..."

"You'd gone home!" Ezekiel finished quickly, knowing their ploy was not going to work with Mariel.

He knew there was no need to look for further proof. The very air reeked of evil and corruption; this was indeed the work of the Shadowean.

He eased Millicent gently ahead of him and closed the door. Moved by Mariel's stricken face, he knew here was another innocent soul he was bound to take into his confidence; it seemed the only fair thing to do.

*

The Shadowean had discovered a new game to play.

It was Mia's misfortune to be asleep in the first room the creature entered. Hunger may have driven the Shadowean from its lair, but it was growing in strength and confidence. Ultimately, time was on its side and it saw nothing against a little diversion.

The cat stirred and sensed the creature's presence, swifter than human prey had ever done, even in the cradle, and the Shadowean was forced to act quickly, penetrating a mind that was less cluttered and virtually free from fear.

Instantly it felt the animal's pride and fierce independence; qualities the Shadowean likened unto itself. Mia was dreaming of moving on, having sensed an alien presence on her territory. The Shadowean delved deeper and discovered her fear of being penned in, of being caged. The Shadowean could relate to that and instantly bombarded the tabby with visions of its own incarceration... the solid walls of the vault, the oppressive silence... the hunger.

The cat began to rock frantically in her sleep, claws working as she tore at imaginary walls, her jaws wide in a panic stricken cry for help, only her tormentor could hear.

The ordeal was short lived. Her spirit broken, Mia died, believing she would never again know freedom.

The Shadowean instantly dismissed the crumpled scrap of fur, eager to investigate a door it had previously noticed, propped slightly open... near where the fat one had grovelled on her belly.

*

Robert Sadler was dreaming, although the beauty of it was nothing like he'd ever experienced before.

Iridescent rivers flowed into valleys brimming with flowers of every hue. Birds of multicoloured plumage nested in the trees and the sun beat down from an azure sky. A light breeze was blowing and the air felt incredibly clear and fresh to breath. Never had his mind's eye shown such amazing textures and colours and he soon became restless in this paradise, wondering if he was being given a taste of heaven; if that was the case, he needed to be up on his feet, experiencing every moment.

It was then he realized he couldn't move... that his limbs were pinioned in some way. At first this proved only slightly annoying; then he started to panic. The wind had dropped and the heat was instantly unbearable. His throat began to close and there was an odd pressure on his ears that quickly became painful. Around him everything began to change. Colours faded as though a dark hand had been laid upon the earth. Leaves withered and died and birds in flight became skeletons against the backdrop of a blackened land.

Humans came, bringing pain and destruction. Rape, murder and pillage; scenes of degradation he had never thought possible in the world he'd inhabited. Everywhere... nothing but the grey pallor of death, stained red with innocent blood.

How could he have believed there was so much that was good and wholesome in the world?

He closed his eyes, but what point was that to a blind man. So he tried, and failed, to turn over, to bury his face in the sand as starving children were paraded before him, maimed and deformed beyond his belief; wasted arms held out to him, bright feverish eyes begging for help that would never come.

What had he worked for all his life? What had he achieved? Why had no one told him the truth?

*

The Shadowean relished this moment. It could tell Robert Sadler had always been a fighter, although this was one battle he would never win. Doubt and despair were now rising in waves from his writhing body. No mere husk to be drained in seconds... the creature would become stronger for this struggle.

It shuddered as Sadler strained against his invisible bonds, his resistance making the ultimate conquest all the more pleasurable. It hissed in ecstasy as Sadler's temperature rose to boiling point beneath the covers, his face turning puce against the sweat-soaked pillows. As his struggles became more erratic, the creature leaned closer, snuffling loudly as it siphoned off the smallest shudder of agony.

"In God's name... why?" The man's last muffled cry was real enough as he finally accepted death, believing his life had been a total failure.

In pure reflex, Robert Sadler's right arm shot sideways and hit the call bell at the side of the bed...

*

Angelica Miers needed a cushion to ease her aching limbs.

The heady scent of jasmine was making her feel sick and she would have given anything to drink a cup of holy water. She'd repeated the invocation so many times it was beginning to sound like a mantra; at least she no longer had to refer to the cue card.

Perhaps the power she'd sensed was no loner present. There *had* been other frail entities, hovering at the edge of the circle; former residents of St Oswald's and briefly, a much stronger force, in ecclesiastical garb, wringing his hands and warning her to desist... not to make the mistakes he had made. But she dismissed them all with the contempt they deserved... even a client she'd driven to suicide; the fool had the temerity to offer her absolution for her sins.

Painfully, she flexed the muscles she could still feel. 'One more try' she told herself, longing for the comfort of her bed... before the candles guttered and left her in total darkness.

*

"We 'ave ta tell Lyons." Mariel could see by Brother Ezekiel's expression her suggestion didn't meet with his approval.

"My dear, he won't believe us," he firmly assured her.

"They'll 'ave ta... after the autopsy."

Ezekiel was pacing up and down, his ginger spikes waving like an out of control antenna, his breath coming in short, painful gasps.

"There's nothing the management can do that we can't... except perhaps cause wholesale panic," he said. "Believe me, the only answer is to send the devil back where it came from..."

"Why bother?" Millicent was sitting beside the Reverend's bed, holding one cold hand as though fervently renewing an old friendship. "Destroy it altogether... so some fool can't call it up again?"

Mariel was nodding at this.

"I don't know 'alf as much as you two and understand even less, but I think Millicent 'as a point."

Ezekiel was beginning to realize Miss Toppler always had a point and he suddenly felt ashamed; there seemed to be no fear in these women.

He had been amazed at Mariel's calm acceptance of the situation, simply saying she had 'known somefing odd' was going on and then doubly thanking him for her rescue the previous evening. Despite her horrific encounter, she went on to show very little anxiety for herself, clearly more worried for her 'old luvvies'.

Suddenly it came home to him he could no longer keep this under wraps; too many lives were at stake. Mariel was right... Lyons would have to be told and the home emptied, just as the Brothers of Conscience had done during his own novitiate.

"Can't you do one of them exercises?" Mariel asked, fidgeting, clearly troubled by a call bell that had long gone unanswered.

"Exorcism," Ezekiel corrected gently.

"Yea... one of them." Mariel stood up. "I'd better get that. We're short staffed... as usual."

"Come straight back if you can." Millicent watched her go with undisguised concern. "I'm sure you have several plans of action, Zeek." Her tone of voice and the new term of endearment suggested she didn't believe that for one moment. "But what we really need is *bait...* a means to temp the thing back into the vault room and possibly all the way to hell."

Ezekiel ceased his pacing and met Millicent's gaze across the room. The twinkle in her eyes told him she had known that had been his need all along.

*

The Shadowean could not believe its luck. A sidelight had flicked on and the fat one was there, leaning over Robert Sadler's body.

The creature moved unhurriedly from its place of concealment. No need for stealth now. It rose up, encompassing them both in the wide curve of its membranes. Freshly fed and totally invincible, it instantly began to weave pictures, sensing the first shudder of contact, that exquisite moment when a fresh mind, full of dreams and desires, teeters on the brink of destruction.

The women's gasp touched every nerve in its body and its snout caressed the back of her neck, savouring her essence for the third time. There would be no escape.

Suddenly the Shadowean felt itself jolted backwards, drawn by an inescapable force...

*

Ignatius Wirrel could not concentrate on the novel he was trying to read; a greater mystery plagued his mind. Those damn orchids!

The long walk he'd taken along the landslipe had cleared his head and set him straight on his own life... and death. No matter how much he loved his family, why relinquish the precious time he had left when their entire lives were ahead of them. They might be struggling financially; but then so had he at their age and it hadn't harmed him one jot. 'Character building' is what his old gran would have called it.

He set the book aside. There was nothing for it... he had to go and have another look.

He had passed the doctor and a harassed looking Lyons on the way in from his walk. Since then, he'd heard several discreet comings and goings. Now all seemed quiet.

The Reverend's door was closed but not locked. Inside, the room was darker than he'd expected, the curtains having been drawn, presumably out of respect. Light from the corridor preceded him and he jumped guiltily as a dark shape moved against the windows and began to back out as another figure approached from behind the door.

"Something you want, Ignatius?"

He recognized Millicent Toppler's voice, but before he could respond, heavy footsteps pounded along the corridor and Mariel fell into the room, dragging Ignatius Wirrel with her.

*

Angelica Miers didn't realize anything was happening until an icy wind buffeted the perimeter of the circle.

The candles flickered, but gamely fought against the shadows swirling around her. Something powerful was out there!

"Show yourself," her voice sounded feeble, drained of all substance. "I command you!" That was a bit better.

She gasped as the Shadowean obliged, towering over her puny efforts at protection. Few had ever witnessed what now confronted her... and lived.

The creature infiltrated every part of the room and it seemed as though all the stars in heaven had descended; some travelling at great speed, while others hovered, blinking on and off like cold, watchful eyes. The chill was incredible; her breath remained, suspended particles of ice trapped within the circle.

Cautiously, she stood up, not to bring herself closer to the creature, but to assert the control she believed she had. She felt the first thrill of excitement... and greed. The thing was immense. She couldn't tell where the creature began or ended, but somewhere in there were hooked talons and a primeval snout... all hers for the bidding.

"You are here because it is my wish," she announced, finding her full voice at last. Vivid colours pulsed between the stars and Angelica read this as some form of acceptance. "Understand... mine will be the controlling mind."

The mass began to undulate, moving faster and faster until she no longer knew in which direction to look. The five points of the pentacle began to blur. Terrified, Angelica Miers fell to her knees, realizing the creature was seeking entry into the circle and that she was powerless to prevent it happening.

*

"Somefing touched me," Mariel gasped, her large frame quivering all over, "and I fink... fink Robert's..." she broke off and collapsed onto the chair Brother Ezekiel had the foresight to slide behind her.

Millicent flicked the nearest light switch and the three residents of St Oswald's glanced at each other and then down at their distraught carer.

Reverend Dimpleton remained unmoved by it all.

*

The audacity of this puny being! The Shadowean growled its defiance. Only one other had succeeded in summoning it, a formidable foe of considerable power; who nonetheless paid the ultimate price for his folly.

This mortal was different; there was nothing here the creature could not destroy with a momentary thought. This human's mind was full of bitterness and self-gratification... already it had sown numerous seeds of pain and discontent, some, the Shadowean could see were almost worthy of its own great deeds. Indeed, they were alike in many ways.

The creature reduced the force of its onslaught and considered its new acquaintance with almost paternal regard; after all, did it not need a host; someone it could feed through at will?

*

Brother Ezekiel hurried breathlessly towards Robert Sadler's room, one hand lifting his habit clear of his ankles while the other clutched his crucifix tightly, to prevent it tangling on its leather thong.

Ignatius had taken charge of Mariel and a recalcitrant Millicent, herding them into his own room, in case the undertakers came for Reverend Dimpleton.

Millicent had insisted on accompanying Ezekiel 'To watch his back,' as she gamely put it, but he just as firmly declined, discreetly suggesting she play a tea and sympathy role until he returned; in truth, he feared the good lady might delay him if a swift get-away was required.

Muttering words of power and protection gleaned long ago from his father's Book of Shadows, Ezekiel flung open the door and instantly recoiled; the chill momentarily stilled his words, freezing the back of his throat and taking his breath away. Before fear totally immobilized him, he forced himself forward and was virtually on his knees by the time he reached the figure huddled beneath the tangled bedclothes, the crucifix wavering erratically between them.

Although Ezekiel had never met Robert Sadler, he was sure the distress etched into the crumpled countenance could not have been his normal demeanour; there was too much pain... too much suffering for one man to carry to the end of his days.

Ezekiels pity was laced with a sigh of relief at finding himself unchallenged; despite his initial bravado, he knew beyond doubt he was *still* not prepared to face the beast.

*

Angelica Miers had never known such peace. Calmly, she resumed the lotus position. The stars were out, a cool breeze was blowing and a new friend was outside, waiting to be let in. All she had to do was reach out a welcoming hand.

There... it was done.

Those bothersome candles were extinguished and the holy water ran in rivulets across the floor. She looked towards the starlit heavens, the red slash of her mouth framing a sickly greeting.

Angelica Miers listened long and hard and then began to rock gently backwards and forwards, giggling insanely at the fun she was going to have.

*

Ignatius Wirrel was not convinced.

Despite Mariel's distraught condition and Millicent Toppler's calm explanation, he just could not accept a demon from the netherworld was roaming the corridors of St Oswald's feeding off the residents. As for Reverend Dimpleton, people his age regularly died. But then there *were* the orchids... and they had yet to know what had happened to Robert Sadler?

Ignatius did not have long to wait; the look on Ezekiel's face confirmed the worst scenario.

"If your suspicions are correct, we have to tell the management. Now!" he insisted. "The authorities must be informed."

Ezekiel looked meaningfully at Millicent.

"Ignatius knows as much as I do." Her tone clearly said, 'Well, what did you expect us to talk about?'

Ezekiel sighed and nodded resignedly.

"Very well."

"Good," Ignatius declared, nonetheless relieved the task was not going to be down to him.

Ezekiel checked his watch.

"Is Lyons likely to be in his office at this hour?" he asked Mariel.

"It's my place ta inform 'im about Robert," she asserted.

"Nevertheless, my dear, we shall all go together!"

*

Angelica Miers had no recollection of moving from the pentacle to the armchair in her bedroom.

She felt strangely relaxed, yet at the same time full of energy, like a mischievous schoolgirl who had woken to an urge to do something forbidden. She stood up and stretched, feeling somehow renewed, more aware of her body than she'd been in a very long time.

She wandered through to the lounge, her supple movements reflecting the feral creature she'd become. The carpet and coffee table were in place. No sign of candle stubs or plastic cups. She glanced up at the ceiling... no stars, no flashes of colour, just the same boring room she was accustomed to; as though none of it had really happened.

Perhaps she *had* been dreaming; yet her body told her differently. She ran her hands sensuously over her sagging breasts and down towards the triangle of her inner thigh, untouched... unheeded for so long. She gasped at the initial contact; even through her clothing, her fingers raised darts that pierced her senses and set her trembling as never before.

She slipped one hand inside her wrap and unexpectedly, a different kind of shudder contained her. God, she was cold... bloody central heating. Temporarily abandoning her pleasures, she gave the radiator a hefty kick and hurried back into the bedroom in search of a cigarette.

Sitting on the edge of her bed, she flicked her lighter and the Shadowean recoiled in terror at the tiny flame.

*

Lyons had been in a foul mood even before Mariel arrived with three residents in tow. Now he was furious.

He would not have been there at all but for the mound of paperwork generated by the demise of Annie Booker and as for Reverend Dimpleton, the undertakers weren't exactly hurrying themselves; but then the old boy wasn't going anywhere. Another time, that thought would have greatly amused him, but not today.

Today was different.

Now Mariel was telling him there'd been another death and amazingly had brought half the Home to confirm it.

"Another one!" Lyons echoed. His face had gone a pasty grey, similar to the colour of his office walls. Instead of enquiring 'whom', he glared fiercely at Brother Ezekiel; he considered all men of the cloth to be born troublemakers. "What's he doing here? You know this office is out of bounds to residents."

"Mariel wanted to come alone," Ezekiel explained, "but I insisted on seeing you."

"And did Wirrel and Tippler..."

"Miss Toppler," Ignatius corrected politely.

"Did they also insist?" Lyons continued regardless, his balding head bobbing aggressively. "Because your job..."

"Don't tell me my job, Mr Lyons," Mariel snapped, her own distress channelling into aggression. "I know it better than you know your own."

Lyons round little body bristled.

"Now look here..."

"Shut up," Ezekiel snapped, uncharacteristically. "Sit down and listen."

Lyons sat.

No one had dared speak to him like that in a very long time. However, it didn't stop him darting a look at Mariel that clearly said "After this, you're out of here."

*

Having satiated both their desires, the Shadowean left its host bruised and exhausted on the rumpled bed, surrounded by the household implements it had encouraged Angelica Miers to use upon herself.

The night was young and it wished to feed again. Then it would go in search of *him*. It relished the idea of destroying that particular human in stages; of taking his mind cell by cell, so *he* would understand what was happening, yet be powerless to prevent it. By the time it was finished, *he* would beg to die... and then his suffering would really begin.

The Shadowean stared in distaste at Angelica Miers tousled ginger hair and the red gash of her mouth... ugly, even in sleep. The creature flexed its membranes, knowing it would eventually become bored with the limits of human confinement. When that time came, at least its present host would provide a convenient opportunity to feed.

*

"Empty St Oswald's?"

"Yes, if you don't want more lives on your hands," Ezekiel reasoned.

"Where do you propose I send them?"

"Local hotels," Millicent suggested. "It's out of season, there must be dozens of vacancies."

"That's insane," Lyons blustered. "You know yourself... some are bedridden, others can't make the stairs. Then there are families to consult. The clearance paperwork alone would take a month."

"They'd all be dead by then," Ignatius stated gravely. The reality of the situation was coming home to him. His normally sleepy expression had taken on a wide-eyed desperation.

"And you'd be outa your job," Mariel added, sounding as though that part of the outcome appealed to her.

"If I agree to your demands?" He made the three of them sound like terrorists. He looked squarely at Brother Ezekiel. "I want a written statement showing the Church takes full responsibility for the consequences."

Before Ezekiel could think of an effective answer, the telephone rang and Lyons took the opportunity to scuttle away to deal with the undertakers.

*

Having seen Reverend Dimpleton off the premises, Lyons paused on the upper corridor and steeled himself for a fresh confrontation.

The medical authorities might demand an autopsy, but having seen Dimpleton's body for the second time, Lyons decided Brother Ezekiel's claims were preposterous; anyone could see the man had expired of old age.

He'd send Toppler and Wirrel away with a flea in their ear; let them relocate if they wished. Mariel he'd dismiss for inciting distress amongst the residents; he'd make sure she never worked in a care home again. Then he'd write a strong letter to Father Abbot, demanding the removal of that meddling priest and the cutting of all religious ties with St Oswald's.

"Demons and Devils... my ass!"

*

It was unfortunate for Lyons and perhaps fortunate for future residents of St Oswald's that their manager decided to descend the back stairway as the Shadowean was coming from Angelica Miers' room.

Unable to believe its luck, the creature instantly sent out a mind trap to confuse its prey and give it time to position itself where the stairs formed a dark alcove between floors.

Lyons paused, frowning. He made a half turn, patted the pockets of his shiny suit, shrugged, hesitated again and continued his descent, straight into the Shadowean's cold embrace.

At first he merely shivered and cursed the staff for leaving an outside door open, a breach in security regulations for which tomorrow someone would be hauled over the carpet. He tried to recall the policy number, but his mind kept side tracking to other things; unexpected scenarios, long forgotten events he hadn't considered for many years. Suppressed painful memories of a shattered childhood.

So... the fool would dare to scoff at devils and demons!

Then the stars came, laced with flashes of colour, falling like a veil before his eyes. Lyons shook his head, believing he was having a mega migraine. Then he saw cold eyes and a drooling, primordial snout. A scream rose in his throat, but a familiar voice ordered him to remain silent, to accept what was happening.

Terrified, he instinctively obeyed his father's wishes, just as he had always done.

"Do this Ronnie. Do that Ronnie. It's cold tonight... I'll just slip in with you to keep us both warm. I won't hurt... Don't cry. Tomorrow we'll buy the fishing rod you've always wanted... Tell your mother and I'll beat you within an inch of your life." The voice droned on, evoking unpleasant flash-backs that brought nothing but physical pain. How could this be happening; hadn't he danced on the old buggers grave?

Lyons sank to his knees as the Shadowean tightened its hold. His limbs felt like heavy blocks of ice and there was a strange pulling sensation at the top of his head, as though his brain was being stretched. Then he began to cry, as his father pitilessly explained how death and damnation waited to claim him.

"Please Daddy, don't let them take me." Great sobs wracked his stocky frame. "I never, *ever* told Mommie what you did." He gave a long hiccupping gurgle and then abruptly all sound ceased.

Lyons' body remained suspended for a moment on the top step. Then it toppled forward... bounced off the wall and slithered down the last flight of stairs into the basement. His baldpate knocked gently against the door of the disposal chute, which obligingly clicked open to receive his mortal remains.

*

Fully fed and at its most powerful since gaining its freedom, the Shadowean roamed at will through the Home.

Lights flickered again at its passing and a deathly chill once more crept into the rooms, making residents and carers alike wonder about the strange antics of the heating since Barry Paterson was taken ill.

No detail, no matter how minute, escaped the Shadowean's sensors. Prospective prey, dark places of concealment where the strange overhead lighting failed to penetrate, every possible entrance and exit and perhaps most important of all, where *he* could be found; a source of latent power that came, not from *him*, but from something in *his* possession... the existence of which the Shadowean instinctively feared.

*

Eventually it became clear to those waiting in Lyons' office, the manager was not about to return.

Brother Ezekiel made use of the phone to leave messages in three different places, insisting Father Abbot contact him on a matter of utmost urgency.

Mariel felt she'd achieved all she could. Robert Sadler's room would be locked and it had to be assumed Lyons would phone IDOC on his return. Despite the badly concealed fear on her round face, she returned to her shift, knowing her 'old luvvies' needed her more now than ever.

Millicent announced she'd spend the remainder of the night alternating between two bed bound, vulnerable residents, while Ignatius and Ezekiel, armed with torches would take turns patrolling the rooms and corridors.

The night seemed endless and Ezekiel longed as much as his colleagues for daylight. In desperation, he had taken time out to once more consult the Book of Shadows, hoping to find an easier, more subtle way of destroying the beast, until he began to wonder whether it was really the Shadowean he feared to face, or the devils that plagued his own soul.

*

By the time the Shadowean returned to its host, it was aware the hunter had also become the hunted.

It had sensed a pattern in the constant movement of humans, repeatedly covering the same ground. Several times it had picked up the essence of where *he* had passed, but all trails led to *his* room and the source of power contained there.

Angelica Miers slept on... unaware of the creature that inhabited her body. The wild thoughts that peppered her dreams were mere seeds of desire... from which the Shadowean was determined terrible things would grow.

DAY FOUR

Todd had decided this would be his last week at St Oswald's.

"I'm not cut out to be a carer," he told himself for the hundredth time, as he dolefully walked to work along the undercliff from St Lawrence towards Ventnor.

In truth, he was disappointed. His entire young life, he'd been intuitively drawn towards the sick and needy. He'd nursed both parents through their last days and still managed to maintain his grades at college, wanting them to be proud of him; the natural step suggested care work, to study for his certificate, perhaps even go into nursing. Finding Reverend Dimpleton's body had changed all that.

He lived with his aunt now, from his mother's side of the family, in a small garden flat on the other side of Ventnor, just until he could afford a place of his own. Against her matronly advice he'd decided to work down the bakery owned by his girlfriend's old man... she'd be pleased about that, make him seem more like one of the family; might even get his leg over at last.

All his mates said they'd done 'it', but with Tracie he'd held back; waiting for the right moment, he guessed, although God knows if he'd recognize it when it came along.

Just to cheer himself up, he hummed one of his mum's old Freddie and the Dreamers favourites, 'She's the girl for me, everybody tells me so,' the rest of the way to work.

At the end of the breakfast shift, he'd explain to Lyons how he felt. He was a good enough judge of character not to expect sympathy; he only hoped the manager wouldn't hold him to his three month trial period.

*

Breakfast turned out to be a shambles.

Mariel had stayed on because of the stream of call-bells from residents disturbed by unaccustomed sounds and movement during the night. The old ones were restless; they knew *something* threatened their peaceful existence and it was being reflected in their demands on the staff.

Besides, Mariel wanted to speak with Lyons as soon as he came in, to insist he gave Brother Ezekiel the support he needed. She would *never* forget the Shadowean's icy embrace or the way it messed with her mind and she couldn't sit at home knowing her friends faced the same terrors. She owed Ezekiel her sanity... if not her life and only wished she could have been there for the Reverend and Robert Sadler and of course, dear old Annie Booker.

Ezekiel had sent Millicent and Ignatius off to get some well-deserved sleep. Now, he sat in his room, the Book of Shadows balanced on his lap, watching dawn break and wondering what this day would bring.

Father Abbot had not returned his call. As soon as the others were rested, he'd start a systematic search for the creature's lair. He knew he lacked the physical strength and faith for this confrontation; but he also knew he had little choice... walking away was no longer an option. The beast had to be stopped, even if it cost him his life.

*

Angelica Miers ran a hot bath as soon as she awoke.

Sinking into the tub, both hands slipped eagerly between her legs. The Shadowean put a stop to her pleasures by asserting its presence, causing the temperature of the bathroom to plummet several more degrees.

Frustrated, Angelica pulled angrily at the call-bell above the bath, determined once and for all that something should be done about the heating.

A ripple of anticipation shuddered through the Shadowean... perhaps the fat one would come? Angelica Miers responded to the creatures heightened expectations. Once more her hands disappeared beneath the waterline.

*

"We daren't wait any longer," Brother Ezekiel announced soberly. After a hurried breakfast, they were again gathered in the manager's office. It was well past nine o'clock and Lyons still hadn't shown. "Every hour of daylight's precious to us."

"More reason I should come with you," Millicent reminded him, not for the first time. "We can spread out and cover the ground quickly."

Ezekiel shook his head.

"Down there, we stick together," he said pointedly.

"Safety in numbers, then." Millicent raised herself to her full diminutive height.

Ezekiel looked kindly upon her.

"Your time would be best served waiting here for Lyons. Tell him what were doing and send him to find us."

Millicent considered this.

"Leave a message on his note pad," she suggested, not to be outdone.

"Ezekiels right." Ignatius nodded at Millicent's walking sticks. "With all these stairs..." he broke off, blanching at the rebellious gleam in her bright blue eyes.

"Has Mariel gone home?" Ezekiel intervened quickly.

Millicent shook her head, still glaring at Ignatius.

"Don't believe she intends to... not until we've nailed this creature."

"Or died in the attempt," Ezekiel muttered ruefully, swinging his satchel carefully over one shoulder. The Book was beginning to feel a weighty burden in more ways than one. "Of which I assure you both, there's a very real possibility."

*

Angelica Miers couldn't believe her luck. There she was, butt naked beneath ice cold water and who should come to her aid, but a fair haired Adonis, tanned, blue-eyed and cute... *very cute!* She gave a long, sensuous sigh and intentionally raised herself until the tips of her breasts bobbed clear of the water.

Todd politely averted his gaze.

"You rang for assistance, Miss Miers?"

"Yes, Todd. It is Todd?" She seemed to savour the name. Her tongue caressed her upper lip.

He nodded.

"Silly of me, I know... but I slipped getting into the bath... and can't seem to get out again." She made a feeble effort to move and raised both arms, imploringly. "Please... do you think *you* help me?"

Todd remained in the doorway.

"I'll fetch one of the girls..."

"NO!" she snapped, her old manner returning. "This water's freezing... I'll catch my death if I have to wait any longer." Her voice softened again as she added, "I need a man's strong arms to raise me."

Todd swallowed.

Until now, Angelica Miers had struck him as nothing more than a jaded, middle aged woman; over dressed, over made-up and over full of her own importance. Here, he was faced with a seemingly vulnerable female, hair concealed beneath a fluffy pink bath towel and green, cat-like eyes appealing to him for help.

There was nothing in regulations preventing him from assisting female residents, as long as they had no objections. He edged forward and the Shadowean watched the young man's approach with interest. Before Todd was aware of it himself, the creature had sensed the sexual frisson between the two and decided it would be amusing to allow this encounter to run it's course. Then *it* would have what it desired.

Todd tried to take the lifting stance he'd been taught, but the woman was heavy and slippery to hold. He leaned sideways to reach for a spare towel and her arms locked round his neck, seemingly in an effort to assist him. He braced himself; but her weight dragged him down, forcing his face close to her own... tantalizingly close. The faintest touch of her lips sent an unbidden fire raging through him.

"Yes, Todd," was all she said.

Her voice sounded husky and inviting.

So this was it; finally it was going to happen... the moment he had been saving himself for. One trembling hand fumbled for his belt buckle, but Angelica was already there, eager to free his straining manhood. He kicked off his trainers and stepped out of his jeans, boxers and tee shirt followed.

He gasped at the touch of her icy fingers and suddenly an unbidden anger engulfed him as the Shadowean began to weave its spell.

He would teach that tight bitch Tracie a lesson... let her know what a man could do with a *real* woman; what he should have done with her ages ago, instead of listening to her simpering, whining excuses. Save themselves... for what? This was all that mattered. And the moment was now.

Taking the initiative, he roughly cupped an eager, upwards thrusting breast and stepped into the bath. He dragged Angelica Miers on top of him, amidst a wave of freezing water.

*

Brother Ezekiel had not realized just how tired he was. It felt like someone had strapped an iron band around his chest. Add to that a rising sense of hopelessness and that summed up the mood of the man leading Ignatius on what was becoming a wild goose chase.

Only when they entered the boiler room had Ezekiel's hopes been lifted, along with his level of dread. Ignatius hadn't noticed anything different, but Ezekiel felt a latent heaviness, as though a more formidable being had tainted the air. Despite standing in the warm, beating heart of the Home, the room had an unpleasant, clammy feel to it; and there was an indefinable mustiness... although they both agreed this could have been coming from the refuge chute.

Ezekiel had flicked on all available lights and checked the up and over shutters where fuel was delivered and rubbish collected. All seemed secure; yet he was certain evil had walked here.

Leaving the lights on to mark their progress and ease Ignatius's formidable fear of the dark, they continued their search.

*

Now on top, Todd reached a heaving, thrashing climax. With sexual release, something else left him... his uncharacteristic urge for violence.

Gasping for breath, he stared into the time-ravaged face of Angelica Miers, seeing the wide cold eyes and leering mouth. He felt her shudder beneath him as she too reached orgasm. The pink towel floated away, setting loose a fiery, orange halo.

'Medusa,' he thought. 'Fucking Medusa!'

Todd levered himself up and over the side of the bath, submerging the gargoyle face as he did so, bare feet seeking purchase on the waterlogged floor. Spluttering and heaving, Miers was up and after him, the Shadowean adding speed and strength to her movements.

Todd only made it to the lounge before he was dragged down with bone crushing force. He rolled over, kicking and punching as their wet bodies collided. Miers didn't flinch. In fact her expression suggested she was getting off on the encounter.

There was something awfully wrong here!

Rising fear broke all barriers of the anger he'd previously felt.

"Dear God... *someone help me!*" he cried, and the Shadowean gleefully lapped up each searing heartbeat.

*

Brother Ezekiel and Ignatius finally reached the top floor.

They'd discovered nothing except the remains of poor Mia, near where Robert Sadler had died. The cat appeared to have died in considerable torment and Ignatius felt it best to say nothing to the others. At the first opportunity, he would bury her in the garden, where those who loved her could later pay their respects.

Of the Shadowean there was still no trace.

"No bloody sign of Lyons either," Ignatius sniffed scornfully. "The man's an ineffectual baboon... probably still skulking in his office."

Ezekiel managed a rare smile.

"Millicent would have given him his marching orders by now. No, my friend, this man's absence is beginning to worry me... he's a big enough egotist not to want us stomping around on his patch unattended..."

"So what now?" Mentally, Ignatius backtracked to remind himself there was *still* a need to do something, the withered orchids, and Robert Sadler's death... Mariel crying, terrified out of her wits.

As if in answer, a piercing scream for help seemed to come at them from all directions. Huffing breathlessly, Mariel turned in at the other end of the corridor and both men followed her, simply because she seemed to know where she was going.

All three came to a stunned halt in Angelica Miers' doorway.

At first sight, two naked figures appeared to be enjoying each other's company on the floor of her lounge. Clearly embarrassed, Ignatius made to turn away, but Ezekiel edged round Mariel, who remained rooted to the spot.

The woman, unknown to him lay on top of a younger man he'd seen working about the place. Her plump arms and legs were curved round, like some wild thing forming a canopy over its prey. A husky, snuffling sound was coming from her throat. Sensing their approach, her head shot back, nostrils flared, orange mane flying as from within her the Shadowean snarled its defiance. It flexed its cramped membranes and the woman's body rippled in response.

HIM AGAIN!

The creature wanted to throw itself forward, to tear through their minds, but its host was not strong enough and alone, daylight would weaken it and make it more vulnerable. The Shadowean had no choice but to play the waiting game.

Spiting and kicking, it took both men to drag Miers from Todd's now motionless body. Mariel fetched blankets and threw one carelessly over Angelica where she crouched in the corner, shuddering, but far from subdued; the other she laid more tenderly over Todd. Gently, she pressed a hand to his shoulder. There was not a flicker of response.

The Shadowean might have been prevented from taking the boy's life, but very little was left of his mind.

*

"I've never seen anything like it," Ignatius declared, standing over Miers. "She's like a wild animal."

Ezekiel studied the women in silence for a moment.

"Perhaps that's what something has made of her."

"Whatever the reason, she should have been sectioned," Mariel shouted bitterly from the bedroom, where Todd was being warmly tucked in. "Not placed amongst vulnerable residents."

"Or carers." Ignatius was still struggling to grasp what he was witnessing.

"*Who* are you?" Ezekiel whispered.

"Angelica Miers," Ignatius informed him for the second time.

"*What* are you?" Ezekiel placed one hand beneath her chin and lifted the bruised face. He flinched as a familiar icy chill ran up his arm. Her gaze, meeting his, instantly became vacant... too vacant, like a cat nonchalantly ignoring the mouse until it was ready to strike. He spun quickly away. "I suggest we lock Miss Miers in the vault. Now... for her own safety."

NEVER! The meddling human *KNEW*.

The Shadowean instantly abandoned its host, eating through her memory banks like acid. The force of its passing knocked Ezekiel from his feet. Ignatius staggered, but managed to right himself, too late however, to prevent Angelica Miers' lifeless body from toppling across Ezekiels outstretched legs.

*

It was nearly midday and three of them sat in Lyons' office, drinking endless cups of coffee and picking half-heartedly over plates of sandwiches.

"We have to phone IDOC and the police," Mariel insisted. "We have two unclassified deaths and a very sick carer on our hands. Lyons appears to be missing..." She glanced at Millicent for corroboration.

"While twiddling my thumbs down here," she cast a meaningful look at Brother Ezekiel, "I phoned Lyons' home every fifteen minutes - no answer. And nobody here has seen him since the undertakers collected dear Reverend Dimpleton last night."

Ezekiel accepted their observations without question. He also had a point of his own to make.

"I believe the Shadowean was using Miss Miers as a host body... that's why Ignatius and I found nothing."

"What's to stop it choosing another one?" Millicent demanded to know with her usual bluntness.

Ezekiel shrugged wearily.

"Depends on how quickly we act." He suppressed a nervous fit of coughing. "We have no option but to search again. The beast *must* have gone to ground. Luckily, we still have the advantage of daylight..."

Ignatius appeared round the doorjamb, having gone to check on Todd. Ezekiel knew he'd also taken time out to bury Mia.

"I think there's something you aught to see," he announced, looking positively animated.

*

Ignatius Wirrel dragged the rug from the pentacle with a somewhat theatrical flourish.

"Must have uncovered part of it in their struggle... didn't notice until I came to fetch Todd's clothing."

"Has the young man said anything?" Ezekiel asked.

Looking down at the crude circle, he sensed his first glimmer of hope. Until now, things were moving too slowly... he was beginning to feel personally responsible for the suffering of so many innocents.

"Nothing. He just lies there starring at the ceiling."

Ezekiel recalled Miers' blank, guarded expression with a renewed surge of determination.

"The poor woman must have used this and got more than she bargained for." He patted Ignatius on the shoulder. "Well done, my friend. You may have just found the answer we've been looking for."

*

Brother Ezekiel would brook no argument.

Within the hour all mobile residents were tempted into the lounge for a prize winning game of bingo, presided over by Mariel. The two most vulnerable had their hospital beds moved together, guarded by Millicent; Ignatius would patrol the corridor between this bedroom and lounge.

A thorough search had revealed candle stubs and a plastic beaker of what Ezekiel assumed was holy water; also the handwritten card Angelica had used, with words similar to those found in his Book of Shadows.

Millicent had been on the verge of tears over fears for his safety, although Ezekiel had no choice but to remain gently adamant; there was room for one only within the circle and that was the safest place for him to finish what old Abbot Gregory had died starting... the added inducement of a willing soul was a point he refused to waste valuable daylight hours discussing with her.

Lighting fresh candles, Ezekiel smiled ruefully, wondering whether Father Abbot had picked up any of his messages... and what the stuffy Church Council would say if they could see him now.

*

The Shadowean sped through the bowels of St Oswald's, desperately seeking the darkness it craved. Everywhere had been violated by overhead lighting and the scent of *him*. Its place of refuge had been tainted beyond endurance.

And now this latest humiliation!

Once again it was being draw towards its entrance to this world. Instinctively the creature knew who it was; *he* was no adept, perhaps even less powerful than its host had been... nonetheless, it was *bound* to answer the summons.

This time it would destroy *him*; and then take the other weaklings at its leisure...

*

Brother Ezekiel had barely completed the incantation when the beast arrived, raging through the room like a winter's storm.

Had Millicent remained, as she wished, she would have been drawn into a whirlwind of destruction. Anything not fixed down began to vibrate and lift, until the room was spinning round Ezekiel like a giant mobile; faster and faster, creating an icy vortex over which the creature straddled in all its terrifying glory.

Despite a strong urge to do so, he didn't look up, even as numerous stars veiled the perimeter of the pentacle, each one independently probing and seeking entry... and miraculously being repelled. He was amazed to find even the candles held their own, the saucers containing holy water reflecting their undiminished flames.

"Go on," Ezekiel muttered, his tense grip on the Book of Shadows easing somewhat. "Burn yourself out... damn you."

All motion abruptly ceased.

Angelica Miers' belongings dropped with a resounding crash that must have shaken the home to its foundations.

"*You* heard me," Ezekiel thought, praying the others would not abandon their posts to investigate the noise.

Colours pulsed between the stars.

"Then you must know I no longer fear you." He said this out loud, amazed at his own temerity and it felt as though his words remained, suspended, frozen like his breath at the edges of the circle. Then he felt it... the first niggling intrusion; the makings of a headache. The colours throbbed again.

It seemed they understood each other.

"Try this for size." Ezekiel turned a page and began to read the Banishment Ritual, silently this time, allowing each word to form a picture in his mind.

The response was instantaneous.

Above him, colours resonated like an out of control laser. The pain in his head increased tenfold, but he continued with agonizing determination... until his vision began to blur and he could no longer see the words. Other thoughts, other feelings began to intrude, filling him with doubts and confusion, taking away his purpose for being there; for existing at all in this world... and replacing it with an insurmountable self-loathing.

He raised his hand, seemingly in a gesture of abandonment.

"Father... help me!" he cried aloud, not knowing if he called upon his father on earth or the one in heaven.

After a countless age, which must only have been a matter of seconds, during which he was shown a cruel caricature of himself, bowed and broken before the Church Committee... the words came again, haltingly and disjointed until the agony and anguish began to recede; then flowing, full of power... spilling from him like liquid fire.

He found himself glaring defiantly upwards, for the first time daring to wonder if he could make out features in the pulsing lights; all the while, his fingers lovingly caressed the illuminated pages as though he were reading braille. It might have been his imagination, but he fancied the canopy quivered like a jellyfish and the stars momentarily lost some of their brilliance.

This seemed almost too easy!

The page appeared to turn itself and he surged on, the words becoming second nature to a true Seventh Son. Too late, he realized he had commenced the ritual for the Exchange of Souls. His lips faltered, yet the sermon continued as clear as a bell in his head. The Shadowean had tricked him, allowing itself to suffer... knowing this moment would come.

Suddenly, for Ezekiel, all became clear. This was as it was meant to be.

Allowing the Book to fall aside, he raised himself up, words still reeling in his mind... words with a different meaning. He accepted it all. The failed Seventh Son... his father's disappointment in him... a life wasted on a misunderstood vocation; even the responsibility for the deaths at St Oswald's. Anything and everything... because none of it mattered anymore!

In this one moment he was going to put all things right.

He held out both hands in a gesture of supplication, tears of release streaming down his cheeks as he edged towards the perimeter of the circle. He gasped as the temperature began to plummet and just before he gave himself willingly to the Shadowean's cruel embrace, it seemed as though a voice spoke to him; it might well have been that of his father... if so, he hoped the old man bestowed a blessing on this, his son's ultimate sacrifice.

*

Millicent Toppler was inconsolable.

"He'd be alive now if I'd stayed with him." She crossed the lounge the carers had just cleared of residents, agitatedly rattling her sticks against the chair backs.

"You mustn't blame yourself," Mariel countenanced. "It wasn't what we expected..."

"But it happened, nonetheless," Millicent rounded, "and I could have prevented it. We *actually* discussed the idea of human bait." She hobbled back towards the two figures seated by the window. "I never dreamt he would do such a thing." She eased herself down into her favourite chair. "One minute he was there, watching the door for me... and then he was gone."

Brother Ezekiel nodded sympathetically, although no one could have been feeling as guilty as himself at that moment. *He* should have died... indeed he had *intended* to do so. Hollow eyed, he listened as Millicent continued;

"Ignatius tried to take an overdose, you know, the night before last. For some reason it didn't work out. It was as if he was meant for other things," she broke off and looked appealingly at Ezekiel, eyes brimming.

"I must have passed out... in that last instant before breaking the circle." It felt as though he was apologizing for being alive. "Ignatius must have come in at that moment. There was nothing for it... the damned creature *had* to take someone..." He gave a rasping cough and noisily cleared his throat. "When I came to, Ignatius was lying on his back, just outside the circle. His eyes were closed and he had the most damnably contented smile on his face."

Millicent gave a small sob and he took her hand. Mariel reached across and held them both. All three jumped as the radiator behind them gurgled.

"I believe Ignatius spoke to me... right at the last," Ezekiel admitted, "and I shall spend the rest of my days wondering what it was he said."

*

Barry Paterson still looked pale and tired. The last thing he needed on his first day back was to be told the oil-fired boilers were on the blink.

He cursed as he descended the stairs; the place was freezing cold and the cellar lights were still on. Obviously someone had been down here poking around. The thought annoyed him beyond reason. This was his territory! Lyons wasn't here, so it must have been one of those bitches from upstairs... good for nothing but wiping asses and a good seeing to behind the shutters. That's all they were fit for...

He broke off, surprised at his own vicious tirade towards a group of girls he was genuinely fond off. Perhaps he'd come back too soon... he still didn't feel right.

As if in confirmation of this thought, his stomach gave an unpleasant lurch and he grabbed for the wall as his world began to spin out of control...

*

Brother Ezekiel decided he was too tired to sleep.

He'd finally persuaded Millicent to take a mild sedative and retire to her room, but this she refused to do until she'd gone outside to inspect Mia's tiny grave; one of the last things Ignatius had spoken to her about.

There was still no sign of Lyons, so Mariel had phoned IDOC before going in to sit with Todd. The police would come... questions would be asked and even now Ezekiel wasn't sure if he had the right answers. So many deaths, and nothing to show for it, except an empty steel vault, a faded pentacle and a young boy who might never talk again.

Perhaps a walk in the gardens would help him unwind; a chance maybe to start enjoying his respite. After the last few days' excitement, the peace and tranquillity of the Carmelite Retirement Home didn't seem such a bad option. He began gathering his belongings. The Book of Shadows was the last item to go into his satchel and here he paused and did something he'd never done before; he reverently kissed the worn cover.

"Be at peace, Ignatius," he whispered. "Bless you my friend, for what you did for me... and for all of us."

Leaving his room, he hovered outside the door of number five. He felt no need to go in; the vault could be dismantled and the proprietor would get the space he wanted. He thought then of the handyman who'd unknowingly released the Shadowean... and decided if the fellow were back on duty, a word as to his health would not come amiss.

*

A simple enquiry indicated Barry Paterson could be found in the boiler room.

As soon as he opened the door Ezekiel knew something was wrong. The lights were off, yet he could hear sounds, like a large animal blundering around. When the screwdriver buried itself in the wall beside him, he knew his hunch was right.

The man he assumed was Paterson came lumbering out of the darkness, metal bar swinging. In that instant, Ezekiel discovered reflexes he didn't know he possessed; unfortunately, the movement took him deeper into the cellar, giving his attacker a chance to block his escape.

"For God's sake!" He dodged again, stumbled and righted himself against the side of the boiler. The bare metal scalded his hand, yet the air around him was icy cold; he had no time to consider the terrifying possibility of this fact as the bar hammered mercilessly into his right shoulder, his cry of pain eliciting a growl of satisfaction from Paterson.

Ezekiel swung away, rolling across the top of the rubbish chute as the weapon descended again with murderous intent. The plastic cover disintegrated and he gagged as foul smelling rubbish erupted around him; his right hand touched something shudderingly like cold flesh and he knew, even down there in the darkness, why Lyons had never returned to his office.

Paterson was on top of him now, the metal bar crushing his windpipe. The lack of air awakened a fire in his lungs and he felt his consciousness begin to slip away. Frantically, Ezekiel's left hand found his satchel and brought it hard against the man's head. Paterson fell sideways, the contents of the bag spilling over him. Then he started to scream, long and loud. A pinpoint of light erupted out of the darkness, growing apace with the man's cries. He virtually levitated against the back wall and hung there, scrabbling at the Book of Shadows where it clung to his chest, flames licking round its gilded edges.

A high pitched keening sound filled the cellar and Paterson literally split open as the Shadowean broke free, showering Ezekiel with gore.

The creature screamed in agony as the fire took hold. Its immense bulk towered over him and just for a moment, Ezekiel caught sight of a long snout and cold, fish-like eyes as silvery membranes snaked out and snatched him up, intentionally drawing him into the inferno. Ezekiel struggled against the crushing tentacles, kicking like a rag doll. Smoke filled his lungs and stung his eyes; yet the flames left him unscathed.

With an ear-shattering roar, the beast flung him aside and weaved an erratic path towards the stairs, seemingly in a bid to escape its torment. Retching and heaving, Ezekiel rolled onto his front and tried to drag himself up the far wall. His legs failed him and he sank down again, blood pouring from a gash in his forehead.

Above his own laboured breathing Ezekiel heard a sharp, metallic screech. He turned over in time to see the shutters swing outwards and up. Late afternoon sunlight slanted into the cellar, bathing Ezekiel and the Shadowean in its blinding brilliance.

Through a red haze, he saw the Shadowean turn almost transparent. He felt a tremendous pressure in his head and the creature suddenly disintegrated in a massive starburst that touched every corner of the cellar... and in each shinning orb Ezekiel was stunned to see a face. Mesmerised, he watched as thousands of souls were at last set free; fleetingly, he thought he saw Ignatius, but perhaps that was just wishful thinking... salve to ease his conscience.

Swiftly the stars dispersed, floating out through the open shutters, dancing in the sunlight. Of the Book of Shadows nothing remained.

The refuse collector starred in disbelief as smoke blackened and covered in blood, Ezekiel finally gained his feet and gasped his unsteady way towards fresh air and reality.

"Er..." Understandably, the man backed off a pace or two.

Somewhere above them a door banged and footsteps clattered on the stairs.

"Brother Ezekiel... are you still down there?"

He croaked an inaudible reply and winched as pain shot through his shoulder.

"Only... there's a Father Abbot on the phone. Wishes to know if you have a problem. What should I tell him?"

End.